Evil Angels Among Them

Kate Charles

*'He cast upon them the furiousness of his
wrath, anger; displeasure, and trouble: and
sent evil angels among them.'*
Psalm 78:50

Ostara Publishing

Dedicated with love to the memory of

GARETH GRIFFITHS
28 March 1954 – 28 August 1994

For while he lived, he counted himself a happy man:
and so long as thou doest well unto thyself, men will
speak good of thee.

Psalm 49:18

Prologue

Their throat is an open sepulchre, with their tongues have they deceived: the poison of asps is under their lips.

Psalm 14:5

The first phone call came just a few days after the Rector and his wife returned from their honeymoon. It was the first evening since their marriage that Stephen had to go out, to a Deanery Synod meeting in a nearby village.

At a loose end, Becca occupied herself with the newly arrived honeymoon photos, slipping them into the clear pockets of an album – a wedding present from one of his parishioners. Stephen had suggested that she write on the backs of the photos, for future reference, but Becca knew that there was no danger of her ever forgetting their honeymoon.

It hadn't been a grand honeymoon, by most standards – on a clergyman's stipend it wasn't really an option to go abroad, to the romance of Paris or Venice or even to some warmer clime than England in midwinter. But the cottage they'd rented in Somerset had been snugly cosy, and the surrounding countryside picturesque even in bleakest January. At off-season rates, they'd been able to afford two weeks, and in the slow time after Christmas it had been possible for Stephen to get away from the parish for that long.

Two blissful weeks. Becca smiled as she flipped through the photos they'd snapped with their rather posh autofocus camera, another wedding present. They'd taken quite a few photos of each other, out of doors on their daily walks over rolling hillsides, and in the cottage in the evenings, in the glow of the log fire. That was one disadvantage of a solitary honeymoon, she reflected wryly – there was no one else to wield the camera so they could both be in the pictures. One day they'd driven into Bath, where they'd found various sympathetic strangers to press the shutter release, so there were a few photos of the newlyweds together in front of the Royal Crescent, viewing the Roman Baths and feasting in a chintzy teashop. And on another day they'd visited Wells, where they'd toured the cathedral, and later they'd climbed Glastonbury Tor. Becca looked at a picture, snapped, she recalled, by a friendly American, of the two of them, arm in arm, at the top of the tor, the countryside spread out beneath them like the map of some wintry fantasy land. Modest as Becca was, she had to admit that they made a handsome couple: both tall and slender and fair-haired, though her hair was a silvery blonde while Stephen's was more golden in colour.

Happy days, exploring the countryside. And if the days were happy, the nights, spent exploring each other, were sheer bliss. Upstairs at the cottage, in the tiny bedroom under the eaves, together they'd discovered joys neither of them had ever even imagined. And that, thought Becca happily, was not going to stop now that the honeymoon had ended. The pleasure of discovery, and the discovery of pleasure, would continue for weeks and months and years to come.

There were no photos of those nights upstairs – taking pictures had been the last thing on either of their minds. But there was one photo that she'd always treasure. One rainy morning Becca had awakened early and slipped downstairs to surprise Stephen with breakfast in bed, delivered on a tray. She'd remembered to bring the camera up with her as well, and had captured his surprise at the unexpected feast. In the photo he looked so young – vulnerable, almost – without his glasses and with his tousled hair flopping onto his forehead so boyishly, in the middle of the rumpled bed. The breakfast, she recalled, had been less than a culinary triumph, the egg yolks broken and the toast burnt, but Stephen had pronounced it the most delicious meal he'd ever eaten. Afterwards they'd made love yet again, as the rain beat steadily on the slanting roof just above their heads. But the bed was so deliciously cosy …

Her happy reminiscences were interrupted by the chirp of the telephone in the hall. Becca tucked the precious photo of Stephen into its polythene pocket and went to answer it.

'Hello?' she ventured.

There was a brief pause, then a slightly muffled male voice responded. 'Hello, my dear. How are you?'

Clearly, thought Becca, the man expected his voice to be recognised – it was something she'd grown used to when acting as secretary to her clergyman father. The voice *did* sound vaguely familiar, but she'd been in the parish such a short time that she was not yet adept at recognising the voices of her husband's parishioners. Embarrassed by her failure, and unwilling to admit it, she played for time, hoping for a clue to the caller's identity. 'Oh, I'm very well, thank you. And you?'

There was a chuckle. 'All the better for talking to you, my dear.'

Still no enlightenment. 'I'm afraid Stephen isn't here,' she offered, certain that the man must be phoning on parish business of some sort. 'He's gone to a Deanery Synod meeting. Would you like me to have him ring you when he gets home?' With sudden inspiration she added, 'Perhaps you'd better give me your number, just to be sure.'

Another soft chuckle. 'Oh, it's you I wanted to talk to. Tell me, how was your honeymoon?'

2

Becca smiled spontaneously at the introduction of her favourite subject. 'Wonderful! We went to Somerset, and had such a lovely time. We went to Bath, and to Wells Cathedral, and spent a lot of time just walking in the countryside and having meals in pubs.'

'The weather was good?'

'Most of the time, though it rained one or two days.'

The chuckle again. 'I don't imagine that bothered you, though, did it? Honeymooners can always find things to do, even when it's raining.'

The first shadow of unease made Becca pause before answering. 'Oh, yes, we didn't have any trouble filling the time.'

'I'm sure you didn't. Would you like to tell me about it?'

Becca found that her mouth was suddenly dry, and her heart gave an uncomfortable thud, 'Well, um, we ...' she began, moistening her lips with her tongue. 'We found things to do.'

'Don't be so shy,' the unemphatic voice urged her. 'Tell me all about it. I want to know all the details. How many times did you do it? Did you do it on the floor, or only on the bed?'

'Please...' Becca whispered, appalled.

Inexorably the voice continued. 'I'll bet the parson loves to touch your pretty titties, doesn't he? I'd like to touch them myself.' Another chuckle. 'Do you want to know what else I'd like to do to you?' He proceeded to tell her, unemotionally and at length.

Becca felt as if she'd been turned to stone, her hand clenching the phone to her ear as the stream of filth poured out unchecked, asking for and receiving no response. Eventually she dropped the receiver, forcing herself to take deep breaths, and covered her face with her hands. The voice went on. She snatched the receiver up again and slammed it into its cradle, then stood staring at it until it began ringing again.

This couldn't be happening, Becca told herself, swallowing hard to control her nausea. She was a married woman, married to the village Rector. Things like this didn't happen to rectors' wives in small Norfolk villages.

Unclean. She felt soiled by the words she'd heard, horrible words made all the more shocking by the calm way in which they were delivered. So many words, all about something filthy that seemed to have nothing to do with the wonderful things that she and Stephen had done in bed.

The phone gave its double chirp a dozen times, stopped, then started again. Rebecca Thorncroft turned and ran up the stairs to the bathroom, slammed the door, stripped off her clothes, got under the shower, and turned on the hot water full blast, drowning the insistent sound of the phone. Perhaps if she stayed in the shower long enough, the phone would stop ringing. And perhaps if she scrubbed herself hard enough, she would be able to feel clean again.

3

Part I

Chapter 1

Ye that stand in the house of the Lord: in the courts of the house of our God.
Psalm 135:2

There was nothing about the woman's appearance that gave any cause for alarm: she was quite an ordinary-looking young woman of an age approaching thirty, neatly dressed, tallish and large-boned with a wide-cheekboned face and honey-coloured hair pulled back in a simple pony tail. And, of course, the child was with her, a smartly turned-out and extremely well-behaved little girl.

Old Harry Gaze was the first one in Walston to meet her, or even to see her. That fact was undeniable, much as it grieved Enid Bletsoe. Enid made up for it later, of course, and claimed that it didn't really count.

Harry was the verger at St Michael and All Angels, an honorary position carrying no remuneration save the use of a cottage, but one which he took quite seriously, and thus he was as usual in the church when the woman and the child came in on a Saturday afternoon at the end of February.

The woman paused just inside the west door of the church, catching her breath at its soaring magnificence. St Michael and All Angels was not the sort of church one might have expected to find in a small, rather undistinguished Norfolk village like Walston; its size bespoke past glories of which scarcely a trace remained. Built in the Perpendicular style, its exterior, crowned by a massive square tower, was a marvel of flushwork in Norfolk flint, and the interior, with its vast expanses of clear glass in the side aisles and the deep clerestory, was irradiated with the sort of light that is found only in East Anglia, as if the sky had somehow found a way to invade the church. The double hammer-beam roof, high above the nave, was the home for a veritable choir of angels, gilded wooden wings outspread and mouths open in eternal song.

The little girl, too, was transfixed. 'Mummy,' she whispered at last, pointing roofwards. 'Look at the angels!'

'It's beautiful,' responded the woman spontaneously, squeezing her daughter's hand.

'Wholly fine work, that,' said a broad Norfolk voice from the shadows, and the woman turned, startled, to see an elderly man coming towards them.

He was quite tall and erect, with a distinguished cast to his features and an impressive head of silvery white hair, and he wore a cassock with an official-looking badge on his chest. 'Harry Gaze,' he introduced himself. 'I'm the verger here.' The woman nodded acknowledgement, and he went on without pause. 'My father was verger here before me, and his father before him, and so on back through the years. I reckon there's been Gazes here as long as this church has been standing, and that's a long time, I can tell you.'

'Do you live here in the church?' asked the little girl, wide-eyed.

Harry chuckled appreciatively. 'That's a good one, bless you. No, my ducks, I live in a little cottage just down the lane.' He gestured vaguely towards the north aisle. 'Between the Rectory and the church, it is. Wholly convenient it is, too – two minutes away. And now that I'm retired – now that my son, young Harry, has taken over the garage – I can spend most of my time here.' The verger lowered his voice to a conspiratorial whisper. 'Can't be too careful, you understand. There's wicked people in this world – people as wouldn't think anything of stealing a church's treasures and flogging them to rich people to decorate their fancy houses. Young tearaways on motorbikes, looking for something to pocket, or even bad 'uns come up all the way from London. You wouldn't feature it, but it's true.'

'I'm sure it is,' said the woman, shaking her head sympathetically. 'And you must have a great many treasures here.'

Harry gave a vigorous nod. 'Aye, that we do. You'll be wanting me to show you around, I reckon.' Without waiting for a reply, he marched up the wide centre aisle, between the majestic arcades of lofty slender pillars and pointed Gothic arches, past the monuments and effigied tomb chests, through the carved screen with its painted panels, and into the chancel. The woman and child followed more slowly, looking around them at the manifold beauties of the church. 'Cromwell's men – Dowsing and that rum lot – busted up all the stained-glass windows,' Harry explained over his shoulder. 'All excepting for the east window. One of the Lovelidge family, them as was lords of the manor, took that out before the Civil War and hid it away, up at Walston Hall, and it didn't get put back till Queen Victoria's time. Here.' He gestured at the magnificent medieval window, the richness of its jewel-like colours belying its age.

'More angels,' said the little girl, pointing to the ranks of winged creatures who ranged along the top of the window.

'Nine orders of angels,' amplified her mother.

'Right you are, my ducks,' Harry nodded. 'There's angels everywhere in this church.' He turned and flourished his arm towards a chair standing by itself against the north wall of the chancel, roped off rather grandly with red cords. 'And this,' he announced, 'is our greatest treasure. King John's chair.'

The woman studied it with interest. The chair was made of age-darkened oak, simple and sturdy in design and carved with Elizabethan strap-work patterns. 'King John?' she said quizzically.

5

Drawing himself up to his full height, Harry launched into a practised patter. 'Bad King John he was known as. Managed to get everyone's backs up – the Pope, foreigners like the Frogs, and even his own true English people. If he wasn't fighting with one, he was fighting with another. Well, you must know the story of how he lost his jewels in the Wash when he was running away from the Frogs.' He glanced at the little girl, who shook her head. 'Don't know what they teach them in school nowadays,' he grumbled to himself. 'In my day, we learned all about history in school – not the sort of nonsense they fill young heads with these days.' Sniffing, he addressed himself to her in a didactic voice. 'King John was running away from the Frogs. He reckoned as he'd take a short cut across the Wash at low tide, and he made it to the other side, but the wagons got bogged down in the mud, and the tide rushed in and swept everything away. Including all of his jewels, and even his crown. It was a wholly bad day for bad King John, I can tell you. Never found none of it again, neither. Not a sausage.'

'Poor King John,' said the little girl, wide-eyed.

'Not a bit of it,' Harry reproved with another sniff. 'He deserved it. I told you, he was a bad king. But the thing about it is, the very day before he lost his jewels, he stopped here in this very church, and he sat himself in that very chair. To pray that he would escape from the Frogs. And he did, too, not forgetting that he lost his jewels as God's punishment for his wicked ways. And that chair has been here in this church ever since, to remind people of the way God answers prayers.' With a decisive nod, the verger went on, 'And King John was by no means the only king to visit this church. Practically every king there ever was, back in the Middle Ages, stopped in Walston on the way to Walsingham, to the Shrine of Our Lady. Right on the way from London it was, a regular stopping-off place for pilgrims, kings included.' He stopped at last and looked the woman up and down, sizing her up. 'These days we get people from all over come just to look at the church. Even folks up from London, who've read or heard about this church. I expect you're from London?' His voice lifted at the end in enquiry.

'Well, sort of.' She smiled, an attractive slow smile that matched her deliberate way of speaking. 'Actually, we're moving to Walston. Today. To Foxglove Cottage. But we got here ahead of the removal van, so we thought we'd have a look around the village. I wanted to see the church – I *have* heard about it.'

For a moment Harry stared at her, his mouth open. 'Foxglove Cottage?' he said at last. 'Old Miss Ivey's place? But that's been empty for months – no one told me that it had been sold!'

'It all happened quite quickly,' she explained. 'It was just what we'd been looking for, and since it offered vacant possession there wasn't any reason to wait – not for me and Bryony, anyway.' Putting out her hand, she added, 'I'm Mrs English, by the way. Gillian English. And my daughter Bryony.'

Harry had regained his composure; he took her hand and shook it with solemn ceremony. 'Very pleased to meet you, Mrs English. Welcome to Walston. This is quite an event – we don't get many newcomers here.' All thoughts of church treasures fled as, with a grin, he went on, 'And you'll be wanting to know all about the village. Well, you've come to the right place, I can tell you. I've been here all my life, bred and born in this village, and there's nothing about Walston that Harry Gaze doesn't know! And about the people in it, I might add.'

'How convenient.' Her tone might have been ironic, but the old man took her words at face value.

'I suppose you've met Enid Bletsoe, across the road from you at The Pines?' She shook her head. 'No, I haven't met anyone yet.'

'Well, I expect it won't be long before you meet Enid,' Harry predicted with a sage nod. 'Enid doesn't let much get past her. Especially these days, since the young doctor's made her retire as his receptionist. She doesn't have anything better to do than look out her window and mind other folks' business for them.'

Gillian, not by nature a curious person, nonetheless saw the value in gleaning a bit of information about her nearest neighbour. 'She lives alone, then?'

'Most of the time. There's a grandson, young Jamie, as she brought up herself from a tiny thing, but he's away at university these days. Oxford or Cambridge or some such – I can't remember. His parents were killed when he was a baby,' Harry added. 'Enid's son and his wife, killed dead in a car crash out on the old Norwich road. Jamie's the apple of Enid's eye, I don't need to tell you.'

'She's a widow, then?'

Harry chuckled, and lowered his voice so that Bryony couldn't hear. 'That's what she'd like you to believe, any road. But there's some of us in this village as remember as clear as yesterday the day when Jack Bletsoe up sticks and left. Years ago, it was – young Jamie's father wasn't more than a baby himself. Jack up sticks and left her to bring up that baby wholly on her own. No one in Walston's seen Jack Bletsoe since – he might be dead for all I know. I suppose that would make her a widow, wouldn't it?' He winked roguishly. 'Not that it makes any difference, mind you – there's not a man in Walston, bachelor or widower, as would take that one on, with or without young Jamie.'

Gillian gave a bemused smile which the verger took as encouragement to continue. 'And her sister, Doris Wrightman. She's not much better, I can tell you. Two of a kind, they are.'

Her expression grew even more bemused as he went on to deliver a succinct and sometimes scurrilous overview of the people she was likely to encounter in her first days in Walston: churchwarden Fred Purdy, proprietor of the village shop, whose wife was suffering from terminal cancer and whose unmarried daughter had presented him with a grandchild, scandalising the village; Roger Staines, the other churchwarden, dismissed as 'an egghead'; Marjorie Talbot-Shaw, clergy widow and the secretary of the PCC; former churchwarden Ernest Wrightman, who still seemed to have his finger in any number of pies; young Doctor McNair, a non-churchgoer who was nevertheless an important and respected member of the village community; Quentin and Diana Mansfield, relative newcomers to the village, who owned Walston Hall; Cyprian Lawrence, the reclusive and unpopular organist. The rapid-fire barrage of unfamiliar names and information was imperfectly absorbed by its recipient, who nonetheless managed to nod her head in the right places.

'So.' Harry paused for breath. 'That's just about everyone who's important. Excepting, of course, for the Rector. I expect as you'd like to know about him.'

'Father Fuller?' said Gillian. 'I saw his name on the notice board outside.'

Harry chuckled. 'Oh, no. Father Fuller was the last rector. Retired near on to two years ago and died last year. We just haven't got around to changing the notice board. New Rector's been here well under a year – name of Stephen Thorncroft. Young fellow, with good solid high churchmanship. But it's always difficult to break in a new rector. Mind you, we haven't had to do it for quite a while – Father Fuller was here near on to thirty years.' He laughed. 'I reckon Father Thorncroft will be all right once we've knocked the corners off him. These young fellows always have wholly grand ideas – takes them a while to learn the facts of life. And,' he added, grinning, 'he's got other things on his mind – like a pretty new wife. Just married, and she's a right corker. No red-blooded young man wants to be worrying about a church and its problems when he's got a pretty new wife to occupy him.'

Gillian thought about the riches of information that Harry Gaze had so freely proffered as she and Bryony walked back through Walston village towards Foxglove Cottage, trying to remember what he'd said about various individuals. It had all come too soon, she reflected ruefully: before she had any faces to attach to the multitude of names that he'd fired at her.

Walston consisted to a large extent of one main street sloping down from the gentle rise on which St Michael's Church had reigned for centuries, past school and almshouses to what passed for the village centre. Gillian looked about her with interest. There, across from the war memorial and the shabby Village Hall, was the village shop. Alfred Purdy, Proprietor, it announced on the cheerful striped awning. Fred Purdy. Yes, she remembered: he was one of the churchwardens. And next to it was Gaze's Garage, clearly once a livery stable, with one petrol pump and a forecourt where middle-aged 'young Harry' sold a few second-hand cars.

The pub beyond, the Queen's Head, featured on its sign the disembodied but otherwise serene face of Anne Boleyn; Gillian recalled from her history books that the Boleyn family had come from Norfolk, not far from Walston. The Queen's Head showed signs of having been smartened up considerably in recent years, probably to its detriment; its former rustic charms had given way to double-glazed windows and other appurtenances of twentieth-century life, including a satellite dish sprouting incongruously from its tile roof.

A discreet brass plaque announced the location of the doctor's surgery, which occupied a beautifully proportioned brick Georgian house set back just a short distance from the pavement. Dr McNair – young Dr McNair, Harry Gaze had called him, Gillian remembered. He'd said that the 'new doctor' had taken over the practice from his uncle, 'old Dr McNair', some fifteen years past, which didn't exactly make him a youngster, she reflected with a wry smile.

Immersed in her own observations, Gillian didn't register the fact that Bryony had been unusually silent during their walk, so the child's voice startled her out of her reverie.

'Mummy,' Bryony said in a thoughtful voice, 'why did Bad King John run away from the frogs? Was it like the plagues of Egypt? Frogs and blood and hail and caterpillars?'

Gillian mastered the impulse to laugh, treating the question with the seriousness it deserved. 'Oh, no, darling. Mr Gaze didn't mean that sort of frogs. You know that we've explained to you about people – ignorant and prejudiced people – who use rude words to describe other people who are – different – than they are? Words like queer, and poufter, and dyke, and Paki, and darky?'

Bryony nodded gravely. 'Yes, I remember.'

'Well, "Frog" is a word like that. It's a word that some people use to refer to French people. Because the French eat frogs' legs.'

'I see.' The girl digested the information. 'Mummy, does that mean that Mr Gaze is ignorant and prejudiced?'

Gillian hesitated. 'Perhaps he's just – uneducated,' she temporised. 'You and I know that it's not nice to use words like that, but it's also important to make allowances for people who don't know any better.'

Relieved, Bryony squeezed her mother's hand. 'I'm glad that Mr Gaze isn't ignorant, Mummy. I thought that he was a nice old man. He knows lots of interesting stories, doesn't he?'

'That he does.'

'But he talks so funny – sometimes I couldn't understand him.'

'That's because he's always lived in Norfolk,' Gillian explained. 'I had a hard time understanding him myself. But he probably thinks that *we* talk funny.'

By this time they had nearly reached Foxglove Cottage, set back a bit from the road, built in grey Norfolk flint. Even in February, the surrounding vegetation still winter-bare, it was a handsome dwelling, showing great promise for the future. There was still, Gillian noted, no sign of the removal van. But there was a woman standing in the drive, peering anxiously at Gillian's red Metro. She looked up as they approached.

'Oh, hello,' she said, her eyes raking them up and down. 'Is this your car? I just looked out of my window and saw it sitting in the drive, and thought I'd better investigate. The house is vacant, you know, and you can't be too careful.'

Gillian replied deliberately. 'Yes, it's my car. We're moving in today, but the removal van doesn't seem to have arrived yet.' She took the house keys from her pocket and jingled them in her hand. 'I'm Gillian English,' she added.

'Oh!' Her neighbour's surprise was evident. 'I didn't even know that the cottage had been sold!' Recollecting herself, she put out her hand. 'I'm Enid Bletsoe. I live just across the road, at The Pines.' She inclined her head towards a modern bungalow, flanked by the eponymous evergreens.

Accepting the proffered hand, Gillian took stock of her new neighbour: well-upholstered figure that couldn't quite be described as stout, a square face with prominent jowls framed by grey hair in a style most reminiscent of the Queen's, sharp dark eyes behind fussy spectacles, a mud-coloured padded three-quarter-length coat over a brown and white crimplene dress. She was aware that she was herself under intense scrutiny, and smiled in what she hoped was a disarming way. 'How nice to meet you.'

Enid Bletsoe found the smile encouraging, reinforcing the woman's ordinary appearance, and the reassuringly domestic name of 'English'. 'Welcome to Walston,' she said, then focused her attention on Bryony, her voice taking on the hearty tone that people often use when speaking to children or foreigners. 'And who is this?'

'This is my daughter, Bryony,' Gillian said.

Enid bent down to study her more closely. 'What a pretty name. How old are you, Bryony?'

'Six.' Her manner was as composed as her mother's.

'Then you'll be going to the village school, won't you?' Straightening up, she addressed Gillian again. 'Why don't you come over and have a cup of coffee while you wait for the removal van? It will be much more comfortable than waiting in an empty house, and we can begin to get acquainted.'

'Yes,' Gillian said. 'That would be very nice, Mrs Bletsoe.'

'Please, call me Enid.'

In short order they were installed in the lounge of The Pines, a room whose double-glazed picture window afforded a panoramic view of Foxglove Cottage. The room was fussily furnished, with a great many china ornaments and a number of framed photos which chronicled the development of a chubby-cheeked little boy into a good-looking young man. Bryony examined them with frank curiosity while Enid was out of the room preparing the coffee.

'I've brought you some orange squash, Bryony,' Enid announced in her hearty voice, bearing a heavily laden tray, 'and some nice choccie biscuits.'

'Thank you very much indeed,' the girl said promptly; such sugar-filled treats did not often come her way at home, and she knew that politeness would not allow her mother to refuse them on her behalf.

'And coffee for the grown-ups.' She handed Gillian a stoneware mug. 'I see you're looking at the pictures of my grandson, Bryony. His name is Jamie.'

'Does he live here?'

10

'This is his home,' Enid explained, 'though he's not here very much these days. He's at Cambridge, and only comes home during the holidays.' She turned to Gillian and explained in a voice full of pride, 'He's a wonderful boy, I don't have to tell you. I raised him from a baby, and he never gave me a moment's trouble. Good as gold, was my Jamie. And now he's at university, doing ever so well. I miss him dreadfully, but there you are. And,' she added confidentially, 'he has such a nice girlfriend. Miss Charlotte Hollingsworth. Her father is Lord Hollingsworth – you've heard of him, I'm sure.'

Gillian gave a noncommittal nod.

'So do you live here by yourself?' Bryony probed, with the unselfconscious curiosity of a child.

Enid took a sip of her coffee and cleared her throat. 'Yes, I'm afraid so, now that Jamie is away. My dear husband has been gone these forty years, God rest his soul.' Taking the offensive, she fixed her eyes on the little girl. 'And what about your daddy, Bryony? When will he be coming to Walston?'

'Oh, Daddy doesn't live with us any more,' she said.

'We're divorced,' Gillian added matter-of-factly.

Another sip of coffee gave Enid a chance to absorb that information. 'So it's just the two of you, then.'

'Oh, no,' replied Bryony. 'There's Lou.'

Enid said nothing, but looked at Gillian, who felt compelled to amplify. 'My – partner. Lou will be joining us in a week or so, when the job in London gets sorted out.'

'I see,' said Enid Bletsoe with a careful smile.

While the removal van was busily disgorging furniture, Enid walked into the village, making straight for the village shop; an invitation for Gillian and Bryony to join her for a simple meal on their first evening in Walston had been accepted, and it was important that she prepare properly for that event.

Fred Purdy was behind the counter as usual. 'Morning, Enid,' he greeted her cheerfully. Fred was a rotund man in his early fifties with a marked resemblance to a garden gnome: his woolly white hair curled about his face and he wore a fluffy goatee on the chin of an otherwise clean-shaven and very pink face. His unvarying good nature was such an accepted fixture of life in Walston that people seldom stopped to ask if he was, indeed, very bright. That question notwithstanding, he had been elected unopposed as churchwarden of St Michael's annually for nearly thirty years. 'What's new?'

Enid chose to dole out her information in small parcels. 'I'm having guests to tea this evening,' she stated, surveying the possibilities on the shelves near the door.

'Lord What's-'is-Name?' Fred chuckled. 'The one whose daughter is keeping company with young Jamie? That'll be something to see – his Roller pulling up in front of The Pines.' Fred was always the first – and often the only one – to laugh at his own jokes.

Enid sniffed to indicate that Lord Hollingsworth was no joking matter, and otherwise chose to ignore Fred's attempt at humour. 'There will be a child,' she said. 'It's been so long since Jamie was six, I'm not sure what to serve.'

'Fish fingers and chips with baked beans,' Fred stated promptly. 'That's my little granddaughter's favourite tea.'

'Hm.' She raised her eyebrows noncommittally. 'That might do, if I had a couple of chops as well.'

Fred prided himself on carrying in his shop everything that residents of Walston might possibly require. 'In the freezer behind you,' he indicated. 'There are some nice ones. But who are these mystery guests?'

'My new neighbours,' Enid told him over her shoulder as she selected the chops. 'Mrs Gillian English and her daughter Bryony. They're moving into Foxglove Cottage today.'

'Oh, yes.' Fred nodded as he rang up her purchases on his ancient till. 'Harry mentioned them when he stopped in for his tobacco a bit ago. Said they'd been up at the church looking around.'

'Did he indeed?' Enid pronounced frostily, extracting some coins from her purse. 'Perhaps Harry Gaze ought to mind his own business for a change.'

Enid's next stop, on her way home, was her sister Doris's house. It wasn't strictly on her way back to The Pines, as Doris and her husband Ernest Wright-man lived in the opposite direction from the village shop, in a small house across from the school and almshouses. But she often stopped by for a cup of tea with Doris, and today she had something worthwhile to tell her.

Ernest had departed on some errand, so Doris and Enid were settled in the kitchen with a pot of tea and a plate of biscuits on the table between them.

'Bryony is the loveliest little girl – so polite and well behaved, and dressed like a little lady, in a frilly little dress and proper shoes,' Enid was saying. 'Not like most of the girls you see these days, all scruffy in jeans and trainers – half the time you can't even tell whether they're girls or boys. It says a lot for her mother, you know, that she's so well turned out. And Gillian herself – she seems such a nice young woman. Nice clothes, well spoken. And why do you think she's come to Walston?'

'I can't imagine.' Doris had a vapid, fleshy face, the chief feature of which was her eyebrows, thin pencilled arches delineating where they would have been had she not plucked them into virtual nonexistence. Her hair was dyed a flat shade of brown and she was fond of telling people that she was Enid's *younger* sister. The same vanity which made that seem an important distinction to her also prompted her to keep her spectacles in her handbag rather than on her face, so Doris observed much of life through a squint.

'Because she grows herbs,' Enid stated self-importantly. 'She has a little business, growing herbs to supply to restaurants in London. But she's done so well that she's outgrown her tiny London garden and decided that she needed to find a place in the country. And Foxglove Cottage was just what she was looking for!'

Doris reached for a biscuit, then remembered that she was supposed to be slimming and withdrew her hand. 'But what about her husband? Doesn't he have a job in London?'

With the air of one who had been saving the best for last, Enid paused. 'She's divorced,' she stated. 'She has a – partner.' The word was said with studied nonchalance.

Doris goggled. 'You mean – a lover? A man she's not married to?'

Taking a sip of her tea, Enid nodded gravely. 'I know it's not quite the thing, Doris. I mean, we're not used to people … living in sin … in Walston. And of course I don't personally approve of such behaviour. But we've got to face the facts – in this day and age I believe it's much more common, and acceptable, than you'd ever think.' Enid was an avid reader of glossy women's magazines, a habit which she'd developed while working in the waiting room of Dr McNair's surgery, and from which she gleaned much of her knowledge of the world outside Walston. 'And far be it from me to cast the first stone,' she added. 'I think that we've got to keep an open mind, don't you? Give them the benefit of the doubt. After all, they may be planning to get married soon.'

'But who *is* this man?' demanded her sister. '*She* may be all right, but what do you know about *him*?'

'His name is Lou, and he's some sort of high-powered computer boffin, according to Gillian,' Enid explained. 'He's been working in London, but now he's going to work from home, from Foxglove Cottage. They call it "telecommuting",' she pronounced self-consciously. 'Quite the new thing, I believe. You never have to leave your house – it's all done with computers and telephones. I read about it recently.'

Doris fastened upon the one thing in her sister's discourse that she'd understood. 'Lou? Isn't that an Italian name? Do you think he's Italian?'

'I don't know.' Enid frowned thoughtfully as she poured herself another cup of tea. 'She didn't say – I suppose it's possible.'

'But that would be awful. Foreigners in Walston! People living in sin is bad enough, but foreigners, Enid!'

'Perhaps he's Welsh,' Enid suggested. 'You know – L E W, short for Lewis, or Llewellyn.'

In her agitation, Doris seized and consumed the forbidden biscuit. 'A Welshman? I don't think that's really very much better than an Eyetie! Honestly, Enid! What is this village coming to?'

Enid judged that it was time to change the subject. 'I've invited her to join the

Mothers' Union,' she announced, adding unnecessarily, 'Gillian, that is. And she's agreed.'

Her sister sputtered in indignation. 'A divorced woman? And one who's living in sin? But we've never had anything like that in the Mothers' Union before! We're a respectable organisation – at least we always were in *my* time.' This was a barbed arrow and a direct hit. Her term of office expired, Doris had recently, and reluctantly, handed over the office of Enrolling Member to her sister; it was inevitably a sore point between them.

'Yes,' Enid said with a smile of sweet malice. 'But weren't you the one who was always trying to attract new, young members? Without any success, I might add. You're just jealous because I've managed to find a young woman to join – not to mention the Rector's wife, who is sure to agree as well, now that she won't be the only young one. Anyway,' she added, retreating to the high moral ground, 'who are we to cast the first stone?'

Chapter 2

When I receive the congregation: I shall judge according unto right.

Psalm 75:3

It was unfortunate for Enid Bletsoe, firmly in possession of her new neighbours on Sunday morning, that their appearance at church, and indeed the entire day, was overshadowed by an event of even more momentousness than the arrival of newcomers in Walston.

They were met at the west door by Ernest Wright-man, whose good luck it was to be on duty as sidesman that day. He spared only a cursory glance for Gillian and Bryony before addressing himself to his sister-in-law as he handed her a hymn book and a service booklet. 'Have you heard the news, then?' he asked, knowing full well that she hadn't, and delighting in the opportunity to tell her.

'What's that?'

'Roger Staines. Had a heart attack last night!'

'What?!'

Wrightman shook his head with lugubrious relish. 'Dreadful news, isn't it? He's in a bad way, they say.'

'Then he's still alive?'

'Oh, yes, it didn't kill him. The ambulance got to him in time, and got him to hospital.' He lowered his voice confidentially. 'Who would have thought it? There didn't seem to be a thing wrong with him yesterday afternoon when I saw him. But that's the way these heart attacks work, isn't it? One minute you're fit as a fiddle, and the next you're flat on your back in a hospital bed. Or in a pine box. Just like what happened to me four years back. Doris didn't think I was going to make it, but here I still am!' His laugh was high-pitched and mirthless.

Gillian, realising that the man was Enid's brother-in-law, took the opportunity to observe him. He was short and rather slight, with thin gingery hair slicked to his skull and pinched features: a narrow nose with small dark eyes above and thin lips below a wisp of a ginger moustache. One might have described him as insignificant, had it not been for the aggressive set of his square jaw, and his unexpectedly deep and resonant voice.

15

Enid recollected herself enough to say, 'Ernest, you haven't yet had the pleasure of meeting my new neighbours, Mrs English and her daughter Bryony.'

He gave them a perfunctory nod and a quick look of inspection before turning to perform his duties with the woman who followed them. 'Marjorie! Have you heard the terrible news?'

Acknowledging defeat, at least in this encounter, Enid hurried them through the empty church and up into the chancel, where a number of chairs were arranged in rows. 'We always have our services up here,' she explained. 'It's cosier – we'd get lost in the nave, as few of us as there are.' Though she usually sat near the back, the better to see, on this occasion she decided to sit near the front, the better to be seen.

Seen they were in spite of the fuss over Roger Staines, and the newcomers were noted by the Rector when he entered from the vestry at the beginning of the service. Stephen Thorncroft was an intelligent young man who didn't miss much, even though on that morning his thoughts were somewhat distracted by concern about the stricken churchwarden. He'd seen Roger Staines the night before, in hospital, shortly after he'd been admitted, and he hadn't looked good at all – as far as Stephen had been able to determine, it had been touch-and-go, and the danger was not past. He wasn't sure how much he ought to say to the congregation about the churchwarden's condition. Realising that Ernest Wrightman was on duty that morning, Stephen had no doubt that the arriving parishioners had been fully informed about the incident; he decided not to make an announcement and instead to wait till the prayers of intercession to mention it. 'The Lord be with you,' he said, raising his hands.

'And also with you,' responded the congregation. Gillian English studied the fair-haired young priest, solemn-faced and looking rather sombre in his purple Lenten chasuble. He had a sensitive mouth, she noted, and his grey eyes, behind gold-rimmed spectacles, seemed intelligent.

That promise didn't disappoint. His homily, just the right length, displayed a quick mind and an articulate way of expressing himself, and he celebrated the Eucharist with reverence and care. Gillian was used to the elaborate ritual of London Anglo-Catholicism; she found the service, with old Harry Gaze as the only server, to be refreshing in its sincere simplicity. And, beyond all expectations, the music was amazingly good: the small choir, conducted by a darkly handsome man, was of a London standard, the unaccompanied voices soaring and resonating through the magnificent building, and the organ was tuneful and rich. She was going to like St Michael's, she decided. And Lou, who wasn't particularly churchy but appreciated good music, would approve as well.

Usually the women, at least, rushed off fairly quickly after the morning service, anxious to get back to their Sunday lunch preparations. But today there was a tendency to linger, possibly to observe or speak to the newcomer or to discuss the condition of Roger Staines and the ramifications of his misfortune.

As soon as decency would allow after the Dismissal and the departure of Father Stephen, Enid got to her feet, crossed the aisle to where Becca Thorncroft still knelt, and waited for her to finish her prayers. Enid scrutinised the Rector's wife with interest: there was something about the droop of her head over her clasped hands, about the dark circles under her closed eyes, that indicated to Enid that perhaps all was not well with the new Mrs Thorncroft. Maybe she was pregnant already, or perhaps Father Stephen wasn't quite what he should be as a husband. Becca would bear closer watching in future, she decided. 'There's someone I want you to meet,' Enid stated as Becca rose.

Becca turned. 'Yes?'

'My new neighbour, Gillian English. And her daughter, Bryony.' She indicated them with a flourish of her arm. 'They've just moved into Foxglove Cottage.'

'How nice to meet you.' Becca's smile was genuine as she greeted the newcomers: there was a dearth of young women in Walston, and instantly she recognised a potential friend.

Gillian experienced a similar relief in discovering that there was at least one person near her own age in the village. She smiled up at Becca; the Rector's wife was even taller than she, and very slender, with silvery blonde hair worn in a short bob, enormous eyes of cornflower blue, and a face that just missed being classically beautiful by virtue of the one feature that actually gave her much of her charm – a rather short, tip-tilted nose.

'Gillian is interested in joining the Mothers' Union,' Enid announced. 'So there will be another young one to keep you company!'

Becca's smile faded. 'I'm not really sure ...'

'Oh, you have plenty of time to decide – the enrolment isn't for a while yet. But I know you'll want to join,' said Enid brightly.

'Do you have any children?' Bryony asked Becca.

Thankful at being rescued from Enid's probing, Becca turned to the little girl, smiling. 'No, I'm afraid not. Not yet, anyway – I've only been married for about two months! So it will be a little while yet.'

'But you don't have to be a mother to join the Mothers' Union,' Enid emphasised. 'You only have to subscribe to its aims and objectives about the importance of marriage and family life.'

Meanwhile Doris Wrightman, torn between her curiosity about Gillian and her determination to ignore her, hovered nearby in conversation with Marjorie Talbot-Shaw, who was holding forth about the shortcomings of the new Rector. This was a favourite theme of Mrs Talbot-Shaw, PCC secretary and herself the widow of a Shropshire clergyman, a man who had by all accounts been nothing short of perfect. Mrs Talbot-Shaw, who had retired alone to Norfolk after her husband's death, was a rather formidable-looking woman, tall and buxom, with a solitary and dramatic streak of silver in her dark hair.

'I just don't understand,' she was saying with a frown, 'Why he didn't even mention poor Roger's heart attack until the prayers. He might have made an announcement at the beginning of the service. My husband Godfrey certainly would have done.'

'Yes,' Doris agreed, darting a glance at the adjoining party. 'Everyone is so concerned about poor Roger. I can't think why Father Stephen didn't say anything.'

Harry Gaze, divested of his server's alb in record time, was expressing similar sentiments to Fred Purdy, a short distance away. 'Wouldn't have happened in Father Fuller's day,' he stated.

'No, indeed.' Fred's amiable smile didn't falter as he brought the conversation round to the question that really interested him. 'Do you reckon that Roger will be able to continue as churchwarden?'

'Don't know. Ernest had to give it up when he had his heart attack, didn't he? Darn near killed him to give it up, but the new doctor said as he had to.'

Fred nodded. 'It's just that Roger hasn't seemed too keen on some of my ideas lately. Things might be easier around here with a new warden.'

'Might be.' Harry was noncommittal; his attention had strayed to the group of women still chatting in the centre aisle. 'Have you met that new lady as has just moved to Foxglove Cottage? Mrs English?'

'Not yet,' Fred admitted. 'But I don't imagine it will be long before she finds her way to the shop.' He chuckled. 'Everyone does, sooner or later.'

'She's a good looker, wouldn't you say?'

'Not bad,' concurred Fred judiciously.

Unaware of the men's scrutiny, Gillian was asking Becca about the music. 'I was really impressed by the choir,' she said.

'They're good, aren't they?' Becca agreed. 'Stephen is really pleased with them.'

'I can't believe that you have so many good singers here in the village.'

'We don't!' Enid interposed indignantly. 'That is, we *do*, but you didn't hear them this morning!'

Gillian turned to her. 'What do you mean?'

'It's a disgrace! He sacked the choir, and a perfectly good choir it was, too, and brought in that lot. All his friends they are, people from Norwich. They just come in for the services, and they're actually *paid*! I can't imagine whyever Father Stephen lets him get away with it! To treat his loyal choir like that – Ernest was really cut up about it, I can tell you.'

Becca flushed at the implied criticism of her husband, and tried to explain. 'Cyprian is a very fine musician – he's an internationally known composer. Stephen says that we're very fortunate to have him. He took on the job mainly because he likes living in the country – it's better for composing, he says – and Stephen was able to offer him a cottage near the church as part of his salary. And the church has an excellent old organ and wonderful acoustics, so those things made it attractive to him as well.'

18

'A disgrace,' interjected Enid.

'He's been able to negotiate several recording contracts using the church because of the acoustics,' Becca continued, doing her best to ignore the interruption. 'And with the money he's made from that, he's been able to hire a professional choir.'

'Father Fuller would never have allowed it,' Enid whispered to Gillian. 'Letting a jumped-up organist like that Cyprian Lawrence sack the choir!'

'Cyprian Lawrence?' Gillian echoed. 'I'm sure I've heard of him.' She looked around, hoping to see the organist; he would be an interesting person to get to know, she reflected. Perhaps Walston was going to be more stimulating than she'd anticipated.

'No use looking for him,' said Enid with a spiteful smile. 'He runs off as soon as the service is over, back to his little cottage to hide. Not that I blame him – he's not exactly a popular person around here.'

But it was a choleric Ernest Wrightman who had the last word on the subject as he joined the women. 'As far as I'm concerned, he can go back to London or wherever he came from and it won't be a minute too soon. Or better yet, he can go to the devil.'

Chapter 3

Over lunch, Stephen Thorncroft made an effort to put aside his concern for Roger Staines, giving his full attention to his wife. She told him about her conversation with his new parishioners, in whom he was of course interested; his own contact with them, on their way out of church, had been necessarily brief. It was good, he reflected, to see Becca enthusiastic about something for a change. Her behaviour since their marriage, or more specifically since the return from their honeymoon, had been a bit puzzling: she often seemed distracted, or depressed, when everything he had known of her before had demonstrated a sunny good nature; what was more disturbing was that she continued to insist that nothing was bothering her. He supposed that it had to do with adjustment to the married state or possibly to life in a village where everyone knew your business and where the Rector's wife had even more restrictions and expectations laid upon her than other people. And he had to remember, Stephen told himself, that Becca, at just twenty-one, was very young for such responsibilities, in spite of her lifetime of training as a vicar's daughter.

'I did think she was ever so nice,' Becca said, passing him the gravy. 'And her little girl is gorgeous.'

'What about her husband? Isn't he a churchgoer?'

'I don't think she's married,' she admitted. 'She called him her "partner" rather than her husband. Apparently he's still in London and won't be getting here until next weekend.'

'That won't go down very well in the village,' Stephen said, half to himself.

'Enid seemed to be all right about it – she's already asked Gillian to join the Mothers' Union.'

Stephen shook his head. 'There's never any telling. Anyway, sweetheart, we'll have to make an effort to welcome them to Walston. Invite them for a meal and that sort of thing.'

Ruefully Becca surveyed their Sunday lunch, adequate but unexciting; cooking had never been one of her interests and her marriage had not brought about any great change of heart on the subject. 'She's probably a really good cook. I'd be embarrassed to invite them.'

'Don't be silly.' He smiled at her fondly; it was fortunate, given Becca's lack of interest in cooking, that Stephen was a rather ascetic young man who didn't consider food to be particularly important. 'It's the hospitality that matters.'

The phone in the hall jangled suddenly; Becca started, then, as her husband went to answer it, clenched her fists on the table and took several deep breaths. It couldn't be the man, she told herself: he had never rung while Stephen was at home. But almost inevitably whenever Stephen was away, the phone would ring and it would be that voice. Soft-spoken, relaxed and just beyond identification. It always began the same – he would ask after her welfare, a friendly and concerned parishioner. And then would come the unspeakable questions, the suggestions, the fantasies. The filth. There was no way to stop it: if she put the phone down, he would only ring again, with a mild, injured rebuke for her discourtesy and continue where he had left off. It wasn't possible to ignore the phone, either – what if it were someone in urgent need of the Rector?

The worst of it was that she couldn't tell Stephen. The first time it had happened, over a month ago, she had managed to convince herself that it was a one-off occurrence, that it couldn't happen again and that there was no reason to worry her husband. And as time had gone on and the calls had continued, she couldn't think of a way to explain to him why she hadn't mentioned it before. Besides, she couldn't possibly bring herself to repeat the foul words, especially not to Stephen. The knowledge of those words, and of her contamination, would come between them, and spoil for ever the beauty of their lovemaking. And it wouldn't be fair to cast such a cloud of suspicion over his relationship with his parishioners – the consciousness that one of them had done such a thing would inevitably colour his feelings towards all of them. So she had borne it on her own, turning aside his concerned enquiries with brave assurances, however unconvincing, that all was well.

'That was Dr McNair,' Stephen said, coming back into the dining room. 'He wanted to let me know that he's just back from Norwich, from hospital, and Roger wants me to bring him the Sacrament. I was thinking that I should go this afternoon in any case, so as soon as we've finished lunch, I'll be off.'

Stephen didn't miss the quickly suppressed look of panic which tensed the muscles of her face. 'I suppose you must,' she agreed bravely. 'If he's asked for the Sacrament.'

'Becca, sweetheart, what's the matter?' He crossed to her and tipped her face up with a finger under her chin.

'Nothing. I'd just – hoped for an afternoon together, that's all.' She forced a smile. 'I mustn't be selfish.'

Stephen bent down and kissed her gently. 'That's my girl. I'll be home in time for tea.'

She went out to the kitchen to fetch the pudding, fighting down the panic. Returning to the dining room, she clutched at an idea. 'Stephen, could I come with you?' she suggested eagerly. 'I'd like to see Mr Staines too.'

He considered the proposal for a moment. 'I don't know why not, sweetheart. The doctor said that he's allowed to have visitors and it might do him some good to see your pretty face. And perhaps we might find a nice teashop somewhere on the way back.'

This time her smile was radiant, startling her husband with its intensity. 'Oh, thank you, Stephen! That would be lovely!'

Stephen had seen him the night before, when he was looking much worse, but Roger Staines's appearance, in his hospital bed in the coronary care unit of the Norfolk and Norwich hospital, shocked Becca deeply. His face was grey, drained of colour, and sensors stuck to his bare chest connected him to the paraphernalia of electronic gadgetry which monitored the degree to which he clung to life, while an intravenous drip sustained that life. But he managed a smile when he saw them. 'What a nice surprise, Rector. You've brought something to brighten my day – your lovely bride.'

Becca crossed to kiss his ashen cheek. 'Hello, Mr Staines. You gave us a scare.'

'It scared me a bit as well.' His smile held a shadow of his customary twinkle. 'I thought for a while there that my number was up. But Fergus McNair tells me that I'm going to pull through.'

'That's wonderful news.' Stephen came to the bedside and touched his hand gently. 'He rang me and said that you wanted the Sacrament.'

'I'm surprised that he passed on the message,' grinned Roger. 'You know what a cynical old heathen he is.'

Becca withdrew to the corner of the room and watched quietly while Stephen administered the Sacrament. Her initial shock had abated, but she couldn't take her eyes off the man in the bed. The bones stood out on a face normally smooth and rounded, and the sickly pallor of his complexion accentuated the height of his forehead with its receding hairline. The normally tidy straight grey hair looked lank and lifeless, and his blue eyes, without their customary silver-rimmed spectacles, seemed smaller. His appearance was all the more startling for its contrast to his usual nattiness: Roger Staines always dressed impeccably if somewhat idiosyncratically in tweed suits with colourful bow ties and patterned silk waistcoats. In anyone else such a garb would have smacked of the *poseur*, but all who knew him were aware that he was incapable of deliberate affectation. He was an intelligent, educated man, trained as an historian; he could have gone far in the academic world, and had indeed been offered more than one Oxbridge fellowship, but he preferred to live in Walston and concentrate on his magnum opus: a comprehensive history of the village

22

and St Michael's Church, a book which had been many years in the researching and the writing.

Roger Staines's interest in that particular Norfolk village was no accident. He was a descendant, in the female line, of the Lovelidge family, who as lords of the manor had dominated the village for centuries. The male line had died out shortly after the Great War; due to the peculiarities of the inheritance system, Walston Hall had been sold, and all that Roger Staines had to show for his illustrious family connection was a modest private income, just enough to enable him to carry out his self-appointed role of village historian without the necessity of earning a living. He lived alone in a cottage on the fringes of the former estate, involved with his research but taking his responsibilities as churchwarden very seriously.

Of all of her husband's parishioners, Becca had so far found Roger Staines to be the most pleasant. His manner towards her was invariably kind, marked with an old-fashioned courtliness; she knew, as well, that Stephen respected him both for his intellect and for his conscientious approach to his duties.

The mission on which he had come fulfilled, Stephen gave Roger a blessing. 'Perhaps we should go now,' he concluded. 'I don't want to tire you.'

'Oh, no.' Roger's face registered disappointment. 'Please stay for a bit and keep me company, both of you. The time passes so slowly – and I feel much better today. I'd really welcome a chat, Father.'

'Yes, all right then.' Stephen pulled two chairs up close to the bed, helped Becca into one, and sat down on the other. 'As long as the doctors don't mind, that is.'

'I'm sure they don't mind. In fact, I'm doing so well that they're likely to send me home any minute.' His smile was wan but determinedly cheerful.

Stephen laughed. 'I'm glad to hear it. I haven't forgotten that you'd promised to clean the church gutters this week and it's about time you got on with it. This malingering can't last for ever, you know.'

'Actually, the gutters are done – Ernest helped me with them yesterday afternoon. But the malingering is what I need to talk to you about.' Roger's smile had faded into a look of pained regret. 'I'm afraid it's going to have to last for ever.'

'What do you mean?' The Rector's voice was sharp with alarm.

'I'm going to pull through this time,' Roger assured him. 'But Dr McNair says that this attack was a warning and that my heart is seriously damaged.' Plucking unconsciously at one of the monitors on his chest, he continued. 'He says that I have to give up the wardenship – that it's too stressful, too much responsibility and too much work. He says that if I want to live for another year or two, you'll have to find another churchwarden. I'm frightfully sorry,' he added.

'Ah.' Stephen exhaled the word on a sigh. 'I see. Well, of course you must stand down immediately, Roger. We shall miss you very much, I don't have to tell you, and I don't know who could possibly replace you, but your health is all that really matters. And we want you around for a good few years yet.'

The man in the bed echoed the sigh. 'So sorry,' he repeated. 'It's a terrible time to leave you in the soup like this.'

Becca leaned forward, alarmed. 'What do you mean?'

With an apologetic laugh, he explained. 'I'd meant to see you this week, Father. I've known that something was afoot for a bit, but I hadn't wanted to alarm you before it was necessary. Now it rather looks as if I won't be able to be much help. It's Fred Purdy,' he amplified. 'He's come up with some hare-brained ideas.'

'About the expansion of Ingram's, you mean?' Stephen raised his eyebrows. 'He's mentioned that to me already.'

'What's this about?' queried Becca, looking back and forth between the two men.

Roger nodded at Stephen, who explained to his wife. 'You know there's a small agricultural business in the village, on a parcel of land that used to belong to the estate? Ingram's?' She shook her head in the negative, so he continued. 'At the moment they just have a few battery hens and sell a bit of seed, but they're looking to expand rather significantly to a proper poultry-packing business. It would make a difference to Walston in several ways, not least of which would be a big increase in traffic – heavy-goods lorries and that sort of thing. They'd need to build a new access road along by the almshouses. Fred thinks it's a good idea.'

'He thinks it would be good for the village,' amplified Roger with a cynical grimace. 'Not to mention good for Fred Purdy, though he doesn't quite put it like that. I think he sees it in terms of a symbiotic relationship between the village shop and a bigger and better Ingram's – he buys in fresh poultry and eggs from them, and all of their new employees help to increase his customer base. He wins both ways. Very neat.'

Becca's puzzlement grew. 'But what does it have to do with you – with either one of you?'

'The Rector and churchwardens are the trustees of the almshouses,' Stephen explained. 'Which means that, in order for him to have a two-to-one majority, at least one of us has to agree with him to grant Ingram's the right-of-way through the almshouses' grounds.'

'And he knows jolly well that I think it's a terrible idea,' put in Roger Staines. 'I've told him so. All that traffic. Not to mention what it would do to the estate. But I'm afraid that's not Fred's only hare-brained scheme,' he went on. 'He's decided that we should stop paying our Diocesan Quota.'

'What!' The Rector's face showed his surprise and alarm. 'This is the first I've heard of it!'

'It's what I wanted to warn you about. He's rather serious about it, I'm afraid – says that there's no justification for sending all that money to Norwich when it's so badly needed in the village.'

Stephen shook his head. 'Ridiculous. But Fred isn't exactly known as an original thinker. Where would he come up with an idea like that?'

Chuckling, the churchwarden explained. 'You're right – he didn't think of it himself.

He was talking to some of the other wardens in the Deanery at the induction of the new vicar of Upper Walston. That's the big Evangelical church,' he added for Becca's benefit. 'Like many Evangelical congregations, they've got more money than they know what to do with, but their wardens have decided that they won't trust the diocese with it, especially after the Church Commissioners lost so much money. They said, according to Fred, "Why throw good money after bad?" So they're withholding their Quota and supporting their own missions instead. If the diocese tries to retaliate by refusing to fund their vicar's stipend, they can well afford to pick up the tab themselves. So they're in a pretty unassailable position. And to make matters worse, the wardens of Walston St Mary – the spikiest Anglo-Catholic church in the Deanery – have also decided not to pay the Quota, in protest at the ordination of women. The Church of England didn't have the authority to take that step, they claim, and so they have no further responsibility to pay their Quota. So, of course, not to be outdone, Fred has decided to follow suit.' He gave a short, cynical laugh.

'But can't the diocese do something to us if we don't pay up?' asked Becca, frowning. 'Can't they refuse to pay Stephen's stipend, or something like that?'

Roger Staines reassured her. 'No, they can't do anything like that. We're fortunate at St Michael's actually. Through an historical fluke, the diocese have to keep an incumbent in Walston.' He paused, trying to simplify the explanation. 'The Loveiidge family used to be patrons of the church, and controlled all the endowments and the rectorial tithes. Some time ago, back in the last century, they set up a trust fund to pay the Rector's stipend through the diocese. But it's only payable if there is an incumbent at St Michael's. If the church should cease to exist – be closed down, for example – or if there were no rector, the diocese would forfeit the trust fund and the money would go instead to one of the Oxford colleges. So it's in the interest of the diocese to keep St Michael's as a going concern with a rector in place. That's the reason that a church like St Michael's has been able to continue in such a small village as Walston and not be swallowed up into some united benefice like so many churches in Norfolk.'

'So Stephen won't lose his job, no matter what Mr Purdy does,' summarised Becca in satisfaction.

Struggling to sit up, Roger's face creased in a fleeting spasm of pain. 'But that's not really the point,' he stated strongly after a moment. 'It would be *wrong* to withhold our Quota. What would happen if every congregation felt that way, and no one paid their Quota?'

'The diocese would be broke,' concluded Stephen thoughtfully.

'Exactly! And if it happened throughout the dioceses, the Church of England would be broke.' He paused and gave his next words all the weight with which he could invest them. 'It's the survival of the parish system we're talking about, Father. Nothing less than that. Or to put it another way, the survival of the Church of England as we know it. It's that important.'

Becca looked horrified. We can't let it happen! Mr Purdy has to be stopped!'

Exhausted with expended emotion, Roger sank back on the bed. 'That, my dear, is why I'm so very sorry that I've let you all down by having this untimely and inconvenient heart attack. It's out of my hands now.'

'Then,' said Stephen, following his train of thought, 'we need to be very careful that your successor as churchwarden is someone … sound. Someone who can be trusted.'

'Yes.' He smiled faintly. 'I've had a few minutes of leisure to think about that, since Dr McNair told me that I wouldn't be able to go on.'

'And do you have any ideas?'

'What do *you* think, Father?' Roger challenged him. 'You've had time to get to know your congregation over the last few months. Who do you think the candidates might be? Good *and* bad?'

Stephen stroked his chin for a moment. 'Surely Ernest Wrightman wouldn't stand again.'

That elicited a breathless bark of a laugh from the man in the bed. 'He'd like nothing better, if he thought that his health – or Doris – would allow it. But he's pretty entrenched now as clerk to the educational trust and the almshouse trust, and he's discovered that being churchwarden isn't the only way to pull strings. I think you can count Ernest out.'

'How about Doris herself, then?' the Rector said, raising his eyebrows in an attempt at humour. 'Don't you think it's time we had a female warden?'

Roger grimaced. 'Very funny. A female warden, yes, but Doris – ? You'll be suggesting Enid Bletsoe next.'

'Well, then.' Stephen was silent as he mentally worked his way through the congregation. 'I think Quentin Mansfield would probably be the best candidate,' he offered eventually. 'He's a shrewd chap and he certainly knows about money – that has to be important in the current circumstances. And now that he's taken early retirement, he would have the time to give to it.' Mansfield was a wealthy businessman who, with his wife Diana, had moved to Walston some five years earlier upon buying Walston Hall with an eye to his future in retirement. That retirement had now taken place, which meant that after years of spending most of his time in London he was now permanently in the village.

Roger nodded in approval. 'Good choice. I don't think he has much imagination, but that's not really what you need right now. As you say, the financial expertise could prove invaluable and he certainly has his head screwed on straight. He won't be pushed around by Fred Purdy or anyone else.'

'When will the election take place?' put in Becca. 'Soon?'

'At the Easter Vestry meeting,' her husband responded. 'That's only a month away, so we won't have long to wait.'

'It will be a great relief to me when it's all over,' said Roger Staines quietly. 'Fred may not be very bright, but I've learned never to underestimate the power of dogged stupidity.'

'Everything will be all right,' the Rector reassured him. 'You can relax now and concentrate on getting better.' He rose and went to the side of the bed. 'You've got that book to finish, you know. We're all waiting for it.'

The other man's face was shadowed with worry at the introduction of this new issue. 'Yes,' he said. 'That's another problem. All these years I've resisted having any help with the book. But what if something were to happen to me? My notes are in no fit shape for anyone else to work from. No one else could even read my writing. I can't bear thinking that all those years of research – my whole life's work – should go to waste if I died tonight. I really can't carry on alone. But who is there in Walston to help me?'

Becca startled both men with her eagerness as she leaned forward and seized Roger Staines's hand. 'Oh, I could do it,' she asserted fervently. 'Please, Mr Staines, let me help you with your book. I could do it. I used to be my father's secretary – I could transcribe your notes and help you get everything in order. Please let me help you.'

Her husband stared at her. 'But Becca!' said an off-balance Stephen. 'I thought you said before we were married that you didn't want a job – that you wanted to stay at home and get used to being a Rector's wife for a while, before you … well, before we started a family.'

'I've changed my mind. Besides, it wouldn't be full time – only for a few hours a week.' She focused all her attention on Roger Staines, willing him to agree. 'Please, Mr Staines?'

The man in the bed smiled and squeezed her hand. 'If you're really that keen, my dear, I accept with pleasure.'

'What's all this carry-on?' The gruff Scots voice at the door affected to sound fierce, but the two men knew Dr Fergus McNair too well to be alarmed.

Stephen turned towards the door. 'Oh, hello, Dr McNair.'

Fergus McNair was small and wiry, with weather-beaten freckled skin and hair that had once been a violent carroty red; he was now nearly fifty and his hair had faded to a more sedate shade, though it was still thick and bushy. He had come to Walston some twenty years earlier to help out with and eventually take over his uncle's practice. In spite of that length of service he was still universally referred to as 'the new doctor', or alternatively 'young Dr McNair', his uncle having long since gone to his eternal reward. 'Don't you realise that this man is very poorly?' he said, drawing his grizzled brows together over shrewd blue eyes. In over twenty years south of the border his Scottish burr had, if anything, intensified rather than faded, and the richly rolled 'r's made Becca smile.

'Isn't it a pity,' spoke the man in question from the bed, sounding far less 'poorly' than he had when they'd arrived, 'that Dr McNair is a heathen Scot, and an unbeliever at that? Wouldn't he make a jolly fine churchwarden? *He'd* see off all this nonsense about not paying the Quota, make no mistake about it!'

Chapter 4

And that because of thine indignation and wrath:for thou hast taken me up, and cast me down.

Psalm 102:10

Roger Staines's heart attack, in and of itself, was a short-lived cause of excitement in Walston, especially as it soon became clear that it wasn't going to prove fatal. However, the consequences of the heart attack, more specifically his resignation as churchwarden, provided an ongoing source of interest for some of the men of the village; Fred Purdy, Ernest Wrightman and Harry Gaze passed many hours in discussion of possible successors.

The women of Walston, though, found far more fascinating the imminent arrival of Gillian English's partner, Lou: according to Enid Bletsoe, the self-professed expert on the newcomers, he was due to make his first appearance in the village on Friday. Furthermore, as Enid delighted to inform her sister Doris and their friend Marjorie Talbot-Shaw, she had secured his presence at her dinner table on his very first night in Walston, ensuring that she would be the first to make his acquaintance.

'I'll be sure to tell you what he's like,' she told them with ill-concealed glee over coffee on Friday morning. 'Knowing Gillian as well as I do, I'm sure he's perfectly delightful.'

Doris shook her head, unconvinced. 'I don't know how you can be so sure he's not a foreigner,' she murmured. 'Italian.'

'He's definitely not Italian,' Enid assured her with triumph. 'I asked Gillian what his surname is, and she said it's Sutherland. That's certainly not an Italian name. Or even a Welsh name, come to that.'

'Scottish, if anything,' pronounced Marjorie judiciously. 'What did you say his job is, Enid?'

'It's got something to do with computers,' the expert explained. 'Telecommuting, you know. Quite the thing these days.'

'How is he getting here?' Doris probed. 'Is he coming to Norwich by train?'

Again Enid replied with authority. 'He has a company car. A BMW, I believe, so it should be easy to spot when he arrives.'

In the event, though, no one witnessed Lou Sutherland's arrival in Walston. Even Enid was not capable of being in two places at once, and meal preparations neccessitated her presence in the kitchen that afternoon over her favoured spot at the front window. So the reunion at Foxglove Cottage was a private one.

Around teatime, though, on one of her periodic peeks through the front window, Enid spotted the car, and took a moment off from peeling potatoes to ring her sister.

'He's here!' she announced. 'He has a dark blue BMW.'

'You saw him, then? You've met him?'

'Well, not exactly,' Enid temporised. 'At least, I might have had a glimpse of him through the window, in their sitting room. Dark hair, it looked like, and of course Gillian and Bryony are fair.'

'You see!' Doris triumphed. 'Italian – I told you so!'

The bell chimed promptly at seven. Uncharacteristically nervous, Enid removed her apron, patted her hair with a quick glance in the hall mirror, and opened the door. Bryony stepped forward, smiling, with a box of chocolates, and her mother, behind her, proffered a bunch of flowers. In London they would have taken a bottle of wine, but Gillian had decided that didn't seem quite the thing in Walston, and especially not for Enid, whose favourite drink seemed to be bitter lemon. 'These are for you,' Gillian said. 'And I'd like you to meet Lou.'

Lou was small and slight, with eyes that would probably be described as hazel in colour, though they were closer to brown than green, and short curly hair of a brown so dark that it was almost black. Lou was also undeniably, unquestionably a female.

Enid didn't speak. 'This is Lou,' Gillian repeated. 'Louise Sutherland.'

The evening had been got through somehow, and it was with a strange mixture of excitement and reluctance that Enid made her way through a chill drizzle to Doris's house on Saturday morning. The news had to be told, yet how could she admit to her sister how wrong she had been?

'A woman!' Doris goggled at her over the coffee, her pencilled eyebrows reaching nearly to her hairline. 'You mean … ? They're – lesbians!'

Jowls quivering, Enid nodded solemnly. 'I've read about women like that in my magazines, but I never thought I'd be forced to entertain them in my own house.'

'But she – Gillian – told you that Lou was a man! She lied to you!'

Thinking back, as she had so often since that horrible moment at the door, Enid acknowledged to herself, if not to Doris, that Gillian had never actually said so. 'She misled me. She let me think so.'

'But that's terrible!' Doris reached for a biscuit and munched on it avidly. 'Poor old you – how did you ever get through the evening with them? They stayed for dinner?'

'It was very difficult.' Enid lifted a brave chin. 'I had to pretend that I'd known it all along. It put me in a very difficult position.'

'I would have thrown them out,' her sister stated with self-righteous relish. 'I wouldn't have allowed those perverts to cross my doorstep!'

'But I couldn't do that – not in front of dear little Bryony!'

'Oh.' Doris's thoughts turned to the unfortunate child. 'Oh, the poor little scrap! How terrible for her.'

'Yes.' For a moment Enid was silent. 'We must have compassion on poor dear Bryony, and try to do everything we can to help her.' She narrowed her eyes as she went on. 'But as for those women … They're evil, Doris. Evil.'

'Wicked,' her sister echoed fervently. 'It wouldn't surprise me if they were witches. I mean, doesn't she grow herbs? Herbs for witches' potions most likely!'

'They'll never cross my threshold again.' Enid reached for the coffee pot and refilled her cup, almost trembling with righteous indignation. 'I have been deceived once, and taken advantage of. My trusting nature has been betrayed. It won't happen again.'

Perhaps to Enid's disappointment, on Saturday no one set foot out of Foxglove Cottage, as Lou spent much of the day sorting out her office and getting her computer system hooked up. Gillian, who found Lou's high-tech setup incomprehensible and considered her office out of bounds, stayed out of her way, busying herself elsewhere in the cottage, preparing lunch and supervising Bryony at play. Her placid nature enabled her to ignore the noises, interspersed with muffled curses, which issued from the direction of the office. Around lunchtime, though, Lou appeared in the kitchen.

'I've had enough,' she announced, waving her hands dramatically. 'That damned hard disk has decided to pack up. It was working fine yesterday, before I moved it. Do you suppose it's trying to tell me something?'

Gillian smiled. 'Like you shouldn't have left London, you mean?'

'Exactly.' Lou flopped into a chair, put her elbows on the pine table and her head in her hands. 'Whose idea was it to move to Norfolk, anyway?'

'I think it was Mummy's,' said Bryony, who was seated at the table, methodically colouring a picture. 'But you thought it was a good idea too, Lou. I remember you said so.'

'More fool me – this place is the pits. Rainy and cold and horrible. I'm sure the sun must be shining in London.' Lou rubbed her forehead. 'I've got a splitting head, Gill.'

'Oh, poor you.' Gill came behind her and massaged the back of her neck with cool, deft fingers. 'Shall I brew you up some marjoram infusion? Or some wood betony?'

Lou relaxed and leaned back into the massage. 'Ugh. You know I don't trust that stuff. You might try to poison me,' she added with a grin.

30

'Shall I get your tablets?' offered Bryony.

'In the drawer of the bedside table,' Lou directed her, gesturing towards the stairs with her expressive hands.

The girl brought them back a moment later, handing her mother the small flat packet of soluble pain-reliever tablets. Gill filled a glass with water and decanted the tablets into it, watching their dervish dance of self-destruction as they whirled and fizzed themselves into nonexistence. 'Here, lovey,' she said, handing the glass to Lou. 'Drink it all down and you'll be better before you know it.'

Lou took it in one gulp, grimacing at the taste. But she smiled at Gill and gave her hand a quick caress as she relieved her of the empty glass. 'Thanks, angelface. You *do* take good care of me.'

At the Rectory, Stephen finished his lunch and looked out at the steady rain without enthusiasm. 'Not much of a day to go out,' he said. 'But I suppose I must.'

'Surely you can wait till the weather's better,' Becca urged.

'No, I'd better go. But I shouldn't be gone long. I've got to pop up to Walston Hall and have a word with Quentin Mansfield, to sound him out about standing for churchwarden. He's expecting me.'

Becca stifled a sigh. 'All right. But hurry back.'

On a fine day, Stephen would have gone to the Hall on foot, taking the ancient path connecting the manor house and the church which the Lovelidge family had utilised for centuries. But the rain was coming down harder than ever and the path was likely to be muddy, so he opted to take the car round via the roads. Mrs Mansfield, he knew, was a rather finicky woman who would view with horror a Rector who tracked muddy footprints into her house.

Walston Hall, even in the rain, was an impressive sight. It was by no means among the largest or grandest of the stately homes of England, but in its compact, all-of-a-piece perfection there was great charm. It was an early Tudor house, built all of small red bricks, with two symmetrical side wings thrusting forward to embrace a courtyard and presided over by majestic zigzagged chimneys. According to Roger Staines, Walston Hall had been built by Cardinal Wolsey, who had acquired the patronage of St Michael's Church, with a view to using its rich revenues to fund his new Ipswich College. John Lovelidge, a man no more high-born than his master Wolsey, had been his local agent in the area, overseeing the collection of tithes. But the first Lovelidge had perceived the way the wind was blowing, and had transferred his allegiance to Henry VIII before Wolsey's downfall. As a reward for his loyalty the newly ennobled Sir John Lovelidge had received Walston Hall, with its surrounding estate, and there he had founded the dynasty that had dominated Walston for nearly four centuries.

Now, of course, it belonged to Quentin Mansfield and his wife. Mansfield had toyed with the whim, when he'd bought the house, of changing its name to Mansfield

Park, but the local outcry had been great, and the idea had been abandoned; Walston Hall it remained, and would as long as it stood.

The Mansfields employed no live-in servants, relying on part-time help from the village to keep the house running smoothly. Stephen was met at the door by Diana Mansfield, who took his wet umbrella gingerly, depositing it in an elaborate brass rack in the entrance hall. 'Come in, Rector,' she said, standing aside. 'Quentin is waiting for you in the library.'

Stephen never knew quite what to make of Diana Mansfield. She was an attractive woman of around fifty, thin as a reed, with champagne-coloured hair, beautifully cut to frame her taut-skinned face. At her age, the village concurred, that smooth skin was either a miracle of genetic good fortune or a marvel of the plastic surgeon's art, but the latter seemed far more likely. Her clothes were clearly expensive, but were much more suitable for wear in and around Sloane Square than for the Norfolk countryside: today, for example, she was wearing a creamy silk shirt above fawn-coloured trousers of some drapey fabric which emphasised her thinness, and a heavy gold chain encircled her neck. Even the Barbour jacket which she occasionally wore around the village, in an attempt to look as if she belonged there, was pristine and unscarred, all too clearly bought in Knightsbridge.

It wasn't as if, Stephen reflected, Diana Mansfield hadn't made the effort to fit in: the Barbour jacket was evidence that she valued the opinion of the village. From the beginning she had proved herself to be a tireless church worker, joining the Mothers' Union and volunteering to organise the annual summer fête. But somehow it hadn't worked; she was never accepted as one of them. She always seemed to be somewhere on the fringes of any group, yearning to belong but never quite making it.

Part of her problem, realised Stephen, was that she had been so much on her own in Walston, her husband living in London during the week and returning to Norfolk only at weekends. Her children had left home before the move to Walston Hall; it was the classic empty-nest syndrome of the middle-aged woman with too much time on her hands, exacerbated by the move to strange surroundings. Stephen felt sorry for Diana Mansfield, but so far had been unable to think of a way to help her.

Quentin Mansfield, who ushered him into the library and offered him a drink, was a different matter. He had always seemed to Stephen to be entirely self-sufficient and self-possessed. A large man with a businessman's paunch, he was conscientious in his church attendance but he seemed uninterested in assuming the role of the village squire.

A fire had been lit against the chill of the day, and Stephen sank gratefully into a comfortable leather chair as he accepted his drink.

His host remained standing, leaning against the carved wooden mantelpiece. 'Well, Rector?' he said. 'What's this all about? I'm not flattering myself that this is a social call.'

'Well, no, not exactly.'

'Money, is it?' he asked bluntly. 'Is the roof leaking? It's no good asking me for money for vestments or any of that High Church rubbish – you know very well that I don't approve of such nonsense.'

Stephen was caught off balance, but recovered quickly. "No, Mr Mansfield. It's not about money. Not directly, anyway.' He smiled. 'And I do know that you don't share my churchmanship, but I don't think that should prevent us working together.' He took a sip of his drink, deciding that the direct approach would be most effective. 'Ill come to the point. Roger Staines has been told by Dr McNair that he can't continue as churchwarden. That means there will be a vacancy to be filled at the Easter Vestry, and I was wondering whether you might be interested in the job.'

'Churchwarden, eh? You do surprise me.' Mansfield turned and scrutinised the young priest. 'Doesn't one have to be born in Walston, or at least in Norfolk, to be considered for such an honour?'

'I don't know about honour,' Stephen demurred. 'It's a great deal of work, and quite a responsibility – legally as well as practically.'

'Then why, I wonder,' the other man mused with a cynical smile, 'does no one ever want to give the job up? Fred Purdy has been churchwarden for so many years that even he has lost count, and from what I hear Ernest Wrightman would have held on for ever if it hadn't been for his health. That probably goes for Roger Staines as well.'

Stephen looked thoughtful. 'There's something in that,' he admitted. 'I suppose it is a very powerful position, and there are people who thrive on power. I wouldn't put Roger in that category, though.'

'And what about me?' Mansfield posed bluntly. 'Is that why you're asking me? Because you think that I thrive on power?'

A question like that, Stephen recognised, deserved an equally straightforward answer. 'I'm asking you because I think you have the financial acumen that we need, and because I believe that I can trust you to act for the good of St Michael's, and for the good of the Church of England. I believe, Mr Mansfield, that you are a man of sense and judgment, all questions of churchmanship aside.'

'Ah.' Mansfield abandoned his position at the mantelpiece and sat down opposite Stephen in a matching leather chair. 'Now we're talking. So it *is* to do with money.'

'Indirectly. As you must know, Mr Mansfield, the Church of England is not in an enviable financial position at the moment.' Stephen smiled wryly. 'The Church Commissioners haven't done us any favours, losing all that money, and the result is that the burden is falling, and will increasingly fall, on the parishes themselves.'

'Obviously.'

'And there are those who, for various reasons, believe that the congregations should owe no allegiance – and send no money – to the diocese, whom they see as money wasters.'

'I've heard that argument,' Mansfield acknowledged. 'There's some merit in it.'

Stephen leaned forward and spoke earnestly. 'Yes,' he said, 'but this is the Church of England we're talking about. The national church. Not a congregationalist confederation, but the national, established church. The only direction this sort of argument will lead is to the breakdown of the parish system, and ultimately the disestablishment of the Church of England. If that's what you want, then fair enough. Tell me now, and we have nothing else to discuss. But if the survival of the Church of England is important to you, as it is to me, then I think you're the man we need as our next churchwarden.'

*   *   *

Back at the Rectory, Becca's nightmare continued. Stephen hadn't been gone more than ten minutes before the phone rang. She picked it up, dreading what was to come, hoping she was wrong.

She wasn't wrong. The call began and continued as all the others, leaving her trembling and sickened. But before he had finished, she put the phone down. Immediately it began ringing again.

Becca covered her face with her hands. She couldn't bear it – not this afternoon. Escape was all she could think about. Escape.

She willed herself to calm down and think clearly about where she might go. The village grapevine had provided her with the information that Gillian English's partner had been due to arrive on the Friday: that would provide her with an excuse, if she needed one, to pay a call of welcome. She'd been meaning all week to call on Gillian, and now she would do it.

But what could she take with her? Becca was well aware that when the Rector's wife went to call she was expected to take along a pot of home-made jam or something fresh from the oven, a fragrant fruitcake or a plate of delicate golden shortbread. Her own shortcomings in that area were all too well known to her. She would just have to make do with something from the village shop – flowers, perhaps.

The phone was still ringing. She plucked up the receiver and laid it down beside the phone, grabbed her coat from the hall stand, snatched up an umbrella and let herself out of the house, breathing deeply.

The rain was a shock, but not an unwelcome one: she found it bracing and strode down the lane with it in her face, not bothering to raise the umbrella. Past Cyprian Lawrence's cottage and Harry Gaze's, then past the church and into the main road through the village.

Fred Purdy was, as usual, behind the counter in the shop. There were no other customers, so he gave her his full attention as she came in.

'Nice day for ducks,' he chuckled. 'But not for village shopkeepers. Not much business today, so I'm glad to see you. But it looks like you've got a bit damp, young lady.'

34

Becca summoned up a smile. 'Yes, it's rather wet out there.'

'Has your brolly sprung a leak, then? It hasn't done you much good.' He looked at her streaming hair, then at the umbrella in her hand, laughing at the sight.

'I just forgot to put it up,' she explained lamely.

'Well, what can I do for you today? Something nice for the Rector's supper, perhaps?'

'Do you have any flowers, Mr Purdy?'

He gestured to a pail behind him. 'Daffs, of course. And some irises, but they're a bit dearer.'

'I'll have the irises,' she decided, reaching for her handbag and realising that she didn't have it. 'Oh! I've left my handbag at home!'

Fred chuckled. 'That's all right, my dear. I'll trust you for it till the next time. If you can't trust the Rector's wife, who can you trust?'

'Thanks awfully,' she said with real gratitude, realising that she couldn't face the thought of going back into the Rectory.

He wrapped the stems of the flowers. 'Having a dinner party, are you?'

'Oh, no. I just thought I'd call at Foxglove Cottage.'

'Ah!' Fred handed the irises across the counter. 'You've heard the news, then? Going to have a look for yourself, are you?'

Becca looked at him blankly. 'I knew that what's-his-name – Lou – was arriving yesterday, but I haven't heard anything else.'

Fred grinned, hugely pleased with himself that he should be the first to tell her. 'Turns out that Lou isn't a he – he's a she, if you know what I mean.'

She wasn't sure that she *did* know what he meant. 'A she?'

'A woman. You know.' He gestured expressively, sketching a pair of oversized breasts with his hands. 'Seems we've got us a pair of queers in Walston. Lesbians – isn't that the word?'

Becca stared at him. 'Oh!'

'Enid Bletsoe had them over for dinner last night, and she wasn't half furious that they'd tricked her like that. Letting her think all this time that Lou was a man.' He chortled with glee. 'She stopped in here earlier to get a big bottle of Dettol to soak her dishes in, so she wouldn't catch anything from them. I've never seen her so upset. Eyes near popping out of her head with rage. To think, she said, that she'd even invited the other one to join the Mothers' Union. Can you imagine it? People like that in the Mothers' Union?'

Becca approached Foxglove Cottage shyly. She didn't think she'd ever met any lesbians before and wasn't quite sure what to expect, though Gillian had seemed perfectly nice and not unusual in any way.

Bryony answered the door. 'Mummy!' she called. 'It's the Rector's wife. She's all wet, and she's got flowers.'

Somehow Becca found herself within a minute or two drying out in the cosy kitchen, sitting at the table with a cup of herbal tea in front of her. Her dripping coat, steaming gently, was draped over the Aga to dry, and Gill fussed over her in her own quiet way. 'You'll catch cold if you're not careful. If you do, you must let me know and I'll brew you up something for it.'

'Lou won't drink Mummy's brews,' Bryony confided. 'She says they're poison.'

'Oh, you haven't met Lou yet, have you?' Gill addressed her daughter. 'Darling, will you please go to Lou's office and tell her that the Rector's wife is here?'

The girl went off on her errand, returning a moment later with Lou. 'Hello,' Lou said warmly, putting her hand out. 'The Rector's wife, is it? I'm glad I was warned – now I know I have to be on my best behaviour. No swearing in front of the Rector's wife. I'm sure Gill sent Bryony to warn me on purpose, so she wouldn't have to be ashamed of me.'

'Oh, Lou, you're terrible.' Gill's slow smile didn't indicate that she meant it.

'Welcome to Walston,' Becca said sincerely. 'It's so nice to have you here.'

Walking back home under the shelter of her umbrella over two hours later, her coat and hair dry again, Becca thought about how much she had enjoyed her afternoon with the two women. Gill was quiet and deliberate while Lou was warm and funny and talkative, with expressive hands that never stopped moving. Once she was there with them, it had never occurred to her that there was anything unusual or strange about their relationship: they treated each other with affection and respect, rather like a married couple.

It was going to be nice having them in Walston. They might become real friends, and that would be wonderful. Stephen was right – they'd have to invite them round for a meal quite soon. Perhaps they should have Cyprian Lawrence as well – he must be lonely, living on his own like that, and snubbed by everyone in the village.

Suddenly she realised, with a jolt, that she'd been enjoying herself so much that she hadn't given another thought to the phone call. As she went up the lane her apprehensiveness returned, like an old familiar dark cloud settling back on top of her.

But the car was in the drive, which meant that Stephen was home and she would be safe.

Stephen was waiting for her at the door, frowning. 'Where have you been?' he demanded with uncharacteristic intensity.

'I've been paying a call at Foxglove Cottage,' she began. 'And they're ...'

'Well, I've been worried witless about you! You weren't here, but your handbag was in the hall, and there wasn't a note or anything. What was I supposed to think?'

Becca clapped her hand to her mouth, stricken. 'I'm sorry. I didn't think.'

'And the telephone was off the hook! I know I've mentioned this to you before, Becca, but it's very important that you don't leave the phone off the hook. I'm the

36

Rector, in case you've forgotten, and people are always needing to get in touch with me. It's very careless of you to do that.'

It was the first time her husband had ever spoken to her sharply, or indeed with anything but tenderness. 'Yes, Stephen,' she said, swallowing hard. 'I'm sorry.' She turned her head away quickly so that he wouldn't see the tears.

Chapter 5

And why? their communing is not for peace: but they imagine deceitful words against them that are quiet in the land.

Psalm 35:20

By the time of the service on Sunday morning, there wasn't anyone at St Michael's, or indeed in Walston, who didn't know about Gillian and Lou – their unorthodox living arrangements and how they had deceived Enid Bletsoe. But as none of them save Enid – and Becca – had actually seen Lou, there was a good turnout for the service in the hope that the women would put in an appearance.

They didn't disappoint. Both of them were there, along with Bryony, oblivious to the fact that they were the most scandalous – and talked-about – thing to hit Walston in a good many years. Sitting near the front, they were unaware, in fact, that they were being shunned by the good folk of Walston by unspoken common consent.

After the service they were not entirely left to their own devices; Becca Thorncroft spoke to them, of course, especially as she had determined to go ahead with her plans for a dinner party the following weekend, and she couldn't wait to issue the invitation.

'It sounds a lovely idea,' Gill assented. 'But what about Bryony? You won't want her to come, and we haven't been here long enough to know any baby-sitters.'

It was a problem which Becca hadn't even considered. 'Oh, I suppose it would be all right if you brought her along,' she said doubtfully.

'Good Lord, no – you wouldn't want this little horror in your house,' Lou laughed, ruffling Bryony's hair with affection.

Enid, who had been lurking within earshot talking to Doris and Marjorie but with her back pointedly turned towards the offending women, spun around and put on a semblance of a friendly smile. 'I couldn't help overhearing,' she began. 'Perhaps I could help – I'd be more than happy to look after dear little Bryony for you.'

With no reason to suspect that Enid, of late their firm friend and champion, was now their sworn enemy, Gill smiled her gratitude. 'That's very kind of you, Enid. Thank you very much. Would you like to come to our house or would you rather have her over with you?'

'Please, Mummy,' interjected Bryony, with visions of the chocolate biscuits and sugared drinks which had been forthcoming whenever she visited The Pines, 'may I go to Mrs Bletsoe's house? I like to go to her house.'

Enid beamed. 'Yes, of course, my darling. You may come to my house.'

'Thank you so much,' Gill reiterated.

'Yes, it will be wonderful to have an evening without the little horror,' grinned Lou. 'You can have her any time you like.'

They walked away with Becca, making arrangements, and Enid turned back to her friends. They were aghast at what she'd done. 'How could you?' gasped Doris. 'And after the way they've treated you!'

'It's taking Christian charity a bit too far,' added Marjorie indignantly.

'Oh,' said Enid with a mysterious smile, 'I have my reasons. You'll see. And as I said to you yesterday, Doris, it's not fair to punish dear little Bryony for what her mother is. She's a victim of her mother's wickedness as much as any of the rest of us.'

Marjorie Talbot-Shaw shook her head and observed their retreat over the tops of half-moon glasses which were secured round her neck with a gold chain. 'I can't imagine what the Rector is thinking about, allowing his wife to invite people like that to dine. Not the done thing. My dear late husband Godfrey would never have sanctioned having people like that at his table.'

'Neither would Father Fuller,' Doris stated. 'Father Fuller would have been shocked. He's probably turning over in his grave right now.'

'And,' Marjorie added with a sniff, 'even if those women weren't … unsuitable, it hardly seems proper for the Rector's wife to invite newcomers like that on the occasion of her first dinner party. I haven't been invited to dinner at the Rectory, and they've been married for months now.'

'Nor have we!' Doris realised indignantly. 'And after all Ernest has done for this church for so many years! Churchwarden, clerk to the trusts – I mean, where would the Rector be without him? He does more work than both of the churchwardens combined!'

They were joined by someone else, a woman called Flora Newall. She was not actually one of their circle as she was some years younger than them and employed full time as a social worker. She lived in Walston, and had done so for several years, though her work carried her to a number of the surrounding towns and villages: Upper Walston, Walston St Mary, Nether Walston and even farther afield in the direction of Norwich. Her involvement at St Michael's was enthusiastic though limited in scope; she was a member of the Mothers' Union and had been known to help with the flowers and even with the Harvest Supper.

Allowing Flora Newall to join the Mothers' Union was a point of pride with Doris, under whose leadership the invitation had been proffered and accepted. It showed how broad-minded and inclusive they were: not only was Flora Newall not a mother, she had never even been married.

She looked, in fact, the very stereotype of the middle-aged English spinster, thin and bony with a pale face that was plain rather than unpleasant, pale, slightly protruberant eyes, large teeth, and hair of an indeterminate hue and nonexistent style. Her personality was inoffensive and her manner was jolly without being pushy.

'You'll never guess,' she announced as she joined their party. 'I've just seen the Rector's wife, and she's invited me to dinner next weekend!'

'Oh!' Marjorie Talbot-Shaw inspected her over her glasses with increased interest. 'She has, has she?'

'Why her, do you suppose?' Doris whispered to Enid.

'Making up numbers, I imagine.' Enid didn't bother to whisper. 'I heard her say she was inviting that Cyprian Lawrence, so presumably she needed another woman.'

'Cyprian Lawrence!' hissed Doris, her eyebrows shooting up. 'It's just as well she didn't invite me and Ernest then! We wouldn't set foot in the same house as that unspeakable man!'

The subject was continued over the well-done joint of beef at the Wrightmans' lunch table.

'I can't understand why she's invited that Flora Newall when she's never asked us to a meal,' Doris said to her husband, spooning peas onto his plate.

Ernest reached for the gravy. 'I thought that Flora Newall was a friend of yours.'

'Oh, she is. At least, a sort of a friend,' she qualified. 'But she has no personality, no spirit. Not like me or Marjorie, or even like Enid. Flora wouldn't say boo to a goose – I just don't know why the Rector's wife would want to invite her.'

'Is that so?' Ernest, who had begun wielding his knife at a slice of beef, stopped and looked thoughtful.

Doris droned on through the meal, not noticing that Ernest was unusually quiet. Nor did she notice that, while she did the washing-up, her husband was in the hall using the telephone.

The week went quickly for Becca as she planned her menu and shopped for food. The former was complicated by her discovery that Flora Newall was a vegetarian, but she managed to find a recipe for stuffed aubergines which Stephen assured her would be acceptable to all.

The phone calls didn't stop entirely, but they seemed less frequent, perhaps because she was out rather more than usual during the day and Stephen's evening meetings were light that week. Without knowing the cause, Stephen was cheered to find his wife in a much better frame of mind; she seemed less nervous and jumpy, which he attributed to the influence of her new friends, and the sudden interest she had developed in cookery and entertaining.

The most momentous event of the week, though it might not have seemed so at the time, was a meeting which took place one evening between Ernest Wrightman and Flora Newall. It happened at Flora's cottage, by Ernest's request, and lasted no more than half-an-hour.

'Would you like a cup of tea?' she offered nervously when she'd taken his coat. 'Or some coffee, perhaps?'

'A cup of tea would go down a treat.'

Flora had been baffled when Ernest phoned asking to see her; she was no more enlightened now that he had arrived and was ensconced in her tiny sitting room waiting for his tea. She switched on the kettle, put a few biscuits on a plate and covered her battered old tea tray with a clean white cloth.

'Here we are,' she said brightly, carrying the tray into the sitting room, settling it on a table and pouring the tea. 'Nothing like a good cup of tea, I always say.'

'I couldn't agree more.' Ernest leaned forward to spoon sugar into his tea, then offered her the sugar bowl.

Flora giggled nervously. 'No, thanks. I always use artificial sweetener.' She produced a dispenser and dropped a small white tablet into her tea, then, at a loss, looked at Ernest.

There was no point in drawing it out, he decided. After a sip of tea he began. 'You're probably wondering what this is all about.'

'Yes …'

Sensing her apprehension, Ernest gave a high-pitched laugh. 'Nothing to worry about, my dear lady,' he assured her.

'Then what …'

'I'll come to the point. I was wondering if you'd ever thought about being churchwarden.'

'Churchwarden?' She stared at him, astonished. 'Me?'

'Someone has to do it, now that Roger Staines is out of action. Why not you?'

'But I don't know anything about being churchwarden. I've only been in Walston for a few years – I don't even know everyone in the congregation.'

He waved a hand, brushing away her arguments like a troublesome fly. 'No matter. You'd have plenty of people – like me, for instance – to help you. To tell you what you needed to know and what you needed to do.'

She sat silently for a moment, absorbing it, getting used to the idea. 'Why me?' she said at last. 'There are other more qualified people, surely.'

'But no one with your talents,' Ernest stated glibly; he'd had several days to prepare his case. 'You're good with people – Doris has told me so. That's very important. And I can tell that you're intelligent.'

Flushing to the roots of her hair, she murmured, 'Oh, Doris is too kind. And you too, of course.'

'And I think it's high time we had a woman as warden, don't you?' He produced a jovial smile. 'After all, this is the end of the twentieth century. We've got to move with the times.'

'But what,' she asked, 'does Father Thorncroft say? Does he think I'd make a good churchwarden?'

Ernest Wrightman's smile never faltered. 'Father Thorncroft doesn't count,' he said dismissively. 'He'll do what I tell him to.'

The dinner party on Saturday night was a great success. Becca's meal was pronounced delicious, to her enormous satisfaction, and the company was a pleasant one. Gillian and Lou, whom Becca found even more delightful on further acquaintance, hit it off very well with Cyprian Lawrence, and they talked about music, life in London and other subjects of mutual interest until well after midnight. Even Flora Newall seemed to enjoy herself, though she didn't have much to contribute to the general conversation. During dinner she was seated next to the Rector; their private chat included, on her part, a number of arcane questions about church policy and government, to which he gave his full and considered attention though their point escaped him.

In the meantime, Bryony was having a most satisfactory, by her standards, evening with Enid Bletsoe. The meal of beefburgers and chips, not allowed at home, was followed by an unlimited quantity of chocolate biscuits and the promise of television programmes that were usually forbidden to her.

But during the chocolate biscuits, and before *You've Been Framed*, Enid sat down with her for a little chat.

'How do you like your new school?' she began.

'Oh, it's very nice. I've made some new friends.'

'Didn't you hate to leave London, and your old school, and your friends?'

'Well,' Bryony considered the question, 'I didn't really want to leave in the middle of the term, but Mummy said it was important, because of her herbs – if we waited until the term was over, it would have been too late to plant them.'

'Yes, I see.' Enid offered her another biscuit. 'What, exactly, does your mummy do with her herbs?'

'She sells them to restaurants, to cook with. And, of course,' the girl added, 'she grows some special ones for when you're sick.'

'Sick?'

'You know – for headaches or tummyaches or things like that. When I don't feel well she puts some herbs in boiling water and makes me drink them.'

'Ah.' Enid sat up straighter. 'Just you, or do other people drink Mummy's herbs as well?'

'Mostly just me,' Bryony admitted. 'And Mummy too. But Lou doesn't like them. She says that Mummy might poison her.'

Enid leaned forward. 'Poison her?'

'I think she's just teasing. But she takes other tablets instead.'

'Tablets?' She tried to keep the eagerness out of her voice. Drug use! She wasn't a bit surprised; she wouldn't put any sort of depravity past those two.

'Yes, she takes them all the time.'

'And do you know where she keeps them?'

Bryony hoped Enid wouldn't notice her hand sneaking towards another biscuit. 'Of course. She usually sends me to fetch them for her – they're in a drawer by the bed. Could I please have some more squash?'

'Of course, darling. I'll get it for you.' While Enid was in the kitchen, Bryony secreted three chocolate biscuits in her pocket.

'Daddy gives me ice creams,' she announced on Enid's return. 'Do *you* have any ice creams, Mrs Bletsoe?'

'Well,' Enid said coyly, 'we'll just have to see. In a bit, after we've finished our little chat.' She put the refilled glass on the table and continued. 'Do you miss your daddy, Bryony?'

'Sometimes.'

'You don't see him very often, do you?'

'No,' Bryony admitted. 'And I won't see him very much at all now that we've left London. Mummy and Daddy don't like each other any more. And Lou hates Daddy,' she added.

Yes, thought Enid. I'll bet she does. 'How long has Mummy been living with Lou instead of with Daddy?' she probed.

The girl considered. 'A while.'

'What do Mummy and Lou call each other?'

Bryony looked at her pityingly. 'Gill and Lou. Those are their names,' she explained, as if to a younger child. 'Gill, short for Gillian, and Lou, short for Louise.'

With a delicate finger Enid edged the plate of biscuits, now almost empty, towards the girl. 'What I mean is, sweetie, do they have any private names for each other? Like "honey" or "darling"?'

'Oh, that!' Bryony took the bait, eating a biscuit. 'Mummy calls Lou "lovey" sometimes, and Lou calls Mummy "angelface". Is that what you meant?' Daintily she licked the chocolate from her fingers.

She was working her way up to the ultimate questions. 'Does Mummy ever kiss Lou?'

'Well, of *course*,' Bryony said scornfully. 'We all kiss each other. Mummy kisses me, and I kiss Mummy, and I kiss Lou, and Lou kisses me, and Mummy kisses Lou, and Lou kisses Mummy. We're a family.'

There was one chocolate biscuit left. Enid indicated it with her head and watched the girl devour it, then asked, 'Do Mummy and Lou sleep in the same bed, Bryony?'

'Of course.'

'And do you sleep in the same bed with them?'

'Not always. Just sometimes, when I've got a tummyache or have a bad dream or something like that.' She looked at Enid expectantly.

'I see the biscuits are all gone,' Enid said brightly. 'Do I know a little girl who would like an ice cream?' She got up. 'And haven't we had a nice chat?'

43

Chapter 6

Which have said, With our tongue will we prevail: we are they that ought to speak, who is lord over us?

Psalm 12:4

On the following Monday afternoon, Becca went to Roger Staines's cottage; he had been discharged from hospital and was eager to get started putting his notes in order. She returned home a few hours later, full of enthusiasm.

'Mr Staines is such an interesting person,' she told Stephen over supper. 'He knows so much about the history of the village. And the church as well. Did you know that this was once a very important area for wool, and that rich wool merchants paid to build the church?'

Stephen was pleased to see her so ebullient for a change. 'Oh, yes?' he encouraged her.

'And did he ever tell you about the Lovelidges? How they were always called John or Thomas? The first son, that is. And how they always managed to back the winning side?'

'What do you mean, the winning side?'

'Well,' Becca explained, 'the first one, Sir John Lovelidge, got to be a noble because he supported Henry VIII just in time, just when Cardinal Wolsey fell out of favour. And he got even richer during the Reformation, when the King gave him the church endowments and rectorial tithes – that meant that the Rector could always be one of the younger Lovelidge sons. Then in the Civil War the Lovelidge of the time – he was a Sir Thomas Lovelidge – changed sides and threw his lot in with the Parliamentarians, just when it looked like they were going to win. That way he got to keep Walston Hall, and he saved the east window of the church from getting destroyed by taking it out and moving it to the Hall. And later on, at the Restoration, his son was a great supporter of Charles II – one of the Gentlemen of the Bedchamber.'

'I think that's called being pragmatic,' observed Stephen. 'That family had a real talent for holding on to power.'

'But it didn't help them in the end. The last Sir John Lovelidge only had one son, called Thomas, and he was killed in France in 1915 when he was just nineteen.

Mr Staines said his father died of a broken heart,' she finished, frowning. 'Isn't that sad? And since there were no more Lovelidges, the estate was sold.'

'It sounds as if you got quite an education this afternoon, sweetheart.' He reached across the table and stroked her hair. 'I'm glad you enjoyed it.'

'I didn't ever like history at school,' Becca admitted. 'But Mr Staines makes it all come alive. The Lovelidges seem like real people to me now.'

Stephen was sufficiently interested in what Becca had told him to spend some time inspecting the Lovelidge tombs in the church when he had a few minutes to spare after lunch on Wednesday afternoon. There was no sign of Harry Gaze, so he was able to wander about undisturbed.

The first Sir John, confidant of Henry VIII, shared an elaborate tomb chest in the chancel with his wife Anne; the full-sized effigies, still bearing traces of their original paintwork, were in remarkably good condition and reminded Stephen of the Larkin poem about the Arundel tomb. 'What will survive of us is love,' he murmured to himself.

Subsequent Lovelidges had taken over the Lady Chapel for their family monuments and Stephen strolled there next to take a closer look at them. The Elizabethan Sir Thomas and his wife Lettice, sporting enormous ruffs, knelt in a curious position, half in and half out of the south wall, hands tented prayerfully in front of them. The Sir John who had been Gentleman of the Bedchamber to Charles II, as proclaimed on his monument, had also evidently spent a fair amount of time in his own bedchamber: he'd had three wives, all of them, confusingly, named Sarah, who had presented him with a total of twenty-three children, most of whom had died at birth or in infancy. The monument showed them all in half-relief, Sir John at the centre, flanked by three women and a bevy of tiny shrouded babies. The matter-of-factness of it was startling.

The monuments became ever more elaborate as succeeding generations of Lovelidges tried to outdo their ancestors at self-commemoration. An eighteenth-century Sir John, reproduced life size in marble, reclined voluptuously, his bewigged head propped up on his hand, while a cloaked allegorical figure of Grief knelt at his feet, head bowed in mourning. According to the florid inscription, he had been nothing short of perfect: liberal, kind-hearted, civic-minded and a wonderful husband and father, as proclaimed by his relict Augusta, daughter of Lord Hollingsworth of the county of Shropshire. Later, Victorian Lovelidges preferred weeping angels to allegorical figures and there were quantities of them in evidence. But as far as Stephen was concerned, the simplest monument was the most moving. It was a small tablet set into the wall; the dignified block lettering said 'Captain Thomas Lovelidge, only son of Sir John Lovelidge and his wife Alice, 1896–1915. His body lies in France, his soul is with God, but he lives in our hearts for ever.'

'Wholly interesting, them monuments,' said Harry Gaze conversationally, materialising behind the Rector. 'Shame the family died out like that.'

'Very sad.' Stephen turned to face the verger.

'Sorry I wasn't here to show them to you, but I popped off home for my dinner. Did you see the one with the three wives?' Harry pointed to the Gentleman of the Bedchamber. 'Didn't have very good luck, did he? I reckon he must have wore them out, one after another, with all them babies.'

'I'm sure you're right.'

Harry seemed, as usual, in the mood for a chat. 'Back in them days that was all women was good for – having babies, and other such related activities in the bedroom. And cooking and cleaning the house, of course.' His tone implied that he considered that a good thing.

'Fortunately we've come a long way from that,' Stephen said reprovingly.

The verger gave Stephen a sly wink. 'I hear your missus has got herself a job of sorts.'

'Only for a few hours a week.' As he said it, Stephen wondered why he sounded so defensive.

'That's how it always starts. Next thing you know you'll be ironing your own albs and cooking your own dinner.'

Stephen forced himself to laugh. 'That wouldn't be the end of the world – I've done it before and it wouldn't kill me to do it again. There are a lot of priests who aren't married, Harry, who don't have wives to cook and iron for them. I've only just got married myself, remember?'

'Yes, but most of them have housekeepers or other women to look after them. Father Fuller had a housekeeper. You wouldn't have caught him ironing his own albs.'

Stephen couldn't help himself. 'The sainted Father Fuller,' he muttered, rolling his eyes. 'Deliver me from Father Fuller.'

'He were a wholly good man,' Harry said severely. 'None better.'

'I'm sure.' The Rector's voice had not a trace of irony.

'I wonder,' Harry meditated, flicking an imaginary speck of dust off the kneeling figure of Grief, 'what Father Fuller would have made of this new scheme of Fred's?'

'What scheme is that?' Stephen asked, knowing the answer.

The verger shot him a speculative look. 'Fred reckons as we shouldn't give any more of our money to the diocese. He says as it's wicked the way they take our money and squander it away and don't give us nothing in return.'

'The money from the Quota helps to pay the clergy's stipends,' Stephen pointed out mildly. 'You're getting *me* in return, Harry.'

'But Fred says as your money comes out of some trust fund, all thanks to the Lovelidge family. Nothing to do with the diocese – you'd get it whether or no.'

'That's not strictly true. And it's not really the point.'

'The point is,' Harry went on stubbornly, 'Fred says that we need that money here in Walston. We've got to look after our own. The Lovelidge family all them

46

years ago made provision for us so as we'd always have a priest. So why should we go throwing good money after bad, sending it off to Norwich every year to pay for some other village's problems? Why can't we just tell them to get on with it and sort themselves out?'

Stephen took a deep breath and tried to be patient. 'Because we're all part of the Church of England,' he explained. 'That's what it's all about. We're all in it together.'

'There's many here as will wholly disagree with you, Father.' Harry folded his arms across his chest. 'Fred's been talking to a lot of folks. He reckons as he's got enough support to raise it at the next PCC meeting.'

'Is that so?' Stephen's exasperation gave way to alarm.

'And by then we'll have a new churchwarden, and she's bound to back Fred up.'

'But—' Stephen began, before one word penetrated his consciousness. 'She? Did you say "she", Harry?'

Harry watched him with sly interest. 'That I did. You don't approve of us having a female churchwarden, and you such a supporter of women and all?'

'Who said we were going to have a female churchwarden?' He was genuinely baffled.

'Everyone knows it by now, Father. Don't tell me you didn't know?'

Stephen frowned. 'Is this another one of Fred's little schemes?'

'Oh, no. This one is Ernest's,' Harry informed him with relish. 'Ernest reckons as it's up to him to decide who ought to be churchwarden, him being so important and all.'

'And who,' asked Stephen, 'is this woman? Or hasn't Ernest decided yet?' he added sarcastically.

'Oh, he's decided, all right. It's Flora Newall, that social worker woman. An interfering female, I reckon, but that's not for me to say. Ernest must know what he's doing.'

At the Rectory, Becca was not having a good afternoon. Stephen hadn't been gone more than a few minutes when the phone rang, and she picked it up with something approaching resignation. The calls were so inevitable, and by now their content was so predictable, that she supposed she was becoming inured to the horror – her revulsion remained unabated, but repetition had taken the edge off her more extreme reactions. But this time there was a difference. After the customary enquiries after her wellbeing, the soft voice took a new tack.

'Does the parson know that he's married such a whore?'

'What?' she gasped, almost as if she'd been physically struck.

'One man isn't enough for you – now you're putting it all around the village. You must have developed a real taste for it, my dear.'

Becca felt herself blushing, though she knew there was no reason. 'What do you mean?' she whispered.

'Off to Roger Staines's cottage every day,' he chuckled. 'Don't wear the poor man out or he'll have another heart attack.'

'But I'm working for Mr Staines!'

The chuckle was repeated. 'Yes, I'm sure you are. And I hope he appreciates it, and pays you well for it – I know I would.'

Becca whimpered, which seemed to encourage him. 'And what about those two bitches at Foxglove Cottage?' he went on softly. 'We all know what they are. And they're your friends, aren't they? Does that mean they've taught you to like it their way as well? Do you all do it together – three in a bed? Does your husband know? And if I promise not to tell him, will you let me watch?'

'No – oh, no!' Her stomach churned; her fingers no longer had the strength to hold the receiver and it clattered to the floor.

The Reverend Stephen Thorncroft was not normally a man given to violent emotions, with a few notable exceptions in his past, but he came close to it that day. He went straight to Ernest Wrightman's house, and the expression on his face must have warned Doris, when she answered the door, that all was not well.

'I'm afraid Ernest isn't here,' she replied to his query, her voice sounding nervous. 'He's gone to a luncheon meeting with the people from Ingram's, and he's not back yet.'

'I'll wait,' the Rector said tersely, 'if you don't mind.'

'Please come in, Father.' She ushered him into her immaculate sitting room. 'Can I get you a cup of tea?'

He would have loved one, but decided it would weaken his position to accept hospitality. 'No, thank you.'

'Well, then.' Doris perched on a chair opposite him and regarded him with an unnerving stare.

'Please,' said Stephen. 'Don't let me keep you from whatever you were doing.'

She rose with alacrity. 'I was hanging out some washing. If you don't mind ...'

'No, of course not. Do carry on.'

Her head swivelled at the faint sound of a key in the front-door lock. 'That must be Ernest now. I'll tell him you're here, Father.'

'Thank you.' Stephen rose, not wishing to be caught at a disadvantage.

A moment later Ernest Wrightman entered the room, rubbing his hands together and feeling quite pleased with himself; the lunch had been a great success. 'Good afternoon, Father,' he said officiously. 'What can I do for you?'

Stephen took a deep breath. 'I've just seen Harry Gaze, and he's told me about your plans for the new churchwarden. I think you owe me an explanation.'

'Well, Father.' Ernest didn't seem at all nonplussed by the Rector's tone; if anything, he sounded more pleased with himself than ever. 'I've asked Miss Newall if she would consider standing as warden. And she has agreed.'

'So Harry told me. And did you not think about discussing this with me before taking a step like that?'

Ernest raised his eyebrows; his voice was aggressive rather than conciliatory. 'Churchwardens are elected by the parish – it has nothing to do with you, Father.'

Controlling his anger with an enormous effort, Stephen spoke coldly; his grey eyes glittered behind his spectacles. 'Everything that happens in my parish has to do with me, not least of all the election of my churchwardens. I trust that you'll remember that in future.' The other man stroked his ginger moustache and looked thoughtful. 'Might I ask, Father, if you happened to have anyone in mind for the vacancy?'

'I did,' Stephen stated. 'And still do. I feel that Quentin Mansfield would make an excellent warden, with his financial expertise and good business sense.'

'Oh, no.' Ernest's response was immediate and authoritative. 'He wouldn't do at all, Father. Not suitable – the parish wouldn't stand for it. I do hope you haven't mentioned the matter to him – that would be embarrassing for all of us. He simply won't do.'

Flora Newall had found already, to her great surprise, that she had never been more popular amongst the good folk of Walston than she now was. Over the past week, as news of her anointing as future churchwarden had spread through the village, she'd been the recipient of numerous phone calls comprising invitations, suggestions and requests, all offered with varying degrees of subtlety. Most of the invitations had been accepted, and the suggestions and requests had been duly noted, with the protest, 'I'm not churchwarden yet, you know.'

The Mothers' Union meeting on Thursday evening was a case in point. Several women, stirred up by Fred Purdy on their visits to the village shop, made a point of mentioning to her the foolishness of sending money off to Norwich to be wasted, and lobbying had also begun on behalf of the sacked choir. 'There must be something that can be done,' Doris Wrightman remarked to Flora in a confidential whisper over tea and biscuits at the conclusion of the meeting. 'That man Cyprian Lawrence is no more than an employee of the church. Surely he can be stopped. Fred Purdy will back you up on it.'

'I haven't been elected yet,' Flora demurred.

'Oh, but you will be. Ernest has promised that you will, and he won't let you down.' Doris's voice was tinged with pride. 'That's one thing about Ernest – he's a man of his word. You can be sure of that. When he says something is going to happen, it happens.'

'But perhaps it's not in Ernest's control,' the other woman pointed out. 'The whole parish has to want me.'

Doris looked smug, though her expression was tinged with pity at the other woman's naïvety. 'The parish will, of course, be guided by Ernest. They always are. He has so many years of experience, and such wisdom. Father Fuller knew that – he would never have done anything without asking for Ernest's blessing.'

When Enid Bletsoe drew her aside for a private conversation a few minutes later, Flora was prepared for a similar approach and was ready with her disclaimer. It was a surprise, therefore, that Enid brushed it aside with a frown. 'This has nothing to do with the parish – it's to do with your professional responsibilities. As a social worker.'

Flora blinked in surprise. 'Yes?'

'I wanted some advice.' Enid lowered her voice. 'About child abuse.'

'Child abuse?' She realised as she echoed Enid's words that she sounded dim-witted, but the subject was the last thing she would have expected the other woman to raise.

'I don't want to name any names, but I just wanted to find out from you, strictly off the record, of course, what the procedure is for reporting cases of suspected child abuse.'

Flora rapidly assumed a professional manner, speaking with a brisk competence that Enid had never before seen her exhibit. 'If there's any question of abuse,' she said in a firm voice, 'then it must be reported immediately. There is no justification for delay when a child is at risk. Who is this child? You must tell me.'

Flustered by this direct reply, Enid retreated; it wouldn't do to show her hand just yet, before the time was right. 'Oh, no one in particular. It was just a theoretical question,' she equivocated. 'I was reading an article about child abuse in a magazine, and I just wondered.'

'Well,' said Flora, no longer the mild spinster. 'I trust that if you ever do hear of any such abuse, you will report it to me straightaway.

Enid nodded. 'You can be sure I will.' As Flora turned away, Enid smiled into her teacup.

Chapter 7

I poured out my complaints before him: and shewed him of my trouble.

Psalm 142:2

Subsequent events of that week did nothing to allay Stephen's fears for the future of his parish; everyone to whom he spoke seemed to regard Flora Newall's election as churchwarden as a foregone conclusion, and the withholding of Diocesan Quota payments as equally certain and equally acceptable. He had the unsettling sensation of being completely out of control, and nothing in his previous experience had prepared him for that.

On Friday night he scarcely slept, replaying all of the scenarios endlessly in his head through the night. Sunday would be Palm Sunday, the beginning of Holy Week, the most dramatic and significant week in the church's year. He should be preparing himself spiritually for it, but he was immobilised by his feeling of utter helplessness in the face of the machinations of Fred Purdy and Ernest Wrightman. How had it happened? he asked himself. How, without even knowing it was happening, had he lost control of his parish?

The question possessed him to such a degree that it eclipsed what otherwise would have been a matter of major concern: the fact that he and Becca had not made love for three days. When he had returned home from seeing Ernest Wrightman on Wednesday, he had been so incensed that he'd scarcely noticed how subdued his wife was. He'd had plenty to say on the subject of Wrightman's arrogance throughout that evening, and Becca had listened quietly. When bedtime had come, she had – for the first time ever – pleaded a headache, retreating to her side of the bed. That wasn't surprising, Stephen had thought – he had a headache himself, and no wonder. Her headache hadn't gone away on Thursday or Friday, but, if he noticed her shrinking from his touch, he attributed it to his own overworked imagination.

As the first light of morning filtered through the bedroom curtains, Stephen turned and looked at his sleeping wife. She was huddled against the edge of the bed, her back to him, but he could see the curve of her pale cheek. Becca *had* been very pale lately – he hoped this headache wasn't a portent of something more serious. Stephen leaned over and brushed the silvery hair back from her cheek with a gentle finger, letting his love for her refresh his troubled soul like a healing balm. How good it was to have a wife. 'Oh, Becca,' he murmured. In her sleep she responded to his voice and turned towards him, dislodging the duvet to give him a tantalising glimpse of breast.

Instantly tenderness was transmuted into desire, fuelled by three days of abstinence. 'Oh, Becca,' he repeated, bending to kiss her as his hand reached for her breast.

Her eyes flew open. 'No!' she gasped, pulling back from him.

'But, Becca sweetheart, what's the matter? I just want to make love to you.'

'No!' Becca's voice was desperate. 'No, I can't!'

It was too terrible – and too embarrassing – to talk about, so they didn't. Sitting at the kitchen table several hours later, after celebrating early Mass at St Michael's, Stephen talked about everything else but what had happened, while Becca prepared his breakfast.

'I do like a fry-up on a Saturday morning,' he remarked as she turned the sausages. 'I know it's not good for me, but I tell myself that it won't kill me if I just have it once a week. And after getting up early on a Saturday to say Mass, I feel I deserve it.'

Becca cracked an egg into the frying pan, then gave a sharp cry. 'Oh, I've broken the yolk.'

'It doesn't matter, sweetheart. I'll take it as it comes.'

She covered her face with her hands. 'It's ruined,' she said softly, her voice catching on a sob. 'Ruined.'

Stephen leaned forward, alarmed. 'I said I don't mind.'

'And the sausages are burnt.' Silent tears trickled down her cheeks. 'I'm a terrible wife to you, Stephen. A hopeless cook and a terrible wife. You shouldn't have married me.'

'Don't be daft, sweetheart. It's only breakfast.' He half rose to go to her, but stopped as she visibly controlled herself and moved away to get a plate.

'Let's talk about something else,' she said with studied calm, dishing up the sorry-looking breakfast and putting it in front of him.

It seemed a good idea, and Stephen didn't need very much encouragement to return to the topic that was so much on his mind. 'I just don't understand how the man's mind works,' he mused. 'Ernest, I mean. In the first place, I can't understand why he thinks he has the right to dictate to me what happens in *my* church. What authority does he have? But that question aside, I can't see what possible objection he could have to Quentin Mansfield as churchwarden. Quentin has all the qualities we need right now, and he's a respected member of the community – after all, he lives at Walston Hall!'

With a silent sigh, Becca welcomed the shift of focus on to external matters, however vexing they were to Stephen. 'But he's only been here for a few years.

People around here are suspicious of anyone who wasn't born in Walston. Or "bred and born", as they say in Norfolk.'

'Exactly my point!' Stephen slapped his palm on the table for emphasis. 'What about Flora Newall? She hasn't been in Walston any longer than the Mans-fields, and she's much more of an unknown quantity. She's very keen, of course, but no one really knows her very well. And she has a full-time job, so she certainly won't be able to devote the time to it that Roger did, or Quentin could.'As he ate his breakfast, oblivious to the broken egg and burnt sausages, he went on to the problem of Fred Purdy and the Quota, while Becca paced restlessly. 'I just don't know what to do,' he concluded some minutes later. 'I don't know where to turn. Nothing I've ever come up against before has prepared me for a situation like this.'

Becca sat down across from him, wrapping her dressing gown across her chest in an unconsciously protective gesture. She tried to think what her father would have done, but realised that her father would never have been in such a situation: no one would ever have presumed to tell him what to do. 'Isn't there anyone you can talk to? The Archdeacon or the Rural Dean? Or a colleague in another parish?'

He shook his head. 'I don't need pastoral advice – what I really need is legal advice. I need to know what steps, if any, I can take to stop Fred Purdy and his chums from doing their best to destroy the Church of England.'

'Legal advice.' Becca frowned thoughtfully. 'You need a lawyer, then.'

They had the idea simultaneously, but Stephen enunciated it first. 'David Middleton-Brown!'

At that moment, David Middleton-Brown was not a happy man. By disposition he was fairly sanguine, through susceptible to occasional moods, and the past year of his life had been by far the most satisfactory to date. After years in the provinces, his career as a solicitor had taken off with a job at a prestigious firm in London. In addition, at forty-two he had found himself dizzyingly in love with the artist Lucy Kingsley, and to his great amazement and gratification he had discovered that the feeling was mutual. Twelve months of sharing her life and six months of sharing her house had convinced him that the arrangement ought to be a permanent one, but Lucy had not proved easy to persuade that marriage should be a part of their future. Now, after three traumatic weeks in which Lucy's stroppy fourteen-year-old niece Ruth had played a prominent part, that morning they'd finally seen Ruth off at Euston station. And a few minutes later Lucy had told him that she wanted to end their relationship: not because she didn't love him, but because she feared that she loved him too much.

David was still in shock as they returned home to Lucy's tiny mews house in South Kensington, having said little in the car. Twelve days: that was all the time he had to change her mind. At the beginning of April, twelve days hence, he would be granted possession of a house which he had inherited, and Lucy would expect him to move out. Unless he could somehow convince her within the next few days that she couldn't live without him. He didn't know where to start, or what to say. In their brief conversation at the station he'd been restrained in his arguments, realising instinctively that emotional blackmail would be counterproductive. But how to change her mind? He was well aware that his happiness now, and for the rest of his life, depended upon his success.

The phone was ringing as they came through the door. Lucy, silent and tearful, picked it up. 'Hello?' Her voice came out sounding nothing like her.

'Is this Lucy?' Stephen enquired tentatively.

'This is Lucy Kingsley,' she confirmed.

'Hello, Aunt Lucy.' It was a joke between them; Lucy had in fact been Stephen's aunt for a few months by virtue of her brief marriage to his uncle some years earlier, though she was only a few years his senior.

'Stephen!' She made an effort to sound enthusiastic. 'How are you? How is Becca?'

His reply required an equal effort. 'Oh, we're both well. And you?'

'Very well.'

After an awkward pause Stephen went on, 'I was hoping for a word with David.'

'He's right here.' Feeling unequal to further small talk, Lucy passed the phone to David, who was standing by with a questioning frown.

Lucy only heard half of the conversation, so David filled in the missing parts later in the kitchen over strong coffee. He would have preferred – indeed he craved – something stronger, but knew Lucy would take a dim view of whisky before noon.

'He's having some real problems with his parish, apparently. Seems he has a headstrong, if somewhat dim, churchwarden, been there for yonks, who wants to stop paying their Diocesan Quota, and the man has managed to sway much of the congregation to back him on it. And there's a vacancy for the other churchwarden, but some self-proclaimed kingmaker in the parish has decided that he knows better than the Rector who ought to be elected. Stephen wants a particular chap who has business experience and money sense, but this Ernest Wrightman's candidate is a woman, a social worker who's apparently only been in the parish for five minutes.'

Lucy listened carefully, twisting a strand of her hair – naturally curly, shoulder-length, and shimmering red-gold in colour – round her finger. She frowned. 'I still don't understand what it has to do with *you*.'

'Neither do I, really.' David's generous mouth curved in a quirky, self-deprecating smile. 'For some reason he seems to think that I can work miracles.'

'He wants you to go?'

'He wants *us* to go,' David amended. 'He says they have a huge old rectory with plenty of room. His idea is that if we go to stay for a few days and see the situation I might be able to give him some advice.'

54

'Do you think you can help him?'

'I think,' said David with a short, unamused laugh, 'that the advice I could give him after seeing the situation would be the same advice I'd give him right now: start looking for another parish.'

Lucy smiled wanly. 'So you don't want to go.'

'I didn't say that.' He took his time refilling his coffee cup as he thought through the implications of Stephen's request. He wasn't at all sure that he could be of any practical assistance to the young priest, recognising that the legal position was fairly straightforward. He could tell Stephen over the phone that overturning a decision by his PCC was nigh to impossible. But getting away to Norfolk for a few days might be just the thing as far as his own situation with Lucy was concerned. David was by nature non-confrontational and dreaded the very thought of spending the next twelve days in discussion of their future, going down the old paths again and again and reaching no happy conclusion. There was one important difference, though: this time he was fighting not for their marriage, but for the very existence of their future together. It was not a joyful prospect. A few days in Norfolk would be a respite from that and might even buy him some time. If Lucy would agree to put the issue on hold until they came back … 'I wouldn't mind going,' he said at last. 'It might be nice to have a holiday in the country, and it would be good to see Stephen and Becca, even if I couldn't do anything to help them. And,' he added with a smile, 'it's a wonderful church. I'd like you to see it – it's one of the most beautiful wool churches ever built, with marvellous Perpendicular architecture and a lovely chapel that's been done up by Comper. What do you think, Lucy love?'

'Yes, it might be nice.' Lucy was already beginning to regret the things she'd said to David earlier that morning. His arguments had been cogent, and she *did* love him. Perhaps a few days away from London would be good for both of them. 'But can you get time off from work?'

'He's suggested that we come next weekend, which is, of course, Easter, with the Bank Holiday on Monday. So we could have a long weekend in Norfolk without my having to take any time off. We could drive up on Saturday morning, and come back late on Monday.'

'Let's go,' she said simply, reaching across the table to cover his hand with hers. 'And in the meantime, let's not talk about … well, you know. I think we can let it rest for a few days.'

'Splendid.' He exhaled in a long, heartfelt sigh and twined his fingers with hers. 'I'll ring Stephen back and tell him to expect us next Saturday.' Suddenly he grinned and pulled Lucy to her feet, leading her towards the stairs. 'Later, that is. For now, my love, if we're not going to talk, I've got a better idea. Actions speak louder than words, anyway.'

Chapter 8

Thou hast made us a very strife unto our neighbours: and our enemies laugh us to scorn.

Psalm 80:6

It was one of Gillian English's chief faults, according to Lou: she was too trusting, too willing to take people at face value. Gill hadn't seen much of Enid Bletsoe lately, but it didn't occur to her to read anything into that other than to theorise that perhaps the novelty of having new neighbours had worn off. So when she ran into Enid in the village shop on the Saturday before Holy Week, she greeted her with unsuspecting friendliness. 'Hello, I haven't seen you for a while,' Gill said, approaching from behind.

Enid, who had just been discussing Gill and Lou with Fred Purdy at the counter, spun round. 'Hello,' she responded grudgingly, not wanting Fred to think that they might be on friendly terms.

'Are you enjoying the nice weather?' Gill gestured outside to a beautiful spring day. 'It's been marvellous this week – I've really been able to get the garden into shape and get most of my herbs planted.'

'Yes, well.' Enid sniffed and gave Fred a significant look; they'd only just been talking about the sinister nature of Gill's business enterprise. Anxious to escape from her neighbour's unwelcome attentions, she began putting her purchases into her shopping basket. 'And I believe I'll take a packet of chocolate biscuits, Fred,' she added deliberately. 'The ones dear little Bryony likes so much.'

Gill's voice was mild but firm; where her daughter was concerned she was capable of taking a stand. 'I'd really rather you didn't give her chocolate biscuits. They're not good for her, you know. I won't let her have them at home.' She smiled in an attempt to soften her words. 'The other week when you so kindly looked after her, she came home with some in her pocket and it didn't half make a mess in the washing machine.'

'I'm sure young Jamie never left anything in his pockets, did he?' chuckled Fred Purdy.

'Well, at least I wasn't daft enough not to check them before I did the wash,' Enid muttered, deliberately placing the biscuits on top of her shopping.

Gill judged that it was time to change the subject and picked one that she thought would further the cause of good neighbourly relations. 'When did you say that the Mothers' Union enrolment would take place? I want to make sure I have the date in my diary.'

The shopping basket landed back on the counter with a thump as Enid turned to stare at Gill. 'Are you serious?' she snapped.

Taken aback, Gill gave a half-apologetic shrug. 'Well, you did invite me to join.'

'That was before I knew what sort of person you really were.' Enid's eyes glittered with outrage and her voice was heated. 'When you deceived me into thinking that you were a mother, a normal mother.'

'But I *am* a mother.'

'A pervert,' Enid spat. 'An evil, twisted pervert. We don't want your kind in the Mothers' Union. We don't want your kind in this village. And all I can say is that I have nothing but pity for your daughter.' Majestically she swept up her basket and stalked from the shop.

Gill arrived home empty-handed and shaking and went into the sitting room, where Bryony was watching a video and Lou was surrounded by the Saturday papers.

'I thought you were going shopping,' observed Lou, glancing up from the newspaper. 'Didn't you buy anything?' She looked at her partner more closely. 'I say, angelface, are you all right? You look like you've seen a ghost.'

Taking a deep breath to compose herself, Gill remembered her daughter's presence. 'Bryony darling, wouldn't you like to go outside and play in the garden for a bit? It's a beautiful day.'

Bryony was more of an indoor child. 'But I'm watching this. You said I could.'

'You can watch the rest of it later, darling. It's too nice to stay inside.'

'But *you're* inside,' pointed out the pedantic child.

'Just go,' ordered Lou.

Bryony went, with a martyred sigh.

'Now tell me what's the matter.' Lou rose as Gill collapsed into the nearest chair.

'Oh, Lou, it was awful.' Quickly she related the substance of her run-in with Enid.

'She called you a pervert?' demanded Lou fiercely.

'A twisted, evil pervert,' Gill amplified with a shaky laugh. 'It was awful.'

'The vicious old cow!' Lou stalked back and forth behind the sofa. 'But honestly, Gill, what did you expect, for God's sake? I warned you before we came that this godforsaken village wasn't going to take kindly to a pair of dykes on their doorstep.'

'But in London it didn't make any difference.'

'London is London,' Lou stated unarguably. 'Norfolk is a different bloody kettle of fish entirely.'

'So I see.' Gill tried to smile. 'But she was so nice to us before – inviting us for meals and offering to watch Bryony. I just don't understand it.'

While this discussion was taking place, Bryony was playing with her skipping rope in the front garden in a half-hearted way. Enid, in one of her periodic peeps from her front window, spotted her and lost no time in making her way across the road. 'Hello there, young lady,' she said in the syrupy voice that she reserved for speaking to Bryony. 'How are you today?'

'Oh, all right.' Bryony stopped skipping. 'But I'd rather be inside. I was watching a video – a really good one – but Mummy wanted to be alone with Lou, so she sent me out to play.'

Enid's smile was triumphant: this was even better than she'd hoped. 'Is that so?'

'Yes, I can always tell when Mummy and Lou want to be left alone. They tell me to go away. And I'm thirsty.'

'Well,' said Enid promptly, 'you must come across the road to my house and have a nice drink of orange squash. And I've just bought some of those lovely choccy biscuits that you like so much.'

'I don't think Mummy would like me to go without telling her,' Bryony demurred.

'Oh, I'm sure Mummy won't even miss you for a few minutes.' Leading the girl across the road, Enid spared one look over her shoulder at the cottage where even at that moment, she was sure, some sort of deviant sex romp was taking place. How dare they leave this poor innocent child outside where any passer-by might snatch her away, she thought indignantly, while they were satisfying their unnatural lusts. People like that didn't deserve to have children.

Bryony was still a bit uncertain, but she followed Enid into her kitchen and soon forgot her unease when the chocolate biscuits and squash were produced.

'So,' said Enid, 'you should be starting your spring school holidays soon.'

'Yes, at the end of this week.'

'Will you be going to London to see your daddy?'

Bryony nibbled daintily on a biscuit. 'No, I don't think so. At least Mummy hasn't said.' The little girl put her head on one side and lowered her voice. 'I don't think Daddy knows where I am.'

'You mean Mummy hasn't told him? That she's moved away without telling him where she was going?' Enid's voice was sharp with excitement.

'I think so. At least, I haven't heard anything from Daddy since we came here.'

Enid was breathing heavily. 'Wouldn't you like to see your daddy?'

'Well, yes. He takes me to fun places like the zoo, and gives me nice treats – like ice creams,' she added slyly.

'Oh, you poor little lamb – to be deprived of your father!' The woman was even more evil than she'd thought, Enid realised.

The ice-cream hint hadn't worked this time, so Bryony took another biscuit with a philosophical shrug. 'I think I'd better be going now, Mrs Bletsoe. Thank you very much indeed for the squash and biscuits, but I don't want Mummy to worry about me.'

'Yes, all right.' Enid ushered her to the door, her mind working furiously. 'Just one other thing, Bryony,' she said in an innocent voice. 'What is your daddy's name? And where does he live?'

A short time after that the phone call came. It was pure bad luck that Gillian was alone in the kitchen and picked up the phone; Lou would have put it straight down again. 'Hello, Gill,' said a smooth voice that was stomach-lurchingly familiar.

Minutes later, for the second time that day, Gill blundered into the sitting room where Bryony had resumed watching her video and Lou was once again engrossed in the papers. 'Oh, God!' she wailed. 'It's happened – he's found us!'

'What?' Lou dropped the paper. 'What are you talking about, Gill? *Who's* found us?'

'Adrian! He's just phoned! Oh, God, Lou, what are we going to do?'

Bryony looked up. 'I'm not leaving this time,' she muttered rebelliously. 'It's just getting to the good part.'

That seemed to help Gill to regain her self-control. Taking a deep breath, she turned to face her daughter and her voice was quiet and resolute. 'No, you're not going anywhere, young lady. You have some explaining to do.'

Lou was on her feet. 'What the hell is this all about?' she demanded.

Gill clasped her hands together to keep them from shaking. 'Adrian has just phoned,' she repeated evenly.

'That bastard! How did he find us?' The venom in Lou's voice was reinforced by the expression of pure loathing on her face.

'He said that our neighbour Mrs Bletsoe had contacted him because she was concerned that Bryony missed her daddy.'

'And how did the nosy old bitch know how to find him?' Lou rounded on Bryony accusingly.

Bryony had the grace to look embarrassed. 'She asked me what his name was and where he lived,' she muttered. 'Awhile ago, when you sent me out to play.'

It was a nightmare come true, reflected Gill, and her own daughter had conspired in it. 'Listen to me, young lady,' she said in a tone that left no doubt as to her intentions. 'I don't want you to speak to Mrs Bletsoe ever again. Not ever. Do you understand me?'

But Lou wasn't content with Bryony's sheepish promise. She stormed out of the house and across the road, banged on the door and stood with her arms akimbo until Enid opened it.

'Listen to me, you interfering old bitch,' Lou shouted, waving an accusing finger within an inch of Enid's nose. 'You leave us alone! Leave Bryony alone and leave Gill and me alone! Stay out of our lives or you'll have me to answer to!'

Enid stared at the apparition of fury, her mouth hanging open; for once in her life she was at a loss for words.

During that busy Holy Week, several meetings of note took place in and around Walston. The Rector found the time – and the courage – to meet Quentin Mansfield and to inform him of the decreasing likelihood of his becoming churchwarden. Ernest and Doris Wrightman spent an enjoyable day sailing on the Broads with the new multinational owners of Ingram's. The village shop being closed on Good Friday, Fred Purdy took advantage of the rare holiday to meet with the wardens of Walston St Mary Church in the afternoon after their respective services, to satisfy himself on the finer points of withholding Quota payments. And another significant meeting also occurred on Good Friday, as Flora Newall, also enjoying a day off from work, lunched at Walston Hall with Diana Mansfield.

When the invitation was issued, Flora objected to the timing: as a likely new churchwarden, she felt that she ought to attend the Liturgical Three Hours in its entirety. But Diana had been insistent not only about the importance of the luncheon but about the timing as well. 'Quentin will be at church, and I need to see you privately,' she'd explained.

Diana reiterated the explanation, with an apology, over the smoked salmon first course. 'I'm sorry to keep you from church on Good Friday,' she said, 'but these days, since Quentin has retired, I don't ever seem to have any time to myself.'

'It must be quite an adjustment for both of you,' Flora sympathised; in the course of her work she'd seen a fair amount of domestic violence with just such a triggering cause.

'Yes, I'm just not used to having him around underfoot.' Diana gave a wry, apologetic smile and waved her hand at their splendid surroundings. 'Not that he's always exactly underfoot in a place like Walston Hall where we both have plenty of places to hide from one another. I can't imagine what it would be like in a council flat.'

Flora looked around at the beautifully appointed dining room, observing her hostess out of the corner of her eye. Diana Mansfield, elegantly dressed and coiffed as usual, had the completely unconscious knack of making Flora feel more than usually plain and awkward by comparison. The uncomfortable sensation she always had in the presence of Diana had contributed to her reluctance to accept this invitation, Flora acknowledged to herself, and her hostess's inability to get to the point of the meeting increased her unease as well. Flora had no illusions that this luncheon had anything to do with friendship on a personal level, but she couldn't imagine what on earth a woman like Diana could want from her.

It took Diana three courses and two bottles of wine to get around to it. By that time, Flora, unused to drinking large quantities of alcohol at any time, or any alcohol at all during daylight hours, was beyond speculating. She shook her head in polite refusal at the offer of liqueur with her coffee, bringing out her supply of artificial sweetener instead, and watched bemused as Diana added a generous dollop of brandy to her own cup. 'I suppose,' said Diana, after taking the first sip, 'you're wondering why I wanted to talk to you.'

Flora inclined her head in acknowledgement.

'Rumour has it that you're going to be the new churchwarden.'

Denial had become automatic. 'It's by no means certain,' Flora temporised, adding modestly, 'there are much more qualified and suitable people than me at St Michael's.'

'But everyone says you're going to be elected,' Diana stated dismissively. 'No one else is going to stand. Quentin was going to, but he's not prepared to have his name put forward if everyone wants you instead. He couldn't bear to be defeated. That's the way Quentin is – if he doesn't know he can win, he won't even play the game.'

Flora thought she could see, at last, what this was all about, and why it was necessary that this discussion should be held before the next week's Vestry meeting. 'You want me to withdraw my name then,' she postulated, 'so that Quentin will have a clear field.'

Diana's stare held amazement. 'No, of course not! I don't *want* Quentin to be churchwarden!'

'Then what ... ?'

Diana looked into her coffee cup and spoke quietly. 'As you're going to be warden, I just wanted to speak to you about something important to ... a friend of mine. Cyprian Lawrence.' Now that she'd started, the words came out in an accelerating stream. 'Everyone hates Cyprian – Mr Lawrence, that is, because he disbanded the choir. They think he's high-handed and arrogant. But he's raised the standard of music at St Michael's so much – now we can be really proud of our choir. They don't seem to realise how much prestige he's brought us in the music world and how much money those recording contracts bring in.'

'But what can *I* do?' Flora interrupted her.

'You can speak up for him and protect him. As churchwarden you'll have a great deal of power – much more than you realise. You'll be trustee of the almshouses and the educational trust, you'll be on all the committees. The Rector explained it all to Quentin. It's a position of enormous power and influence.' Diana continued rapidly, 'Roger Staines was all in favour of everything that Cyprian – Mr Lawrence – has done to raise the standard of the music. Fred Purdy hates him, just like Ernest Wrightman, because he chucked them out of the choir. Quentin would have been against him as well, because he doesn't see any value in intangible things like music. But you – you're an intelligent, cultured woman. You can see how important it is that Mr Lawrence be allowed to continue here in Walston. Please – you must make sure that they don't manage to sack him!'

Chapter 9

Thine adversaries roar in the midst of thy congregations: and set up their banners for tokens.

Psalm 74:5

In the Church of England the day between Good Friday and Easter Sunday is traditionally a quiet one, save for the army of tireless workers, usually women, who transform their churches from sombre places of mourning to buildings fit for joyous celebration. The altars; stripped bare on Maundy Thursday, are, by Easter Sunday, bedecked with shining white frontals, the plain wooden crosses have given way to the best silver or silver gilt and, after a long flowerless Lent, lilies spill in profligate splendour from pedestals and are crammed into every nook and cranny. For the average churchgoer the transformation seems nothing short of a miracle, but for those to whom the performance of the miracle is entrusted it involves a great deal of hard work and careful planning.

St Michael's Church, Walston was no exception; Enid and her team of flower arrangers had an early start on the Saturday morning, armed with chunks of Oasis, pails of water and every spare receptacle on which they could lay their collective hands. It was one time during the year when no expense was spared: the garden flowers and modest sprays of florist's carnations with which they made do at other times gave way to exuberant displays of lilies and other expensive cut blooms, supplemented with daffodils, tulips and potted hyacinths.

In the ordinary course of things, Enid would have been there first, but on this Holy Saturday she timed her entrance very carefully. Her sister Doris had arrived, as had Marjorie Talbot-Shaw and Flora Newall; they stood about waiting for their orders like an army waiting for its general. Doris monopolised the conversation, describing in some detail her day on the Broads. 'And the weather was just perfect – sunny and warm,' she rhapsodised, sticking out a scrawny leg for their inspection. 'Just look at my suntan.'

It was at that moment that Enid arrived. They all knew her well enough to realise, as she swooped down upon them in the chancel, that she had something significant to impart, and they weren't disappointed.

'What do you think?' she began breathlessly. 'I've just had a phone call from my Jamie.' She paused for maximum effect.

Doris rather spoiled the moment. 'Where *is* Jamie?' she queried. 'I would have thought he'd be home for Easter.'

Her sister spared her a brief dirty look before going on. 'Jamie is spending the holiday at Hollingsworth Park with Lord Hollingsworth and his family. He's just announced his engagement to Charlotte Hollingsworth! They're going to be married!'

David and Lucy arrived in Walston rather later that morning than they'd planned, having taken an unintentional detour, but they decided to stop at the church on their way to the Rectory. 'It's such a beautiful sunny morning,' David pointed out. 'The church will look spectacular with the sun coming in through that marvellous medieval east window.'

'Will it be open?'

'These East Anglian churches are always open,' David predicted confidently. 'It seems mad to Londoners, but I've yet to find a locked church in Norfolk.'

He was right on both counts: St Michael's was open, and it looked magnificent in the spring sunlight. Stepping into the church, Lucy almost gasped aloud. 'It's wonderful!'

'The quality of light is quite incredible.' David gave her a moment to drink it all in, then pointed out a few things from their vantage point at the west end. 'Over the chancel arch,' he indicated with his finger, 'you can just about see the medieval Doom painting. It was whitewashed out and the royal coat of arms painted over it, but over the years it's begun to re-emerge, as the arms have flaked off. See the devils on the one side, dragging sinners off to hell, and the angels on the other, receiving the blessed into eternal bliss?'

'It's wonderful,' she repeated.

'Do you like them angels on the roof?' Harry Gaze had spotted the visitors and lost no time in hurrying up to them.

'Wonderful,' Lucy echoed once again.

'I reckon you'd like to see the rest of our treasures.'

David would have preferred to show Lucy round himself, but recognised the inevitability of Harry's guided tour and gave in gracefully. 'Yes, of course.'

He took them down the centre aisle at a good pace and would have led them straight into the chancel, but David paused at the chancel gates and pointed the screen out to Lucy. 'Take a close look at the panels. The Puritans painted them over with Protestant texts, but there are saints underneath.'

She scrutinised the painted panels and was thrilled to find the faint but unmistakable outlines of figures under the fading blackletter texts.

'You can tell who they are by their attributes,' he showed her. 'See, this one has a scallop shell, so it must be St James. And the one with the chalice is St John the Evangelist.'

Harry Gaze regarded him with suspicion. 'How is it that you know so much about this church?'

'Oh, I've been here once or twice,' David explained, adding diplomatically, 'but of course we're anxious to learn all you have to tell us.'

Mollified, Harry led them into the chancel and gave them the benefit of the full story of King John's chair. Lucy looked questioningly at David once or twice, but with an almost imperceptible shake of his head he directed her attention back to the verger, realising the folly – and the futility – of questioning Harry Gaze's version of history.

'Are you interested in the monuments?' Harry queried hopefully when the tale of Bad King John had been told and the medieval east window had been admired. 'The Lovelidge family, them as was lords of the manor for nigh onto four hundred years, is all buried here in the church, and some of their monuments are wholly interesting.'

'Yes, of course,' David assented, following him to the Lady Chapel. 'You see,' he whispered to Lucy. 'Comper – I told you he'd redone the chapel.'

The flower arrangers, having finished in the chancel, were now concentrating their efforts on the chapel, but they looked up with interest as the visitors entered. Enid noted for later discussion the pleasant-looking brown-haired man of average height and build and the extremely attractive woman with him, slightly younger, beautifully dressed, and with shoulder-length curls of an extraordinary colour as they caught the light which streamed through the east window.

'This here Lovelidge, Sir John he was, had three wives, and all of them named Sarah,' Harry pointed out. 'He must have been wholly fond of that name, but I would of thought it might of been wholly confusing.'

'How odd,' remarked Lucy. 'What a coincidence.'

'Gentleman of the Bedchamber to King Charles II,' David read from the monument. 'Quite an important man, it would seem.'

Mindful of the number of women within earshot, Harry toned down the suggestive remark that he would have indulged in had David been alone, contenting himself with a wink in David's direction as he repeated, 'Gentleman of the Bedchamber, indeed. And twenty-three children to show for it.'

Enid produced a disapproving sniff and gave the extravagantly curled wig of the eighteenth-century Sir John a reflective pat. 'Speaking of coincidences,' she interjected, seeing her opportunity, 'this Sir John Lovelidge was married to Augusta, daughter of Lord Hollingsworth. See, it says it right here. And my grandson Jamie is engaged to Charlotte Hollingsworth, daughter of the current Lord Hollingsworth. They've just announced it. Isn't that an amazing coincidence?' This coincidence had already been pointed out to Doris, Marjorie and Flora, but she felt it worth disseminating to a wider audience.

Lucy made the appropriate congratulatory response and Enid beamed. Oblivious to Harry's glower at having his monopoly of the visitors infringed, she edged closer to them. 'Visiting Walston, are you?' she asked in a chatty manner, stating the obvious.

'We've just come up from London,' David replied. It occurred to him that this might provide a useful opportunity to meet a few of Stephen's parishioners before their connection to the Rector became known, so he went on quickly, 'And we thought for a while that we weren't going to make it. We went off the main road one turning too soon, at Nether Walston, only to discover that you can't get to Walston from there. We wandered around for quite a while before we got back to the main road.'

'My fault,' Lucy put in with a rueful shake of her head. 'I'm not a very good navigator.'

'Nether Walston!' Enid sniffed. 'No reason to go there from here, is there? Not a very nice place.'

'Nasty,' agreed Doris, joining in.

Harry took it upon himself to explain. 'Folks from Walston have never got on with folks from Nether Walston. Not for hundreds of years, since Dowsing's men came and busted up our windows, and afterwards them folks in Nether Walston fed and watered them. Not a neighbourly way to behave.'

'And,' said Enid indignantly, more concerned with slights within living memory, 'a few years ago they won the Best Kept Village competition when anyone with eyes in their head could see that we were better. I'm sure the judges were bribed.'

Flora entered the conversation. 'It's not really so bad,' she dissented, directing her remarks to David and Lucy. 'Though it *is* difficult to get there from Walston. I go there quite regularly for my work.'

'*I* wouldn't go there,' Enid stated with magisterial conviction, as though that ended the discussion.

Doris, like younger sisters the world over, knew exactly how to needle her. 'But didn't Jamie work there?' she asked, all wide-eyed innocence. 'I was sure he had a summer job there a year or two back. Didn't he, Enid?'

It had the desired effect. Enid scowled at her sister and replied in a clipped voice. 'Only because there weren't any jobs going in Walston.'

'He tried to get taken on at Ingram's, I remember, but they wouldn't have him.' Doris couldn't hide her satisfaction; she was tired of having the Hollingsworth connection shoved down her throat and she savoured this moment of revenge. 'If he wants a job there this summer, Ernest can put in a word for him. They think ever such a lot of Ernest at Ingram's.'

'Don't be ridiculous!' Enid snapped. 'Jamie hardly needs a job at Ingram's now that he's going to marry Charlotte Hollingsworth!'

Flora, embarrassed by the sisterly squabbling, tried to distract Enid. 'So he'll be spending the summer at Hollingsworth Park then?'

'Most of it, I should think.' Enid nodded, somewhat mollified.

'I know Hollingsworth Park well,' Flora said in an aside to David and Lucy. 'I lived near there for some years.'

'Oh, in Shropshire?' Lucy turned to her with a smile. 'I grew up in Shropshire myself. Near Ludlow.'

That sparked off an animated exchange in which they tried to establish whether they shared any mutual acquaintances. Before they were able to discover any, though, Harry interrupted in an attempt to regain their attention. 'Do you see that armour?' he said loudly, pointing to an ancient breastplate and helmet which hung on the stone wall above one of the Lovelidge tombs. 'It belonged to one of the younger Lovelidge sons as was a soldier and fought at Naseby. That armour has been there ever since he died, from that day to this. And do you know what?' He paused impressively, waiting until he had everyone's attention before he continued. 'The story has it, that if that armour ever falls down, there will be a violent death in Walston!'

David and Lucy hadn't made it to the wedding; they hadn't seen Stephen and Becca since the previous summer when matters had been anything but pleasant for either of them. Given the circumstances of their summons to Walston, they were expecting to find Stephen, at least, in a depressed state of mind, but they were surprised at how low they both seemed.

Stephen took David into his study for a long talk in the afternoon while Lucy accompanied Becca on a shopping expedition. Later in the guest room, after a dispirited evening meal, David and Lucy compared notes, their own problems pushed into the background.

'His parishioners are obviously a real pain in the posterior,' David said, shaking his head. 'All this nonsense about withholding Quota and sacking the organist. It's really getting to him, poor chap. But I can't help feeling there's more to it than he's told me.'

'And Becca,' Lucy put in. 'She's a loyal wife, of course, but surely her husband's parochial problems couldn't be affecting her to such an extent. Did you see the dark circles under her eyes? She looks terrible and she seems so nervous and jumpy.'

David was pacing while Lucy sat on the edge of the bed. 'Did you ask her what the matter is?'

'I couldn't ask her directly, of course.' Thoughtfully Lucy twisted a curl round her finger. 'But I tried to tell her that if she wanted to talk to me about anything, I would be happy to listen. I had the feeling that she really wanted to tell me something but couldn't quite bring herself to do it.'

'Stephen was the same,' David observed. 'He was very forthcoming about the parish problems, but shied away from talking about anything personal. I made some little joke about the happy newlyweds and he flinched as if I'd struck him. There's something very wrong there, Lucy love.'

She couldn't resist a barbed comment. 'And that's after three months of marriage!'

Not feeling equal to shifting the battleground, David ignored the remark and its implications. 'Don't forget, love, that Becca is very young. It may be taking her a while to adjust.'

'And,' Lucy added thoughtfully, 'it's less than a year since her father was murdered. He may have richly deserved it, but it was still a great shock for her. She was always so dependent on him for approval. Somehow, though, I think there's more to it than that.'

David nodded. 'I'm sure you're right. I just wish there was something we could do to help them.'

'What about Stephen's parish problems? Couldn't you give him any advice about them?'

He shook his head. 'Not really, at least as far as withholding the Quota. I'm afraid the churchwardens really *do* have a great deal of power in making policy decisions, especially if they're able to sway the PCC to their way of thinking. The Rector's hands are pretty much tied unless he has the sort of personality to bully everyone into giving him his way.'

'Like Becca's father,' Lucy put in dryly.

'Exactly. But, as we know, Stephen isn't like that. He's far too reasonable a chap and works by consensus.'

'What about sacking the organist? Becca explained a bit of the situation to me, but I can't say that I understand what's going on.'

David sat down next to her on the edge of the bed. 'It seems he's an excellent musician, but most of the congregation resent him for various reasons – because he's an outsider, I suspect, and because he hasn't made any effort to mingle or to integrate himself into the community as much as for anything he's done musically. But in this instance Stephen *does* have a bit more going for him. Legally, the organist is employed by the Rector, not by the PCC, and they can't get rid of him unless Stephen wants to. So I'd say that in spite of the hate campaign against him, the organist's job is quite secure.'

'That must have made Stephen feel better.'

'I suppose.' Restless, David got up again and went to the window. 'The other thing that's bothering him, of course, is the election of the new churchwarden. He feels so helpless that he's not being allowed to choose his own warden.'

'But I thought he *could* do that – you told me before that he could appoint one warden and allow the parish to elect the other.'

'Theoretically he could do,' David explained. 'But the person he wants as warden has indicated that he won't accept under those circumstances. Fair enough – I suppose the man feels he doesn't want to stand if he doesn't have the backing of the congregation. So that makes the election pretty much a foregone conclusion.'

Lucy got up and went to stand beside him. 'And doesn't Stephen like the other person who's standing?'

'It's not that he doesn't like her – I don't think he has anything against her. But he feels that she's an unknown quantity, that he doesn't know her well enough to get her measure. And he very much resents having the matter taken out of his hands by an interfering parishioner.'

'I met the one warden today' Lucy told him. 'At the village shop with Becca. Fred Purdy, the one who wants to stop paying the Quota.'

'And?'

'He seemed a complete prat to me – he couldn't stop laughing at his own jokes. I wasn't impressed,' she admitted. 'I would have said he was harmless, but evidently not. At least not when it comes to the Quota.'

'He's been warden for years, according to Stephen. And his word carries a lot of weight in the parish.'

'At the risk of sounding politically incorrect, "weight" is a good operative word when it comes to Mr Purdy,' Lucy said with a wry smile. 'He's a bit on the tubby side. And he looks like a garden gnome.'

David laughed, a spontaneous laugh of amusement; it seemed to him that it was the first time he'd laughed in weeks. A sensation of wellbeing enveloped him; for no particular reason, he suddenly felt that things were going to be all right, at least as far as he and Lucy were concerned. He took her hand. 'I love you, Lucy,' he said quietly. 'So very much.'

Her reply was so soft that he held his breath, straining to hear. 'Yes, I know.' She gave his hand a squeeze. 'But I'm not used to it yet – I need more time. I just hope you can bear with me for a bit longer.'

He exhaled his breath on a sigh, somewhere between relief and disappointment. 'Take as long as you need, my love. I'll be here.'

Chapter 10

I labour for peace, but when I speak unto them thereof: they make them ready to battle.

Psalm 120:6

Easter Sunday dawned as brilliantly sunny and cloudless as the previous day and there was a full congregation at St Michael's to celebrate the Resurrection, the most joyful and important festival of the church year; many of them had brought out their spring best, and the dark garb of winter had given way to pastel dresses and even an occasional hat.

In recent weeks there had been a subtle reshuffling of the seating arrangements at St Michael's, reflecting the polarisation of the congregation. Gillian English and Lou Sutherland, along with Bryony, usually sat on the south side, and Becca Thorncroft sat with them. In consequence, those who disapproved of the women – and their number was substantial – had shifted to sitting on the north side, as if afraid of contamination.

The exception to this was Ernest Wrightman, who was genuinely torn between his desire to support his wife and all right-thinking members of the congregation, and the irresistible opportunity to fill, if only for a brief time, the vacant churchwarden's seat on the south side. Roger Staines had not yet come back to church, so the seat was there for the taking, and it seemed only right that its temporary occupant should be a man who had served faithfully as warden for many years. In the end his desire to sit in that seat and to carry the wand again had won over other considerations, and Ernest Wrightman was the sole hostile presence on the south side of St Michael's.

Unfortunately for Ernest, on this Easter Sunday Roger Staines had made an effort to come to church. Preparing himself to his customary standard of sartorial splendour after weeks of relative inactivity had taken rather longer than he'd anticipated, and he arrived a few minutes before the service was to begin to find Ernest ensconced in his seat, churchwarden's wand firmly in his hand.

'Oh, excuse me,' Roger said in a mild, surprised voice.

Ernest turned; his gingery eyebrows drew together in alarm. 'I wasn't expecting to see *you* here,' he growled aggressively.

Happily Roger apprehended at once what was happening. He would have quite liked to have sat in the churchwarden's seat for one last time, thus fulfilling his term of office, but it wasn't worth an embarrassing scene. 'No problem, my dear chap,' he said gracefully. 'Carry on.' With a wave of his hand he moved forward and took a seat behind Gill and Lou.

The service was followed by an event which emphasised the polarity of the congregation: a grand Easter luncheon party at Foxglove Cottage, to which Gill and Lou had invited Stephen and Becca, along with their weekend guests, as well as Cyprian Lawrence and Roger Staines, whom they had met through Becca. After some thought, and in a spirit of solidarity, they had also included the Mansfields, though they scarcely knew them; Ernest Wrightman's treatment of Quentin Mansfield's candidacy for churchwarden qualified them as outcasts of the congregation. Stephen had been a bit reluctant to accept the invitation, pointing out with some justification that the Rector shouldn't be seen to be siding with one faction over another, but Becca had replied, unarguably, that no one else had invited them.

Seating that many people around the dining-room table was out of the question, so Gill had produced an impressive buffet, with the added advantage of allowing their guests to circulate freely during the meal.

The party was a great success, everyone agreed. The food was excellent and the company congenial. David and Lucy found it interesting as a way of getting to know a few more of Stephen's congregation, and from them to glean information about the others. While Lucy had a long chat about music with the organist, David enjoyed talking to Roger; it was rare, in his experience, to find a person whose interest in things of the past was as great as his own. Roger filled him in on the finer points of the history of Walston, eventually moving on to the present.

'I saw what happened this morning,' David commented. 'When you came in.'

Roger grimaced. 'Ernest, you mean.'

'What was that all about?'

'It seems that Ernest has rather enjoyed being the surrogate churchwarden while I've been ill. I decided it wasn't worth making a scene over.' His smile was not unkind. 'Ernest means well, I think. And I'm not about to disparage the work he's done for the church over the years, but he's pompous, self-important and more than a bit tedious. I find him difficult going.'

'Sounds a charming fellow,' remarked David ironically. 'What a shame I haven't had the pleasure of his acquaintance.'

'Quite.' Roger raised his eyebrows. 'But tedious as he is, I don't think he's as dangerous as Fred Purdy. I don't mind telling you this business about the Quota has got me worried.'

Stephen wasn't very good company for anyone on Monday as he prepared himself for that evening's meeting. In the afternoon he shut himself in his study to think and pray about his response to his congregation's intransigence. The Annual Parochial Church Meeting, much as he dreaded it, would provide him with a forum to address his parishioners in a way that had not been appropriate or possible during Holy Week and Easter. It was customary, during the APCM, for the Rector to speak at some length, reviewing the past year, assessing the present and looking forward to the future. This, Stephen realised, was his opportunity to articulate some painful truths.

They wouldn't be expecting it, he knew; he'd been through the minutes of past APCMs, and it seemed that Father Fuller's annual talks had always been of a positive nature, congratulating the parish on making it through another year and predicting continued prosperity and maintenance of the status quo. Since this was Stephen's first such meeting, they would be expecting nothing short of gratitude at his good fortune in being granted the living of Walston and praise for their role in making him welcome in their midst. They would get something quite different, he resolved, reaching for his Bible. Perhaps he couldn't do anything to stop them doing what they pleased, but at least he could give them something to think about.

As evening drew in, they all gathered for the meeting in a corner of the nave which Harry Gaze had prepared in advance with chairs arranged in a semicircle around a table where the Rector presided. The meeting was, legally, two meetings. The first, open to anyone resident in the parish whether they ever attended church or not, was the Vestry meeting for the election of churchwardens; the second, limited to those on the electoral roll, was the APCM. In practice, of course, the two meetings flowed together seamlessly.

The Vestry meeting went very much according to expectation. After the necessary preliminaries, nominations for the office of churchwarden were called for and Ernest Wrightman got to his feet with alacrity. 'Mr Chairman,' he boomed pompously, 'I nominate Mr Alfred Purdy and Miss Flora Newall.'

There were no other nominations, and the candidates were declared elected. After the frenzied goings-on of the past weeks, it was almost disappointingly anticlimactic, thought Becca in her front-row seat.

But even she was not prepared for what followed. The technicalities of the minutes and the electoral roll report out of the way, Stephen rose to his feet. He took his time, looking over the assembled parishioners with unsmiling gravity.

'I understand,' he began at last, 'that it is the custom for the Rector to spend just a few minutes reviewing the past year and looking forward to the next one.' There were a few confirmatory nods. 'And I'm sure you haven't come here to listen to a sermon from me.'

'Too right,' Fred Purdy whispered to Ernest Wrightman with a quiet chuckle and an elbow in the ribs. 'We get enough of those on Sunday, don't we?'

'But I'd like to read you a few of Our Lord's words.' Stephen picked up his Bible from the table and opened it to the marker he'd placed earlier. 'From the Gospel according to St Matthew, Chapter Seven. The Sermon on the Mount. "Ye shall know them by their fruits. Do men gather grapes of thorns, or figs of thistles? Even so every good tree bringeth forth good fruits; but a corrupt tree bringeth forth evil fruit. A good tree cannot bring forth evil fruit, neither can a corrupt tree bring forth good fruit. Every tree that bringeth not forth good fruit is hewn down, and cast into the fire. Wherefore by their fruits ye shall know them."

In the dim light of the nave he could see the puzzlement on the faces of his congregation, but at least he had their attention. 'Since I came here to Walston last autumn, I've heard of nothing but Father Fuller. You've all told me what a fine priest he was, how compassionate and caring, how much time he spent in prayer and meditation.' There were nods of agreement. 'You've told me how privileged I am to follow in the footsteps of a man like Father Fuller.' More nods.

Stephen paused, then slammed his Bible shut with an abrupt ferocity that made his listeners jump. 'But look at you!' he said, his voice quiet but intense. 'Since I've been here I've seen scant evidence of Christian charity, of even basic human kindness. This parish is a cesspit of sin. Squabbling, jockeying for position, backbiting. What would Our Lord think of such shameful behaviour? What would Father Fuller think?'

The restrained passion of his tone gave his words an impact that shouting could not have achieved; puzzlement gave way to shock. But the ultimate reaction was one which Stephen had not anticipated. He was prepared for defensiveness and resentment, for arms folded across chests and for eyes staring back at him defiantly or even cast down in penitence. Instead, though, eyes swivelled around to look at their neighbours, Doris looked at Enid, while Enid, hearing only the part about sin, stared at Gill and Lou. Ernest scowled at Quentin Mansfield, then at Cyprian Lawrence. Becca flushed and looked down at her clasped hands, then cast a quick glance over her shoulder at the men of the congregation, hoping in vain to catch a guilty look on someone's face.

Nonplussed but determined to persevere, Stephen amplified his theme. 'The fruits of Father Fuller's long ministry here are not very healthy. Not least of them seems to be a widespread lack of understanding of our role as part of the Church of England. We at St Michael's are not some congregationalist sect – we're a part of the national Church, and have been for centuries. Don't we owe something to that Church which has nurtured us for so long? Don't we owe her our loyalty, our support? In these difficult times …' He was interrupted by a loud metallic crashing noise sounding almost like a car smash, but it came from within the church and reverberated deafeningly through the stone building.

'Oh!' Harry Gaze was up, and moving more quickly than anyone had seen him move for years, towards the chapel. Everyone else sat as if frozen; the noise still echoed as Harry scuttled back, his face a picture of horror. 'Father!' he gasped, addressing Stephen in a portentous, awe-struck voice. 'It's happened! The armour's come down!' He collapsed into the nearest chair, clutching his chest. 'It's a sign, Father. We're wholly in for it now!'

Chapter 11

For he shall give his angels charge over thee: to keep thee in all thy ways.

Psalm 91:11

The beginning of Flora Newall's career as churchwarden was as eventful as the run-up had been, as she found that her popularity had increased even further. During her first week in office, even before her swearing-in by the Archdeacon, she met with Ernest Wrightman, who lost no time in letting her know what was expected of her as warden, and with Fred Purdy, still determined to carry on with his plans, while other parishioners stopped her in the street to put forth their own agendas.

She'd scarcely had time to get used to her new role, however, before an unrelated development unfolded that was to have lasting repercussions on a number of lives. As so often happens, the event that set everything in motion was of itself unremarkable.

It happened like this: one day Gillian, usually so deft with her hands, was preparing lunch for herself and Lou when her knife slipped, cutting deeply into a finger. She gave an involuntary cry which brought Lou out of her office.

'What's the matter?' she asked at the door of the kitchen.

'I've cut myself.' She held up the finger, spurting blood, for Lou's inspection.

'Oh, God!' Lou threw her hands into the air and covered the distance between them rapidly. 'How can you be so calm? You could bleed to death! Oh, God!'

Gill gave a shaky laugh. 'It's not that bad.'

'The hell it's not! Look how deep it is!' She grabbed a piece of kitchen roll and tried to stop the bleeding. 'You've got to see a doctor right away.'

'All right, then. I'll go down to the surgery.'

'I'll ring to make sure he's there,' Lou decided. A quick phone call to the surgery elicited the information that Dr McNair wasn't immediately available; the receptionist suggested that they should, if possible, make their way as quickly as they could to casualty at the hospital in Norwich to have the wound stitched.

'Come on, then,' Lou ordered, picking up her handbag and reaching for her car keys. 'Let's go, for God's sake.'

Gill hesitated. 'But what about Bryony? You know how long these things can take – I might not be back in time to collect her from school.' She thought quickly. 'Could you ring Becca and ask her to collect Bryony and keep her at the Rectory until we get back?'

Impatiently Lou followed orders, recognising the probable truth behind Gill's concern, but instead of Becca she got Stephen.

'I'm sorry, but Becca's not here right now,' he said in response to Lou's query. 'She's at Roger's. You can ring her there, or I can give her a message.'

'I don't have time to make another call, and I don't have time to explain.' Her words tumbled over each other and her voice was high-pitched with urgency. 'But could you ask Becca to collect Bryony from school this afternoon and to keep her until we come to fetch her?'

Reading the panic in her voice, Stephen was concerned. 'Is something wrong? Can I do anything to help?'

Lou looked at Gill; the blood was beginning to seep through the kitchen roll. 'I don't have time to explain,' she repeated frantically. 'See you later.'

Unfortunately, the message didn't reach Becca; Stephen went out and left her a note on the kitchen table, but when she came in she dropped a bag of shopping on top of it without seeing it. As a consequence, no one met Bryony at the school gate that afternoon. She waited for a few minutes, unalarmed, then decided that perhaps her mother had forgotten her and concluded that she was quite capable of finding her own way home: after all, it was a short and now familiar walk through Walston from the school to Foxglove Cottage.

Her journey was accomplished without incident, but when she reached Foxglove Cottage and knocked at the door, there was no reply. She went round to the drive and checked the cars: her mother's Metro was there, but Lou's BMW was missing.

Bryony wasn't really worried in spite of the unfamiliar situation. They would be back any minute, she was sure, and she could wait in the garden. A few minutes later, though, it began to rain, a persistent chill rain which soaked her uniform. Shivering, she huddled against the front door, taking advantage of the slight protection offered by the overhang of the roof.

Across the road at The Pines, Enid carried a cup of tea into the lounge, selected a new magazine from the table and settled down by the window. What she saw when she looked out sent her scurrying for an umbrella, tea and magazine forgotten. She made her way across the road and let herself in through the gate. 'Bryony, my darling!' she exclaimed in her heartiest voice. 'Whatever are you doing out here in the rain?'

Bryony smiled, then remembered her solemn promise to her mother that she would never speak to Mrs Bletsoe again. But she couldn't very well not answer her – that would be rude, and Mummy wouldn't want her to be rude. 'There's no one at home,' she explained. 'Mummy didn't come to collect me at school, so I came home by myself, but there's no one here.'

75

'Oh, you poor darling girl! Come on over to my house – I'll make you some hot chocolate and you can dry off by the fire.'

This was a little more difficult. Not being rude was one thing, but Bryony knew that Mummy would be terribly cross if she went to Mrs Bletsoe's house, even to get out of the rain. She squared her thin shoulders and spoke with formal politeness. 'No, thank you, Mrs Bletsoe. I'll just wait here. Mummy is sure to be home soon.'

'Don't be silly, darling!' Enid gushed. 'You're getting soaked, and there's no telling how long Mummy will be away.'

'No, thank you,' Bryony repeated. Feeling some explanation was necessary, she added, 'It's very kind of you to offer, but Mummy wouldn't want me to. She's told me never to talk to you, and she'd be very cross if I went to your house.'

'Oh!' Enid drew back and stared at the girl.

'Thank you anyway,' Bryony said, wrapping her arms round her chest in an effort to control her shivering. 'You'd better go home now, Mrs Bletsoe. I wouldn't want Mummy to come home and find you here.'

Enid's tea was cold, but she made a fresh pot and stationed herself by the window to see what would happen. It was nearly a quarter of an hour later that the dark blue BMW pulled into the drive; the two women got out, rushed up to the soaking wet child by the door, and in a moment they were all inside and out of Enid's view.

She poured herself another cup of tea and thought carefully about the best way to handle the next step. Should she put it all in writing and lodge a formal complaint, or would a word in the ear of Flora Newall be sufficient? As a compromise, she decided to make sure she was prepared by making a list, getting all of her facts straight in her own mind, and then she would talk to Flora. She found some lined writing paper and a blue Biro in the bureau and settled down to make a list headed 'Abuse of Bryony English'.

The list having been drafted, amended and copied out in her best hand, she gave Flora enough time to get back from work before ringing her at home.

'I was just having my supper,' Flora said. 'I've got to go out this evening to an important meeting of the almshouses trust. Being churchwarden really does cut into my evenings,' she added, half-humorously.

'But this is important – I need to see you straightaway,' Enid insisted. 'Something has come up that just can't wait.'

Flora hesitated. 'I can't miss this meeting. Can't you tell me what it's about?'

'Child abuse,' Enid stated baldly.

Flora was startled; it wasn't what she'd been expecting. 'Oh! You must give me the name right now, Enid. I'll file a report tomorrow.'

Enid wasn't to be put off. 'I want to talk to you tonight – I need to explain.'

'After the meeting, then,' Flora promised. 'Shall I come to you when we've finished? It will probably be nearly ten.'

'I'll be waiting,' affirmed Enid with satisfaction.

Flora didn't arrive at The Pines until after ten, by which time Enid was in a fever of impatience. She ushered her into the lounge and offered her refreshment. 'Tea? Coffee?'

'I don't suppose,' said Flora with a sigh, 'that you've got any gin?' She gave a shaky laugh. 'No, forget I said that. Tea would be lovely.'

By the time the tea appeared, Flora had composed herself and focused her attention on the reason for this visit. 'You said,' she began without preliminary, 'that it was about child abuse. Please do tell me.'

Enid was equally to the point. 'Bryony English,' she stated. 'The child is being abused and should be taken into care immediately.'

Flora knew that appearances could never be relied on when it came to child abuse, but this surprised her. She stared at Enid. 'Bryony? But Gillian English seems to be an exemplary mother.'

'Hmph.' Enid crossed her arms and narrowed her eyes. 'I don't know how you can say that, when you know that she's living with that other woman. Lesbians,' she enunciated self-consciously. 'Depraved, it is. They ought to be locked up.'

Relieved that the accusations weren't any more serious than that, Flora shook her head. 'It's not a crime, you know. Never has been, not even when male homosexuality was illegal. And Social Services don't regard it as sufficient reason to take a child into care. Not any longer, anyway – lesbian couples are even being allowed to foster and adopt children these days.' She glanced at the clock and put her teacup down. 'I do appreciate your conscientiousness in drawing my attention to this, but I've had a difficult day, and it's quite late …'

'Oh, no, you mustn't go!' Enid reached across and put her hand on Flora's arm. 'That is by no means the end of it! I tell you, that dear little girl has been abused in many different ways.' The list had been put in the bureau for safekeeping; she got up and retrieved it.

'Well …'

'Today,' she began, 'the poor child was abandoned. Left out in the rain, and I shouldn't wonder if she caught her death of cold. Shivering, she was, the poor little mite, locked out of the house, and that mother of hers out in the car somewhere with her – lover.'

Flora frowned thoughtfully. 'I agree that's worrying, but there could be a perfectly reasonable explanation.'

'A reasonable explanation for leaving a child of six to walk home from school by herself, and to spend half-an-hour standing in the rain?' Enid said scathingly. 'That's, not the way we brought up children in *my* day. And it's not the first time she's been abandoned. I found her outside in the garden, all on her own, another time. She said that her mother had sent her out so she could be alone with that other woman. Shocking to think someone could endanger her own child like that, just to satisfy her unnatural lusts – I mean, these days it just isn't safe to leave a child unattended. The things I read would curl your hair!'

Inclining her head in acknowledgement, Flora encouraged her to continue. 'You said there were other things?'

Enid scanned her list, looking for a damning indictment to follow on with. 'They take drugs,' she announced. 'Bryony told me so herself. And she knows where they're kept, and even participates in their drug-taking rituals.'

'Oh!'

'Not to mention,' Enid added, 'all those poisonous herbs that Mrs English grows. I believe many of them have hallucinogenic properties. She's probably even got a bed of cannabis tucked somewhere in that garden.'

'I hardly think …'

Enid went back to the list. 'I've heard that Lou say terrible things about Bryony – she called her a little horror, and said she'd be glad to be rid of her.'

Flora frowned. 'Oh, dear.'

'And one of the worst things of all – Bryony's father has been denied access to her. It's just like one of those things that you read in magazines, or see on the telly – they moved away and didn't even tell her father where they were. So it was quite deliberate. Obviously he disapproves of his ex-wife's deviant lifestyle, and they've punished him by taking his daughter away – away from her home and her school and her friends, not to mention her father. And if depriving a little girl of her father's love and companionship isn't abuse, I don't know what is,' she finished on a note of self-righteous triumph.

'That's not good,' Flora acknowledged, troubled. 'Is there more?'

'There certainly is.' Enid had saved what she considered to be the best for last, and she delivered it with relish masked with disgust. 'Sexual abuse. They take the child to bed with them. She told me so herself – they all kiss each other.' She got up and went to the window, looking across the road at the darkened cottage. 'I shouldn't wonder that they're all at it at this very moment – in bed kissing and fondling each other.' This was the extent of her knowledge of what women did in bed together, so she had to be content with a rather vague epithet. 'Unnatural practices!' she spat, waving her list at Flora. 'Surely you can't stand by and allow an innocent child to be abused so shamefully! It's just a good thing for her that she has a neighbour who cares about her and who isn't afraid to get involved.'

Chapter 12

For they shall soon be cut down like the grass: and be withered even as the green herb.

Psalm 37:2

Flora didn't sleep very well that night; she felt slightly nauseous, as though she were coming down with some kind of tummy bug or flu, and she was not easy in her mind. Her visit to Enid's, troubling as it was, had been the latest in a series of difficult encounters of a sort that didn't sit comfortably upon a woman who was as essentially amiable as Flora Newall. Her problem, she'd analysed long ago, was that she wanted to be liked and hated making enemies, but she was also highly principled and unwilling to compromise her strong sense of right and wrong. When she undertook something, whether it be the office of churchwarden or her job as a social worker, she was determined to carry it out to the best of her ability; that meant, though, that she would inevitably end up on the wrong side of someone whose good opinion she craved.

The situation with Bryony English was a case in point: no matter what she did about it, she would alienate either Enid or Gillian English, or both. Enid's allegations of abuse would have to be followed up and investigated, for they were serious charges and could scarcely be ignored, especially if there were any question of the child being at risk. But Flora knew from experience that once the machinery of Social Services ground into action it was likely to get out of control and the consequences for everyone could be disastrous. She wished with all her heart that Enid had not dragged her into this. Since she had, though, Flora's duty was clear: she would have to inform her supervisor and let things take their course. She could declare a personal interest in the case and avoid being directly involved in it, but she couldn't stop it.

Through the night, as her stomach churned, she turned all these things over in her mind, with resultant scenarios of case meetings, medical examinations, care orders, custody battles and almighty rows resounding through the village of Walston. In spite of her desire to be accepted by Enid and her group of cronies, she had never been among those who had declared enmity towards Gillian and Lou; her encounter with them at Becca's dinner party, and subsequent meetings at church and around the village, had convinced her that they were well-meaning and civilised people, and she was open-minded about their sexuality. She was very much afraid, however, that Gill would assume that her carrying out of her responsibilities in following up Enid's allegations was motivated by malice or some equally reprehensible emotion. But if she couldn't stop what Enid had set in motion, at least she could assure Gill of her personal neutrality. She would call on her in the morning, as a friend and neighbour as well as a social worker, and explain her dilemma. Perhaps, with Gill's understanding and cooperation, things wouldn't have to get out of hand.

She rose early and made herself a cup of tea; usually her appetite was hearty, but this morning, with her queasy stomach, she couldn't face the thought of breakfast. After a shower and another cup of tea it was still too early to be out and about, so she busied herself with some paperwork, bringing her notes on her current caseload up to date. The activity served to pass the time as well as taking her mind momentarily off her other concerns.

A great believer in the efficacy of tea, and hoping to settle her stomach, Flora made herself yet another cup which she sipped while she made her final preparations. Her resolve to call on Gill crystallised her determination to carry out another action which she'd contemplated and vacillated over for several days. Checking her watch to make sure it wasn't unsociably early for a phone call, she rang Directory Enquiries and obtained the London number of Lucy Kingsley.

It was now a fact commonly known in Walston that one of the Rector's recent visitors was the artist Lucy Kingsley. Lucy's name was not a household word in many of the homes of Walston, not known as a hotbed of artistic appreciation, but Enid Bletsoe had once read something about her in a magazine, and was suitably impressed to discover that she was a friend of the Rector's; the information had spread from her circle of friends to the village at large. In addition, the word had got out that the man with Lucy Kingsley was some sort of lawyer, with a special expertise in church law. Flora had found the information especially interesting, given the conversation she'd had with Lucy about Shropshire. Now she was determined to make use of the connection.

Lucy answered after several rings. 'Hello?'

Nervously, Flora stammered out a greeting. 'Hello, Miss Kingsley. I don't know if you remember me, but we met in Walston last month. In the church. We talked about Shropshire. My name is Flora Newall,' she added.

'Oh, yes, Miss Newall. Of course.'

'I'm sorry to bother you,' Flora apologised. 'I'm sure you're very busy. But I was just wondering something – I didn't find out your name until after we'd talked, and I wondered if you were by any chance related to John Kingsley, the clergyman. I believe he's a canon at the cathedral now, but when I knew him he was a parish priest.'

'He's my father,' said Lucy, her voice warming. 'And he *is* a canon at Malbury Cathedral. How did you know him? Were you a parishioner?'

'Oh, I didn't live in his parish, but my job took me there, and our paths crossed a number of times. He's a wonderful man, Miss Kingsley,' she said earnestly.

'Yes, I know,' Lucy agreed, smiling down the phone. 'You don't have to tell me that, but it's nice to hear that other people realise it.'

Now that the preliminary excuse had been got out of the way, Flora hesitated. 'I understand, Miss Kingsley,' she began tentatively, 'that your friend – the one who was with you in Walston – is a lawyer, and knows about church law.'

'David *is* a solicitor,' Lucy confirmed. 'And he deals with churches rather a lot, but he'd be the first to say that he was no expert in canon law. Why?'

'I just sort of wondered if ...' she floundered then went on. Well, you might have heard that I've recently been elected as churchwarden of St Michael's. And I know that there are legal responsibilities and duties to being churchwarden, but I'm not sure what they all are.'

'If you'd like to have a word with David,' Lucy suggested, her curiosity aroused, 'I'm sure he'd be happy to talk to you. I could give him a message to ring you, or you might ring back this evening.'

'Thank you. Perhaps I'll ring back then, if you think he won't mind.'

'I'm sure he won't,' she assured the other woman, and couldn't resist adding, 'Was there anything specific?'

'Well,' Flora hesitated; her words were punctuated with careful pauses as she sought the appropriate phrases. 'I wondered what a church-warden's ... legal duties might be if they were to discover something ... compromising ... about someone ... with an important role in the church. One of the ... officers, or employees, for example. Something fairly ... unpleasant. If the warden were legally bound, for example, to ... inform the Rector, or the Bishop, I wondered ...'

'I don't know about legally bound,' Lucy stated pragmatically. 'David could put you right about that. But it only seems good sense to talk to the Rector about it. Stephen – Father Thorncroft – is a good man, Miss Newall. I've known him for years and I have great respect for his pastoral skills. I think you ought to talk to him.'

Flora's sigh was audible down the phone. 'Thank you, Miss Kingsley. That's good advice, I'm sure. And I'll be in touch later this evening if you're sure your friend David won't mind.'

*   *   *

It was not with a great deal of enthusiasm that Flora approached Foxglove Cottage. Her queasiness seemed worse rather than better, and she was aware that this might be a difficult meeting.

The beginning was propitious enough; Gill, pleased at what seemed to be a neighbourly call, invited her in warmly, taking her into the kitchen. 'It's cosier in here,' she explained, 'and I was just about to make myself a cup of herbal tea. Would you join me?'

Flora would rather have had a cup of ordinary PG Tips, but Gill's hospitality could not be refused. 'Oh, yes, please,' she affirmed, trying to sound enthusiastic.

'It's my own blend,' Gill confided as she scooped an assortment of dried leaves into the teapot. 'I find it very relaxing.'

When served up, the tea was an unappetising yellow-green colour, and Flora looked at it dubiously before taking a polite sip of what proved to be, at least to her palate, an extremely bitter beverage. 'Very nice.' She didn't think she'd managed to make it sound very convincing, but it must have satisfied Gill, who smiled.

'I'm glad you like it. Now, how about something to eat? Some biscuits, or a sliver of cake?' She disappeared into the pantry for a moment, just long enough for Flora to whip out her ever-present dispenser of artificial sweetener and decant three tablets into the cup. She gave it a quick stir to dissolve them, and by the time Gill returned she was able to take another sip without fear that an involuntary grimace would cause her to blot her copybook. 'Cake?' Gill urged her.

She accepted a piece, but was unable to do any more than toy with it on the plate. Sensing Gill's curious gaze, she apologised for her lack of appetite. 'I'm sorry not to do this justice – it looks delicious. But I'm afraid I'm not really feeling very well this morning. My tummy is feeling a bit … delicate.'

'Oh, you should have said!' Gill chided her gently. 'I can give you something for it. Costmary is the best – not a very well-known herb, but nothing is better for settling the stomach. I give it to Bryony whenever she complains of tummyache.' She filled the kettle and went back to the pantry, returning with a jar of dried leaves. 'Fresh leaves are better, of course, but it's too early in the year for that.' Putting some of the leaves in a cup, she poured the boiling water over them and set it in front of Flora. 'That will soon set you to rights,' she predicted with confidence.

Perhaps to put off getting to the point of her visit, Flora accepted her ministrations meekly. The costmary tea was even more bitter than the other herbal tea, but once again she was successful in surreptitiously sweetening it while Gill cut herself another sliver of cake.

'It's very kind of you to go to so much trouble,' she said, meaning it.

'Not at all. It's very kind of you to call. We don't get many visitors,' Gill confided with a shy smile.

This made Flora feel even more guilty; she decided she should get to the point of her visit as soon as possible. 'Actually,' she said, this isn't really a social call.'

Gill blinked and her smile faded. 'No?'

'I've come more or less in my official capacity, but thought it would be nice to have an informal chat.'

Uncomprehending, Gillian hazarded, 'Is this some sort of church business?'

'Oh, no,' Flora said quickly. 'I'm not here as a churchwarden, I'm here as a social worker.'

82

Gill tensed, though she wasn't yet aware of it and couldn't have articulated a reason for it. 'A social worker?' she echoed. 'Whatever for?'

Buying herself a few seconds to collect her thoughts, Flora took a large gulp of the costmary tea. 'It's about your daughter, Mrs English,' she said at last. 'Bryony.'

'Bryony?' Gill's voice was suddenly shrill with alarm. 'Has something happened to Bryony? Tell me!'

Flora plunged in. 'I've received a complaint on her behalf – an allegation of child abuse.'

'Child abuse?' Gill stared at her blankly. 'I don't know what you're talking about.'

'A complaint has been lodged,' Flora repeated. 'By Mrs Bletsoe.' She braced herself for Gill's reaction, but was startled when that reaction proved to be sudden peals of laughter.

'That nosy old shrew!' Gill laughed, on the edge of hysteria. 'I might have known. Surely, Miss Newall, you can't be silly enough to believe anything that woman tells you!'

'It is a serious allegation and it will have to be looked into,' Flora stated.

The laughter stopped as abruptly as it had begun. 'Looked into?' Gill echoed.

'I'm afraid so. I believe that you're a good mother, Mrs English,' she said belatedly. 'But Mrs Bletsoe has documented several instances of what could only be called neglect, in addition to a number of other charges.'

'Tell me.' Gill's voice was deadly in its intensity.

Flora produced the list from her handbag and passed it across to her. 'These are the things that Mrs Bletsoe has observed, or been told by Bryony herself. I'm not saying that I believe them, but surely you must see that …'

'Lies!' The shrieked word cut across Flora's explanations. Scanning the list quickly, Gill repeated, 'Lies, wicked lies!' and she tore the list to bits, tossing the fragments onto the floor.

Trying to ignore the histrionic gesture, Flora kept her voice calm. 'I'd like to suggest that we put off the case hearing for a few days, with your cooperation. If you'll agree to have Bryony examined by Dr McNair, say this afternoon or tomorrow …'

'Never!' Gill was angrier than she had ever been in her life. 'Dr McNair isn't coming near my child, not today and not ever!'

'But if you'll cooperate,' Flora pleaded, 'it will be so much easier for everyone. Otherwise I'll have to seek an order to have Bryony taken into care.'

Gill was on her feet. 'How dare you come into my home and suggest such a thing! Get out of here, right now, before I do something we'll both regret!'

'I'm just doing my job,' Flora said softly. 'I'm trying to make things easier for you, Mrs English.'

'Get out!' Gill shrieked; no tigress could have been more fierce in defending her cub. 'And don't even think about coming back. And if you try to take my child into care, I'll kill you! I swear to God – I'll see you dead before I'll let you touch my child!'

Flora rose; as she did so, her stomach gave a painful lurch, she felt suddenly faint and her chest tightened as if in a vice. 'Oh!' she gasped, clutching her chest with one hand and her stomach with the other. 'Oh, I'm not a bit well.'

Gill was unmoved, seeing it as a ploy for sympathy. 'Get out!' she repeated resolutely.

'Please …' Flora choked. 'Please, call Dr McNair. Or call an ambulance. I think I'm dying!'

Flora's colour was ashen and her skin was visibly clammy, but Gill was in the grip of an anger beyond rational thought. 'Well, you can do it in the road, then,' she shrilled, grabbing her arm and propelling her to the door. 'I don't want you in my house for another minute!'

Flora managed somehow to stumble across the road to The Pines, and to lean on the bell, but Enid was at that moment drinking coffee at Doris's house. Unable to go any further, Flora collapsed on the front step in agony, gasping for breath as the pressure in her chest increased to a point beyond bearing before she mercifully lost consciousness.

Enid found her some time later when she returned home. Her first natural impulse was to call for an ambulance, but Flora had fallen in such a way as to block Enid's access to the door. In desperation she rushed across the road and banged on the door of Foxglove Cottage.

'It's Flora!' she cried to a startled Gill. 'Ring 999 – I think she's dead!'

'Oh, God!' Gill's hands flew to her mouth. 'Oh, God – I've killed her!'

Part II

Chapter 13

False witnesses did rise up: they laid to my charge things that I knew not.

Psalm 35:11

It wouldn't be fair to say that David Middleton-Brown forgot completely about Walston in the weeks following his visit there, but the people and problems of that Norfolk village were certainly pushed to the back of his mind by more immediate concerns.

On the first of April, just after David and Lucy's return to London, he at last came into possession of the house he had inherited near Kensington Gardens. And while Lucy didn't insist on his complete removal from her house, she was firm that he should at least make some pretence of settling into his new house. That meant, on a practical level, that his books and records and most of his clothes had to be moved. Lucy's house was so tiny that the majority of his books and records, transported there when he left Wymondham, were boxed in the loft, almost untouched, so moving them was a simple matter of a car journey. The removal of his clothes from her wardrobe was a more symbolic act and not accomplished without some pain, but Lucy assured him that it didn't mean a complete break, just the putting of some psychological distance between them for a time to give her space to rethink the relationship. His actual physical presence in her house during the evening – and the nights – was to be negotiable.

The fact that he wasn't being rejected completely or ejected from her life made it just about possible for David to cope with the removal process. He sent for the remainder of his belongings, the contents of the family home in Wymondham which had been left in storage after the house had been sold some six months earlier; it took some time, and a great deal of emotional energy, to integrate those remnants of his past life into his new surroundings; his relationship with his mother in particular had been difficult, and this process of re-examining things that were so closely associated with his life with her brought many long-suppressed feelings to the surface.

In addition, David found that, in spite of himself, he couldn't help taking an interest in the new house as he explored its gracious rooms and beautiful furnishings; a sense of ownership began to take hold of him, and a sort of delight in the exquisite quality of what he had inherited as well as a feeling of responsibility for its survival. And, to his delight, Lucy became involved too; they spent a number of evenings sorting through the contents of drawers and rearranging furniture, and consequently it seemed that most nights they were together in the new king-sized bed which he'd installed in the spacious master bedroom.

And so it was, thus employed in various pursuits, that Lucy neglected to mention Flora Newall's odd phone call to David, and when the promised follow-up call to him never arrived, she forgot the matter entirely.

*   *   *

In Walston, though, things were anything but tranquil. Flora's death was a tremendous shock to the community, but greater shocks were yet to come.

The postmortem examination, required by law in the instance of sudden death, revealed that Flora Newall had died of a massive heart attack; this was consistent with Gillian's contrite statement to Dr McNair that Flora had complained of indigestion, had been ashen in colour, and had clutched at her chest as well as her stomach.

But shortly after the news of the postmortem findings made its way round the village, on a Monday afternoon, Enid Bletsoe popped into the waiting room of Dr McNair's surgery. 'I'd like to see the doctor,' she informed the woman who had replaced her – usurped her position, she said to herself – as receptionist.

The woman looked at Enid, in high colour but not in any evident distress that would qualify as a medical emergency, then consulted the appointment book. 'I'm afraid there aren't any appointments available today. I'll try to squeeze you in tomorrow, shall I?'

Enid gave a haughty sniff and glared at the usurper. 'I don't require an appointment, thank you. I need to see Dr McNair, as I said.' She added, 'I've never been ill a day in my life, I'll have you know. And Dr McNair will not be amused if you keep me waiting.'

Recognising the inevitability of defeat, the usurper gave in gracefully. 'Dr McNair is with a patient right now. If you'll take a seat for a moment, I'll let him know you're here.'

A few minutes later Enid entered the consulting room; the doctor, knowing her well, raised his eyebrows and crossed his arms across his chest. 'Well?' he growled. 'What's all this palaver? I'm a busy man, and there are sick people waiting to see me. What is so important that you couldn't wait until a more convenient time?'

Enid was not intimidated by Fergus McNair; she had, after all, worked for him since he was a mere callow youth, and to her way of thinking, she had 'broken him in' to the job. 'Flora Newall,' she announced. 'I've heard that the postmortem results are in.'

'Yes?' His tone was noncommittal, though his eyebrows inched even higher.

'Heart attack, I heard.'

'Yes?' he repeated, questioningly.

'Well, surely you don't believe it!' Enid challenged.

Dr McNair's brows drew together. 'It is what the postmortem shows. And it is consistent with what we know of her symptoms from Mrs English.'

'Yes, if you believe *her*!' Enid put her hands on her hips. 'What would you expect her to say?'

'Just what exactly are you suggesting? Is there some reason I shouldn't believe Mrs English?'

It was Enid's big moment, and she savoured it. 'Because,' she announced, 'I think that she had every reason to lie to you. I think that Gillian English murdered Flora Newall!'

'Murder?' The doctor took a step backwards, staring at her. 'What are you talking about, woman? It was a heart attack!'

Enid stood her ground. 'I didn't work in this office for so many years for nothing – I know very well that there are things you can give people to make them have a heart attack.'

'Yes?'

'Foxglove!' she proclaimed triumphantly. 'Digitalis, from foxglove. Doesn't she live at Foxglove Cottage, and know about all those poisonous plants? And when I told her that Flora was dead, didn't she say, "Oh, God, I've killed her!"? That's what she said, you know – I was there and I heard her, clear as day! She killed her – I promise you!'

Fergus McNair was troubled. He knew that Enid Bletsoe was a spiteful woman who could hold a grudge for years and would stop at nothing to discredit someone whom she felt had done her wrong, but there was something in what she had said that had planted a seed of doubt in his mind. The story of Gillian's spontaneous exclamation of guilt had gained wide circulation in the village; he had already heard it from more than one source. And when he had spoken to Gillian English about Flora's symptoms, her manner had been reticent, as though she weren't telling him the whole story.

His unease increased when he consulted his reference book on toxicology. As he'd suspected, digitalis, a product of the foxglove plant, would not show up in a routine postmortem test for poison. It mimicked the symptoms of a natural heart attack perfectly: indeed, in its medical form it was given to regulate heart rhythm, and an overdose would stimulate heart contractions to the point that a heart attack was induced. He learned from his book that a specific test for digitalis poisoning was possible, but you would have to be looking for it in order to find it.

To set his mind at rest, Dr McNair determined to have another word with Gillian

English. Perhaps this time she would be more forthcoming and the matter could be cleared up with no more fuss.

He dropped by Foxglove Cottage after completing his early evening surgery, finding them at the end of their meal. 'I'm sorry if it's a bad time,' he apologised to Gill at the door.

'No, that's all right,' she said. 'We were just finishing. Do come in and join us for coffee.'

Lou was clearing the table as they entered the kitchen. 'Hi, Doc,' she greeted him cheerily. 'Is there something I don't know? Is one of us sick?'

'You tell me.' He sat down in the chair indicated by Gill. 'Isn't the doctor allowed to pay a social call?'

'Not jolly likely,' Lou grinned.

'Go upstairs and clean your teeth, darling,' Gill addressed Bryony. 'Then you can watch a video for a bit before bedtime if you like.'

'Can't I stay?' pleaded Bryony, who found Dr McNair fascinating; she loved his strange Scottish accent and was intrigued by the freckles that covered the backs of his capable square hands.

Gill was firm. 'No, darling. If you don't want to watch a video, you can play in your room.'

Bryony went sulkily, but she went. Gill busied herself making the coffee, giving herself a few minutes to think. She had a terrible feeling that Dr McNair's visit was connected with Flora's death, and she didn't know what she could say to him. Her own behaviour in turning Flora out into the street when she was so obviously ill was inexplicable unless she told the whole story, including the allegations of child abuse, and she wasn't about to do that. Since Flora's death, no further action had been taken on that front, and Gill could only assume that Enid hadn't mentioned it to anyone else; perhaps she had changed her mind and would pursue it no further. To mention it to Dr McNair at this point would be to reopen the whole dreadful business, perhaps unnecessarily, and he would be bound to follow through on it. Besides, she hadn't told Lou about what had passed between her and Flora that day: Lou, she knew, would go completely spare over it, and would quite probably do something drastic to Enid. So she couldn't possibly tell the truth about Flora's visit. Her smile was strained as she poured a cup of coffee for the doctor. 'Cream or milk?' she queried.

'Just black, thanks.' He accepted the coffee, turning to Lou. 'Actually, you're right. This isn't strictly a social call, though I do like to keep tabs on my patients – even the ones who are too healthy to come in to see me. How is that finger, by the way?' he asked Gill.

'Oh, it's better – it's healing very well.' She held it up for his inspection. 'I think the stitches can come out soon.'

'No doubt.' He took a sip of coffee, then put the cup back in the saucer, smacking his lips with satisfaction. 'Ah, that's grand. I do like a good cup of coffee.'

Gill rubbed the cut finger in an unconscious nervous gesture. 'But you didn't come about my finger,' she prompted, half wanting to get it over with.

He shot her a shrewd look. 'Actually, I wanted to ask you a bit more about Miss Flora Newall – about the day she died.'

'I told you everything.' She looked into her coffee, unable to meet his eyes. 'She came in for a cup of tea, and then she felt ill.'

'She only had tea, then?'

It wasn't the question she'd been expecting. 'Why – yes,' she said uncertainly. 'Herbal tea, that is. A cup of my special herbal mixture, and then when I'd given her a piece of cake she said she wasn't feeling well, so I made her a cup of costmary tea, to settle her stomach. I don't think she ate any of the cake – because of her upset stomach – but she drank both cups of tea.'

'I see.' Dr McNair considered the answer thoughtfully. 'And was *her* visit a social call?'

'Well …' Gill floundered, unused to telling less than the truth. 'Yes, it was.'

He turned to Lou. 'You weren't here that day, Miss Sutherland?'

Startled, Lou stammered, 'Why, no. I was – away that day.'

The discomfort of both women wasn't lost on Dr McNair. He turned back to Gill. 'A social call, you say. So you didn't – disagree about anything, or have a row?' he probed.

'No, of course not. I didn't know her well enough to disagree with her about anything,' Gill stated with as much conviction as she could muster.

'Then why,' asked Dr McNair, 'did you say, when you heard that she was dead, "Oh, God, I've killed her."? That is what you said, isn't it?'

Gill swallowed hard. 'I – felt guilty because I'd let her leave the house when she wasn't feeling well. I should have insisted that I ring you, or called for an ambulance.'

'And why didn't you?' he pressed. 'Wasn't it evident that she was quite poorly, was in fact in considerable distress? You said that she clutched at her chest and her stomach and that her colour was very bad. Why on earth did you let a woman in that condition leave your house on her own?'

Again she couldn't meet his eyes. 'I can't explain it,' she said softly. 'It was inexcusable of me, I know. And I shall have to live with the guilt for the rest of my life.'

Lou had been uncharacteristically silent throughout the doctor's questioning; it wasn't until after Fergus McNair had gone that she tackled Gill. 'I've been wondering about it as well,' she said. 'What *did* go on here that morning, angelface?'

'I can't tell you,' Gill whispered miserably. 'I wish I could, but I can't tell you. You'll have to trust me.'

'Of course, I trust you,' Lou assured her, putting her arms round her in a comforting, tender hug. But at the back of her mind a nagging question remained: what was Gill hiding? And at the back of Gill's mind a corresponding alarm bell began to sound: where *had* Lou been that day?

Dr McNair went away with the same questions unanswered and his spirit even more troubled than it had been before his visit. The more he thought about it, the more convinced he became that Gillian English's story didn't hold water. She was hiding something: was it a minor matter, or was it complicity in murder?

After a restless night, he rose early the next morning, dressed in his old comfortable tweeds, called his dog and went out for a walk through the countryside, wrestling with his conscience. What should he do? Fergus McNair was not a religious man, but he was a scrupulous one, with a strong sense of justice as well as a sense of loyalty. How could he balance the loyalty he felt to his patient Gillian English with the responsibility to seek justice for Flora Newall, who had also been a patient? What would be the consequences, either way, if he did the wrong thing? If he failed to order the test, the truth – positive or negative – would never be known. Flora Newall would be dead and buried, the victim of an unfortunate heart attack, and no one the wiser. No one but Enid would reproach him for allowing that course of action, and he wasn't any more afraid of Enid than she was of him. But if he ordered the test, and the results were negative, questions would be asked. The police would want to know why he had even suggested such a thing, and suspicion would certainly attach itself to Gillian, if only among the inhabitants of Walston, who seemed to find out about these things by osmosis. He could hear them now: 'no smoke without fire,' they would say, and the village would take it as an excuse to marginalise and exclude the women at Foxglove Cottage to an even greater extent than was already happening. Could he bear to be responsible for that? But if there were any truth in it, and he did nothing …

He wished that there were someone with whom he could talk over his dilemma without prejudice. In spite of his own lack of faith, Fergus McNair liked and respected the young Rector, but he knew that Stephen would view the situation in an entirely different way, within a religious framework. And he considered Roger Staines to be a friend with whom he could be honest, but Roger's current fragile state of health precluded any such stressful communication.

'What do you think I should do, Jock, old boy?' he asked his faithful retriever. But Jock, who was predisposed to believe that anything his master did was just fine, only wagged his tail.

Their walk had taken them down a country lane, along a public footpath and through the wooded pathway that ran between Walston Hall and St Michael's – a path which was theoretically private, but which residents of Walston had always used as a short cut when necessary. They were now within view of the church; on impulse, Fergus McNair strode to the door and tried it. It was unlocked. 'Bide here a wee while,' he commanded the obedient Jock, and slipped into the church.

It had been quite some time since he'd been inside St Michael's, he realised; occasionally he deigned to attend the funeral of one of his patients, but he hadn't lost one for a while – not until Flora Newall. That death was very much on his mind as he stood quietly at the back of the church. A soft murmur from behind the rood screen – the Rector saying the Morning Office, presumably – warned Fergus that he was not alone, but it only provided a muted background for his thoughts. The sun streamed through the east window, dappling the chancel floor with pools of liquid colour, striking sparks off the brass eagle lectern and illuminating the dust motes which danced in the air; a faint whiff of polish mixed with flowers and overlaid with the memory of incense provided a complex bouquet of fragrance. It was such a tranquil, almost timeless, place that for just a moment Fergus McNair wished that he could be a part of it, wished that he could have faith. He looked at the life-sized figure on the cross that topped the screen; there was nothing of the tortured struggle in that limp, resigned body, fixed with gilded nails to a foliated cross, more an object of beauty than an instrument of torture and death. Was it really like that? he wondered. Did He die so serenely, then? Fergus McNair's own experience of death, viewed up close and in a variety of circumstances, had shown him nothing like this. That, he knew, was why he couldn't have faith. Then his eyes were drawn above the rood screen to the Doom painting, a vivid medieval vision of the Last Judgment: an impassive God presided over the division of the sheep and the goats as red-eyed devils pulled struggling sinners down on the one side and white-robed angels waited with open arms on the other for the tiny souls of the blessed. How comforting in some ways, and terrifying in others, to think of this ultimate meting out of justice. No escape …

With a shrug, Fergus McNair knew what he had to do. Unpleasant as might be the consequences, justice and truth must be served. As quietly as he had come, he left the church, whistled for Jock and went home to ring the pathologist.

The test would take a couple of days, Dr McNair was told. So he did his best to put the matter out of his mind as he devoted himself to his routine of surgeries and home visits, looking after the physical wellbeing of Walston with as much conscientious ownership as the Rector with his cure of souls.

On Thursday, between his morning and afternoon surgeries, he decided to pop round and see Roger Staines with the excuse of monitoring his progress. Roger's cottage, on the edge of the old estate and within view of the unsightly clutter of buildings that comprised Ingram's agricultural processing plant, was a rather substantial dwelling surrounded by an immaculate garden. The interior of the house was equally tidy, in keeping with Roger's rather fussy bachelor standards; the sole exception to this was his study, the room in which he spent much of his time, and over which was strewn an incredible tangle of papers and books, the tools of his life's work.

He found Roger looking well – almost like his old self, he thought, in a lemon-yellow silk waistcoat and matching bow tie under a smart tweed jacket with leather elbow patches. Roger seemed delighted to see him, showing him into the sitting room and offering to make him a cup of coffee.

'Don't go to any trouble,' Fergus cautioned. 'I'm quite happy with instant.'

Roger made a rueful face. 'I know you think I'm an invalid, but I assure you that making a proper cup of coffee isn't going to kill me. Drinking vile instant is much more likely to be the death of me – that's why I never touch the stuff.'

Settled with their steaming cups a few minutes later, they chatted about general matters, avoiding the topic that was on both their minds. 'Young Becca is working out well, I take it?' asked the doctor.

'Oh, yes. She's been a great help in getting things sorted. She's a bright girl, and has had secretarial experience.' Roger hesitated. 'But to tell you the truth, I'm rather worried about her. She hasn't seemed herself lately, if you know what I mean. A bit distracted and jumpy. And tired, as though she hasn't been sleeping well.'

Fergus grinned. 'That seems entirely natural for a newlywed. I don't mean to be indelicate, but she and the Rector probably have better things to do at night than sleep. And I'm not talking about praying or reading the Bible to each other either.'

'Perhaps.' Roger shook his head. 'Though in that case she ought to be happy and bubbly, but she's not.'

'Pregnant, then,' Fergus diagnosed succinctly. 'It often has that effect. Has she been sick in the mornings?'

'Not that I've noticed.'

'Och well.' As he took a sip of the excellent coffee, his beeper went off, startling him into spilling a few drops on his jacket. 'Hellfire and damnation!' he swore.

Roger rose instantly and went to him. 'Are you all right? You haven't burned yourself?'

'No, I'm fine. But I need to use your phone, if you don't mind.'

'Please, be my guest.'

He made the call to his office in Roger's cluttered study, sitting at a desk covered with incomprehensible bits of paper. The receptionist apologised for bothering him, but there had been an urgent call from the pathologist, who wanted to speak to him as soon as possible.

In a fever of apprehensive impatience, he dialled the pathologist's number. 'Positive,' was the pathologist's terse statement. 'It was digitalis poisoning, without a doubt. The police have been notified, but I wanted to let you know right away.'

'Bloody hell,' Fergus McNair said to himself as he put the phone down. His action had been justified, but he didn't feel any better about it than he had before. A case of sudden accidental death had suddenly become a murder enquiry, and there would be no turning back.

Chapter 14

O go not from me, for trouble is hard at hand: and there is none to help me.

Psalm 22:11

It wasn't long after that, of course – only a matter of an hour or two – that a police officer called at Foxglove Cottage to ask Gill a few questions. She told him exactly the same story that she'd related to Dr McNair: Flora Newall had dropped in to pay a neighbourly call, had drunk some herbal tea and had been taken ill. She, Gill, should have insisted that the doctor be called, but she had failed to do so, and so blamed herself for Flora's death.

Sergeant John Spring, a well-built man with a trim brown moustache and a disconcerting stare, made her nervous, but by now she'd told the story several times, so it came out sounding more calm and coherent. Nevertheless, he took away her jars of herbal teas for analysis, and advised Gill that it was possible that she would be required for further questioning. 'In other words, don't leave the area,' he told her with a grin.

Inevitably, through some mysterious process it was soon common knowledge in Walston that Flora's death had indeed been murder, and that the police had been to Foxglove Cottage.

Enid could scarcely contain her glee. 'Quite right, too,' she told Fred Purdy in the village shop that afternoon, nodding in satisfaction. 'It's quite clear to me that she did it – I said so from the first. I always did say, didn't I, that all those herbs were something sinister? She brewed up a big pot of foxglove leaves, I reckon, and gave it to poor unsuspecting Flora to drink.'

'But why?' Fred wanted to know as he sliced four rashers of bacon for her. 'Why would she want to kill off poor old Flora? She seemed a harmless enough sort to me.'

'Well,' Enid lowered her voice conspiratorially, 'I happen to know that she had a very good motive. I can't tell you what it was, mind you, but if that nice young policeman were to come round and ask me …'

The shop door swung open and Becca entered; Enid broke off and looked at her suspiciously, but Fred had no such compunction. 'Did you hear?' he said.

93

'Poor old Flora was murdered, just like Enid thought. Poisoned. And the police have been round to Foxglove Cottage. I don't need to tell you what they were looking for,' he chuckled.

'Oh!' Becca gasped, appalled. 'That's not very funny.'

'Not meant to be,' Enid put in crisply. 'It's God's own truth – that perverted woman murdered poor Flora! I've always said so, and now my words have been proved true.'

'Oh, poor Gill!' cried Becca, leaving the shop abruptly.

Well.' Enid looked disapproving as Fred wrapped her bacon. 'That's a fine thing – more concern for the murderer than for the victim. What about poor Flora, I ask you?'

Becca went straight to Foxglove Cottage, knowing that she could do little but offer sympathy and support but feeling she must do that much. Becca had felt a certain constraint with the women, particularly Gill, since the unfortunate incident in which Bryony had been abandoned, though she had been freely forgiven for something that was not her fault; this new development, though, swept away any awkwardness in a rush of empathetic friendship.

She found Gill subdued, almost in a state of shock. 'I'm just glad that Bryony was still at school when he came,' she said calmly. 'It would have been dreadfully upsetting for her to know that Mummy was being questioned by the police. I don't know how she'll cope if I'm … arrested.'

Lou was anything but calm. 'Arrested?' she raged, pacing the kitchen. 'They wouldn't dare arrest you – you haven't done a bloody thing except give a woman a cup of tea, for God's sake!'

'Herbal tea,' Gill corrected. 'Two cups.'

'Bloody herbal tea, then! She could have drunk a gallon of the stuff and it still wouldn't have killed her!'

'Is there any chance …' Becca hesitated and tried to phrase it delicately. 'Is it possible that something poisonous could have got mixed in accidentally? Some leaves of something else?'

Gill laughed, unoffended. 'I think I'm a bit more careful than that. And don't forget that I drank some of the tea myself – and have been drinking tea made from the leaves in that jar for months. It's never harmed me or anyone else. You've had it yourself, Becca, and you're still here to tell the tale.'

'It was just a thought,' she sighed.

They all jumped as the phone rang. Lou, who was on her feet, went to pick it up, passing it over to to Gill.

'The police,' Gill reported a moment later, her voice noticeably shakier. 'That Sergeant Spring. He said that he has a few more questions to ask me. This time he wants to bring a colleague along to take some notes, he said.'

'You should have told him to piss off,' Lou declared.

Gill shook her head. 'Not a very constructive response.'

'Have you got a solicitor?' Becca asked with sudden urgency. 'It sounds to me as though you need one.'

'But I haven't done anything.'

'It doesn't matter whether you have or not – as long as the police suspect you, it's important to have legal advice and representation. And they must think there's reason to suspect something or they wouldn't be coming back so soon.'

'She's right,' Lou agreed. 'But you can't be having some Norfolk hick representing you.'

'David,' said Becca firmly. 'That's who you need – David Middleton-Brown. You remember – he was here at Easter.'

'Of course I remember,' Gill agreed. 'But do you think …'

Becca gave a vigorous nod and said with conviction, 'He's the man you need. You must believe me – he's wonderful. I'll get in touch with him, if you like.'

Lou handed her the phone. 'Do it right now, and tell him to get himself here as soon as he can. I don't think there's any time to be wasted.'

Lucy took the call, listening in amazement as Becca related the events that had unfolded in Walston since their visit a few weeks earlier. 'I don't know,' Lucy said when Becca had finished. 'I'll give you his number at work and you can talk to him, but I can't promise anything. You know how he is – he'll tell you to get someone better.'

'But there isn't anyone better!'

'You know that and I know that.' Lucy gave a wry laugh. 'But David is so modest.'

'You must convince him that he *has* to come!' Becca pleaded. 'And you must come too, of course, and stay with us – both of you. Gill needs David, but I need *you.*'

Lucy read the urgency in her voice, realising that there was more to it than Becca was saying. 'I'll do my best,' she promised.

As predicted, David was not easy to convince; it took the combined persuasive powers of Becca and Lucy to make him agree.

'She should get someone more local,' he said to Lucy on the phone after speaking to Becca. 'Someone from my old Norwich firm – I'd be happy to recommend someone good.'

'She wants *you*,' stated Lucy.

'But I keep saying – I'm not a criminal lawyer!' David argued plaintively. 'No one ever listens to me.'

'I think,' Lucy confided, 'that there are personal reasons why Becca wants us to come. She said that she needs me – I'm sure she wants to talk to me about something. Remember – I thought before that she wanted to tell me something, but couldn't quite manage it. Perhaps now she's ready.'

David sighed, knowing in his heart that he couldn't hold out against Lucy. 'That doesn't mean that I have to get involved professionally,' he pointed out. 'We could go down for the weekend and you could have your little heart-to-heart with Becca.'

'There's one other thing,' she said slyly, playing her trump card. 'I completely forgot to tell you before, but Flora Newall, the woman who was killed, rang a week or ten days ago and wanted to talk to you. She wanted to ask you about her legal position as churchwarden, and hinted that she'd found out something damaging about someone important in the church. She wondered if she had a legal responsibility to inform the Bishop or the Rector.'

'Good Lord. What did you tell her?'

'I told her to talk to Stephen.'

'And did she?'

'I don't know. As I said, I just remembered it now.'

'Well.' David tapped his pencil on his desk and took a quick look through his diary. 'I'll need to rearrange some appointments, but if all goes well we ought to be able to go up to Walston tomorrow morning. Tomorrow's Friday – perhaps we can get it sorted over the weekend.'

'I'll ring Becca,' offered Lucy, smiling down the phone.

And for his part, David was not as displeased as he would have liked Lucy to believe; the prospect of a few days away with her, working together with a common goal and sleeping together every night, held a certain attraction for him. Perhaps this was what they needed to cement their relationship back together once and for all.

*   *   *

'Let me get this straight.' David sat at the kitchen table at Foxglove Cottage on Friday afternoon drinking black coffee; herbal tea didn't appeal to him at the best of times and this was certainly not the best of times. 'All you know for sure is that for some reason the police believe that this Flora Newall was poisoned, and they've been questioning you because you were the last person to see her alive.'

Lou had been simmering, containing herself; now she boiled over. 'That little shit of a policeman has been treating Gill like some sort of criminal,' she fulminated. 'Implying that she poisoned the old bag, just because she bloody gave her a cup of herbal tea.'

'He took away my jars of tea leaves,' Gill explained. She had regained her composure and sat with her hands folded in her lap. 'And he questioned me quite closely about what she'd eaten and drunk when she was here, so I can only assume that he suspects I poisoned her.'

'And you don't know any more than that?'

She gave a wry smile. 'I'm sure that everyone else in Walston knows far more about what's going on than I do, but they don't talk to us. Maybe they'll talk to you, but probably not if they know you're my solicitor.'

David laughed. 'Maybe Lucy will be able to get something out of them. She's good at that.' He took a sip of coffee. 'What else did the policeman ask you?'

'Mostly about times. He wanted to know what time she came and what time she left – that sort of thing.' Gill shrugged. 'And he wanted me to describe what she looked like when she left, and what she'd said about not feeling well. You know the sort of thing I mean.'

'And now he wants to talk to you again?'

'He rang up yesterday afternoon and said he had a few more questions and would like to bring a colleague along to take notes.' She sighed. 'But then Becca and Lou convinced me that I needed a solicitor, so he said that he could wait until you got here. Tomorrow, he said. Saturday.'

David frowned, biting his thumb nail thoughtfully. 'That doesn't sound good – it means that he intends to talk to you under caution. But none of this makes much sense to me,' he admitted. 'I can see that if the woman was poisoned they would need to question you, since you were the last one to see her, and you did give her something to drink. But surely they can't believe that it could be anything other than an accidental poisoning? I mean, you couldn't possibly have a reason for wanting to murder Flora Newall, could you?'

'Don't be bloody ridiculous!' snapped Lou. 'Of course she didn't. Did you, angelface?'

'No, of course not,' Gill said quietly, but she was unable to meet either of their eyes.

Lou didn't seem to notice. 'So you'll sort out that little shit Sergeant Spring, won't you?' she demanded of David. 'Tell him to go to hell?'

David had noticed Gill's reticence, but something else now caught his attention. 'Spring, did you say?' he asked eagerly. 'John Spring?'

'We're not on a first-name basis,' Gill interposed with a dry smile.

'Well-built chap? With dark hair and a moustache?'

Gill nodded.

'And doesn't half fancy himself,' Lou put in scornfully. 'Tight trousers and a smug grin on his stupid face.'

'Ah.' David smiled in satisfaction. 'This puts an entirely different complexion on things. I've known John Spring for a long time, and I can tell you that his bark is far worse than his bite.' He sat for a moment, deep in thought, then turned to Gill with a serious expression. 'Before you speak to the police again, I must tell you not to talk to anyone, especially not the police, unless I'm present.'

'Yes, all right.'

'And I've got to ask you one question before I'm able to represent you. Are you absolutely sure that you've told me everything?'

'Yes,' said Gill, a bit too quickly; once again her eyes were averted.

Lucy, meanwhile, was with Becca. In the several weeks which had elapsed since Lucy's last visit, Becca had become even more drawn and pale than before, with dark hollows under her eyes, and Lucy was resolved to get to the bottom of the problem as quickly as possible. There was more to it, she was sure, than the admitted shock of a sudden death in the village and the suspicion which had attached itself to Becca's friends in Foxglove Cottage.

Guessing that Becca wanted to talk but was unwilling to volunteer anything, she tackled the issue head on, with a bluntness that was not characteristic. 'Something is wrong,' she said as gently as she could. 'Don't you think you'd better tell me about it?'

Tears sprang to Becca's eyes, but she managed to keep her voice steady. 'Not here,' she said. 'I need to talk to you, but not at the Rectory. Let's take a walk.'

Lucy assented readily; it was a beautiful spring day and the prospect of a walk through the country lanes was an attractive one. They set off away from the village. 'Have you seen Walston Hall?' Becca asked. 'We'll walk in that direction. Beyond the Hall there's a good public footpath.'

The path between the church and Walston Hall, through a wooded area which served to screen the manor house from general view, was a fairly narrow one, not wide enough for two abreast, and this precluded much conversation. Coming round a bend, Becca in the lead, they met Diana Mansfield, who was as usual beautifully dressed in a fashion that seemed even more incongruous on a country path than it did in the village.

'Hello,' said Becca, drawing aside for Diana to pass. 'You've met my friend Lucy Kingsley, I believe.'

Diana seemed more nonplussed by the encounter than was warranted. 'Oh – hello,' she said awkwardly. 'Yes, of course we've met. Easter, wasn't it? Lunch at Foxglove Cottage?'

'That's right,' Lucy affirmed.

'I'm on my way to the church,' Diana explained in a somewhat breathless voice. 'The flowers for Sunday, you know. This path is very handy for me, especially when the weather is fine. Saves taking the car out – it's a long way round by road.'

The mention of the church reminded Becca that she had left no note for Stephen; if he came home to find the house empty he might be worried. 'Oh, Stephen will be in church, saying Evensong,' she said. 'Could you please tell him when you see him that I've gone out for a walk with Lucy and supper might be a bit late?'

There was a fractional hesitation before Diana nodded. 'Yes, of course, I'll tell him.'

'Thanks awfully.'

Diana edged round them, wafting a delicate and expensive scent. 'Are you going to be staying in Walston for long, Miss Kingsley?' she asked.

'Possibly a few days.'

'Perhaps the two of you might come and have tea with me one afternoon.' She offered the suggestion tentatively, with a shy smile. 'Tomorrow?'

Lucy looked at Becca, who nodded. 'How kind – I'd like that,' Lucy said, returning the smile.

'I'll expect you about four then.' Diana, hurrying on her way, waved at them over her shoulder.

In a few minutes they were out of the trees and in view of Walston Hall: mellow brick, towering chimneys and leaded-glass windows glittering like diamonds in the afternoon sunshine. 'It's beautiful,' Lucy observed enthusiastically. 'I can't wait to see the interior.'

'It's very nice,' admitted Becca, adding, 'the footpath is over here.' It was a wider path, bounded by grasses and early wildflowers rather than trees; soon they were walking side by side.

'Now tell me what's bothering you,' Lucy prompted after a few minutes of silence.

Becca, striding along with her head down, sighed deeply. 'It's very difficult,' she said softly. 'I hardly know how to tell you.'

For weeks Lucy had been trying to imagine what it was that had caused such a change in her friend; Becca had never been the most assertive or self-confident person Lucy had known, but her current state of nervous agitation defied explanation. 'Does it have anything to do with that woman's ... death?'

There was a sharp indrawn breath. 'I don't know. That is, I'm not sure. I think that it must do. There can't be that much ... evil ... in one village unless it's all connected.'

'Tell me.'

It all came out then, in a rush, related in Becca's quiet voice: the telephone calls, their general content, their frequency, their escalating degree of intimacy and the corresponding horror.

Lucy listened in silence until Becca had finished; all of her imaginings had produced nothing like the truth. 'But what about Stephen?' she asked at last. 'What does he say?'

Again an indrawn breath. 'Oh, I couldn't possibly tell Stephen. Don't you see? It would spoil everything – our marriage, and his relationship with his parishioners. To know that one of them ...'

'Yes, I see.' Lucy understood Becca's thinking, though she thought that she was wrong, and her heart went out to the young girl who had borne such a burden alone, and for such selfless reasons. 'But wasn't there anyone else you could talk to? Gill and Lou, for instance?'

Becca shuddered. 'Not after the things he said. About ... well, you know. All of us doing it together. I thought at one time that I might be able to tell them, but not after that. And I don't have any other friends, not in Walston. You were the only one

I could talk to – I wanted to tell you at Easter, but I just couldn't. And now Flora is dead, and I feel so terrible.'

'What do you mean?'

For the first time she turned to look at Lucy. 'What if Flora found out who it was? And what if he killed her to keep her from exposing him? If that were true, it would be all my fault.'

Lucy put a hand on Becca's arm. 'That seems very unlikely. How would Flora have found out, if she didn't even know about the phone calls?'

'She might have caught him in the act or something. I don't know.'

'I don't think that seems likely,' Lucy repeated reassuringly, but in her mind she was replaying her telephone conversation with Flora: the woman *had* known something, it was clear, and perhaps Becca was right. She looked forward to talking it over with David.

Walking back towards the Rectory, Becca was silent again. After a while Lucy said. 'You must tell Stephen, you know.'

'But I can't!'

'You must.' Her voice was reasonable but firm. 'I know it's difficult, Becca, but you must let him help you through this. That's what he's there for, not just as a priest but also as a husband. That's what marriage is all about – sharing the painful things as well as the good things.'

'But I told you – it would spoil everything!'

'Listen to me, Becca.' Lucy stopped and once again put her hand on Becca's arm. 'I understand what you're saying, but don't you think that it's spoiling things between you already? Keeping that kind of a secret to yourself is bound to poison your relationship. Surely Stephen must have noticed how upset you've been. Surely it's made a difference to the way you behave towards him?'

Becca blushed and turned her head away. 'I can hardly bear him to touch me,' she confided in an agonised whisper. 'I want him to make love to me – of course I do. I love him so much, and before … all this … it was wonderful. But now when he comes near me, I just cringe.'

'Oh, Becca!'

'I can't help it,' she gulped, near tears.

Lucy was appalled by the revelation. 'Can't you see how important it is to tell him everything? That's the only way you're going to get through this with your marriage intact. Becca, love, you must tell him – right away!'

Chapter 15

O let not mine heart be inclined to any evil thing: let me not be occupied in ungodly works with the men that work wickedness, lest I eat of such things as please them.

Psalm 141:4

Lucy's conversation with David was destined to be delayed; David had plans for the early part of that evening.

He used the phone at Foxglove Cottage to ring Sergeant Spring, who was only too eager to accept his invitation to meet for a drink later on. 'The Queen's Head?' Spring suggested.

The Queen's Head in Walston would be convenient, but David didn't want to risk being overheard by the villagers; he remembered, suddenly, that no one from Walston ever went to Nether Walston. 'Is there a pub in Nether Walston?' he asked. 'That might be better.'

'The Crown and Mitre,' Spring supplied promptly. 'Nice pub across from the village green – you can't miss it. See you in a bit, then.'

And so it was that John Spring, casual in an open-necked shirt, leather jacket and tight trousers, waited for David, ensconced in a booth, in the lounge bar of the Crown and Mitre. He professed himself delighted to renew the acquaintance. 'Great to see you again, Dave,' he said, getting to his feet. 'An unexpected pleasure. I'd heard that you'd left Norfolk for the big city.'

David took the proffered hand and shook it. 'I was a bit surprised to hear your name as well. This is a bit off your patch, isn't it?'

'That's a long story, mate, and it can keep for a minute.' Spring had already made inroads on his first drink and was thinking about a second; he picked up his glass and drained it. 'What can I get you to drink? Whisky, as usual?'

'Thanks.' David sat down and waited for Spring to return with the drinks, watching him in action as the policeman eyed up the women he passed coming and going from the bar. Some things never changed, David reflected wryly, and one of those was John Spring's insatiable appetite for the opposite sex.

'Here you go, Dave.' Spring eased himself onto the opposite seat. 'Cheers.'

David raised his glass. 'Cheers.'

After a deep draught of his beer, Spring leaned back with a satisfied sigh. 'Good beer,' he pronounced. 'The local brew. And the scenery here is worth seeing,' he added, nodding towards a nearby table inhabited by a gaggle of young women.

'You were going to tell me why you're so far from Fakenham?' David prompted, anxious to change the subject.

Spring grinned, unrepentant. 'I've had a transfer to Upper Walston. A change of scenery is sometimes not a bad thing for a bloke, Dave. Truth is, the wife chucked me out. Didn't take too kindly to me screwing her best friend.' He shrugged philosophically. 'Win a few, lose a few. I shouldn't have got caught, but there you are. So I may be needing your services again soon myself – another tidy little divorce, just like the last one you fixed up for me.'

'I'll recommend someone local,' David said with haste.

'Oh, but you did such a good job for me before. And it's always good to do business with a mate,' Spring said, giving him a wink. 'If you understand me.'

David understood all too well: this was the *quid pro quo* for any information Spring might be willing to part with about the poisoning of Flora Newall. 'I'll do what I can,' he promised, sighing.

'Good.' Spring winked again. 'How about you, Dave?' he went on. 'Are you still with that smasher, the one with the reddish hair? 'Cause if you've finished with her, I wouldn't mind having a go myself.'

'Lucy and I are still – together,' David said stiffly.

'Married?'

'Not yet,' he admitted. 'But I'm working on it.'

'Marriage.' Spring took another long drink, then went on in an expansive tone. 'It's a great institution, mate. I highly recommend it. Just as long as you get a woman who's willing to give you a bit of – freedom. Trouble is, most women tend to get possessive.'

David could see that they'd be there all night if he didn't turn the conversation away from Spring's favourite topic. 'Can I get you another drink?' he suggested.

'Wouldn't say no – ta very much.'

'About this Newall case,' David said hastily on his return from the bar, shoving a foamy glass in front of John Spring. 'As I told you on the phone, I've just come into it, and don't have any idea what's going on. I was hoping you could fill me in a bit. Off the record, of course.'

'Of course.' Spring's wink was exaggerated. 'You know me, Dave. Always willing to give a mate a helping hand.'

'What can you tell me? All I know is that the woman is supposed to have been poisoned.'

'She was poisoned, all right.' Spring wiped the foam from his mouth with the back of his hand and prepared to talk business. 'Digitalis, it was. At first they thought it was a heart attack, and that's what the postmortem showed. Heart attack, end of chapter. But the local doctor bloke rang up the pathologist and asked him to run a test for digitalis poisoning. Seems that a routine test won't show digitalis poisoning – you have to be looking for it. So they looked for it, and there it was.'

David frowned, perplexed. 'But why on earth would the doctor ask for the test? Why would he even think of it? If it looked like a natural heart attack, that is?'

Spring shrugged. 'He said that he'd had a tip-off that it might be digitalis. And he had enough doubts himself to ask for the test. Seems he was right.'

'Who tipped him off, then?'

'Don't know,' Spring admitted. 'He won't say – some sort of ethical rubbish about professional confidentiality. But don't worry, we'll sort him out. I'll put the heavies on him tomorrow and get a name out of him one way or another.'

'And so you've been questioning my client, Mrs English. Because she was the last person to see Miss Newall alive, presumably?'

Taking a prim sip, Spring looked at him over the rim of his glass. 'It's worse than that, mate. The pathologist reckons that she must have taken the digitalis no more than thirty minutes or so before she died. Which means that she was at Mrs English's house when she took it.'

David stared at him, stunned. 'But that's outrageous! Are you suggesting that my client deliberately poisoned her?'

'Hold on to your hair, Dave.' Spring grinned. 'I didn't say anything about deliberate, did I? The powers that be reckon that some foxglove leaves could have got mixed up in that herbal tea muck that she served the lady. Seems she grew all the stuff herself, so it could have happened. That's why I took away her jars of leaves – so they could be tested.'

'But I don't understand.' David thought aloud. 'Why wouldn't it have affected anyone else? That doesn't make any sense to me. Either Gillian English gave her poisoned tea or she didn't, but if she did I can't see how it could have been accidental.'

'You said it, mate, not me.' Spring drained his glass. 'Trouble is, there doesn't seem to be any reason for your Mrs English to poison Miss Newall – not on purpose, anyway. And until someone comes up with a reason, we don't have anything but circumstantial evidence to go on.'

'So what exactly is her position?'

'Let's just say,' Spring stated in a self-conscious police voice, 'that we'd prefer Mrs English not to leave the area. Not until we've had a chance to ask her a few more questions. And until we get the results of the tests on those tea leaves. Funny woman, your Mrs English,' he added in a more normal tone, shaking his head. 'I just don't get it.'

'What do you mean?'

'Not a bad looker. And she's had a bloke, or she wouldn't be a Mrs and have a kiddie.'

David understood what he was getting at. 'Ah,' he said noncommittally.

'I know that there are women like that, who prefer other women, just like there are blokes who go with blokes, but I don't understand it. What a waste. Maybe,' he added with a speculative look into his empty glass, 'after this is all over I could have a go. Get her to change her mind, do her a good turn. Maybe she's just never had a good bloke.'

David registered the empty glass. 'Another beer, John?'

'My round.' Spring looked at the nearby table, where the gaggle of girls was reduced to just two, a delicate blonde and a robust brunette. 'And maybe it's time for some company,' he said, rising and going to the table before David could stop him. 'Hello,' he addressed the girls. 'Could I buy you two lovely ladies a drink?'

'Yes, please,' said the dark-haired girl as the blonde shook her head. 'I'll have a pint of lager, thank you very much. And my friend is drinking lager shandy.'

'Cynth!' the blonde whispered frantically. 'I said no!'

'Oh, don't be such a spoilsport.' The dark-haired girl shrugged and reached for her handbag. 'Let's join them.' She arrived at their booth just as John Spring returned with the drinks, sliding in next to him. 'My name's Cynth,' she announced.

'I'm John, and this is my mate Dave,' Spring said, clearly delighted.

David was appalled; joining John Spring in picking up girls was the last thing he wanted to do, tonight or any other night. He wondered how on earth he could get out of it.

The blonde girl seemed to share his feelings; she hung back at the other table, joining them only when it was obvious that her friend would not be returning.

'This is Lisa,' Cynth said. 'Lisa, John and Dave.'

Lisa gave a jerky, shy nod and perched on the end of the seat as far from David as she could manage. 'Cynth, I really need to get home,' she said quietly but urgently.

'Oh, don't be so silly' Cynth's voice was scornful; she was evidently enjoying herself and had no intention of being moved in the immediate future. 'You got a light, mate?' She took a cigarette from her handbag and leaned closer to John Spring.

'You bet, sweetheart.'

David looked across at the girl. She was not unattractive, he decided, though that coarse sort of beauty appealed to him not at all. Her hair was thick and shiny and dyed a deep purplish shade of brown, and the lavish mouth which held the cigarette was painted purple to match. She was well-endowed, and dressed to show it, in a low-cut ribbed black body under which she clearly wore nothing at all, and a short leather skirt revealing well-muscled legs.

Her friend, on the other hand, had a face which would have looked more at home in a Gainsborough painting than in a country pub: Lisa was fine-boned and pale, with a luminous beauty that her shyness couldn't disguise. Her downcast eyes were a shade between grey and blue, and her fair hair was as fine and straight as silk thread. She looked about twelve, though she was surely at least eighteen, and David didn't have a clue what to say to her.

Cynth took a deep drag of her cigarette, then put it in the ashtray while she concentrated on her lager and on smiling at her admirer. 'Do you come here often, John?' she asked, ignoring David.

'Not often enough, sweetheart.' He inched closer to her; the two of them might have been alone for all the attention they paid their companions.

'I didn't think so. I would have remembered if I'd seen you before – a real man like you stands out a mile from all the local lads.'

'Cynth, I really do have to get home,' Lisa interrupted yet again, tucking her hair behind her ear in a nervous gesture. 'I told Mum that I'd be back in time to read Janie a bedtime story.'

Cynth frowned, turning to her friend. 'Let your mum read the bloody story,' she snapped. 'I'm not ready to go. Besides,' she relented, 'you don't get out of the house enough, Lisa. You deserve a night out.' She swivelled to face Spring again. 'I had to practically drag her out,' she explained virtuously. 'All she wants to do is stay at home with the bloody baby. The girl needs a bit of fun. And I'm the one to see she gets it. Me, her best friend.'

Embarrassed, Lisa averted her head over her shandy. 'That's not fair,' she protested. 'Janie is my responsibility.'

'That's what your mum says, isn't it?' Cynth felt called upon to explain to Spring, as though Lisa weren't there. 'She's got this baby, see. Made a mistake, and now she's stuck with it.' She took another drag of her cigarette and blew the smoke at him provocatively. 'She didn't take my advice, see. I always say, "if you can't be good, be careful." Well, she wasn't good, and she wasn't careful either, and what's she got to show for it? A bloody baby. Now me, I may not always be good, but I'm always careful. If you understand me.' She patted her handbag in a meaningful way. 'Be prepared, that's my motto. Just like a bloody boy scout, that's me.'

'You don't look much like a boy scout to me,' Spring murmured; Cynth giggled.

David cleared his throat, wondering how on earth he could escape from this nightmare, then inspiration struck. 'I really must be going as well,' he said. 'My girlfriend will be expecting me. Perhaps,' he addressed Lisa, 'you might allow me to see you home?'

Lisa seemed doubtful, but Spring was delighted at the opportunity to solve all their problems. 'You don't have anything to worry about with Dave,' he assured her. 'He's a perfect gent, is Dave. I don't know where he's gone wrong,' he added for Cynth's benefit, squeezing her thigh.

'Oh, you're terrible, you are.' She leaned against him and looked up into his eyes; neither of them even noticed when the other two left.

'My car is in the car park,' said David at the door of the Crown and Mitre.

'I can walk – I live just the other side of the village,' Lisa explained, still refusing to look at him.

'I'll walk with you, to make sure you get home safely.'

'You don't need to bother – nothing will happen to me in Nether Walston,' said Lisa, with her first smile of the evening. Afraid that perhaps he might find her ungracious, she added, 'It's very kind of you, I'm sure.'

'Not at all.'

They walked through the village in silence till she stopped at the door of a small, modern terraced cottage. 'Here,' she said. 'This is home. Thank you very much, Mr ...' Her voice faded away as she opened the door and stepped inside.

David stood for a moment, bemused, looking at the door. Behind it he could hear a woman's voice raised in anger and the wail of a baby. Shaking himself out of his reverie, he went back through Nether Walston to retrieve his car.

Meanwhile, at The Pines, Enid Bletsoe was entertaining her sister and brother-in-law to supper. It was part of a long-standing arrangement, enshrined in tradition, whereby they reciprocated supper visits on a weekly basis, routinely and without any particular enjoyment on either side. At one time there had been a bit of culinary rivalry between the sisters, and they had tried to outdo each other with tasty concoctions, but that was far in the past: the meals had long since sunk into a sort of samey mediocrity, featuring whatever Fred had on hand in the shop and was easiest to prepare.

This evening, though, Enid was very glad that it was her turn. The comings and goings at Foxglove Cottage over the last couple of days had been of intense interest to her, and she would have hated to have gone out that night, when even yet something exciting might happen across the road. And it certainly provided a more than adequate subject for conversation.

Fortunately the menu – sausages and mash, with mandarin Angel Delight for afters – hadn't required Enid's presence in the kitchen for very long during the day, and she'd managed to keep a close eye on Foxglove Cottage. 'That friend of the Rector's was there this afternoon,' she told Doris avidly. 'Remember – the one who was visiting from London at Easter, with Lucy Kingsley, the artist?'

Doris nodded, more interested in Lucy than in David. 'She had such pretty ginger hair.'

'The actual term is "strawberry blonde",' Enid corrected her, pursing her lips in a superior way.

'Whatever. You don't think that colour could be natural, do you?' Unconsciously, Doris's hand went to her own dyed hair.

Enid sniffed. 'I don't see why not. Some of us don't see the need to tamper with Mother Nature.' She took a sip of her bitter lemon, looking pointedly over the rim of her glass at her sister's hair.

There was no reply to that, nothing to be done but to shift the subject. 'Was she with him? When he was across the road this afternoon, I mean?'

106

'No,' Enid admitted. 'But I wonder what he was doing there. I know he went to that lunch at Foxglove Cottage at Easter, but …'

Doris interrupted her. 'He's from London, isn't he? And those women came from London, too. So maybe they know each other from London.'

'London isn't like Walston, Doris,' her sister said with triumphant scorn. 'It's just a bit bigger. Not everybody in London knows each other.'

'But didn't someone tell me that he was a lawyer?' recalled Doris, ignoring her sister's tone. 'Maybe that's why he was there.'

'Of course!' Enid crowed. 'If anyone needs a lawyer, it's that woman. I mean, it's just lucky for her that they don't hang people any longer. You can depend on it – that's why he was there.'

Ernest had been silent up to this point, concentrating on his sausages and mash. He was far less interested in the comings and goings at Foxglove Cottage than he was in the death that had brought it all about, and the consequences of that death. He took a breath and jumped into the pause in the conversation. 'What I'd like to know is what the Rector is going to do about the vacancy.'

'Vacancy?' Enid echoed, not following him.

'Churchwarden,' he stated succinctly. 'It's my understanding that the Rector can call a special parish meeting to fill the vacancy, or he can make do with one warden and wait until next year's Easter Vestry.'

Enid understood what he was getting at; on Sunday he had rushed to fill the vacant seat once more. 'I suppose you'd like it if he waited a year,' she said in a snide tone. 'Then you can play at being churchwarden again.'

He refused to be drawn. 'Trouble is,' he went on as if she hadn't spoken, 'I can't think of anyone suitable. And you know how the Rector relies on me to find the right person.'

'Of course, there's always Roger Staines,' Enid continued, ignoring him as he'd ignored her. 'There's no reason why he couldn't do the ceremonial parts of the job – fill in on a Sunday, carry the wand and so forth.'

'But Roger Staines is ill!' Doris reminded her sharply. 'He had a heart attack, remember? He's under doctor's orders!'

'Yes …' Enid's eyes glittered as she turned to her sister, her malicious needling forgotten. 'He *did* have a heart attack, didn't he? I just suddenly thought – what if she poisoned him as well? What if his heart attack was nothing more or less than digitalis poisoning, but the first time she didn't get the dosage right? What if Roger Staines had a lucky escape from that witch at Foxglove Cottage?'

Chapter 16

That thou mayest take the matter into thine hand: the poor committeth himself unto thee; for thou art the helper of the friendless.

Psalm 10:16

Breakfast at the Rectory the next morning, Saturday, was a somewhat dispirited affair; Stephen was already up and gone, Becca was silently miserable, and David and Lucy, who had talked late into the night in the privacy of their room – not entirely harmoniously – were tired.

'You haven't talked to Stephen, then,' said Lucy, as a statement rather than a question.

'Not yet – I thought about it, but I just couldn't.' Becca stirred her cornflakes with a defensive frown. 'I will, though. Soon.'

'You must,' Lucy reiterated firmly. 'It will be difficult to tell him, but things will be better when you have.'

David helped himself to another cup of coffee. 'You can do something for *me*, Becca,' he said.

She gave him an enquiring look.

'It's Gill,' he explained. 'I have the strongest feeling that she's keeping something back from me. And until I know everything, I feel that I'm operating in the dark. Could you talk to her and see if you can find out anything?'

'Yes, all right.' Becca was glad to have a specific task, something that would take her mind off her own dilemma and enable her to feel useful. 'I'll go this morning, if you like.'

'I'd appreciate it. And while you're doing that, Lucy and I will have a little nose around Walston – see if we can unearth any village gossip.'

'The village shop is always good,' Becca suggested. 'And someone will be doing the flowers in church, of course.'

David and Lucy had gone when the phone rang. Becca looked at it with a feeling of sick loathing, but picked it up nevertheless, knowing from long experience that there was no escape.

'Hello, Becca – it's Gill,' said a voice that was not the one Becca had expected. 'Could I speak to David, please?'

'He's not here – he's gone out for a bit. Can I give him a message?'

Gill sighed. 'I thought he ought to know – that policeman has just been here. Without any warning, he just showed up on the doorstep.'

'And what happened?'

'Lou sent him away with a flea in his ear.' Gill gave a dry laugh. 'But that doesn't mean he won't come back, and I'd feel better about it if David were here. Could you tell him?'

Becca made a quick decision. 'I'll come,' she said. 'I know I won't be much help if the policeman comes back, but I need to talk to you. I'll leave a note for David, telling him to come as soon as he gets back.'

*   *   *

'Let's stop in the church first,' David suggested to Lucy as they left the Rectory.

'All right.' She didn't sound very enthusiastic.

There was a slight but palpable air of awkwardness between them that morning, following their discussion of the night before. David had not responded to Lucy's revelations about Becca's tribulations in quite the way she anticipated: he had felt that perhaps Becca was overreacting to what was after all not a very uncommon occurrence. 'Don't you think she's being just a bit ... wet ... about the whole thing?' he'd suggested.

Lucy's reaction had been anger on Becca's behalf. 'Now you sound just like a man,' she'd accused. 'You just have no idea how traumatic something like that can be for a woman, especially one as young as Becca, and one who has led the sort of sheltered life she has. Don't forget, David, her father insulated her from anything resembling real life. And Stephen hasn't exactly encouraged her to grow up either.'

'So it's all the fault of men,' he'd snapped back uncharacteristically. In the end he'd apologised for his insensitivity, had promised to bend over backwards to be understanding and they'd kissed and made up in a rather satisfying way. But the memory of their disagreement lingered.

'Sorry about last night,' he said awkwardly as they walked towards the church.

Lucy turned to him and smiled in a conciliatory way. 'Me too, darling. I didn't mean to jump down your throat like that. And I appreciate what you said to Becca this morning – it's good of you to try to get her involved and make her feel useful.'

Gratified, David returned her smile; it was going to be all right after all.

They went in through the west door. As Becca had predicted, the church was not empty: Marjorie Talbot-Shaw was in the chancel, poking stripy pink tulips into a pedestal arrangement. After each addition she stepped back, removed her glasses and allowed them to fall to her ample chest where they hung suspended by a gold chain, viewed the overall effect, then replaced her glasses and moved closer to add yet another tulip.

'Very nice,' said David, moving into the chancel.

'Oh!' She turned and peered at them over her glasses. 'You startled me – I didn't hear you come in.'

'Sorry,' David offered with his most ingratiating smile. 'I always think that this is one of the nicest times of the year to do flowers,' he added. 'Those tulips are lovely – where did you get them?'

Marjorie began to thaw visibly. 'From my garden. They *are* rather nice, aren't they?' She removed her glasses and prepared for a chat.

With her imposing height and the dramatic streak of silver in her dark hair, she was a memorable woman. 'We've met before, I believe,' said Lucy. 'At Easter. You were doing the flowers then as well, on Holy Saturday.'

'Yes, of course.' Marjorie scrutinised them. 'Friends of the Thorncrofts, aren't you?'

'That's right,' Lucy confirmed, adding unnecessarily, 'we've come back for another visit.'

'I see.' Marjorie thought for a moment, then said, 'You seem sensible people. Perhaps you'll be able to sort that young woman out. She's got a great deal to learn about being a Rector's wife, I'm afraid.'

'Becca? What do you mean?'

Marjorie contemplated her flower arrangement. 'Very standoffish, for one thing. Doesn't make any effort to become involved with things at church – things like the Mothers' Union and flower arranging. She doesn't entertain at all to speak of, except for her own little circle of friends, including those women at Foxglove Cottage, and that just won't do. A Rector's wife should set an example for the parish in her involvement with the church as well as her hospitality. And this idea that she has about having a job – well!' She turned away from the flowers and faced Lucy. 'I'm not being critical, mind you. I'm just trying to help. The girl is very young, and needs taking in hand. But she won't listen to anyone in the parish. Perhaps she'll listen to you.'

Lucy was astonished and didn't know what to say. But David, shrewdly, understood. 'You are – were – a rector's wife, then?' he guessed.

'Yes, indeed.' She smiled. 'My dear late husband Godfrey spent all his life in the service of the Church of England. And I like to think that I was a worthy helpmeet for him. I ran the Sunday School, sang in the choir, helped with the flowers, and, of course, was involved in the Mothers' Union. And the amount of entertaining I did! My dinner parties were famous throughout Shropshire.'

'Shropshire!' Lucy exclaimed. 'But I grew up in Shropshire. My father had a parish near Ludlow. John Kingsley – do you know him?'

Marjorie frowned. 'No, I don't believe so. Though perhaps the name sounds familiar.'

They were interrupted at that moment by the approach of the Rector, who had spotted David and Lucy in the chancel. 'Sorry to bother you,' he said, 'but I wondered if you were going to be going back to the Rectory soon?'

David turned to look at him; Stephen, like Becca, was looking much worse since their last visit. His cheeks had hollows that hadn't been there before and there were tiny lines around his eyes. His smile was strained, as though it required a great effort to produce. Before Lucy's illuminating talk with Becca, David and Lucy had attributed it to the problems within the parish; now they knew better. 'We could be,' David said, willing to make a special trip if necessary.

'I wondered, then, if you could tell Becca that I'll be home for lunch, around one. I didn't see her this morning,' he added. Stephen had in fact seen his wife increasingly little over the past several weeks: being around her was just too painful, and it was easier for his peace of mind to stay away from home. Concerns about his parish – even the death of a churchwarden – had paled into insignificance amidst the horror of his crumbling marriage. Becca wouldn't talk to him, wouldn't let him touch her – could scarcely bear to have him in the same room, it seemed. What had happened to the lovely and loving young woman he had married only a few months ago? At the bottom of his agony was the fear that it had something to do with him – that somehow he was responsible for killing her love and her spirit. He couldn't ask her what was wrong for dread of what she might tell him.

'Yes, of course,' said David. 'We'll go right now.'

Becca found Gill calm and Lou in a state verging on frenzy. 'I sorted the little shit out,' Lou told Becca. 'I told him to piss off, in no uncertain terms.' She gave a demonstration, hands on hips and a ferocious look on her face. '"Bugger off," I said, "and don't come back! Mrs English and her solicitor will come to you when they're good and ready."'

The thought of Lou, tiny and fierce, seeing off a large policeman was so funny that Becca had consciously to keep from smiling.

'It was a sight to behold,' Gill said dryly. 'She was more than a match for him, I can tell you. But I thought I'd better let David know.'

Lucy and David, having found Becca's note, arrived shortly after she did, and had the story repeated to them. 'And he'd better not come back,' Lou finished, scowling. 'I'm not afraid of him, with his tight trousers and his big truncheon. He obviously thinks with his truncheon, that one.'

David laughed. 'Well put.'

Gill, mindful of Bryony, gave them a warning look. 'Would you like some coffee?' she asked quickly.

While Gill went to put the kettle on, David drew Becca to one side. 'You haven't had a chance to talk to her, have you?'

'Not yet,' Becca admitted. 'But I was thinking – have you talked to her on her own? Maybe there's something she doesn't want to say in front of Lou.'

He recognised the truth in that as soon as she'd said it. 'You're brilliant!' he whispered. 'If I can only get her alone …'

Becca thought for a minute. 'I could take Lou to the Rectory,' she offered. 'Would that help?'

'Perfect. If you can see to that, I can take care of the rest.'

They followed the others into the kitchen. 'I was just about to offer everyone some sandwiches for lunch,' Gill was saying. 'But I've suddenly realised that in all the excitement this week, I haven't been to the shops and I'm just about out of bread.'

Becca seized the opportunity. 'You can all come to the Rectory for lunch,' she offered.

'Me, too?' asked Bryony.

'Of course.'

The little girl beamed. 'Yes, please.'

'It's very kind of you,' said Gill.

But as they prepared to go, David put a detaining hand on Gill's arm. 'We'll be along in a few minutes,' he said. 'I need to have a private word with my client.'

In a short while the others had gone; Gill carried on making coffee as though nothing had happened. 'Milk? Sugar?' she offered.

'Just black, thanks.' David waited while she poured out the coffee and sat down across from him, cupping her large, capable hands around her mug and looking at him questioningly. 'Now, then,' he said. 'I think you know what this is about, Gill. I think you're keeping something from me, and I reckon that it's because of Lou.'

'What do you mean?' she asked calmly.

'I think that there's something you don't want her to know, or that you're trying to protect her from. Am I right?'

Gill sighed and sipped her coffee. 'You're right,' she said. 'At least partly.'

'I'm waiting.'

'It's just that – well, in spite of what I said before, I had what some people might construe as a good motive, or at least some sort of a motive, for killing Flora.'

'What people?' David asked sharply. 'The police, for instance?'

'Possibly,' she acknowledged.

He leaned back in his chair, fighting the impulse to rush her. 'Start at the beginning,' he ordered.

Gill related the whole story, rationally and composedly. She had a good memory for such things and was able to recall the substance of her conversation with Flora in some detail. 'I don't suppose you can imagine me in a towering rage,' she concluded with a small smile. 'But I can assure you that I was in one. It was almost as if I were outside myself, watching myself screaming at her. But she was threatening my child, threatening the security of our family. I think I *could* have killed her at that moment. But I didn't. I just let her die instead, and I've got to live with that.'

David wasn't going to let her forget her subsequent sins. 'And you lied to the police, and lied to me.'

'Well.' She ran her finger around the rim of her coffee mug, considering. 'I prefer to think of it as not telling the whole truth.'

'Same thing.' David leaned forward to emphasise his words. 'You've got to come clean now, you know. You've got to make a statement to the police telling the whole truth, and you've got to tell Lou.'

'Oh, no!' For a moment she seemed startled out of her self-possession. 'I can't tell Lou! She would – well, you heard what she did to that policeman this morning. Can you imagine what she'd do to Enid Bletsoe if she knew?'

'You can't protect her from the truth,' he said insistently. 'Surely you can see that? For one thing, these allegations of Enid's: they involve Lou as well. She needs to know about them. And it can't be a good thing for your relationship to keep secrets like that. In the end it will only come between you.'

'Yes, I see.' Gill sighed. 'I'll have to tell her, then.'

'Today, soon. And then we'll draft a statement for the police.'

She was silent for a moment, thinking. 'Will you come with me when I tell her? I think it would be better if we weren't alone. Bryony mustn't know, of course, but – I think I'd like to tell Lucy and Becca as well. They'll have to know eventually, and it would be better if I told them all.'

David nodded. 'The sooner the better. Why don't we go to the Rectory right now and get it over with?'

Things didn't go strictly to plan, though. As they were leaving Foxglove Cottage, David spotted a police car in the drive of The Pines and a moment later Sergeant John Spring emerged, a bemused grin on his face.

'Why don't you go on ahead to the Rectory and I'll catch up with you in a few minutes?' David suggested to Gill in a hurried whisper. 'I'd like to have a word with the sergeant.'

Gill complied, and David crossed the road.

'Dave!' John Spring greeted him. 'Just the bloke I wanted to see, and here you are!'

'Have you got a few minutes for a chat?' suggested David.

'You bet, mate. Fancy a drink at the Queen's Head?'

'All right,' David agreed. 'I'm buying.'

It was an unseasonably warm day, so they were able to carry their pints to a table in the garden of the Queen's Head where they were unlikely to be overheard. David knew that some report of the previous night's conquest was inevitable, and it wasn't long in coming.

'Not that I wouldn't rather go back to the Crown and Mitre,' Spring mused. 'Jolly good pub, that, and a smashing clientele.' He shook his head reminiscently. 'What a corker, that Cynth. Knows how to give a bloke a good time, I don't have to tell you. The things that girl doesn't know about pleasing a man just aren't worth knowing. The windows of my car are still steamed up,' he added with a grin.

'A very nice-looking girl,' David said neutrally.

'Nice-looking! Dave, that's not the word. Didn't you get a look at her knockers? Weren't they the most smashing pair you've ever seen?' Fortunately no reply was required; Spring went on, 'Trouble with you, Dave, is you're too strait-laced. You need to break out a bit, have a bit of fun. Now I could see that Cynth's friend Lisa really fancied you. Quiet little thing, seemed prim and proper, but she had a kid, didn't she? So she wasn't as pure as she'd like to let on. You could have had it off with her, Dave, and your Lucy none the wiser for it. Stick around with me a bit, mate. 'I'll see to it that you have a bit of fun now and again.'

David moved his glass around on the weathered pine table, leaving damp stains on the wood. 'I'm not really in Walston to have fun,' he reminded Spring with a wry smile to take the sting out of his words. 'I'm here on business, and it's serious business.'

'Ah, yes. That client of yours.' Spring lowered his voice and looked around. 'That's what I wanted to talk to you about. She's in a hell of a lot of trouble, Dave.'

'How so?'

'Well, you know that she told me she didn't have any motive for poisoning the old bag? Turns out she had a hell of a motive.'

'Oh, yes?' David raised his eyebrows, inviting him to go on.

'I suppose you heard how I went there this morning and that little gal sent me packing?' He laughed, amused by the situation. 'A real little spitfire she is – I wouldn't want to cross her. I was afraid she'd scratch my eyes out, or kick me in the family jewels. So I cut my losses and went to see the doc, like I told you I was going to. He didn't want to tell me, but I finally got it out of him. It was the old bag across the street, Enid Bletsoe, that gave him the tip-off, told him that Flora Newall had been poisoned. So I dropped in to see her, and you won't believe what she told me.'

'Try me,' David invited.

'She told me that she knew all along that your client had poisoned her, and why. Flora Newall was a social worker and she was threatening to take Mrs English's kiddie into care. Because the old bag Mrs Bletsoe had filed a complaint to say that the kiddie was being abused. That's it in a nutshell, Dave.' He grinned with relish.

David, profoundly glad that he wasn't as surprised by this information as Spring had hoped, decided not to reveal how much he knew. 'That's very interesting,' he said cautiously.

'And besides that, she said, your client grows poisonous plants – just look at the name of her cottage.'

'That doesn't prove anything,' David pointed out. 'From what I understand, she inherited the name of the cottage when she bought it.'

'And,' Spring went on, undeterred, 'apparently some other bloke in the village had a heart attack not long ago. Mrs Bletsoe reckons he was poisoned too, only he didn't die.'

'That,' said David, beginning to get angry, 'is a malicious and unsupported lie. Mrs Bletsoe ought to be ashamed of herself for spreading such rubbish.'

'Hold on to your hair, Dave,' Spring grinned. 'I'm just telling you what she said. I didn't say that I believed her. But any way you cut it, mate, your client is in trouble.' He spread his hands on the table for emphasis. 'I'll put it to you straight, Dave. There's no one else in the picture. Everything points to your Mrs English and no one else. The timing – Miss Newall had to have been poisoned during the time she was at Foxglove Cottage, according to the toxicologist. And we know it was no accident. All those jars of leaves have been tested and there was no trace of foxglove in them.'

'I could have told you that.' David tried not to sound scornful. 'Don't forget that Mrs English drank some of the tea herself and didn't seem to have suffered any ill effects.'

'The first lot, yes,' Spring pointed out with unusual perspicacity. 'But she says she made up a special brew to settle Miss Newall's upset stomach. They've tested that jar as well, and it was perfectly okay. No foxglove. That means no accident. And now that we've got a motive, your Mrs English is well and truly stitched up, Dave.'

David digested the information for a moment. 'But you have no proof,' he said at last. 'Nothing but circumstantial evidence. You haven't got enough to charge her.'

'Don't worry, mate. We'll get it. It's only a matter of time.'

'Why are you telling me this?' David asked shrewdly. 'It's not just because we're friends, is it?'

'Dave!' Spring put on a hurt expression. 'How can you doubt me?' When David continued to regard him with a sceptical smile, he lowered his voice. 'Okay, Dave, I'll put it to you straight. I want you to get her to confess.'

'Confess?' David echoed, unbelieving.

'Don't you see, it's the best way? She's obviously guilty as hell, and we'll get her in the end. But if she confesses now, we can do a deal. Go easy on her. Manslaughter, and she'd be out in a few years.'

David shook his head. 'She's not guilty, John.'

'Come, on, Dave! It's as plain as the nose on your face that she did it – the old bag was going to take her kiddie away, so she poisoned her. Just get her to confess and we'll all be better off. And do it soon or it will be too late.'

'What's in it for you?' David wanted to know. 'I can't believe that you're that interested in my client's welfare.'

Spring sighed and drained his glass. 'If you want to know the truth, Dave, I'd like to get it all sorted while I'm still on this case,' he admitted. 'It'll look good for me if I can get a confession – help me to get promotion. Now that this has developed into a full murder enquiry, one of the chief inspectors will be taking over soon and it will be out of my hands.' He gave David a sly look over the rim of the empty glass. 'And I won't be able to help *you* any longer, mate, if I'm not on the case. No more information.'

David understood exactly the position in which Spring found himself. 'I'll see,' he said noncommittally, standing up and offering his hand. 'Thanks for being honest with me. And 'I'll be in touch, John.'

'Just a minute, Dave.' Spring scrabbled in his pockets for a scrap of paper and a stub of a pencil, then wrote down a number and handed it to David. 'My home number,' he said. 'Ring me any time, day or night. But you'd better make sure you do it soon.'

By the time David got to the Rectory, Gill had managed to impart the crucial information to Lou in the presence of Lucy, Becca and Stephen, while Bryony played in the garden. Lou was, of course, upset, but the public nature of the confession made it difficult for her to react as she would have done in private, and Gill was cheered by everyone's warm support.

Encouraged by this, Becca decided to make her own confession, cushioned by the presence of her friends. Catching Lucy's eye, she began, 'I have something to say as well. Stephen, I just haven't known how to tell you this, but perhaps it will be easier with everyone else here.'

'What is it?' he asked bravely, fearing the answer.

She reached across the table and gave his hand a squeeze, looked briefly into his eyes, then stared down at the table as she related, amidst tears, the substance of the telephone calls and their impact on her. 'I should have told you, Stephen,' she finished softly, 'but I just couldn't. Can you forgive me?'

'Forgive you!' He'd been motionless with shock; now he rose, went round the table, and took her in his arms. 'Becca, love!' Words failed him as his heart overflowed with strong yet conflicting emotions: anger, sorrow, relief, and above all love. 'Let's go upstairs, love,' he urged, oblivious to the others around his table. 'I think we need to be alone.'

'Wait just a minute,' David interjected reluctantly, unwilling to intrude on this private moment. 'Something has to be done about this. You'll have to report it to the police. File a complaint.'

'No!' Becca turned panic-filled eyes to him. 'Then everyone would know!'

'But it's the only way he'll ever be caught,' he pointed out. 'The only way he'll be stopped.'

'David is right,' agreed Stephen. 'The monster must be caught. I know it's difficult, love, but it's the only way.'

'Don't forget,' Lucy added gently, 'what you said yourself. It probably has something to do with Flora's murder. The man may be something worse than a nasty phone caller.'

Becca bit her lip, fighting back more tears. 'Do I have to go myself? Do I have to tell the police in person? It's just too awful.'

David gave her an encouraging smile. 'I'm quite happy to represent you,' he said. 'If you'll allow me to take a statement, I can file it for you. I'm sure the police will want to ask you some questions, but that can wait.'

She sighed, relieved. 'All right, then.'

After an intensive session with pen and paper, they dispersed: Becca and Stephen went upstairs to make their private reparations while David accompanied Gill and Lou to the police station. Lucy, happy to be useful, took Bryony back to Foxglove Cottage and read to her from her favourite book of fairy stories.

Chapter 17

For thou hast maintained my right and my cause: thou art set in the throne that judgest right.

Psalm 9:4

The trip to the police station was accomplished without incident; David handed over Gill and Lou's carefully prepared statements and had a word with the officer on duty regarding Becca's complaint. 'I'd appreciate it if you could send a WPC to interview her,' he suggested, anxious to avoid the nightmare of John Spring or someone of his ilk salivating over Becca and the lurid details of the phone calls. 'It's a fairly delicate matter, as you'll appreciate, and I think that a woman is called for.' The officer nodded. 'And perhaps she might come in plain clothes,' David added. 'Judging from the timing of the calls, it seems fairly evident that the house is being watched. We don't want to alert the caller that the police have been involved.'

Later he dropped Gill and Lou off at Foxglove Cottage, refusing the offer of refreshment but going in to collect Lucy. Gill saw them off at the door. 'Thanks for everything,' she said with a rueful smile. 'You've made it all comparatively painless.'

David returned her smile, raising his eyebrows. 'Sounds like a tooth extraction.'

'Something like that.'

'But it's not over yet, you know,' he reminded her. 'Just beginning, I'd say.'

Gill sighed. 'Where do we go from here, then?'

He thought for a moment. 'That depends on the police, to a great extent. But we have a lot more talking to do, you and I.'

'Come back tonight,' Gill invited. 'Both of you. Come for some supper and we'll talk.'

At the Rectory, Stephen and Becca were waiting for them in the kitchen, his arm protectively and tenderly around her shoulders.

'How did it go?' Stephen demanded. 'Tell us what happened.'

David interpreted correctly that he was referring not to Gill and Lou but to Becca's statement. 'There was no problem,' he assured them. 'They'll be sending someone along to talk to Becca — a woman, I asked for. And it won't be until tomorrow.'

Becca nodded bravely, drawing on her husband's strength. 'All right. I can cope.' She looked at the clock. 'I was beginning to worry that you wouldn't be back in time.'

They looked at her blankly.

'Tea at Walston Hall, Lucy. Remember? We're meant to be there at four. We'll have to leave in a few minutes.'

Going to tea at Walston Hall wasn't exactly what either Becca or Lucy wanted to do at that moment, but as they traversed the footpath between the Rectory and the Hall they agreed that it was perhaps a useful way to take their minds off everything else.

Diana Mansfield welcomed them warmly and ushered them into a drawing room which was cosy and liveable but at the same time large enough not to be dominated by the massive grand piano in the corner. The decor and furnishings reflected the availability of a great deal of money and a corresponding quantity of good taste – if not on the part of Diana herself, at least that of some expensive interior designer. The genius of it, though, was in its managing to look as though it had always been that way, from time immemorial, or at least since the time of the first Lovelidges: everything just a bit faded, with nothing raw and obviously new to mar the mellow beauty of the sixteenth-century linenfold oak panelling and the leaded glass windows. Lucy's admiration of the room was unfeigned. 'It's absolutely beautiful,' she said with spontaneous enthusiasm.

'You like it?' Diana's smile of pleasure lit up her face in an extraordinary way, just as the late afternoon sun, slanting through the ancient diamond-shaped panes of glass, bathed the room in a quality of light that was almost palpable.

'I love it,' Lucy assured her hostess. 'You won't think me rude if I look at your pictures?'

'Oh, please do.'

The walls were covered with time-darkened oil paintings, a mixture of landscapes, still lifes and portraits. 'It's the people I like,' Lucy admitted, examining a portrait of a woman in a stiff brocade bodice, every thread distinctly rendered and the pearls of her brooch so creamily luminous that it looked as though they could be plucked from the canvas. The woman's face, heart-shaped and dark-eyed, framed by wings of centre-parted auburn hair, had a look of sad nobility, with an unsmiling mouth conveying endurance and a quality of strength. 'Who was she, do you know? She has a marvellous face, hasn't she?'

Diana shook her head with a small smile. 'I don't know who she was. They're not my ancestors, I'm afraid. Not even Quentin's ancestors. Our instant forebears, he calls them – bought and paid for.' She joined Lucy in front of the portrait. 'But she's one I especially like. There's something about her face that I find quite haunting. I sometimes sit here looking at her, wondering why she was so sad. Did all her children die in infancy, or did her husband spend all his time wenching with the village maidens?' She gave an apologetic laugh, as if embarrassed by her fancifulness, and moved around the room almost restlessly. 'And this one,' she said, standing in front of a swashbuckling cavalier, dressed in blue satin and striking a pose with a sword. His luxuriant dark hair tumbled to his shoulders, his eyes stared out boldly and the extravagant drooping moustache did nothing to conceal a mouth that was frankly sensual, lips parted slightly in a confident smirk. 'I wonder how many hearts he broke,' Diana mused, almost to herself.

'He was certainly aware of his own attractions,' Lucy agreed. 'Probably not what you'd describe as unduly modest. Some women find that appealing.' She thought of her own David, modest and self-deprecating almost to a fault. And what, she wondered, was Quentin Mansfield like? She'd formed no great impression of him during their brief meeting at Foxglove Cottage, other than that of a man who knew his own mind, and most probably his own worth: not one to hold an inflated opinion of his own importance, but not one for false modesty either. She looked again at the proud cavalier, moving closer. There was something about his flashing eyes that reminded her of someone, but she couldn't quite think who it might be. Certainly not the solid if not stolid Quentin Mansfield; of that much she could be sure.

With an involuntary sigh, Diana seemed to make an effort to recall herself, turning towards Lucy. 'But you've come for tea, haven't you? And here I am wittering on about portraits while the two of you are gasping.'

The tea, when it came, was everything that it should be: a proper afternoon tea, with delicate sandwiches of thinly cut bread, crumbly scones and jam, and slices of rich fruit cake, all accompanied by fragrant China tea poured from a Georgian silver teapot into delicate antique bone-china cups. But Lucy found conversation difficult; their hostess seemed distracted and Becca proved to be no help in keeping things moving.

Casting about for a suitable topic of conversation, Lucy looked round the room. 'That's a lovely piano,' she said. 'Do you play?'

Diana flushed. 'A bit,' she confessed, almost reluctantly. 'It's something I've always wanted to do, and recently I've been taking lessons. I'm not very good yet. But I enjoy it.'

'I think that's splendid,' Lucy enthused. 'Your husband must be proud of you.'

'Yes, well.' Diana lifted the teapot. 'This seems to be almost empty. Shall I make another pot?'

It wasn't until they were well into the next pot of tea that Diana got around to the subject that seemed to Lucy to have been the reason for the invitation to tea – and perhaps the reason for her nervousness as well – though Lucy couldn't quite understand why. 'I understand that you're a famous artist,' Diana began.

'Well, I don't know about the famous bit.' Lucy smiled, twisting a curl round her finger. 'But I do make my living as an artist, yes. Watercolours, but not very traditional ones.'

'Yes, I know.' Diana looked into her teacup, embarrassed. 'I've checked up on you a bit, you see. I saw some of your paintings at a gallery in Norwich.'

'That would be the Bridewell Gallery,' Lucy guessed. 'I had an exhibition there last year, and they usually have a few of my things.'

'Yes. And I liked them very much. But I wondered – do you ever undertake special commissions?'

'Yes, of course.' Lucy leaned forward and put her teacup on the table. 'I love doing commission work – I find it very satisfying. What did you have in mind?'

'Something … special. For a gift.' Diana twisted her fingers together in her lap. 'For … a friend.' She looked up at Lucy, suddenly imploring. 'But you won't mention anything to Quentin, will you?'

While the women were away, Stephen made a pot of strong tea which he and David consumed at the kitchen table along with a packet of shop-bought shortbread biscuits. David found the young priest distracted and upset, not surprisingly, and his efforts to draw him out were not very successful. 'I know you haven't had much time to think about it,' he said, 'but do you have any ideas at all about who might be making the phone calls?'

Stephen looked at him blankly. 'No. I can't think.'

'No one in the parish?' David prompted. 'No one who has a grudge against you, for instance?'

'No. None of my parishioners are … like that. Some of them may be a bit difficult, but not … sick.' He looked into the depths of his mug of tea, then turned a tortured face to David. 'How could anyone do it?' he said, his voice husky with pain. 'Whoever he is, he's almost destroyed her. He's taken away her lovely innocence, and almost managed to kill our marriage. We had so much. And now …' He shook his head. 'I don't know how long it will take to put the pieces back together. If we ever can. Becca was right – nothing will ever really be the same between us again. I just don't understand why someone would want to do that.'

At a loss for words, David shook his head, then watched helplessly as the tears trickled from the corners of Stephen's eyes.

'I love her,' Stephen said softly. 'So much.' His voice caught on a sob, and for a few minutes he wept into his hands while David patted his shoulder in an awkward display of sympathy. Coping with women's tears was difficult enough; David found this situation completely beyond his control.

'Sorry,' Stephen muttered, pulling himself together with visible effort; he removed his gold-rimmed glasses and polished them on his sleeve. 'Not fair to burden you, David. But I've got to be strong with Becca – I can't let her see how much this is tearing me apart.'

'That's what I'm here for,' David assured him.

Walking back to the Rectory from Walston Hall, Lucy took the opportunity to ask

Becca a question which had been on her mind for some time; it was the same question that David had asked Stephen. 'Surely,' she said, 'you must have some idea who it is? The man who's making the phone calls?'

'No.' Becca spoke abruptly, with a brusqueness that was not characteristic. She softened it by adding, 'Actually, Lucy, I've tried not to think about it. In some ways I don't *want* to know. The thought that it's someone here in the village, someone I know, whom I see every day ...' She shuddered. 'It just doesn't bear thinking about. Can't you understand that?'

'Yes, of course, I can,' Lucy assured her, giving her arm a sympathetic squeeze. 'But you realise that the police will ask you. They'll need all the help they can get to catch him. He's sick, Becca love. He's got to be caught, so that he won't ever do it again.'

'Yes, I see.' Becca was silent for a moment, deep in thought.

'It's someone who knows when you're alone,' Lucy prompted. 'That much is obvious.'

'But the Rectory is fairly isolated – it isn't really overlooked by any other houses,' Becca pointed out. 'Unless someone is using a telescope, I suppose.' She paused, and when she resumed, her voice was quiet. 'When Stephen goes out, even to the church, he has to pass Harry Gaze's cottage. I thought – at first – it might be Harry. But Harry's voice is so ... Norfolk. I think I would have recognised him if it had been Harry.'

'You said that the voice was muffled,' Lucy reminded her. 'And you don't know how much of Harry's broad Norfolk accent is put on. I've noticed that it gets stronger when he's talking to outsiders like us, almost as if he's making a point.'

Becca nodded thoughtfully. 'That's true.' She gave a sudden shudder. 'Oh, Lucy. I just wish it was all over. It's better now that Stephen knows. But I wish it was over and we could just get on with our lives.'

David and Lucy agreed that it was just as well that they were going to Foxglove Cottage for supper that night: it seemed a good thing to leave Stephen and Becca to have an evening alone together, without any necessity for polite conversation or hospitable behaviour. But the backlit face of Enid, peering avidly from her front window as she observed their arrival, cast a pall on the evening from the outset. In addition, Lou seemed unusually subdued, and Bryony's presence during the meal added an air of constraint and meant that nothing of significance could be discussed.

Gill, though, made an effort at cheerfulness. 'I've remembered that you're vegetarian, Lucy,' she said as she served the pasta. 'It's mushroom sauce. And lest you fear that I'm trying to poison you, I can assure you that I didn't pick the mushrooms myself – they came from the supermarket.'

Lou's voice was sharp. 'That's not very funny, angelface.'

'No, I don't suppose it is.' Gill sat down and unfurled her napkin. 'Flora was vegetarian as well, I think,' she said in a conversational tone. 'When we went to dinner at the Rectory, Becca made stuffed aubergines. Very nice they were, too.'

'Yes, she's made them for us as well,' Lucy recalled. 'I feel sorry for people who have to cater for vegetarians when they're not used to it.'

'I want to be a vegetarian,' Bryony announced, looking for approval to Lucy, who had made a great hit with her by reading endless stories that afternoon. 'Eating dead animals is horrible, Mummy.'

'Oh, don't be so silly,' snapped Lou. 'You've been eating meat all your life.'

Gill raised her eyebrows at Lou, then smiled patiently at her daughter. 'We'll talk about it later, darling.'

Bryony, usually a fairly docile child, seemed out-of-sorts and stroppy that evening; it wasn't surprising that she resisted going to bed when the time came. 'But I don't *want* to go to bed,' she whined, clinging to Lucy. 'I want Lucy to read me a story.'

'Go upstairs and clean your teeth and get into your nightie,' her mother said in a mild but firm voice. 'And if you do it double-quick, perhaps Lucy will tuck you into bed and read you a story.' She looked at Lucy, who nodded.

'Coffee?' Gill offered, drawing the curtains, as they settled down in the sitting room after supper.

'As far as I'm concerned, you can keep the bloody coffee till later,' Lou said bluntly. 'I'm not finished with the wine yet.' Throughout the meal a good quantity of cheap and cheerful red wine had been consumed, but there was still some in the bottle, and another bottle of a rather better wine which David had brought was still on the sideboard.

'Wine sounds good to me,' David agreed, retrieving his empty glass and refilling it. 'As I said this afternoon, the time has come to talk. We can't put it off any longer, I'm afraid.'

'Yes.' Gill sat down on the sofa next to Lou. 'You're right, of course. Though it seems we've already done rather a lot of talking today.'

'A hell of a lot of talking,' Lou echoed truculently. 'And I don't know what else there is to be said.'

David took a seat across from them and leaned forward; his voice was mild. 'Well, in case you haven't realised it, there's the little matter of a murderer loose in Walston. I believe you, Gill, when you say that you didn't poison Flora Newall. But that means that someone else did.'

'Oh.' Lou looked thoughtful. 'Yes, I see what you mean.'

'It couldn't have been an accident,' Gill stated, hoping to be contradicted.

David shook his head. 'I don't see how.'

'But Gill didn't bloody do it,' Lou said insistently. 'So what does it have to do with us?'

'You and I may know that Gill didn't do it, but I don't think that the police are at all convinced.' He leaned back. 'They don't have any other suspects, and the time of death is pretty damning. And now that they think they've got a motive ...'

'But what can *we* do?' Gill interjected. 'I can't prove that I didn't do it, can I?'

'Trust David.' Lucy, her task upstairs completed, came into the room and paused behind David's chair for a moment, smoothing his hair with a gently intimate gesture as she spoke in a matter-of-fact, unemphatic tone. 'He won't let you down. He's done this sort of thing before, you know.'

Embarrassed, yet touched by her faith in him, David cleared his throat. 'With Lucy's help, of course.'

Lucy curled up in the remaining chair and reached for the wine. 'We've got to find out who killed her,' she said. 'The police aren't going to do it – it's up to us.'

For a moment no one said anything as they pondered the truth – and the implications – of Lucy's statement.

'All right,' Gill said at last, with a nod of resignation. 'But where do we start? I mean, who could have had a reason to poison poor old Flora? – apart from me, of course,' she added, smiling wryly.

Lou scowled. 'That's not funny.'

'Sorry.'

'It seems to me that we should start with the phone calls – Becca's obscene caller,' Lucy suggested. 'When we've found him, we might have an answer.'

'You think there's a connection?' Lou turned to her eagerly. 'You think that the ratbag who's been calling Becca is the murderer?'

'It would make sense.' Lucy twisted a curl round her finger, working through it in her mind as she spoke. 'Becca's the one who suggested it. What if Flora found out who was making the calls somehow – say, caught him in the act? Wouldn't that be a good motive for murder? To keep her from telling anyone?'

'But that's just supposition,' Gill pointed out.

'Not entirely,' David put in. 'Lucy had a phone call herself, from Flora.' He explained about the mysterious call. 'Of course we'll never know if that was the deep dark secret that Flora had managed to find out about someone,' he added. 'But it's a good guess. And it gives us a place to start looking.'

'Did she ever talk to Stephen, I wonder?' Gill asked. 'As Lucy suggested? That would make things easier.'

David shook his head. 'I asked Stephen about it this afternoon while Becca and Lucy were out. The last time he saw Flora alive was at a meeting the night before she died. And she didn't say anything about it then or any other time.'

'Too bad.' Lou tipped the rest of the wine into her glass, emptied it, then got up to fetch the other bottle. 'So how do we catch the obscene caller, then?'

'I suspect that the police will have a few ideas about that,' cautioned David. 'We'd better leave it to them.'

Lou poked the tip of the corkscrew into the cork and gave it a vicious twist. 'Then we're back to square one: what you're saying is there is nothing we can do.

So why don't we just drink up this wine and call it a night?'

Thoughtfully, David put the tips of his fingers together and contemplated them. 'I'd like to hear your story, Gill,' he said. 'From the beginning. About the day that Flora died.'

'She's told you already. More than once.' Lou glared at him, putting a protective hand on Gill's knee. 'Can't you just leave her alone? You're as bad as the bloody police.'

'It's all right,' Gill said.

'I just want to hear it all again, in order, the way it happened. There's something about it that's bothering me,' he admitted. 'Something that doesn't quite add up.'

Gill rubbed her eyes wearily. 'I've told you the truth. All of it.'

'I'm not suggesting you haven't,' he assured her. 'I'm just afraid that I'm missing something important.'

'All right, then.' They all listened carefully as Gill related her story in meticulous detail, beginning with Flora's arrival and continuing through the row to Flora's ejection from the house. 'And the next thing I knew of it was when Enid banged on the door and said that she was dead,' she finished.

'Ah.' David smiled in satisfaction. 'I've got it – now I know what was bothering me.' He leaned back in his chair. 'You offered her tea as soon as she arrived.'

'That's right,' Gill confirmed, puzzled.

'And she drank it.'

'Yes … ?'

'And she didn't tell you why she'd come until after she'd drunk both cups of tea?' he probed. 'You're sure about that?'

Gill nodded as Lucy clapped her hands together. 'Oh, I see! Darling, that's brilliant!' She turned to Gill and Lou and explained. 'She drank the tea *before* she told you why she'd come. So that means that you didn't have a motive when you're supposed to have poisoned her! When you gave her the tea, you had no reason to think that it was anything but a social call!'

'He's right, angelface!' Lou suddenly became animated. 'Those bloody police haven't got a leg to stand on!'

'*If* they believe me,' Gill cautioned. 'Which they haven't shown much inclination to do up till now.'

'They'll *have* to believe you,' Lou asserted. 'It's true!'

Chapter 18

Their soul abhorred all manner of meat: and they were even hard at death's door.
Psalm 107:18

Lucy woke before David the next morning with that momentary disorientation, almost subliminal, which often comes when waking in a strange bed. Before she opened her eyes she was aware that she was neither in her own bed nor at David's house. Then it came to her: the Rectory.

She feared she'd drunk rather too much wine the night before, and the coffee had come too late to be of much help. Gingerly she stretched her toes to the end of the bed and opened one eye, attempting to judge from the amount of light just how early it might be. Very early, she reckoned: there were no sounds that betrayed life in the house and very few that indicated life outside. Deep in sleep, David stirred and turned towards her, putting an arm around her and drawing her closer.

She snuggled into the curve of his body and gave herself up to the sleepy enjoyment of what she had always felt was one of the nicest – and most underrated – pleasures that life had to offer: waking up next to the person she loved, sharing the warmth of his body and knowing she didn't have to get up at any time in the immediate future. Drowsing in contentment on the edge of sleep, David's regular deep breathing lulling her back towards slumber, she found herself suddenly jolted into wakefulness by an unwelcome, intrusive thought as she realised that something was nagging at the back of her mind.

The night before. The great relief and celebration when they'd all realised that David had stumbled on something important: the timing of Flora's death. Gill couldn't have poisoned Flora, or perhaps more accurately wouldn't have poisoned Flora, because she'd had no reason to do so until after she'd had the opportunity. Surely the police would see that, would recognise the truth of it.

But something about it still wasn't quite right. Something niggled at the edge of her consciousness. Timing. It had something to do with timing. With a sick jolt in the pit of her stomach she knew what it was: the timing of Flora's death in relation to the poison. David had said he'd been told the toxicology report indicated that the digitalis must have been ingested during the time she was at Foxglove Cottage.

How much margin for error could there be? And how could they all have ignored it last night when they were so jubilant?

They'd ignored it because it didn't fit, because it wasn't convenient. But the police wouldn't ignore it, and the Crown Prosecution Service wouldn't ignore it. The CPS would use it to put Gillian English behind bars for a very long time.

Lucy turned over and David grunted in protest. 'Darling,' she whispered urgently. He groaned and turned his back to her, still asleep.

'David, darling,' she repeated, giving his arm a gentle shake. 'Wake up. It's important.'

'Hm?' He wasn't awake yet, but Lucy could tell he was beginning to surface.

She leaned over him. 'Darling, it's about Gill. About Flora's murder.'

David opened his eyes. 'What on earth are you going on about?' he grumbled. 'And what ungodly hour is it anyway?'

'About the timing,' she said.

'Time? What time is it?'

'No, not time – timing!'

He covered his face with his hands, groaning in mock horror. 'Woman, why are you waking me up with this nonsense?' he muttered. 'In case you don't remember, we didn't get to bed until quite late. And it now appears to be quite early. I love you to distraction, but there are limits.'

Lucy giggled. 'All right, darling, you've made your point. Now wake up and listen to me.'

With a deep sigh he turned over and looked at her, his eyebrows raised. 'I'm listening. This had better be good.'

Succinctly she told him of her doubts. 'I just don't understand it,' she finished. 'I believe Gill, of course. But how could the toxicology report be wrong? Are these things ever wrong? Or is there some sort of leeway in it?'

David listened thoughtfully. 'You're right, of course,' he admitted. 'We were all so excited about the motive bit last night that we managed to ignore the question of opportunity – the fact that no one else seems to have had one, whereas Gill certainly did.'

'But what can we do? Is there any way you can get a copy of the toxicology report?'

He pondered the question for a moment. 'I think it might be possible,' he said at last. 'John Spring is really keen for Gill to confess. I'm sure I can use that as a lever to get it out of him.'

'I knew you'd think of something.'

'And then we'll have to see where it goes from there.' David closed his eyes for a moment. 'I'd hoped that we'd be able to get things cleared up this weekend, and be back in London by tonight,' he admitted. 'But there's no chance of that. Too many loose ends. All this business with the toxicology, and the inquest opens tomorrow – not that it will be anything but a formality, but I'd better be there.'

'What about Flora's funeral, then?' Lucy asked.

'Stephen tells me that it will be on Wednesday. I suppose it would be a good idea for us to stay for that, if nothing else. Don't you think so?'

She nodded. 'So, in other words, we'll be imposing on Becca's hospitality for a few more days yet.'

'I feel badly about that,' David said.

'I'm sure she doesn't mind, though I think the cooking is a bit of a burden for her. Perhaps I could offer to help,' Lucy thought aloud. 'At least it would give me something useful to do. Though 'I'll have to be careful not to offend her with any implied criticism of her cooking.' With a contented sigh, she settled back down.

'Just what do you think you're doing?' David demanded.

'Trying to go back to sleep. It's too early to get up.'

'Oh, no, you don't, Lucy love,' he said with a wicked chuckle, reaching for her and pulling her close. 'You're the one who woke me up. And now you've got to deal with the consequences.'

*　　*　　*

That morning's church service was uneventful; much to the disappointment of the congregation, Gillian and Lou stayed away, mainly because of the excess of wine and the late night. But Enid managed to put the worst possible construction on their absence. 'A guilty conscience,' she whispered to Doris. 'She doesn't dare appear in the house of Almighty God with murder on her conscience. Not now that we all *know*.'

'She came when she had perversion on her conscience,' was Doris's rejoinder. '*Both of* them did.'

Enid withered her sister with a look. 'Not the same thing at all!'

Becca made a real effort with Sunday lunch and Lucy offered some discreet help, making a vegetable casserole for herself to supplement the roast chicken that the others would have, and concocting a pudding out of odds and ends in the pantry.

'It's very kind of you to help,' Becca said gratefully. 'I feel guilty letting a guest do so much work.'

'It's my pleasure.' Lucy's smile conveyed sincerity. 'I love cooking – I don't consider it work at all. And we're the ones who should feel guilty, outstaying our welcome like this. David reckons we may have to stay for a few more days at least.'

'Oh, I don't mind!' Becca assured her. 'It's lovely to have the company.' She smiled shyly, her eyes down-cast. 'I've never had many friends,' she admitted. 'And I think of you as a real friend, Lucy. I wish you could stay for ever.'

Too touched for words, Lucy squeezed her arm.

Taking advantage of the lull between church and the production of the meal on the table, David rang John Spring at home.

The sergeant's voice was hopeful. 'What can I do for you, Dave?'

'Well, John,' David put on his heartiest tone, 'you know what you told me yesterday? That you thought my client would be much better off if she confessed?'

'She's agreed, then?' Spring responded eagerly.

'Well, not exactly. Not yet, anyway.' Choosing his words with care, David went on. 'I've explained to her what you told me – that you've got her pretty well stitched up, and that you could cut a deal for her that would get her out in a few years. But she's not convinced.'

Spring interrupted, indignant. 'I'm a man of my word, Dave. If I say I could cut a deal, I mean it.'

'That's not the problem,' David assured him. 'She's just not sure how much you've got on her. I told her that the toxicology report was what did it – no room to manoeuvre around that one.'

'Damn right,' Spring confirmed.

'But she's not convinced – she says she wants me to have a look at it. Just to be sure. I'm sorry to have to ask you this, John.' David's voice became apologetic and chummy. 'You know how clients can be. They've got minds of their own, that's the trouble.'

Spring chuckled. 'I understand, Dave. A bit like chief inspectors.' He laughed again, then went on thoughtfully. 'So you'll want to see the toxicology report, then. On the q.t. and straightaway.'

'If it's not too much trouble, John. I think it will make all the difference.'

'No problem, Dave.' There was a brief pause while Spring worked out the logistics. 'I'll have to go by the station and make a copy. Just as well it's a Sunday – not so many nosy parkers hanging around the photocopier. How about if I meet you at the Queen's Head for a quick one in – say – an hour? Half past twelve? Then I can slip you the goods.'

'Thanks, John.' David grinned into the phone. 'I'll look forward to seeing you then.'

David was back just in time for lunch, with only a brief opportunity to peruse the crucial document. 'It doesn't look good at all,' he whispered to Lucy as they went into the dining room. 'There doesn't seem to be any room for doubt.'

'What will you do?'

'I'm not sure,' he admitted.

Naturally enough, he was preoccupied during lunch as he puzzled about what he might do next. Becca, too, was silent, dreading the visit of the police officer which was promised for that afternoon; that left the burden of conversation on Lucy and Stephen. They managed to struggle through the meal, but everyone was almost relieved when the doorbell rang during coffee in the sitting room.

Becca jumped. 'Oh! That must be the police!'

'I'll get it,' Stephen said firmly, pausing to give Becca's hand a comforting squeeze. 'It will be all right, love,' he whispered to her.

The WPC, when she was ushered in, had a reassuringly normal appearance, dressed in a colourful jumper and a pair of faded blue jeans. 'Plain clothes, you said.' She grinned, indicating the jeans. 'So I've made the most of it.' Belatedly, she introduced herself. 'WPC Karen Stimpson, Norfolk CID.' Her voice had a hint of Norfolk in it, reinforcing the open face of a country girl. She was young, with an unruly mop of sandy-coloured curls defying the efforts of a pair of hair-slides to keep it under control.

'You're Mrs Thorncroft?' she addressed Becca.

'Yes, that's right.' Becca summoned up the ghost of a smile which WPC Stimpson returned in the form of an infectious grin.

David identified himself. 'And I'm Mrs Thorncroft's solicitor, David Middleton-Brown.'

Realising suddenly that she was the one person without a right to be there, Lucy said awkwardly, 'Would you like some coffee, officer? Or tea?'

'Thanks, I'd love a cup of tea,' Karen Stimpson declared. 'If it's no trouble.' She took some papers and a notebook out of her handbag and sat down. 'I'll try to make this painless,' she promised.

'Thanks.' Now that the moment had come, Becca was outwardly calm, but she looked down at her hands and realised they were shaking. Stephen sat beside her on the sofa, taking her hand firmly in his.

'Here is a copy of your complaint, as filed by your solicitor,' WPC Stimpson said, passing a paper across to Becca. 'If you wouldn't mind reading through it, I'd appreciate it.'

Hiding her distaste, Becca read the statement. David had done a wonderful job of rendering the horrible unpleasantness into almost antiseptic language, but Becca knew that she would have to relate the specifics to this nice woman. 'Yes,' she said when she'd finished. 'It's quite accurate.'

'Poor old you,' Karen Stimpson said warmly, with real sympathy. 'How awful. It's never happened to me, but my Auntie Jean had some loony ringing her every day for months, and she was in a right state about it.'

'Did they catch him, then?'

'Oh, yes. It was some dirty-minded old bugger across the road. Don't worry, love,' she added. 'We'll catch this one too.'

Becca relaxed a bit, cheered by the young woman's openness and warmth. 'Do I have to tell you what he said? So that you can write it all down?'

The policewoman tapped the paper. 'It's all here, isn't it? No need to go through it all again – it will only get you upset.'

'Thank you.' Becca sighed with profound relief.

'What is the procedure, then?' Stephen asked.

'We'll need to put a tap on your phone, Mr Thorncroft,' WPC Stimpson explained.

'It's quite straightforward. Then your calls can be traced, and we just wait for the bugger to ring. I know it's unpleasant for you, Mrs Thorncroft, but the longer you can keep him on the line, the better chance we have to trace him.'

Stephen frowned. 'I'm afraid that's out of the question,' he said. 'This is a Rectory. It's essential that all calls should be completely confidential. My parishioners often ring with matters of a private nature, and it just wouldn't do to have the police listening in. It would be unethical.'

Leaning forward, David intervened. 'I can certainly understand your concern, Stephen, but don't you see how important this is? It's your wife we're talking about – her peace of mind, even her sanity. My God, man, you've seen what this has done to her. You've got to let them do it.'

'Please, Stephen,' Becca begged; it was as if she'd suddenly seen a light at the end of the tunnel, only to have the darkness descend again.

'With any luck it won't be for long,' Karen Stimpson added. 'Just a day or two, and we should have him.'

He wrestled with his conscience, but only for a moment; of course Becca was the most important thing, he told himself. And besides, the man might not stop with Becca: every woman in the village was a potential victim. He owed it to all of them to ensure that the man was caught. 'Yes, all right,' he agreed. 'But only for as long as it's absolutely necessary.'

'Thank you,' Becca murmured.

WPC Stimpson nodded. 'And I need to ask you,' she went on, 'if either of you has any idea who might be behind this. Mr Thorncroft?' She turned to Stephen. 'Do you know of any parishioners who bear a grudge against you? Or have you noticed anyone taking an unnatural interest in your wife?'

He considered the question; it was something he'd thought about quite a lot since David first posed the query on the previous afternoon. 'No,' he said at last. 'I can't think of anyone. I've had my differences with one or two of my parishioners, but nothing that could even be remotely construed as a grudge. In fact,' he added with a wry smile, 'I'm the one who's come out rather the worse from my skirmishes with my difficult parishioners. If anyone has a grudge, it should be me.'

Lucy reappeared with a mug of tea, which the WPC acknowledged with a nod. 'Ta ever so much.' She turned to Becca. 'Mrs Thorncroft? Do you have any thoughts? Is there anyone in the village who makes you uncomfortable – who stares at you or says things that bother you?'

'No,' Becca stated, though without a great deal of conviction. 'Everyone has been very nice to me.'

'And is there anything at all you can think of that you haven't told us?' She took a gulp of tea. 'Ah, that's magic. Cheers.'

Becca handed back the statement. 'It's all there. I can't tell you any more than that.'

'If you do happen to think of anything, Mrs Thorncroft, don't hesitate to give me a call.' She passed across a business card. 'And I'll arrange to have everything done tomorrow. Then we'll have him in no time at all – I promise you.'

'That wasn't so bad, was it?' Stephen said a few minutes later when the WPC had gone.

'I liked her,' Becca responded. 'She was nice. And I believed her when she said they'd catch him.' She sighed. 'I'll just be glad when it's all over.'

'So will we all,' Lucy put in. 'There's something very wrong in this village, you know. Nasty phone calls, murder – someone who's very disturbed is on the loose, and the sooner he's caught the better.'

David looked thoughtful. 'But what I wonder,' he said quietly, 'is what he'll do next?'

The idea came to David as they all shared a cup of tea. Suddenly he remembered his firm's Christmas dinner, an event he'd not enjoyed and had managed to put out of his mind. Lucy had been busy that night so he'd been on his own; at the dinner he'd been seated next to the wife of one of the junior partners, a rather dull, plain woman who had been extraordinarily taciturn through most of the evening. All David's conversational gambits had fallen flat – it had been jolly hard work, he recalled. And then she'd begun talking about her job and she'd become a different person. Poison: it was a subject she'd seemed able to talk about indefinitely, with animation and profound interest and in mind-numbing detail. She was, he recalled now, an assistant in the toxicology department of a major London hospital. Just the person he needed.

'May I use the phone?' he said without preamble.

Stephen looked up from his tea, surprised. 'Of course. If you want some privacy, use the one in my study.'

'Thanks.' David raised his eyebrows to Lucy's questioning look and went off to make the call. What was that woman's name? he asked himself. He'd managed to block it quite effectively. Tom Lansing's wife. Chloe Lansing.

A call to Directory Enquiries got him the number he needed, and in a few minutes he was speaking to Chloe Lansing. 'We were sitting together at the firm's Christmas dinner,' he explained to her. 'David Middleton-Brown.'

'Yes, of course,' she recalled.

'And you were telling me about your job. About poison.'

'Yes?'

He took the toxicology report out of his pocket, unfolded it and put it in front of him on Stephen's desk. 'I was just wondering if you might spare me a few minutes and a bit of your expertise to help me with a case I'm working on,' he began.

'If I can. It has to do with poison?'

'That's right. Digitalis,' David explained.

'Obtained from the leaves of the foxglove plant,' she said promptly. 'Actually, the whole plant is poisonous, but the leaves are especially so. Scientific name *Digitalis purpurea*. Highly toxic – nasty stuff.'

He'd come to the right person, David reflected. 'You say it's highly toxic. What does that mean in terms of reaction time? In other words, if you took a massive dose of it, enough to kill you, how long would it take?'

'How long would it take you to die?' she asked dispassionately. 'Twenty minutes, maximum. If you took enough of it, that is. Possibly less time, but no longer than twenty minutes.'

He sighed. 'I was afraid you were going to say that.'

'And it wouldn't be a nice death either,' Chloe went on. 'Nausea, headache, irregular heartbeat. A heart attack, in short.'

'And how soon after taking the poison would these effects start?'

'Oh, not long,' she said with confidence. 'No more than a few minutes. And then it would be downhill quickly.'

'Well.' David scribbled a few notes on the toxicology report. 'Thanks for your help. I really do appreciate it.'

'Any time,' she assured him. 'If you need help in killing someone off, just let me know.'

Later that evening, late enough to ensure that Bryony would be in bed, David and Lucy returned to Foxglove Cottage to share the disheartening news. They'd rung ahead and alerted the women of their intention to drop in, so the wine was already open and the glasses waiting in the sitting room.

'Hair of the dog,' muttered Lou. 'We had enough wine last night to last us a while, but we may as well start all over again.'

Gill motioned them to sit down, then poured the wine. 'Sorry we missed church this morning,' she apologised. 'We just didn't make it up in time.' She sat down and raised her own wine glass. 'What's up? I have a dreadful feeling this isn't a social call.'

While David thought how to begin, Lucy plunged in. 'We've been doing some thinking about the timing, David and I, and I'm afraid that it doesn't look very good.' Lou frowned and Gill gave her an enquiring look. 'I mean,' she explained, 'it isn't really enough to talk about motive – about what motive you might or might not have had, or whether there was anyone else with a motive. At the end of the day it still comes down to opportunity. And whether we like it or not, the police say that the tests show she must have ingested the poison that killed her – the digitalis – during the time she was in this house. That's what we're up against.'

Lou slammed her glass down on the table, spilling wine. 'Bloody hell!'

'Lucy's right,' Gill said, looking at David for confirmation. 'I'm still in trouble, aren't I?'

He nodded. 'I've seen the toxicology report myself, and I've confirmed the findings with a toxicologist. A dose of digitalis of the amount Flora ingested would have killed her in no more than twenty minutes. And she was here longer than that. In fact the symptoms would have manifested themselves pretty quickly – the nausea and chest pains and so on.'

133

Gill shivered suddenly. 'It's cold in here,' she said. 'Is anyone else cold?' Not waiting for a reply, she got up and switched on the gas fire. It hissed into life, the flame caught, and within a moment the realistic-looking coals were bathed in dancing blue flames which took the chill off the air and cast surrealistic shadows in the darkened room. 'That's better,' Gill said, resuming her seat on the sofa.

No one spoke for a moment. Lucy stared into the fire, Lou took one of Gill's hands between her own and chafed it, and David sat with his eyes closed, biting his thumb nail. 'Tell us again,' he said into the silence, not opening his eyes. 'Tell us what happened that day.'

'Oh, for God's sake,' Lou fulminated. 'Haven't we been through this enough times?'

'Obviously not.' David opened his eyes and looked at her. 'Obviously we're missing something crucial. If the tests show that she couldn't possibly have taken the digitalis *before* she got here, and Gill didn't give it to her while she was here, there must be an explanation.'

Gill sighed in resignation. 'I offered her some herbal tea,' she began obediently. 'Straightaway. She tasted it and said it was very nice, though I wasn't convinced that she was all that keen on it. Then I offered her something to eat, some biscuits or cake, and she took a piece of cake, but she just played with it.'

'You're sure she didn't eat any?' David probed.

'No. She pushed it around on her plate and apologised. That's when she said that she wasn't feeling very well, that her tummy was a bit delicate.'

'Already!' Lucy interrupted her. 'There was something wrong with her already!'

David frowned. 'It doesn't make sense. If she'd taken the digitalis before she came, she would have been dead by then. She wouldn't have been merely unwell – she would have been dead.' He turned to Gill. 'Go on.'

'So then I made her some special costmary tea, to settle her stomach. I think she found it a bit bitter,' Gill recalled with a smile. 'She added some artificial sweetener tablets to it when she thought I wasn't looking.'

David, in the midst of taking a sip of wine, started, sputtered and managed to spill half a glass of wine on the arm of the chair and the carpet; the red stain spread like blood. 'Damnation!' he muttered, reaching for his handkerchief in a vain effort to mop up the stain. 'Sorry.'

'Oh, don't worry,' Gill assured him. 'But are you all right? What on earth is the matter?'

He collected himself, then fixed her with an intense look. 'Repeat what you just said,' he commanded.

'I said, don't worry.' Gill frowned, puzzled.

'Before that.'

Gill wrinkled her brow, trying to remember what had happened immediately before David's little fit. 'I said that she added some artificial sweetener tablets,' she repeated slowly. 'Oh! I see!'

134

Chapter 19

For he spake, and it was done: he commanded, and it stood fast.

Psalm 33:9

It was too late that evening, David judged, to ring Chloe Lansing again, but the next morning he did so as early as seemed civilised, hoping to catch her before she left for work.

'Oh, hello,' she greeted him. 'Actually, I was going to ring you back today. After I talked to you last night, I thought of something else I should have mentioned about digitalis poisoning.'

'What's that, then?'

'Well, I was a bit more definite than I should have been about the timing,' Chloe admitted cheerfully. 'There are certain things that would make the poison work much more quickly and more effectively. Quinine, for instance – digitalis administered in gin and tonic would be a most effective way to kill someone. And, of course, there are also factors that would slow the reaction time. Tea is the obvious one – tannic acid and caffeine are both antidotes to digitalis poisoning, so if the victim were drinking tea, it could take considerably longer for them to die.'

'Tea?' David echoed, dismayed. Was this going to undermine his theory? 'But the person in my case drank some tea,' he blurted. 'Herbal tea.'

'Oh, well, that's different, isn't it?' Chloe pointed out. 'That's the whole point of herbal tea, it seems to me: no caffeine and no tannic acid. I mean, most of it tastes like washing-up water. You certainly wouldn't drink it for its flavour.'

He sighed in relief; the theory was still hanging together, but there were some crucial pieces missing. 'I suppose you're right.'

'But I don't suppose you rang me to discuss the flavour of herbal tea,' Chloe went on. 'Is there something else I can help you with?'

'Well.' David thought how best to frame his question; he knew so little about it that it was difficult to know what to ask. 'It's still about digitalis,' he said. 'Is it always in the form of leaves? Or is there any way it can be given as a tablet? Don't people take it for heart trouble?'

'Digitoxin,' she responded promptly. 'Also digoxin, and a few others. They're all derived from the foxglove plant and are used to treat congestive heart failure.'

135

'And what exactly do these tablets look like?' he asked, holding his breath. 'Do any of them, for instance, resemble artificial sweetener tablets?'

'Let me think.' There was a pause, excruciating for David. 'Digitoxin are a bit on the large side – say, ten millimetres. But digoxin are only about five millimetres. They're actually quite similar in appearance to some brands of artificial sweetener tablets.'

'Ah.' David exhaled his breath on a satisfied sigh. 'So it would be possible to take digoxin by mistake, if you thought they were sweeteners?'

'Well, they wouldn't taste very nice,' Chloe cautioned. 'Quite bitter, I'd think, rather than sweet.'

'But if you'd put them in something that was bitter anyway …' he thought aloud.

'Like herbal tea!' she finished for him on a note of triumph. 'Yes, you might not notice the bitterness.'

'Well.'

Chloe sensed the excitement in that single syllable. 'Is that what you wanted to hear, then?' she probed.

'It is so far,' he admitted cautiously. 'But I have a few more questions for you.'

'Go ahead.'

'What would constitute a toxic dose of digoxin?' David asked. 'In other words, how many tablets would you have to take to kill you?'

'Difficult to say,' she temporised. 'I mean, we haven't yet got to the point of experimenting like that on humans, giving them increasing doses of poisons to see how much it takes to kill them!'

David laughed. 'I see what you mean.'

'Ten tablets of digoxin, taken over a fairly short period of time, would almost certainly kill you. Possibly quite a bit less would do the job as well.'

Again he thought aloud. 'And if you were drinking bitter herbal tea, something you weren't used to drinking, and adding sweeteners that didn't seem to be making much difference …'

'You'd probably add a few more for good measure,' she concluded in satisfaction.

It was all falling into place. But before he rang off, David had another question. 'One other thing. If you were testing for digitalis poisoning, would you be able to tell what the source of it was? Could you tell whether it had come from the leaves of the plant, or from one of the drugs derived from it?'

'No,' Chloe stated. 'The test would only pick up the presence of digitalis, not its source. Digoxin or digitalis leaves – it would make no difference. From the point of view of the toxicologist they're indistinguishable from each other, chemically identical. And,' she added humorously, 'from the point of view of the victim as well. They'd be equally dead either way.'

'So you think I'm on to a winner, then?' he allowed himself to ask.

'I think,' Chloe replied, 'that you've found yourself the perfect murder.'

Thanking her for her help, David put the phone down and turned to Lucy. 'Good

Lord,' he said. 'I think we've got it.'

'Tell me!' she demanded eagerly, though she'd been able to follow things pretty well from listening to his side of the conversation.

'Digoxin. A medical form of digitalis, and chemically indistinguishable from it.'

'Tablets, then.'

'Tablets.' He grinned. 'Virtually the same size as various brands of artificial sweeteners. And the bitterness of herbal tea would mask the taste, as well as probably induce you to use more of them.'

'Oh!' Lucy hugged him. 'Darling, you're so clever.'

On this occasion, at least, it wasn't modesty that caused David to shake his head. 'I'm not the clever one,' he said, suddenly sober. 'It was the murderer who was clever. All he had to do was substitute digoxin for the artificial sweetener tablets that Flora always carried around in her handbag, and wait for her to use them. Apparently everyone in the village knew about Flora's sweeteners.'

'He was lucky, though, with the herbal tea,' Lucy pointed out. 'If it had been ordinary tea, it might not have worked.'

'True. It might have taken much longer, or only made her ill. But he wasn't taking any risk,' David reasoned. 'If it didn't work, he could always try again. But as it turned out, it worked spectacularly well – better than he could ever have anticipated. There was the herbal tea, and the added bonus of having it happen at Gill's, so suspicion fell on her immediately.'

'He was jolly lucky, wasn't he?'

David sighed and shook his head. 'Lucky or clever, love, the result is the same. I'm afraid that Chloe was right: she called it the perfect murder. And right now, if our murderer is just clever enough to lie low and not try anything stupid, I don't see any way at all that we're going to catch him.'

Matters moved quickly after that; David, aware that the inquest was scheduled for that afternoon, lost no time in ringing John Spring.

Hoping to forestall the sergeant's inevitable hopeful enquiry about a confession, he said, 'I've come across something that could prove to be significant, John.'

'What's that, then, mate?'

'I think I might have found out how the murder was committed.' David paused. 'And you might not be too happy to hear that if I'm right, as far as I'm concerned it puts my client in the clear. But it might do you just as much good as if she were to confess.'

'Oh, yes?' Spring sounded distinctly sceptical. 'And just how do you reckon that?'

'I'm assuming that you'll have Miss Newall's handbag at the station,' he replied obliquely. 'And I'm willing to bet that inside it you'll find a dispenser for artificial sweeteners. If I were you, John, I'd have the contents of that dispenser tested – and immediately. I'd send it to the lab by courier if I were you, and ask that it be tested on the spot. The results might interest one or two people, especially with the inquest opening this afternoon.'

John Spring was baffled. 'Just what are you talking about, Dave?'

'Your superiors will be impressed when you pull this one out of the hat, Inspector,' David said smoothly, with a tiny stress on the title. 'There's no need to tell them that you had any help – we'll keep that just between us, if you understand me.' He hoped that Spring, not known for being quick on the uptake, *did* understand him.

'Oh. *Oh*.' David could almost hear the wheels turning as the sergeant went for the bait which he'd dangled so invitingly. 'Oh, I see. Well, thanks for the tip, Dave. I'll be in touch.'

'Let me know when you get the results,' David requested. 'That's all I ask, John.'

'Will do, Dave,' he promised, and he was as good as his word.

His voice held admiration and a certain amount of bafflement when he rang back early in the afternoon. 'You were right on target about the tablets, Dave,' he said. 'Digitalis. Or something like it, anyway.'

'Digoxin,' David supplied. 'Essentially the same thing.'

'That's it. But how did you know?'

'It was a good guess,' David claimed with characteristic modesty.

'The boss is dead impressed, mate. Hasn't done me any harm at all, I can tell you.'

'Congratulations, then, Sergeant.' David's voice held not a trace of irony. 'You've done well.'

John Spring was essentially a fair man. 'All down to you, mate. Ta ever so much.'

'Well, you know what they say, John.' David smiled. 'That's what friends are for.'

The inquest later that afternoon was a mere formality, a preliminary hearing only. Fergus McNair provided evidence of identity and the coroner gave permission for the body to be released for the funeral. 'It is clear,' said the coroner, 'that a great deal more needs to be known about this death before we can consider its causes. Only today some additional evidence has come to light which substantially alters this case. I therefore adjourn this inquest for three weeks, or until such time as I feel that we are ready to proceed.'

'Much ado about nothing,' David said to Lucy later. 'Now we can go back to London. I suppose I'll have to come back in a few weeks when the inquest is reopened, to give moral support to Gill when she testifies. But I don't think we can really justify staying any longer. And I dread to think what will be waiting for me back at my office – my secretary will not be best pleased that I wasn't back at my desk this morning as I promised.'

'But there's still a murderer on the loose in Walston,' Lucy pointed out. 'We can't just walk away from that, can we?'

David shook his head. 'It's out of our hands now, love. As I said this morning,

I don't see any way for us to catch him. We've done all we can – we've more or less put Gill in the clear, and that's what we set out to do. Now I think we'll have to leave it to the police to take it from here.'

'Sergeant Spring?' Lucy's voice was dismissive, scornful. 'As Lou so pithily said, he thinks with his truncheon. How do you think he's going to catch someone who was clever enough to commit a murder like that?'

He laughed. 'That may be so, but he'll have plenty of help with this one. Now that they know how it happened, it will be a full-blown murder enquiry. There's no room for us in that.'

For whatever reason, Lucy realised that she was extremely reluctant to leave Walston. She wasn't sure why, and wasn't sure that she even wanted to know why, but she acknowledged to herself that she was in no hurry to return to London. 'Maybe you're right, darling. But we *will* stay for the funeral, won't we?'

'I suppose we must,' David agreed. 'And who knows – perhaps if we keep our eyes and ears open, we'll learn something important.'

'Poor old Flora,' said Lucy. 'I think we owe it to her to stay for the funeral.'

'Yes, poor old Flora.' David nodded thoughtfully; he didn't really want to go back to London either, though his conscience was bothering him about it, and this seemed as good an excuse as any to stay away for a bit longer. 'I suppose it's the least we can do for her.'

If the day of the inquest and the day of the funeral were days of remembering Flora in various ways, the intervening day was one given over to the trappings of death, in which Flora and her memory figured scarcely at all.

Harry Gaze was very much in his element, preparing the church for the funeral. He was there from early on Tuesday morning, carrying out a ritual as formalised in its way as the funeral service itself would be. First he got out the wrought-iron bier candlesticks, used no other time than at funerals, when they stood at the four corners of the coffin. Wax had dripped down onto the metal of the candlesticks, and Harry busied himself removing it with boiling water. He congratulated himself that he'd remembered to bring his electric kettle from home to boil the water. 'Good job, that,' he muttered. 'Candle wax is the very devil to get off any other way but with boiling water.'

The candlesticks tidy and in place, his next task was preparing the candles themselves. They were, of course, proper beeswax candles – unbleached and yellow as honey. Harry took the bundle from his storage cupboard and unwrapped them carefully; beeswax candles were expensive, reserved only for funerals, and reused as necessary. The wax had guttered over them, leaving unsightly runnels. 'Don't know why I didn't clean them before I put them away the last time,' Harry grumbled, getting out his pocket knife to remove the wax dribbles.

It was thus occupied that David found him when he popped into the church. David was at a bit of a loose end that morning; Lucy had gone off with Becca to gather wildflowers for the funeral pedestals and Stephen had gone out to pay a call on Roger Staines. This would be Stephen's first funeral – a Requiem Mass – since he'd been in Walston, and he wanted to confer with his respected former churchwarden to find out how things were usually done at St Michael's.

'Those are lovely candles,' David commented, for something to say.

'Ay, wholly lovely,' Harry agreed. 'For all that they cost an arm and a leg.' Glad for someone to talk to, he paused in his labours, cocked his head and looked at David. 'Well I remember the last time as these candles were used.'

'Back in Father Fuller's time?' David hazarded, remembering Harry's reverential respect for Stephen's predecessor.

'No – for Father Fuller himself.' Harry crossed himself. 'God rest his soul. Last year it was when he passed over to his eternal reward. We won't see his like again,' he added with regret.

Deciding that subject was something better not opened for discussion, David offered, 'Can I help you with that?'

'I'm just about finished with the candles. But you can help me get the frontal up on the high altar, if you like – that's a job as goes better with two.'

'Yes, of course.' David followed the old man to the sacristy and helped him to lift the heavy lid of the chest where the altar hangings were stored.

'It's way at the back, seeing as it's used so seldom,' Harry explained. 'Even less than the rose pink.' He reached behind purple and red and green and rose-pink frontals and dragged forth the pole on which the black frontal was hanging. 'Beautiful piece of work,' he said proudly. 'Shame it isn't used more often.'

David examined it: black moire trimmed with slightly tarnished silver braid. 'Yes, it's lovely,' he agreed. It was as well he was there, he thought, as he helped the verger with the heavy pole. This really was a job for two, especially if one of them was an old man.

They carried the frontal out to the high altar; between the two of them they removed the white Easter frontal and replaced it with the sombre black. 'Got to do them as well, of course,' Harry said, pointing to the curtains around the sides and back of the altar. 'But I can do that myself, if needs be.'

'It's a great deal of work for just one day,' David sympathised.

'Oh, I don't mind.' Harry grinned. 'To tell you the truth, I do like a good funeral. Especially if it's done wholly proper, like we've always done it here. As I said before, we haven't had one for a deal of time here at St Michael's. Not since Father Fuller, and before him old Miss Ivey. We're all too healthy here in Walston, that's the trouble.' He gave a chuckle. 'Though I suppose as I shouldn't say that, since by rights I ought to be the next to go.'

David said what was expected of him. 'I dare say you'll be around for a good many years yet.'

'I'm counting on it. I'll tell you one thing, young man,' Harry confided. 'I'm not ready to go yet. Not by a long chalk. Don't suppose as anyone ever is – excepting maybe

140

Father Fuller, God rest his soul. He were a good man, and lived his life so as he'd always be ready to meet his maker.'

Father Fuller again, thought David. 'There, that's done,' he said, helping to spread the fair linen cloth across the top of the altar and replacing the candlesticks.

'And a wholly fine job we've made of it, young man.' Harry nodded in satisfaction. 'Now it's time to get the pall ready.'

Once again David accompanied him to the sacristy; he had nothing better to do, and this at least was an interesting way of passing the time. Harry took a black chasuble from a drawer and put it on top of the vestment chest, smoothing out the folds. 'Father Fuller looked wonderful in this,' he confided. 'Just how a priest ought to look.' The chasuble, lined in red silk, matched the altar frontal; the workmanship was beautiful, but it looked to David as if it should be worn by Count Dracula rather than a priest of God. 'No one could do a funeral quite like Father Fuller, I can tell you.' Another drawer yielded a black pall, carefully folded.

'That looks like it's been around a few years,' David said.

Harry nodded in confirmation. 'You're right about that, young man. No one knows quite how old it is. A gift from the Lovelidge family, of course, a long time ago. Used to bury every Lovelidge for generations. And everyone else in Walston, since the Lovelidges died out.' He took it out of the drawer and carried it to the ironing board which he'd set up in the corner of the sacristy. 'Got to get the creases out,' he explained unnecessarily. 'It gets creased, sitting in that drawer year in and year out. Can't have a churchwarden buried from this church with a wrinkled pall.'

He worked methodically and with care, David watching. But before the job was done, the sacristy door flew open. 'Don't believe in knocking, eh?' Harry muttered when he saw that it was Enid Bletsoe.

'Isn't the Rector here?' Enid demanded as her companions, Doris Wrightman and Marjorie Talbot-Shaw, crowded into the small room behind her.

Harry raised his eyebrows. 'I thought as your eyes were better than that, Enid. You don't see him, do you?'

'Well, where is he, then?'

'He's not here,' Harry stated. 'Hasn't been here since early Mass, neither.'

'But where is he?' Doris echoed. 'We need to ask him about the flowers.'

Used to being the unquestioned spokesperson, Enid glared at her sister. 'We need to ask him about the flowers,' she repeated as if Doris hadn't spoken, then elaborated. 'If he has anything special in mind for the funeral flowers. It's time to get on with them, and I haven't been able to reach him. He's not answering his phone, and neither is that wife of his. And no one seems to be home at the Rectory – we've just been there, and no one came to the door when we rang the bell.'

'I think that we should just carry on,' Marjorie asserted. 'After all, we've done enough of this sort of thing to know what's appropriate. *I* certainly have, in my years as a rector's wife.'

David debated whether he ought to speak; he didn't want to interfere, but in the end he decided that it might save a fair amount of unnecessary effort to say something now. 'I think, actually, that Mrs Thorncroft is planning to do the flowers herself,' he said, as tactfully as possible. 'She's gone out to get some things now, I believe.'

Enid, who had up to that point managed to ignore his presence in the sacristy, turned her attention to him. 'Mrs Thorncroft! But she doesn't know the first thing about arranging flowers! She'll be wanting our help, of course.'

'Lucy is with her,' David said. 'She's asked Lucy to help.'

'It *is* the privilege of the Rector's wife to do the flowers at times like this,' Marjorie admitted.

'With the help of the ladies of the parish, of course!' Enid amended, frowning. 'And what do you mean, she's gone out to get some things? *Where* has she gone? To the florist's shop in Upper Walston?'

'Actually,' David replied, wishing now that he'd kept his mouth shut, 'they've gone into the country. To collect things from the hedgerows and fields, she said.'

'What!' Enid looked horrified. 'I've never heard of such a thing in my life!'

'Father Thorncroft seemed to think that it would be more appropriate than cut flowers from the florist,' David tried to explain.

'How ridiculous!'

'We'll just have to do our wreaths instead,' Doris intervened. 'From the Mothers' Union, they'll be. Wreaths and crosses. Our own tribute to poor dear Flora, a faithful member of the Mothers' Union.'

'If the Rector spurns our help,' added Marjorie. 'And that wife of his.'

Harry frowned. 'They're not going on my pall,' he warned. 'Them wreaths leave stains on my pall. You can put them at the foot of the coffin, but not on my pall.'

'We'll have to go to Upper Walston for the chrysanths,' said Doris. 'And if they haven't got purple ones there we may have to go even farther. So we'd better get started.'

David could picture all too vividly what the women were proposing to make: purple chrysanthemum heads cut off and poked into polystyrene wreaths, the blooms tightly packed together in an opulent, extravagant display of bad taste.

Doris and Marjorie turned to go, but Enid wasn't quite finished yet. She confronted David yet again. 'Since you seem to be in the Rector's confidence,' she sneered, 'perhaps you might know what he and his wife have planned for the catering. For the funeral lunch. Since poor dear Flora didn't have any family here, I'm assuming that the funeral lunch will be at the Rectory.'

'And we want to help, of course,' Marjorie added in a conciliatory tone.

'*If* we're wanted, that is,' Enid concluded.

Now David really did wish that he'd never started the conversation; he knew that a truthful response would not be popular. The venue of the funeral lunch had been discussed over breakfast, and Becca for once had been adamant: she

142

didn't want to have it at the Rectory. Her reason was simple: the phone caller would be among the mourners, and she didn't want him in her house under any circumstances. Stephen, sympathetic, had agreed that the food could be served at the back of the church instead. People wouldn't like it, Stephen admitted, but it was high time they got used to the idea of change. 'Father Fuller is dead and buried,' Stephen had said. 'And it's about time that Walston accepts that.'

David wasn't going to tell the women about that conversation, but they'd find out the results sooner rather than later. It was better to get it over with now, he decided, and spoke as firmly as possible. 'I believe that it's all under control. The lunch will be here in the church.'

'Food in church!' Harry was as horrified as the women. 'But that's wicked! We wouldn't have had so much as a cup of tea in church in Father Fuller's time!'

Enid's face showed her astonishment. 'Food in church!' she echoed. 'I'm not having anything to do with such a thing!' The expression of astonishment gave way to one of smug cunning as she realised her position. 'She can go down on her knees and beg me, and I shall still say no. Then she'll have to change her mind. She can't manage without our help – we all know that Becca Thorncroft is no cook!'

'She's never even invited Ernest and I for a meal,' Doris interjected ungrammatically. 'And after all that Ernest has done for this church.'

'Perhaps Miss Kingsley will be helping her with the catering as well as the flowers,' suggested Marjorie.

David took a deep breath and plunged ahead. 'Actually, she's asked Mrs English and her friend Miss Sutherland to do the food.'

For a moment it seemed that Enid was at last at a loss for words. Then she exploded. 'Well! Now I've heard everything!' Turning on her heel, she stalked out of the sacristy, followed by her faithful minions.

After lunch, Stephen went to the church to see how the preparations were advancing.

'It's all under control, Father,' Harry assured him. 'That young fellow as is staying with you gave me a hand with the frontal, the candles is all fixed and the pall is pressed and good as new.'

Stephen looked at the high altar and frowned. 'I wish you'd asked me before you changed the frontal, Harry,' he said mildly. 'I don't like black altar hangings for funerals. I much prefer white – the Easter set. That symbolises the Resurrection and eternal life. Flora died in Christ, Harry. We must give thanks for her life, rather than concentrating on her death.'

'White for funerals! Pardon me, Father, but I've never heard of such a thing!' Harry's voice was scornful.

Stephen responded with a conciliatory smile. 'I'm sorry to put you to the trouble, since you've already done it, but I'll be happy to give you a hand to get it changed back.'

The old man frowned. 'It just won't do,' he said stubbornly. 'Black it is, and black it will stay. Father Fuller would turn in his grave at the thought of white altar hangings for a funeral!'

Pressing his lips together, Stephen spoke firmly. 'But Father Fuller isn't the Rector any longer. *I* am. And I want the white set.'

Harry sat down and folded his arms across his chest. 'I'm an old man,' he said. 'And I've worked hard today. Harder than many as is half my age. If you want that frontal changing, Father, you'll have to do it yourself!'

David spent the rest of the afternoon trying to stay out of the way of the various activities which occupied both the Rectory and the church. It was an almost summer-like day, so being out of doors was no hardship; he spent some time exploring the churchyard, deciphering the inscriptions on ancient lichen-encrusted gravestones and admiring the Victorian angels on several of the tomb chests, their marble wings outspread as they watched over the church with eternal vigilance.

Later, when all the people seemed to have gone from the church, and even Harry had been observed to slope off home for a cup of tea, David crept back in through the west door to survey the results of their labours. Becca and Lucy had been busy: the pedestals, overflowing with froths of cow parsley and wild flowers, adorned the chancel, artful and lovely in their innocent artlessness, and tables covered with snowy white cloths stood ready along the west wall. More cow parsley and flowers had been arranged on the tables, and the effect was a pleasing one. The afternoon sun slanted through the west window, irradiating the chancel with light; the white altar hangings and the foamy flowers spoke to David of a kind of divine purity, of hope and resurrection. But at the crossing, in the shadows where the sun didn't reach, huddled a small mound of hideous purple floral wreaths and crosses, like a malevolent cancer in their morbid ugliness. Involuntarily, his eyes went up to the Doom painting: the sheep and the goats. He shivered, as if the sun had gone behind a cloud suddenly, then turned and left the church. In the slanting afternoon light the marble angels who had seemed so friendly a few hours ago, guarding the churchyard, now looked sinister, their smooth faces ambiguous and the shadows of their wings exaggerated and elongated as they fell over the decaying vegetation and crumbling gravestones.

Shortly after David left, Ernest Wrightman crossed the churchyard and went in through the west door. His eyes flicked round the church: it seemed that all was in readiness for tomorrow's events. The bier candlesticks were in place, the flowers had been done and the purple wreaths and crosses were finished, waiting for the coffin. Harry had been busy, and so had a number of other people. Then Ernest noticed the white altar hangings and frowned. What was Harry thinking of? Was he that far past it that he'd forgotten to put up the black hangings?

Or had he just not got around to it yet? 'Harry?' he said enquiringly, but there was no answer.

'Oh, well.' Ernest spoke to himself in the echoing silence of the ancient stone building. 'Nothing to prevent me giving old Harry a helping hand. Won't be the first time I've put up a frontal, and probably won't be the last either.' He went back to the sacristy, hauled out the black frontal from the chest, and carried it to the sanctuary.

It was a difficult job for one man to accomplish on his own, but Ernest took satisfaction in doing it well, and in the feeling of importance it gave him to do Harry's job for him. Before he'd finished, though, a noise in the church alerted him that he wasn't alone. 'Is that you, Harry?' he called.

'No, it's me.' Stephen walked up the aisle into the chancel. 'I've come to say Evensong. And what do you think you're doing?'

'Putting up the black frontal. Harry seems to have forgot.' Ernest tapped his forehead. 'I don't mean to say anything against him, but sometimes I wonder about old Harry.'

'It wasn't Harry,' Stephen said. 'I wanted the white hangings up – to symbolise the Resurrection.'

'Oh, but that's not the way things are done here, Father.' Ernest spoke in a tone that was both pompous and condescending. 'We always have black. Someone should have told you.'

'Harry *did* tell me. I still want the white.' Stephen's smile was courteous, but his voice was firm. 'And as I reminded you once before, I am the Rector here.'

Ernest stopped, gave him a measured look, then turned and deliberately continued putting up the black frontal.

Chapter 20

Thou hast loved to speak all words that may do hurt: O thou false tongue.

Psalm 52:5

The day after the funeral, things had a slow start at the Rectory. Stephen was as always up and about early, going off to church to celebrate the daily Mass, but Becca was in no hurry to get up, waiting until she heard their guests stirring before she went down-stairs to attempt some breakfast.

'Umm, bacon!' David sniffed appreciatively, appearing in the kitchen in his dressing gown. 'You don't know what a treat it is for me to have bacon for breakfast.'

Lucy, coming in behind him, pulled a face of exaggerated pity. 'Poor deprived darling. But I must admit it smells good.'

David ate his breakfast with evident enjoyment. 'Thanks, Becca,' he said. 'The bacon is splendid. I'll patronise this restaurant any time.'

'But I'm such a terrible cook,' Becca protested. 'And Lucy is such a wonderful cook.'

He grinned. 'As long as you don't miss bacon. Which I do, occasionally.' With a sigh he went on, 'Tomorrow it will be back to toast and cereal. I feel like a condemned man eating his last meal.'

'Very funny.' Lucy kicked him under the table and spoke tartly. 'You know the answer to that one, mate. You've got your own house now – if you don't like the catering at my house, you're quite free to make other arrangements.'

'Ouch.' He reached across the table for her hand. 'Literally and metaphorically speaking. You know that's not what I want, love.'

Lucy disengaged her hand. She was feeling somewhat prickly and unsettled that morning, and David's jibes about her vegetarianism had worn a bit thin. Mortified by her reaction, David tried to think of something to say. Neither of them noticed that Becca had gone very quiet.

It wasn't until after David had gone back upstairs to shave and Lucy went to pour herself another cup of coffee that she took a proper look at Becca. Still standing by the cooker, Becca had turned her back to Lucy, but her head drooped and her shoulders were shaking. Lucy went to her instantly and put an arm round

146

her, forgetting everything else in a rush of warm sympathy. 'Becca, love, are you all right? Tell me what's the matter.'

Tears trickled from the corners of Becca's eyes, but she attempted a brave smile as she faced Lucy. 'You're leaving today, then?' she whispered.

'David has to get back to work,' Lucy explained gently. 'He thinks that we've already outstayed our welcome here.'

'Of course you haven't!' There could be no doubt of the sincerity of Becca's words.

'We'll be back, love,' Lucy promised. 'Before too long. And you must come to London to see us as well. David has enough room in his new house to put up the entire village of Walston.'

'But I thought you'd stay until they've caught that … horrible man!' Becca's voice was anguished; she clung to Lucy's arm.

'David says there's nothing more we can do here,' she reiterated. 'And he really does need to get back to his office.'

Becca's head drooped. 'I just wish you didn't have to go,' she gulped. 'You promise you'll come back? Soon?'

'Soon.' Lucy drew her over towards the calendar on the wall. 'Let's look at this, shall we, and find a good weekend?' Studying the calendar, she suddenly gave a yelp of dismay. 'Oh, Lord, that's not really the date today, is it?'

Becca pointed and nodded. 'That's today.'

'Oh, help. It's my father's birthday, and I haven't even sent him a card, let alone a present.' She ran her fingers through her hair in agitation. 'I completely lost track of the days, being away from home like this.'

'You must ring him right now,' Becca urged. 'You can wish him a happy birthday on the phone, and explain what's happened.'

'Thanks. I think I will.' Lucy went to the phone in the hall and dialled her father's number; in a moment he answered.

'Happy birthday, Daddy.'

'Lucy, my dear! How lovely to hear from you.' His voice was warmly sincere, not the least bit reproachful. 'How are you, my dear, and how is David?'

'Oh, we're both well.' Lucy launched into a contrite explanation. 'I'm sorry I haven't sent you anything for your birthday. But we were called away to Norfolk last week, and haven't been able to get back to London yet.'

'Nothing serious, I hope?'

'It's a case of David's. Murder, I'm afraid – pretty serious for the woman who was murdered, as well as for David's client.' Suddenly she remembered Flora's connection with her father. 'Actually, Daddy, I'd met the woman who was murdered, and she told me that she knew you. She was a social worker named Flora Newall.'

'Social worker?' John Kingsley echoed. 'Flora Newall? Oh, yes, I remember. It's been a few years ago, of course. But I remember her as a nice woman. Very conscientious – I had professional dealings with her a few times. She's been murdered?' he realised belatedly, distressed. 'But how dreadful, my dear.'

'Terrible,' she agreed. 'I only met her once or twice, but I quite liked her.'

'Murder – I just can't believe it.'

To take her father's mind off the stark fact of murder, Lucy went on, 'It's quite a coincidence that you knew her. But as a matter of fact, I keep running across people with Shropshire connections, and they all seem to know you. There's another woman here in the parish: Mrs Talbot-Shaw, her name is. Her husband was a clergyman in the Malbury diocese.'

'Oh, yes. Godfrey Talbot-Shaw. I knew him years ago,' John Kingsley recalled. 'He had a parish next to mine for a while, before he moved on to the other end of the diocese. He was a great big tall chap, dark and very serious, and his wife was tiny and blonde and rather silly – Marjorie, she was called. They made a very strange couple – couldn't have been more different from one another.'

'But Marjorie Talbot-Shaw isn't tiny and blonde,' Lucy protested. 'She's tall and dark-haired. And very formidable. You must be thinking of someone else, Daddy.'

He laughed in a gentle, self-mocking way. 'I know I can be a bit absent-minded at times, my dear, but I *do* remember faces quite well – it's a knack that clergymen develop. And I remember Marjorie Talbot-Shaw quite clearly. She was one of those women who never seem to have grown up – Godfrey treated her more like his child than his wife. I didn't mind her, myself, but I remember that your dear mother couldn't abide her. She used to say that no one could really be that naïve and dim.'

At the end of the conversation Lucy put the phone down, frowning in puzzlement. It didn't make sense: a woman could change her hair colour, she accepted, but how could she change her size and her personality?

Stephen came back from the church a few minutes later. 'There's still a fair bit of clearing up that needs to be done,' he said ruefully to Becca. 'Especially from the lunch. You and Lucy did the washing-up, of course, but everything needs to be put away, and the tables taken down. And Harry refuses to have anything to do with it. So that means it's down to us.'

Seeing a way to help, and to delay their departure, Lucy offered assistance. 'David and I can give you a hand,' she proposed. 'We don't have to leave for a bit, do we, darling?'

'As long as I get back to the office by some time this afternoon,' assented David.

Becca hesitated. 'Is anyone else in church? Besides Harry?'

'Enid is around,' Stephen admitted. 'Fiddling with the flowers. And Fred is being the interfering church-warden, helping Harry to shift chairs. Out making a few deliveries, he said, and just thought he'd call into the church to see if Harry needed any help. I'm surprised that Ernest wasn't there as well.'

'But why can't Fred help you with the tables, then?' Becca asked.

'Not a churchwarden's job.' Stephen smiled wryly. He sensed Becca's reluctance to risk another run-in with Enid, who had been curt to the point of rudeness the day before. 'You don't have to come, love. The three of us can manage just fine.'

'You need a nice relaxing hot bubble bath,' Lucy prescribed. 'Go up and take one right now. We'll be back in a bit for coffee.'

Becca didn't require much persuasion. 'Yes, all right,' she assented.

'But keep an ear out for the phone,' Stephen said as they left. 'Gill called by the church to collect her serving dishes, and I told her that you'd brought them home to wash. She said she'd give you a ring later this morning.'

Becca relaxed in the hot bath, idly popping the bubbles and trying to keep her mind blank. It wasn't working very well: Stephen's remark about Gill reminded Becca of the events of the day before. Gill and Lou had worked terribly hard preparing and serving the food, and had been rewarded with out-and-out rudeness on the part of Enid and her cronies. There were mutterings of contamination, and even the word 'poison' had been heard. In fact, Enid had started with the avowed – and loudly declared – intention not to eat anything, but the men had no such compunction, and their enjoyment of the food was so evident that Enid eventually relented. Though Gill and Lou had seemed to take it all in their stride, Becca was embarrassed on behalf of her friends, and wondered how she might make amends to them.

So when the phone rang, Becca was ready with words of commiseration and apology for Gill. Anxious not to miss the call, she hurried out of the bath, grabbed a towel, and rushed for the extension in the bedroom. 'Sorry, Gill,' she gasped breathlessly into the phone. 'You caught me in the bath. I'm dripping all over the bedroom floor.'

There was a brief pause, then a muffled voice chuckled. 'What a charming picture, my dear. Sorry you thought I was your queer friend – I was hoping you were naked just for me.'

'Oh!' Instinctively clutching her towel around her, Becca slammed the phone down without thinking, then collapsed on the bed in tears. When Stephen returned a short while later she was still there, damp and shivering, wailing into the pillow.

'Becca, love!' Terrified, he covered the distance to the bed in a few long strides. 'Whatever is wrong?'

'The phone!' she howled. 'It rang. It was … him. And I ruined it! That policewoman told me to keep him talking as long as I could, but I put the phone down straightaway. I'm sorry, Stephen. I ruined it. But it was so awful – I just couldn't bear it!'

Not long afterwards, Quentin Mansfield drove his Mercedes up the long lane leading to Walston Hall and pulled up in the circular drive in front of the house. Taking his overnight bag from the boot, he let himself in with his key. His wife, descending the stairs, looked surprised. 'Oh – hello, Quentin,' she said uncertainly. 'I wasn't expecting you back quite so early.'

'No traffic at all,' Mansfield explained in a hearty voice. 'I just zipped up the motorway and straight across to Walston.'

'Did you have a good … meeting?' Diana asked dutifully.

'Oh, you know.' He gave a dismissive laugh. 'How was the funeral?' he added. 'I was sorry to have had to miss it. A nuisance that the meeting should have been scheduled for that day.'

'It was all right,' she shrugged. 'Of course I didn't know Miss Newall very well. Sad what happened to her. But they gave her a good send-off. It wasn't just a funeral – it was a proper Requiem Mass.'

Mansfield snorted. 'High church nonsense, in other words. Mincing about with incense and all that rot. And all that airy-fairy music instead of good old-fashioned hymns. "Crimond", that's what's wanted, and "Abide with me". Perhaps it's just as well that I missed it.'

'The music was very good,' Diana said, flushing. 'The choir sang a Latin Requiem.'

Quentin Mansfield lifted a sardonic eyebrow, but before he could comment on the Latin Requiem the doorbell rang. He swung round and opened the door to find two uniformed police officers. 'What can I do for you?' he demanded in his most authoritative voice.

The younger of the two policemen gulped and looked over Mansfield's shoulder, awe-struck at the splendour of Walston Hall. 'So sorry to bother you, sir,' he stammered.

The other policeman produced a warrant card. 'Sergeant John Spring,' he introduced himself, ignoring his companion. 'Are you the gentleman of the house?' he went on in an aggressive voice, designed to show that he was not at all intimidated.

'Quentin Mansfield,' he confirmed, frowning. 'What is this all about, Sergeant?'

Spring chose not to reply directly. 'If you wouldn't mind, Mr Mansfield, we'd like you to come to the station with us and answer a few questions.'

'I'm afraid I *do* mind, Sergeant.' Mansfield cast his mind back over the past couple of hours and the way he had exceeded the speed limit by a rather wide margin, but decided that it wasn't possible that minor infraction could have caught up with him in this way. 'I'm a very busy man, and I've just returned home from a rather tiring trip. If you have anything you'd like to ask me, you can do it right here.'

'Been on a trip, have you?' Sergeant Spring echoed, nodding significantly.

Quentin Mansfield's heart sank; perhaps there *had* been some sort of a speed trap in operation. He'd read about these new methods of photographing number plates, but he'd had no idea that such sophistication had reached rural Norfolk. 'What of it?' he challenged belligerently, his voice still firm.

Spring decided to come to the point. 'We're investigating a phone call made

150

from this house within the past thirty minutes. A phone call of an obscene nature. And we'd like to ask you a few questions about it.'

'An obscene phone call!' Mansfield's face showed utter bafflement. 'From this house? Don't be daft, man!' He laughed and started to shut the door.

Spring intervened with his muscular shoulder. 'Not so fast, sir.'

'You're suggesting that *I* made an obscene phone call?' Quentin Mansfield demanded, suddenly angry. 'Sergeant, I don't find that very funny!'

'Not meant to be funny, sir.' Spring stood his ground. 'And not just one phone call, but a whole lot of them. But this time we've caught you. If you'll just come with us …'

The younger policeman spoke at last. 'Perhaps there's another explanation,' he offered diffidently.

'Such as?' Mansfield challenged.

Cringing, the young policeman continued. 'Is there by any chance another man in the house? A butler or some other servant or even a gardener?'

Mansfield shook his head. 'No one! You've got the wrong house, you fatheads!' He turned for confirmation to his wife, who stood in the shadows, her hand over her mouth and her eyes staring at him in horror. 'Tell him, Diana!' he demanded. 'Tell him that I wasn't here!'

'He wasn't here,' she said faintly from the shadows. 'And there isn't another man in the house. You must have come to the wrong house.'

Spring stepped forward into the entrance hall. For a moment his attention was caught by the woman, who was beautifully dressed and, while not young, was at least well preserved; her body, under the drapey silk garments, looked firm and supple. In his experience, sometimes these older women were the hottest thing going, and for an instant he allowed himself to imagine the feel of the slithery silk between his fingers, imagine what she would look like without her clothes. Under other circumstances he might have been interested in finding out whether her rich husband kept her satisfied, but this was not the time; he turned back to Quentin Mansfield. 'Then you won't mind coming to the station with us while we get this all cleared up,' he asserted. 'And you won't mind telling us where you've been, sir.'

'None of your damn business,' Mansfield exploded as his right fist shot out and caught John Spring neatly on the jaw.

'I didn't know where else to turn.' Diana Mansfield, shaking, had been led to a chair in the Rectory kitchen and provided with black coffee, but she still wasn't making much sense. 'When they took him away, he told me to get him a solicitor. But his solicitor is in London. And then I thought of you. Thank goodness you're still here. You'll come, won't you?'

'Let me get this straight.' David sat beside her, frowning in concentration. 'Your husband has been arrested for making obscene phone calls?' He looked around to make sure that Stephen had taken Becca from the room; Lucy caught his eye and nodded.

Diana didn't notice. 'I don't think so. I think he was arrested for assaulting a police officer. Didn't I say? Quentin hit that policeman – Sergeant Spring, I think he said his name was – so hard that he knocked him to the floor. I think he's in big trouble.'

David covered his mouth with his hand so that Diana wouldn't see his involuntary smile. 'Assaulting a police officer is a serious offence,' he concurred hastily. 'But what about the obscene phone calls? Why did they want to question him about that?'

'They – or at least that Sergeant Spring – insisted that they'd traced a phone call to Walston Hall a bit earlier this morning. But they couldn't have,' she explained in an earnest voice. 'Quentin wasn't at home. He'd just come in not five minutes before the police arrived.'

'You're sure about that?' David exchanged a look with Lucy.

'Positive,' Diana stated. 'I tell you, he couldn't have done it.' She cupped her trembling hands round the coffee mug and stared into its depths. 'They must have made a mistake. The call *couldn't* have come from Walston Hall.'

Chapter 21

That he may bring food out of the earth, and wine that maketh glad the heart of man: and oil to make a cheerful countenance, and bread to strengthen man's heart.

Psalm 104:15

Needless to say, David's plans to return to London were abandoned. He rang his secretary that afternoon, full of abject apologies and promises to come back as soon as was humanly possible.

Before that, though, he went to the police station to bail out Quentin Mansfield. Since he was representing Becca's interests in the matter of the phone calls, David didn't feel that it would be appropriate to get involved with Mansfield's defence against any possible charges stemming from the traced call, and he had told Diana so, without mentioning any names. But she'd been so distraught that at last he'd agreed to represent her husband when it came to the assault charge.

A subdued-looking John Spring, nursing a nastily bruised jaw, greeted him at the station. 'Dave – I suppose I shouldn't be surprised to see you,' he said. 'You've got a finger in everything that goes on in that blasted village, mate. The local blokes don't get a look-in with you around.'

David composed his face to a suitable expression of concern. 'I was really sorry to hear what happened, John.'

'He decked me,' Spring admitted, rubbing his jaw ruefully. 'I'd like to lock the bugger up and throw away the key. But seeing as he's a client of yours, I suppose I'll have to let him out.'

'Once I get him sorted out,' suggested David, 'how about a drink? You haven't had lunch yet, have you? I'll buy you a sandwich and a pint – it seems like the least I can do.'

'Too right.' Spring grimaced. 'It's a deal, Dave. Nether Walston? The Crown and Mitre?'

'It's a deal.'

Once again John Spring waited for David in a booth at the Crown and Mitre; his early arrival meant that he'd already had time to check out the local talent, and he had evidently found it wanting, as his face was buried in his pint when David arrived.

Unusually for him, Spring was subdued, drinking his beer and munching his sandwich in silence. David resolved to draw him out; he wanted to know whether the police had any evidence, or indeed any suspicion, that would link the phone caller and the murder. 'Funny thing, those phone calls,' he remarked conversationally.

Spring acknowledged the statement by looking up at David. 'So you don't reckon that we've got the right bloke, then?'

'I'm afraid not.' David shook his head. 'Quentin Mansfield may be a hot-tempered so-and-so, but he certainly didn't make the call that was traced. His wife's evidence puts him in the clear. He didn't get home until nearly thirty minutes after that call was made.'

The sergeant touched his discoloured jaw with a grimace. 'Hot-tempered is putting in mildly, Dave! No one's ever done that to me before. And you don't think his wife could be lying?' he added. 'I really fancy putting this bloke behind bars for a long time.'

'I don't think so.'

'That's what I was afraid of,' said Spring morosely. 'And to tell you the truth, Dave, the wife's not the only one who puts him in the clear. The constable has been back to the house and had a word with the daily. She says he was away last night and she heard his car in the drive just a few minutes before the police car arrived.'

'Ah.' David looked thoughtful. 'And she wouldn't have any reason to lie, no reason to protect him. Not like a wife might.'

'Which leaves us right back where we started, mate. With two nutcases on the loose in Walston, and us no closer to catching either one of them than we were before. Who'd be a policeman, I ask you?' Spring scratched his head. 'And speaking of the wife, Dave, what do you make of her?'

David deliberately misunderstood him. 'Diana Mansfield seems a very nice woman.'

'And a damn good-looking one,' Spring added with a lascivious grin. 'I wonder if she plays around? She looks the type to me – all proper on the outside and a real tiger in the bedroom. I'd like to find out for myself.'

'She's a respectable married woman, Sergeant,' David reminded him. 'With a husband who packs a pretty powerful punch, I might add.'

Spring groaned. 'You're telling me, mate!'

The publican arrived at the table with David's sandwich, which he delivered without ceremony and which David received without enthusiasm. The bread seemed to have reached its prime of life some days earlier, and the filling, which was meant to be beef, was almost unrecognisable as such, composed as it was of large slabs of unappetising white fat with tiny brown bits in between. 'Almost enough to turn me vegetarian,' he muttered to himself. 'At least there's not too much they could do to cheese.'

'Don't be too sure about that, mate.' Spring grinned, more like himself again now that the stirrings of lust had reasserted themselves, and lifted the corner of his sandwich to reveal shrivelled scrapings of a luridly orange cheddar. He laughed and raised his glass. 'Never mind, Dave. At least the beer is drinkable.'

'No one ever said that we came here for the food,' David admitted.

'Too right.' Reminded of his reasons for patronising the Crown and Mitre, Spring looked around the bar.

Right on cue, as if she were conjured up by his thought processes, the dark-haired girl named Cynth came through the door, dressed quite differently from the last time they'd seen her, in jeans and sweatshirt and with her hair pulled back and bunched together in a pony tail. She spotted them right away and headed for their booth. 'John!'

'Hello, sweetheart.' He gave her a welcoming leer and moved over to make room for her.

She slid in beside him. 'I've been hoping you'd be back,' she said, with a dazzling smile directed at the policeman.

David realised that he was once again surplus to requirements. 'What can I get you to drink?' he offered lamely.

'Just a soft drink,' Cynth grimaced. 'Lemonade and lime will do fine. With ice, ta very much. I'm on my lunch hour,' she explained to John Spring in David's absence. 'Can't drink on my lunch hour or I'll sleep all afternoon. Ta,' she repeated when David returned with her drink, without taking her eyes off Spring.

'What do you do, sweetheart?' the policeman asked.

Cynth favoured him with another smile. 'I work at the agricultural processing plant,' she said. 'Most people in Nether Walston do – there's not much else going.'

'That sounds ... interesting,' David attempted.

She turned to him for the first time. 'Dead boring,' she said succinctly. 'If you want to know the truth, what I do is pluck turkeys. It's horrible – the feathers get everywhere, and it's the very devil getting them all out. But it's a living, and, as I said, about the only one going in Nether Walston.'

Spring whispered in her ear, a suggestion for where he might later look for stray turkey feathers. Cynth giggled. 'Oh, you are naughty.' She fumbled in the pocket of her jeans for a cigarette and held it out for Spring to light.

'Your friend isn't with you today?' David asked, then was immediately sorry; he didn't want either of them to get the idea that he was interested in Lisa.

But Cynth took the question at face value. 'No, Lisa doesn't come to the pub at lunchtime – she goes home to feed her bloody baby. She's no fun at all these days,' she complained, drawing on her cigarette. 'Nothing but bloody Janie, day in and day out. It's all I can do to get her to come out with me in the evening once in a while.'

155

David thought that Lisa's shouldering of responsibility for her baby daughter was admirable. 'Janie's father isn't … around? To help Lisa with the baby?'

Cynth gave a cynical laugh and blew smoke out through her nostrils. 'Fat bloody chance of that.' She lowered her voice to a confidential whisper and leaned across the table towards David. 'To tell you the truth, I don't even know for sure who Janie's father is. I have my suspicions – I wasn't born yesterday, you know – but she won't tell me. Me, her best friend! She won't tell *anyone* - says he'd be in big trouble if people found out. I don't know why she's so bloody keen to protect him after he went and got her in the club like that, then took off.'

'But what about Social Services?' David asked. 'Aren't they involved?'

'Oh, Lisa had herself a bloody interfering social worker all right.' Cynth shrugged, unconcerned. 'But then she went and got herself killed, didn't she? Lisa's in a right state about that, I can tell you.'

Lucy told Becca that, in view of their extended visit, she would prepare the meal that evening. It was no reflection on Becca's cooking, she emphasised, but it was the least she could do; she would enjoy it, she added, and it would give her something to do to feel useful. Becca protested half-heartedly, but in truth her repertoire of vegetarian dishes had been stretched to the limit over the previous week, and she welcomed the break.

'Just relax. Put your feet up and have a cup of tea,' Lucy instructed her in a motherly way, setting off for the village shop. She didn't hold out very high hopes that she would be able to find all of the ingredients she needed to prepare even a moderately interesting meal amongst Fred Purdy's stock but David had not yet returned with the car and until he did the village shop would have to be the extent of her shopping expedition.

She found Marjorie Talbot-Shaw at the counter chatting with Fred while he totalled her purchases. Rather, Marjorie was listening to Fred, who didn't seem to find any difficulty in talking non-stop as he punched the prices out on the old-fashioned till. 'She never let on a thing,' he was saying as Lucy came through the door. 'I don't know how long it's been going on, but you would have thought she might have said something.'

'*I* certainly would have,' Marjorie agreed.

Fred turned to Lucy. 'We were just talking about your friend, young Becca,' he filled her in. 'I suppose you know about the phone calls. Someone's been bothering that poor young girl with nasty calls. The news is all over the village – Quentin Mansfield has been arrested, but his wife says that he didn't do it.'

Lucy nodded tersely, unwilling to discuss Becca's distress with the font of village gossip. 'Yes, I know.'

'Did you just find out, along with the rest of us, or did she tell you before?' Fred questioned her. 'Since you're friends, I mean.'

'I've known for … a while,' Lucy admitted.

156

Fred wasn't going to let this source of firsthand information escape unpumped. 'How is Becca taking it all? Is she very upset?'

'Becca is understandably ... distressed,' Lucy said in a repressive voice.

'Poor little scrap,' pronounced Fred with relish and a totally inappropriate chuckle. 'Did she tell you what he said?'

To Lucy's relief, Marjorie intervened. 'I don't think we really want to know that, Fred,' she stated. 'All I know is that he'd better not try it with *me*. I'd give that nasty pervert something to think about.'

Fred raised his eyebrows and chuckled again. 'I'll bet you would, Marjorie.' He tried to catch Lucy's eye, but she resolutely avoided it, going to the back of the shop to scan the shelves for possible ingredients for supper.

By the time she got back to the Rectory, David had returned with the car. 'How do you fancy a shopping trip?' she greeted him. 'The village shop was a dead loss, though I can't say that I ever had much hope of finding decent bread or even good fresh veg there, let alone some of the exotic ingredients I've got in mind: pine nuts, artichoke hearts or fresh coriander.'

'Hardly a good bet,' David agreed. 'What, pray tell, are we having tonight, then?'

'Carrot and coriander soup, followed by pasta with pine nuts and artichoke hearts with salad and French bread, and tiramisu for pud.'

'I don't think that in my wildest imaginings I would expect Fred Purdy to carry mascarpone cheese,' David laughed. 'Even olive oil would be pushing your luck.'

'No: just a fund of nasty gossip,' Lucy said soberly. 'That seems to be Fred Purdy's main stock.'

They drove to Upper Walston, a thriving market town which far eclipsed its neighbouring village; it boasted a prosperous middle-class population, a well-stocked town centre and even a brand new out-of-town supermarket. After the paucity in the Walston village shop, Lucy enjoyed pushing a trolley up and down the aisles of Tesco and loading it up with goodies the likes of which Fred Purdy had probably never even heard of. The French bread was still warm, and there was coriander growing in little pots and packets of fresh pasta. 'Quorn,' Lucy pointed out with satisfaction. 'If you asked Fred for quorn, he'd probably bring out a stack of tatty old naughty magazines from under the counter.'

'Well-thumbed,' David agreed.

While they shopped, they discussed the events of the day. 'Did you learn anything from Sergeant Spring?' Lucy wanted to know. 'Anything useful, that is?'

'I found out the one thing I was fishing for,' he said with satisfaction. 'The police haven't made the possible connection between the phone calls and the murder. That is to say, John Spring hasn't made the connection,' he amended. 'He's assuming that they're dealing with two separate people.'

'So let me get this straight.' Lucy paused by the cheese counter, her mind not registering what she was looking at. 'We're still assuming that the phone caller is also the murderer.'

'That hypothesis still makes sense.'

'But you don't think that Quentin Mansfield is the phone caller.'

'No.' David picked up a large wedge of Stilton and tossed it into the trolley. 'Even if his wife were lying, which I don't think she is, Spring tells me there's another witness who's provided independent confirmation that he wasn't in the house when the call was made.'

'Who?' Lucy demanded.

'The housekeeper. Or daily, I think he said. Anyway, she's confirmed it.'

'Then he's definitely in the clear. Which means he's not the murderer either. But it doesn't make sense …'

'Slow down a minute, love,' David interrupted, adding, 'Let's go and get some wine.' As he pushed the trolley towards the wine aisle, he went on, 'I really think we ought to go back to London tomorrow. There's nothing more we can do here.'

'Nothing we can do?' Lucy echoed indignantly. 'The thing is, darling, I just don't see how on earth the police are ever going to catch him now. I told you that Spring would manage to throw a spanner in the works somehow, and I was right.'

'How do you reckon that one?'

'Well, thanks to Spring's bungling, and Fred Purdy the town crier spreading the news, now everyone in the village knows about the calls and knows that the police have a tap on the Rectory line. No one in their right mind would make another call now.'

David stopped the trolley and scanned the shelves of wine. 'Claret, do you think?' he asked. 'Or something Italian? Maybe white would be better – Frascati, perhaps.'

'Oh, you're infuriating,' Lucy snapped. 'Aren't you listening to me? The police have blown their only chance to catch the obscene caller, and perhaps their best chance to catch the murderer!'

He turned and gave her his full attention. 'Which is why I'm saying, love, that it's time for us to go home.'

'But that's exactly why we need to stay!' she insisted. 'For Becca's sake, if nothing else. She's put herself through a great deal so that the horrible pervert can be caught. Are we going to tell her now that it's all for nothing? That they'll never catch him now, but she shouldn't worry because he won't be bothering her any more? How do you think she'll feel, living in the village when it's never been cleared up?'

'Calm down, Lucy love.' He put a hand on her arm. 'I can see that it means a lot to you. If it means that much …'

Lucy took a deep breath. 'Oh, it does. To me, and to Becca.'

'Then we'll stay. But I still don't know what we can do.'

She pushed the trolley along a little further, to the shelves of champagne. 'I know what I'm going to do first,' she told him with a small smile. 'I'm going to talk to Diana Mansfield's daily. Tomorrow. Because if Quentin Mansfield wasn't in the house to make that phone call, some other man was, and she's the one who will tell me who it was.' She plucked the most expensive bottle of champagne from the shelf and settled it in the trolley with a gesture of confident triumph. 'And this is what we'll drink to celebrate when we've solved it.'

David shook his head, but his bemused look held admiration. 'I hate to admit it, love,' he said, 'but you just might be on to something.'

Chapter 22

Thou hast set our misdeeds before thee: and our secret sins in the light of thy countenance.

Psalm 90:8

As she traversed the footpath between the church and Walston Hall the next morning, Lucy pondered what she might say to Diana Mansfield. David had pointed out, with some justification, that Diana was scarcely likely to welcome a visit from Lucy with the avowed purpose of questioning her daily, especially when it was a matter of checking up on Diana's story. She would just have to think of something plausible when the time came.

But Lucy was in luck: it was not the mistress of Walston Hall who opened the door to her, but a young woman – little more than a girl, really – in a pinny, with a strangely familiar round face under a corona of golden curls. As the young woman spoke, Lucy tried to think where she might have encountered her before, but couldn't place her. 'I'm sorry,' she said in a voice that bespoke her Walston roots, 'but if you're wanting Mrs Mansfield, she's not here right now.'

'Actually,' Lucy replied with a dazzling smile, 'it was you I wanted to see. If you're not too busy, that is. I won't take up much of your time, but I'd really appreciate the chance of a few words.'

'Me?' The young woman stared at her, baffled. She was wary as well; usually people who wanted to see her were interested in selling something. Curiosity got the better of her; she looked at her watch. 'Actually, I was about to make myself a cup of coffee. Elevenses. Do you want to join me?'

'Very kind,' Lucy murmured, following her through the house to a part she hadn't seen before: the servants' quarters. In its time, during the glory days of the Lovelidge family, the house must have been run by an army of servants, and the size of the servants' hall reflected this. Lucy had a brief, fanciful vision of the room as it must have been a hundred years ago: a beehive of frantic activity, with fresh-faced house-maids in black dresses and frilly white caps scurrying about, and uniformed footmen going about their business, all under the watchful eyes of the much-feared cook and the stern-but-fair butler. Now, though, there was only this one woman in a pinny, her lone coffee mug dwarfed by the vast deal table on which it sat, her footsteps echoing in the enormous room.

'Big, innit?' the woman said cheerfully, switching on the electric kettle. 'And there's masses more rooms, for when the servants used to live in.'

'You don't live in, then?' Lucy asked, though she knew the answer.

'Not me,' she confirmed, shaking her head. 'I've got my little girl to look after. Jessica. I just come in for a few hours a day while she's at school.'

The woman scarcely looked old enough to have a daughter at all, Lucy thought, let alone one of school age, though her figure was mature, wide-hipped and large-breasted under her pinny.

Spooning instant-coffee granules into a spare mug, the daily asked, 'Do you take milk, then, Mrs – Miss …' Her voice tailed off as she looked enquiringly at Lucy's bare ring finger.

'Oh, I'm so sorry, I haven't introduced myself. I'm Lucy Kingsley. Miss, if it makes any difference,' she added with a smile. 'But please call me Lucy.'

The woman nodded. 'I knew who you were, of course – everyone in Walston does by now. I just wasn't sure if you were a Mrs or a Miss. And my name is Sally Purdy, if you didn't know.'

'Sally Purdy!' Lucy tried to keep the surprise out of her voice. 'Then you must be related to Fred Purdy. His daughter-in-law?' she hazarded.

'Daughter,' Sally grinned. 'I'm not married either.'

Lucy realised, then, why the woman looked so familiar: her round face strongly resembled that of her father. Fortunately for her, though, on her it looked much more attractive, and somehow she managed to escape looking like a garden gnome, or even the daughter of one.

While they sipped the hot coffee, Sally filled her in on her story; she proved to be a voluble talker who appreciated a good audience. 'I like this job,' she said. 'It gives me some independence, gets me out of the shop. I live with Dad, up above the shop, me and Jessica. Always have done. When Jessica was only little, I couldn't get out much. I helped Dad out in the shop a bit, of course, and Mum looked after Jessica. I still help him, when I can – so he can get out and make his deliveries. Doesn't have as many of those as he used to, of course, now that people have cars.'

'What about your mother?' Lucy asked. 'I don't think I've ever seen her – does she help in the shop as well?'

A shadow fell over Sally's face. 'Not any more. She used to, of course. For years and years. But Mum is sick now – cancer. She's in a hospice. They don't reckon she'll last much longer.'

'Oh, I'm sorry.' Lucy's quick sympathy was genuine; she had lost her own mother when she was still in her teens. 'That must be rough for you and your father.'

Sally blinked back tears. 'Oh, Dad's coping all right. At least he says so. But it's been going on for quite a while now. Sometimes I think it would be easier if she would just die. It's a terrible thing to say, but …'

'I understand.' Lucy patted her arm awkwardly, establishing a bond between them. 'But losing a mother is never easy.'

'I worry about Dad,' she admitted. 'It takes so much of his time, running back and forth to the hospice, and he's still got to keep the shop going.' She frowned. 'And there's that bloody church, of course. He's not willing to give up any of that churchwarden nonsense, and he's used to spending hours and hours doing anything that no one else wants to do. To hear him talk, the Rector can't even find his way to the loo without asking Dad to show him the way – he relies on Dad for everything.'

Lucy welcomed the change of subject. 'You don't go to church, then?'

'Not bloody likely!' Sally snorted derisively. 'I used to, of course. Every Sunday, all my life. But then I had Jessica. And you would have thought I was the biggest sinner who ever lived, a real slut, instead of just a girl who made a mistake. Doris Wrightman, and Enid Bletsoe, and the bloody Mothers' Union – you would have thought they would have liked to have a young mum around, to add a bit of life. You would have thought they could have given me a bit of help.'

'But they didn't?'

'No chance!' Her voice was bitter. 'Enid Bletsoe told my mum that she should be ashamed, letting her daughter go off and get herself in the club like that. She told her that she was a bad mother. My *mum* – the best mum there ever was, and still is! And after that my mum got sick, and do you think those old cows ever lifted a finger to help her, or to help me and Dad and Jessica?'

Lucy shook her head.

'Too bloody right they didn't! Not then, and not to this day. They don't ever visit her in the hospice, and they don't even talk about her any more – it's as if she's already dead. And they don't do a bloody thing for Dad – they say it's up to me to look after him. After he stood by me in my disgrace – that's what that Enid Bletsoe told me. If that's what the church is all about, I don't want any part of it.' Sally took several deep breaths and made an effort to collect herself. 'Sorry,' she said in a less heated voice. 'That's not what you came for – to hear me let off steam about the church.' She glanced at her watch, signalling the passage of time, then looked up at Lucy. 'What did you want to talk to me about exactly?'

The moment of truth had arrived. Lucy, who had found her talk with Sally illuminating – if not in the areas expected – also had to make an effort to change mental gears. 'It was about yesterday. I understand that the police were here, asking you questions.'

Instantly Sally's face lost its openness. 'Yes?' she confirmed in a neutral voice, ending the single word in an uplift of enquiry that implied 'what is it to you?'.

Lucy tried to make her smile both confiding and confidence-inspiring. 'I'm interested because it was my friend Becca Thorncroft who was on the other end of the phone call. But you know that, I'm sure.'

Sally's expression of unfeigned surprise belied that assumption. 'No, I didn't. The policeman just said that they had traced a phone call to this house. He didn't tell me any more about it. What was the phone call about, then?'

'Let's just say it wasn't very nice. And it wasn't the first one she'd had, either.' Lucy hurried on. 'You said that Mr Mansfield wasn't at home at the time.'

'He wasn't,' Sally stated, defensive. 'I was telling the truth. He didn't get home until just before the police came.'

'I believe you,' Lucy assured her. 'But what I wanted to ask you was if, to your knowledge, there was any other man in the house at the time.'

Sally sat very still for a moment. 'Why do you ask?' she queried warily.

'Because,' Lucy explained, deciding to be honest, 'if Mr Mansfield didn't make that phone call, someone else did.'

'Is there any reason why it couldn't have been Mrs Mansfield?' Sally asked. 'I just figured that it must have been her if it wasn't Mr Mansfield.'

Lucy shook her head. 'It couldn't have been Mrs Mansfield – or you, either,' she added hastily, afraid that Sally might misinterpret her words as an accusation of guilt. 'The call was definitely made by a man.'

'Then I can't explain it,' Sally said, too quickly.

'You're sure there wasn't any other man in the house?'

'Why should there be?' she countered.

Why, indeed? Lucy asked herself. Unless …

Suddenly, with an instantaneous and blinding intuition, a great many little things fell into place. There was the accidental encounter she and Becca had had with Diana Mansfield on the path between the Hall and the church. Diana had been flustered, and had said that she was going to the church to see about the flowers. But the next morning it was Marjorie Talbot-Shaw who had been doing the flowers, not Diana Mansfield. And there was the piano, and Diana's awkwardness about it, and her request that Lucy undertake a commission for a painting 'for a friend' and not tell Quentin. Above all, there was the painting of the proud cavalier. Those flashing, self-confident eyes: now Lucy knew without a doubt whose eyes they resembled. 'Diana Mansfield is having an affair with Cyprian Lawrence,' she blurted aloud even as the thought confirmed itself unshakably in her mind.

Sally Purdy let out a gusty sigh, and her face changed. 'Well, since you know …'

'It's true, isn't it?'

'It's true,' Sally admitted reluctantly. 'Mrs Mansfield thinks that I don't know.' Her mouth twisted in a wry smile. 'That's what she wants to believe, any road. But I'd have to be deaf, dumb and blind to work in this house every day and not know what was going on. The closed doors, the whispers. The way she looks at him, like she wants to eat him up. And who does she think washes the sheets, I ask you?' she finished, grinning, her palms upturned in a gesture of amusement.

Lucy's mind leapt ahead to the next conclusion. 'And he was here that night, wasn't he? While Mr Mansfield was away?'

Sally nodded. 'I didn't see him, of course – they were at least too careful for that. But as I say, I do wash the sheets.'

'So he could have made the phone call …' Lucy thought aloud. 'If he was still in the house …'

'I didn't go upstairs right away yesterday morning,' Sally confirmed. 'He – Mr Lawrence – usually stays over when Mr Mansfield is away, and I like to give him plenty of time to sneak out before I go upstairs.'

'Very discreet,' Lucy approved.

'Oh, but she'd die if she thought I knew!' Sally's face changed again, assumed a worried look, and her volubility returned. 'You won't tell her, will you? I'd hate Mrs Mansfield to think I was talking out of turn. You can see why I couldn't tell the police when they asked me if anyone else was in the house. I couldn't do that to Mrs Mansfield! She's a nice lady, and she's been ever so good to me, giving me things for Jessica – toys that used to belong to her kiddies years ago, and even clothes and things. She's even offered me some of her own clothes, those lovely silk things that she wears, but of course I could never get into them.' She looked down at her ample bosom ruefully, mentally comparing it with Diana Mansfield's sylphlike shape, then continued her litany of praise. 'And she never complains when I'm late, or when Jessica is sick and I can't come. And even him – that Mr Lawrence. I know that Dad hates him, because of him sacking the choir and all, but he's never been anything but nice to me. He even said that he'd give Jessica piano lessons free of charge, but Dad said no.'

Buying her silence, the cynic in Lucy said. Both of them. But she merely nodded reassuringly. 'Don't worry,' she said. 'I won't tell anyone what you've told me.' Or at least no one but David, she added to herself. That didn't count.

She told David as soon as they had a moment alone, doing the washing-up together after lunch, having shooed Becca out of the kitchen.

'Good Lord,' was his response. He stood for a moment in abstracted thought, rubbing the tea towel round and round on the plate until it squeaked. 'Well, love, you were right,' he said at last. 'I admit it, freely and with nothing but admiration. There *was* another man at Walston Hall yesterday morning.'

Lucy inclined her head in modest acknowledgement of her genius.

'But what are you going to do about it?' he queried. 'You've promised that you won't tell the police.'

'I'll tell you what *we're* going to do about it.' Lucy outlined her plan, the only one she'd been able to come up with: she would talk to Diana Mansfield, and David would talk to Cyprian Lawrence. They would see what they could find out, then compare notes later.

She went off to fulfil her part of the plan later that afternoon. This time Diana Mansfield herself came to the door, and professed herself delighted to see Lucy. 'Lucy! What a nice surprise! Would you like some tea?'

'That would be lovely,' Lucy said sincerely; it was exactly what she'd hoped Diana would say.

'Is Becca all right?' Diana asked, finding it odd that Lucy had come on her own.

'Oh, she's just about coping.' That elicited a rather puzzled look, so Lucy elaborated. 'The phone calls, you know.'

'Oh!' Diana stared at her, comprehension coming slowly. 'Oh, I didn't know that it was Becca. The police didn't say. And David wouldn't tell me.'

Lucy tried to laugh it off. 'I thought you knew. I thought that *everyone* in Walston knew by now.'

Diana showed Lucy into the drawing room, then went off to see about the tea. When she returned, she found Lucy standing in front of the portrait of the cavalier. 'Admiring our friend again, I see,' she said with a small laugh.

'He's very handsome,' Lucy agreed. She turned to face Diana and added deliberately, 'Don't you think he's very like Cyprian Lawrence? Especially around the eyes?'

Diana gasped. 'I've never ... I've never seen a resemblance. But perhaps ... You could be right. The eyes ...' Under Lucy's unblinking, knowing gaze she sank onto the sofa, staring back at her with horror.

'He was here that night, wasn't he?' Lucy said gently.

'Oh, God.' Diana covered her face with her hands. 'Who told you? Surely Cyprian didn't tell you. And no one else knows.' Then as another, more horrible, thought occurred to her, she looked at Lucy again and demanded urgently, 'It wasn't Quentin, was it? Oh, God, please don't tell me that Quentin knows!'

'No one told me,' Lucy assured her, going to sit beside her on the sofa. 'I just ... noticed a few things. Like the cavalier's eyes, and the way you looked at the painting.'

'Oh, God.' Diana took a deep, shuddering breath.

Lucy reached for her hand and squeezed it. 'Do you want to tell me about it?' she offered. 'I promise that I'll respect your wish for secrecy, but it might make you feel better to talk about it. And to someone from outside the village.'

Withdrawing her hand, Diana gave her a long, measured look, then got up and poured the tea with hands that were only very slightly shaking. She passed Lucy a cup of tea and sat down in a chair across from her; she seemed to have regained her composure. 'All right,' she said, taking a deep breath. She related her story simply, without emotion and in a calm voice, her eyes only occasionally flickering to the portrait on the wall. 'It started last year, shortly after Cyprian came to Walston. I'd always wanted to play the piano, as I told you, and I asked him to give me some lessons. That was before Quentin retired, and he was always in London during the week. So Cyprian started giving me lessons here, in this room. And one day ... something happened. A spark, I don't know. We ... ended up in bed. It's been going on ever since, whenever we get the chance. It was easy at first – Quentin was never here, and Cyprian could stay the night with no one the

165

wiser. But since Quentin's retired … it's become a bit more difficult. Most of the time it has to be at Cyprian's cottage, during the day, though we've managed a few nights here when Quentin's been away. Like Wednesday.' She allowed herself a half-embarrassed smile. 'And even a few times here during the day, practically under Quentin's nose. I suppose we've been foolish once or twice, but we've never been caught. We're very fortunate in having the footpath between the Hall and the church – I suppose you've realised that it goes right past Cyprian's cottage. We can go back and forth without anyone in the village seeing us. That day, last week, when we met on the footpath … but I suppose you've guessed that,' she said lamely.

Lucy nodded, unwilling to interrupt.

And then came the rationalisations. 'I love him, you see,' Diana explained calmly. 'I know that he's … younger than I am, but I love him. And I need him. Quentin hasn't been interested in me for years. Not in that way, anyway. We haven't shared a bed since … oh, I can't remember, it's been so long. Not that *he's* been celibate,' she added, her voice taking on a note of bitterness for the first time. 'Quentin has always kept a mistress. One of the perks of being a rich, influential businessman, no doubt. We never talk about it, you understand, but I'm sure that he knows I know, and I'm also sure that he isn't particularly bothered that I know, as long as I don't mention it. We've been keeping up this polite fiction for years. All the time I was living here while Quentin was still in London – that suited him very well, I should think. A nice, presentable wife who only had to be seen at weekends, and a young mistress to entertain him for the rest of the week.' She put her teacup into the saucer with a strident rattle. 'That's where he was on Wednesday night, of course – in London with her. He said that it was a business meeting, and of course I let him pretend. He goes off to see her once or twice a month. And what sort of a fool does he take me for? I can smell her on his clothes when he comes home. I don't suppose he cares. Not that I mind,' she added, attempting to be fair. 'It gives me a chance to spend the night with Cyprian.' That brought a smile to her face. 'And that's the best of all. An hour here and an hour there is fine, when that's all you can get, but there's nothing quite like spending the night in the arms of the man you love.'

In spite of herself, and in spite of the fact that she concurred with the last sentiment, Lucy found Diana's frankness somewhat embarrassing. 'But if Quentin has a mistress …' she said, leaving Diana to draw the inference.

'Oh, but you don't understand.' The bitterness was back, evident in Diana's brittle smile. 'It's all very well for Quentin to have a mistress. He's a *man*. But he would go spare if he even suspected that I had someone else. Women aren't *supposed* to enjoy sex, or to want it, especially women of my age. How little he knows,' she added; her smile held contempt mingled with a sort of triumphant reminiscence.

Diana got up and went to stand in front of the portrait, devouring it with her eyes. 'Cyprian is a wonderful lover,' she said softly. 'I had no idea what it could be like, not with Quentin, not for all those years. All those years wasted …' Her voice became so soft that it was almost as if she were talking to herself; Lucy had to strain to hear. 'And now that I've found him … I just couldn't bear to lose him. If someone else … younger … came along, or if he grew tired of me, I couldn't bear it.'

It was Doris Wrightman's turn to entertain her sister to supper that Friday night. There was nothing special about that evening; it was one of many such Friday evenings, with mediocre food eaten in indifferent company, stretching behind them and ahead of them in an unbroken line. If anything distinguished this week from its many fellows, it was the potential rich mine of conversational topics, centring on the week's extraordinary happenings in Walston, replacing their usual exchange of bits of stale gossip. Enid sipped her customary bitter lemon before supper, considering which delicious titbit of conversation she would offer up first.

'It was a lovely funeral, wasn't it?' she said with a sigh.

'Lovely,' agreed Ernest. 'Though not as good as in Father Fuller's time.'

'And serving the food in church – that was a disgrace,' Doris put in, her pencilled eyebrows raised to her hairline. 'Not to mention who prepared it. It's a wonder we didn't all come down with food poisoning, at the very least. Or digitalis poisoning! Just like poor dear Flora!'

'You're forgetting,' Enid reminded her. 'Those women *didn't* poison Flora. Or so everyone is saying now.'

'First I've heard of it.' Ernest frowned. 'I thought they'd given her foxglove leaves instead of tea.'

'Oh, you're way behind the times!' Enid said with a condescending smile. 'Dr McNair told me earlier this week. It was tablets, not foxglove leaves. And I know what that means – I didn't work in a doctor's surgery for all those years for nothing!'

'What?' demanded Doris. 'What does it mean?'

Enid laughed coyly. 'Oh, let's just say that I have an idea or two about it. More to it than meets the eye, at any rate. I don't want to say any more just yet.' She savoured the self-important feeling of knowing more than she was telling – or at least of being able to give that impression. 'I wouldn't want to say any more than that before I have a chance to discuss my theory with Dr McNair. Or the police.'

'Enid, you're horrid,' her sister sulked. 'I think you should tell us.'

'She's just winding you up,' Ernest growled. 'You ought to know that by now. She doesn't know anything more about it than we do.'

'I wouldn't be so sure of that.' Enid looked superior. 'My medical background gives me certain advantages.'

Seeing that she wasn't going to get any further with her sister, Doris changed the subject. 'And what about poor Becca Thorncroft? Fred says that she's very upset about those nasty phone calls. He told me all about it when I went in for the ham this afternoon.' In deference to the warm weather, it was to be a salad supper: flabby slices of ham served with cucumber, wedges of hard greenish tomatoes and limp lettuce leaves.

Enid tried to hide her annoyance that Doris had broached that toothsome topic before she judged that it was time. 'I knew about it *yesterday*,' she said smugly. 'Fred told me all about it, how she's been getting these horrid calls for *months*. And she never said a word to any of us. I just can't understand it.'

'Damn sensible, if you ask me,' muttered Ernest.

'I just don't know what I'd do if someone rang *me* and said nasty things like that!' Doris gave a delicious shudder. 'I'd be so upset. But I'd send Ernest round to sort them out. You'd sort them out, wouldn't you, Ernest?' A husband was the one thing that she had over Enid, and she never missed an opportunity to rub it in.

'He'd tell them they wanted their head examined,' Enid said tartly. 'No one in their right mind would say things like that to *you*, when there's someone like Becca Thorncroft around. Or even that Sally Purdy, and her no better than she should be.'

'Humph.' Doris knew when she'd been bested; once again she changed the subject. 'I think it's time to eat, don't you?' They were already at the kitchen table and the ham salads were prepared, so it was only a matter of transferring the plates from the counter to the table.

'I've been giving some thought to what you said last week, Ernest,' Enid remarked in a conversational tone as she wielded her knife and fork over the ham.

He looked up from his plate. 'What's that, then?'

'About the vacancy for churchwarden.' She paused, then went on impressively, 'I've been giving some thought to standing myself.'

'You?' he said, in a tone that was far from flattering.

'Why not? We've just had a woman warden, even if it only was for a few weeks. I think it's a good thing to have the woman's point of view represented, don't you? Correct me if I'm wrong, but you were the one who wanted Flora, weren't you?' she challenged her brother-in-law.

'But Enid – you re much too busy with the Mothers' Union,' Doris interposed.

'The Mothers' Union is a big commitment,' her sister admitted. 'But now that I'm retired from my job, I have plenty of time to give. Perhaps,' she mused, 'I'll have a word with the Rector about it. See what he thinks.'

'Speaking of the Rector,' said Ernest, 'did I tell you what he said to me about the black frontal? Shocking isn't too strong a word for the way he spoke to me. And my back hadn't been turned five minutes before he changed it back to the white set.'

David and Lucy didn't have a chance to compare notes until much later that night, in the privacy of the guest room.

David told Lucy that he had found the organist in the church practising the organ. 'And I didn't have much trouble getting him to talk.'

'He admitted the affair, then?' Lucy queried, sitting in front of the dressing-table mirror in her dressing gown, brushing her hair.

'Oh, he admitted it, all right.' David gave a little laugh. 'He almost bragged about it, in fact. Sort of a wink, wink, nudge, nudge thing – boys together and all that.'

She wrinkled her nose in distaste. 'That doesn't sound very nice.'

'It *wasn't* very nice, quite frankly.' David took the brush from her hand and began pulling it through her hair tenderly, careful not to tangle the red-gold curls; it was something he loved doing, and she found it both relaxing and sensuous.

Lucy leaned back into the regular strokes. 'You don't think he loves her, then?'

'Love isn't the word,' he told her. 'According to him, she's the one who initiated the affair – threw herself at him, practically raped him, to hear him tell it. Not that he's complaining, mind you. He says that she's great in bed: "insatiable and completely uninhibited" were his words, if I recall.'

'Charming,' Lucy said ironically. 'Whatever happened to gentlemanly discretion?'

'And apparently when it started he was particularly vulnerable. Lonely, at any rate, if not brokenhearted – he'd been left at the altar, virtually, by his fiancée, he told me, and he more or less came to Walston to get away from all of that. Diana Mansfield provided physical relief with no emotional ties.'

'That may be what *he* thinks,' Lucy declared, taking the brush from his hand and turning to him with a frown. 'But she's in love with him, David. Deeply in love. It will kill her if he dumps her.'

'I have the distinct feeling that he's growing tired of her already,' David admitted, troubled. 'He hinted as much.'

'Oh, poor Diana!' Lucy threw herself into his arms with unaccustomed fierceness; catching her mood, he responded and pulled her towards the bed.

Some time later, unable to sleep, Lucy sat up and wrapped her arms around her knees. 'Are you still awake?' she asked gently.

'Mm.' David turned and smiled at her. 'That was nice.'

'Nice isn't the word.'

He stroked her thigh. 'Aren't you sleepy?'

'I can't stop thinking about Cyprian Lawrence,' she admitted. 'He was in the right place at the right time to make that call yesterday. And I'm sure that Diana realises that as well. If you want to know what I think, I think she's terrified that he did it. Remember how she insisted, when she first came to see you yesterday, that the call couldn't possibly have come from Walston Hall?'

'And,' David added, 'he lives in a cottage overlooking the Rectory. Of all people, with the possible exception of Harry Gaze, he had the best opportunity to know when Becca was alone.'

'And if he's getting bored with Diana, maybe he's developed a thing about Becca,' she speculated.

'Or maybe she reminds him of his fiancée and it's his way of getting back at her for dumping him.'

'And he's not very nice,' David concluded. He was quiet for a long moment, so long that Lucy thought he'd fallen asleep. Suddenly he spoke, his voice drowsy. 'But do you know what, Lucy love? Somehow I don't think he did it. In spite of all those things, it just doesn't feel right.'

Lucy sighed. 'No,' she said. 'I don't think he did it either.' She hugged her knees. 'Do you know what I *do* think?' she went on, hesitantly, after a while.

But there was no reply; David's breathing had become deep and regular.

Sighing again, she settled down next to him, pillowing her head on his shoulder, though she knew that sleep was still far away for her. 'Never mind,' she whispered. 'Sleep well, my love.'

Chapter 23

The righteous will consider this, and rejoice: and the mouth of all wickedness shall be stopped.

Psalm 107:42

When Lucy woke the next morning, groggy after a heavy sleep which had come to her very late, she stretched out her arm towards the other side of the bed, yearning instinctively for David's comforting warmth. But her hand encountered only cold emptiness; her eyes flew open in alarm. 'David?' she queried. 'Darling?' There was no reply.

She struggled to sit up, still shaking off the lingering effects of deep sleep. What time was it? The curtains were drawn, offering no hint; she reached for the alarm clock on the bedside table and her hand grazed the edge of a teacup.

David had brought her some tea, she realised. She dipped an exploratory finger into the cup to gauge how long it had been there: it was tepid but not yet cold. Then she saw the note, tucked between the cup and the saucer.

It was written on the back of an envelope in David's neat handwriting. 'Lucy love: You were sleeping so soundly and peacefully that I didn't want to wake you,' she read. 'I'm assuming that things haven't changed, and you're not prepared to go back to London yet. Fair enough – you feel that Becca needs you. But I can't put it off any longer – I'm leaving right now to take care of a few urgent matters at the office and will be back as soon as I can, tonight if possible or tomorrow at the latest. Look after Becca, and I'll see you soon. Love, David. P.S. Last night was wonderful – will you marry me?'

Lucy smiled to herself at the last bit, both in reminiscence and in bemusement that he should choose such a method for his latest proposal. At least it was something different, she thought, realising that it had been some weeks since he had last proposed to her. This note – and last night – provided proof that he hadn't tired of her. As Cyprian Lawrence had tired of Diana Mansfield, or at any rate was sure to do soon. Lucy shivered, aware suddenly of the vulnerability of her nakedness, and fumbled on the floor for her discarded dressing gown.

She had a quick shower and dressed before she went downstairs. Becca was sitting at the kitchen table, still in her dressing gown, looking pale and drawn.

'Good morning,' Becca said, summoning up a smile. 'David's gone. But I suppose you know that.'

'You saw him, then?'

Becca got up and poured Lucy some coffee. 'Yes, I gave him some breakfast. He said that you were still sleeping and he didn't want to wake you.'

'He left me a note.' Lucy drank the coffee gratefully, feeling in need of the caffeine. 'But I wish I'd known he was going – I would have asked him to bring back my sketchbook.' It was something she'd only just realised: art was for her more than her livelihood, it was also her way of dealing with tension and conflict. Assuming that she'd only be away from home for the weekend, she had left all her art materials behind, and was now longing for the familiar feel of a pencil or a paintbrush in her hand. 'And I could have used a few more clothes as well,' she added. 'Everyone must be getting tired of seeing me in the same two Laura Ashley skirts.'

'I don't care what you wear – I'm glad that you're still here,' Becca said, her voice low and intense. She put her elbows on the table and cupped her chin in her hands. 'But he won't be ringing again, will he?'

Lucy knew very well to whom she was referring, but she replied with caution. 'What do you mean?'

'He'd be a fool if he did – even I can see that! Now that everyone knows that the police have a tracer on the line!'

'I think you're right,' Lucy admitted. 'How do you feel about that, Becca?'

'I've been thinking about it, sitting here,' she mused. 'And I'm not sure. Part of me feels relief, knowing that I'll never have to be afraid to pick the phone up again. But the rest of me knows that in some ways it will be even worse, not ever knowing who it was. I've still got to live here in Walston, amongst them all, and one of them is … him. And I'll always wonder who. And maybe sometime later, when all the excitement has died down and the police have given up, it will start all over again – with me, or with someone else. It's a horrible thought.'

'I understand,' Lucy said. 'That's what I told David.' She still hadn't decided whether she would tell Becca the results of her sleepless night: Lucy was almost positive that she knew who the phone caller was. But she had no proof, and there didn't seem to be any way to get any unless he was foolish, or driven, enough to ring again. She'd meant to discuss it with David this morning, to share her suspicions and ask his advice. Now it would have to wait.

'But if …' Becca began; she was interrupted by the chirp of the phone in the hall. Instinctively she tensed, then forced herself to relax. 'It couldn't be,' she said, as much to convince herself as for Lucy's benefit. 'Just see how paranoid this has made me?'

'I'll get it,' Lucy offered on impulse. 'Just in case.'

And just in case, she answered in a whisper. 'Hello?'

'Did you think I'd forgotten you?' the muffled voice said. 'Not a chance of that,

172

my dear. I just had to wait for those guests of yours to leave, and overcome a few … technical problems.'

Lucy took a deep breath; she found, to her surprise, that her hand was suddenly clammy. 'Oh!' she gasped, requiring no effort at all to sound like Becca. Technical problems? she thought with the portion of her mind that remained detached and analytical. What was he talking about? Then, hearing the faint traffic noises in the background, she realised that he was ringing from a public call box.

'They finally left this morning, those guests of yours – I was glad to see their car leaving Walston. Now we can resume our little … chats … my dear. As long as we're careful, that is.'

Careful – to use a call box, presumably. How long would it take the police to trace the call and reach the call box? she wondered. It depended, of course, on where the call box was located. It was up to her, Lucy realised, to keep him on the line for as long as possible, to give the police a fair chance. She looked at her watch to mark the time.

'You're very quiet this morning, my dear. Aren't you glad to hear from me, then?'

'Why don't you just leave me alone?' Lucy moaned.

'Your maidenly reluctance is most becoming,' he said with a chuckle. 'Though we both know you don't mean it.'

The analytical part of her mind registered that chuckle; it confirmed to Lucy that she had been right about the identity of the caller.

'I've got a new fantasy that I want to share with you,' the voice went on. 'I hope you'll like it. This one takes place in church. Your husband is at the altar with his back to the congregation, so he can't see. During the prayers you look at me across the church and I can tell that you want me. You get up and go to the sacristy, telling me with your eyes to follow you. I know that I shouldn't, but I can't help myself. Once we're in the sacristy, you lock the door from the inside. I stand there and watch you as you unbutton your blouse …' On and on the voice went, all the more horrible for its unemotional, matter-of-fact tone; all that was required from her was the occasional moan, and she discovered to her surprise that the moans were not feigned.

Lucy had been prepared to find the call unpleasant; what she wasn't prepared for was the strength of her visceral reaction of nausea and revulsion. Even though the man's filth wasn't really directed at her, she found herself shaking, her flesh creeping in repugnance, and she had to fight the impulse to slam down the receiver. Endure it for Becca, she told herself, her eyes fixed on the dial of her watch. Only a few more minutes.

Before, she had had a great deal of sympathy for Becca in her continuing ordeal; now she suffered with her in a way that went even beyond empathy. It was demeaning, it was abominable, it was worse than obscene. No one should have to put up with such a violation of their personhood. With a great force of will, Lucy channelled her feeling of disgust, of defilement, and turned it to anger.

173

What would he do if she accused him by name? Put down the phone, perhaps, or hang on to find out how she knew. At that moment Lucy knew that it was a chance she had to take: she couldn't bear to listen to another single sickening detail of what this man wanted to do to Becca in the sacristy.

'You ought to be ashamed of yourself, Mr Purdy,' she said scathingly, her voice cutting across his soft tones.

There was a gasp, a sharp intake of breath and an agonising period of silence. 'Who … is this?' he asked at last, cautious.

'Never mind that. The shoe is on the other foot for a change, isn't it, Mr Purdy? I know who you are, and you don't know who I am.' She paused for breath. 'How dare you terrorise a poor young woman like Becca? Don't you realise what you've done to her?'

'I never meant any harm,' he whimpered, then began sobbing. 'I'm sorry. Please don't tell.' His sobs were breathy, pathetic.

'Never meant any harm?' Then, as rapidly as the anger had come, it was gone, transmuted into a profound pity, as she reminded herself that she was talking to a deeply disturbed man. 'Oh, Mr Purdy,' Lucy said, her voice sorrowful. 'Don't you know what you've done?'

'I've been a very bad man,' he sobbed. 'I'm sorry. I couldn't help it. I've been so … frustrated.'

She understood only too well: the sick wife who was neither one thing nor the other, neither dead nor really a wife; the daughter, voluptuous and always around, but not sexually available to him; and the final ingredient in the recipe for disaster, the new Rector's wife, young and innocent and beautiful, the perfect object for sexual obsession. Lucy realised, too, that talking about it was the way to keep him on the line. 'Your wife,' she said. 'She's been ill.'

'For years – nearly five years it's been, since she's been a real wife to me.' His voice now became self-pitying. 'And I've been faithful to her. But I'm a man, with … urges, like any other man. What am I supposed to do?'

Lucy decided not to mention his daughter; that would be touching on a taboo so deep that it might cause him to put the phone down in denial. 'And then Becca came to Walston.'

'It wasn't fair,' he whined. 'Why should the Rector have her all to himself? It just started as … a bit of harmless fun. I just … wanted to know.'

Voyeurism, Lucy thought. Voyeurism, and the need for an essentially weak and powerless man to exercise power, to be in control. That's how it had started, but the charge he'd got from Becca's reaction had rapidly turned it into an obsession, one so strong that it had nearly wrecked a young girl's life and destroyed a marriage.

'Don't you see?' he went on. 'It wasn't meant to hurt anyone. I thought she knew that. I thought she was … playing along with me.'

But he'd known – he must have known – how distressed Becca was. Could he really have convinced himself that she was only play-acting? Was his capacity for self-deception, for self-justification, that great? Lucy reminded herself that he was a sick man.

It was at that moment that another voice was heard: the faint, polite voice of a policeman. 'Sir, if you wouldn't mind coming with me ...' There was a sudden, strangled cry, and then only a dial tone.

The wait seemed interminable, but in reality it wasn't much more than an hour before WPC Karen Stimpson arrived at the Rectory. 'I'm here to let you know,' she told Becca, 'that Mr Alfred Purdy has been taken into custody and is being charged in connection with a series of phone calls made to you over the last several months. I just wanted to tell you in person,' she added, less formally. 'And I wanted to congratulate you for keeping him on the line for so long. We never would have got him otherwise, at a public call box like that.'

Becca gave credit where it was due. 'It wasn't me,' she said, her voice full of admiration. 'It was my friend Lucy. She can tell you all about it. She knew who it was, and she kept him talking.'

Over the past hour a great deal of coffee had been drunk as Lucy had explained to Becca how she'd guessed the identity of the caller, though she hadn't related her insights into Fred Purdy's psychosexual problems. Now the kettle was put back on and Lucy repeated her story to the WPC. 'It was only a little thing,' she explained, 'but it was the key to everything. When I was in the village shop on Thursday, Fred Purdy was discussing the calls, and Quentin Mansfield's arrest, with a customer. He mentioned Becca specifically and said that she'd been upset by the calls. I assumed at the time that the information had come from Diana Mansfield – that she'd found out from the police. But she told me later that she hadn't known that Becca was the recipient of the calls.' She took a sip of coffee. 'And the other person who might have told him was his daughter Sally, who works at Walston Hall. But she told me that the police hadn't told her anything at all about the calls – she didn't even know that there was more than one, or that they were obscene.'

'It was so clever of you,' Becca said admiringly. 'I would never have thought of that.'

Lucy laughed. 'It took me a while, I'm afraid. It wasn't until last night, when I was too keyed up to sleep, that I started putting the pieces together. The other day, when I was talking to David about it, I called Fred the font of village gossip – and last night I suddenly realised how apt that was. He wasn't just passing it on: he was the source of it. And he slipped up by telling other people something that no one but the caller – and the police – knew: the identity of the victim.'

'*You* knew who the victim was,' Karen Stimpson pointed out.

'Yes,' Lucy admitted. 'And I also knew that I hadn't told anyone else, and neither had David. Or Stephen.'

'How *did* he make the call from Walston Hall?' Becca asked suddenly. 'I'd forgotten about that.'

The WPC nodded. 'We asked him about that. It seems he was delivering some groceries there, and asked his daughter if he could use the phone – as Lucy said, she works at Walston Hall, and I'm sure she wouldn't have thought anything of it. Probably didn't even remember it when the constable talked to her.'

Lucy twisted a curl round her finger thoughtfully; she wasn't so sure that Karen Stimpson was right about that. There was one other thing that she'd remembered in the middle of the night and that she couldn't disclose to Becca or the policewoman without betraying a confidence: Sally Purdy's reaction when Lucy had stumbled on the truth about Cyprian Lawrence and his presence in the house on Thursday morning. She had looked … relieved, Lucy analysed in retrospect. She must have realised, once she knew the nature of the phone call and recalled that her father had both been in the house and had used the phone, that he was the guilty party; she had seized on Cyprian Lawrence as a way to deflect Lucy's suspicion. It had worked, if only briefly, and had caused considerable unnecessary heartache to Diana Mansfield, but Lucy knew that she couldn't judge Sally too harshly for shielding her father. In the completely unlikely event that John Kingsley had ever done something culpable, wouldn't Lucy have done the same?

After WPC Stimpson had gone, after Stephen had returned home and the story related yet again, Lucy managed to reach David at his office. 'What's the matter?' he asked, alarmed.

She told him.

'Good Lord,' he said, stunned. 'Fred Purdy! But he always seemed such a … harmless buffoon.'

'Don't forget,' Lucy reminded him, 'you didn't have any trouble picturing him with naughty magazines, when I made that joke about the quorn in the supermarket.'

'I suppose you're right – that should have told me something,' he admitted. 'I suppose I shouldn't be surprised. But how brave of you, love, to hang on till they caught him!'

It was something Lucy didn't really want to dwell on, though she was afraid that the recollection of the way it had made her feel – the creeping of the flesh, the sick sensation of being unclean – would stay with her for a long time. 'Never mind that,' she said briskly. 'But I thought you'd want to know as soon as possible, and I thought you might want to consider whether you need to say something to John Spring.'

'About the possible connection to the murder, you mean.' David sounded thoughtful. 'Yes, I see what you mean. You didn't mention it to the WPC?'

'No. I thought that you might be able to get some … mileage … out of it with Spring. Like you did before, with the tip about the artificial sweeteners.'

'Clever you,' David said with real admiration. 'I'll see what I can do. And I'll be back in Walston as quickly as I can – this evening at the latest. But don't wait supper for me.'

David was as good as his word, arriving at the Rectory just as they were sitting down to supper in the dining room. It promised to be a delicious meal: cooking had seemed a good way to pass the hours until David's return, and Lucy had outdone herself with goat's cheese in filo pastry parcels, accompanied by tiny spring vegetables, delicately steamed.

'I'm glad I didn't miss this,' he said as he joined them at the table. 'It looks wonderful.'

Lucy indicated the empty glasses. 'We were just wondering whether we should break out the bottle of champagne that I bought the other day or if we should save it until after supper. We didn't want to drink it without you.'

'I think you'd better wait until you hear what I've found out,' David said soberly. Three alarmed faces turned towards him. 'Oh, it's not that bad,' he assured them, 'but I'm afraid it's not quite over yet.'

'Tell us,' Lucy insisted.

'Just a sec.' He went to the kitchen, retrieved a bottle of white wine from the fridge, brought it back into the dining room, opened it and poured it out while they waited. 'I rang John Spring from London,' he began, 'and suggested that he might want to talk to Fred Purdy about the murder. I mentioned our theory that Flora Newall had discovered he was making the phone calls and he'd killed her to keep her from talking. Spring was over the moon – he was sure I was right, that there was a connection and that he was on his way to promotion.' He sat down and took a sip of the wine. 'Not bad,' he judged.

'And?' Lucy prompted him.

'I went by the station to see him on my way back. He said that they'd questioned Purdy about the murder and he denied knowing anything about it. The man was terrified, Spring said. He admitted everything about the phone calls, but insisted that he'd had nothing to do with the murder.'

'Well, he would, wouldn't he?' said Stephen.

'Yes,' David agreed. 'But the thing is, Spring believed him. And no one had more at stake in getting a confession out of Fred Purdy than John Spring – no one could have wanted it to be true more fervently than he did. My friend the sergeant isn't best pleased, but he told me that he doesn't think Purdy did it. And I believe him.'

'So that means,' Becca said slowly, articulating the thoughts of all of them, 'that there's still a murderer loose in Walston.'

'I'm afraid so,' David admitted.

'And the police are no closer to catching him than they ever were,' added Lucy with a thoughtful frown.

The meal was characterised by periods of silence as each of them tried to absorb the implications of the day's happenings, punctuated with comments in the form of random observations and questions.

'One thing I don't understand,' mused Stephen, 'is how he always seemed to know when Becca was home alone.'

'I suppose he could see you when you drove past the shop, going out,' David suggested. 'Then he would know you weren't at home.'

Lucy smiled wryly. 'I think there's a bit more to it than that. Didn't you confide in him a great deal as your churchwarden?'

Stephen stared at her for a moment as the truth of her question sank in. 'Of course!' he said. 'I used to go through my diary with him at least once a week and tell him what appointments I had! I started doing it, I suppose, because I was defensive – I wanted him to know that I was working as hard as Father Fuller ever did. Fred said to me one time that he wouldn't blame me if I never went out, if I just skived off home to be with my beautiful new wife. After that I made a point of telling him exactly where I was going, and when.'

'And played right into his hands,' Lucy said ironically.

'But how did you know that?' Stephen queried, baffled.

Lucy gave a short laugh. 'Something his daughter said to me – she said you wouldn't go to the loo without asking Fred the way. On reflection, that didn't sound like you, but I suppose that's the interpretation Fred might put on it, especially if he were trying to impress people with his importance.'

After another silence, Stephen spoke again. 'What I *really* don't understand is why he did it. Why did he make those horrible phone calls? And why did he pick on Becca?' They were rhetorical questions for which he expected no answers.

Lucy knew that Stephen deserved the truth, but she was constrained by Becca's presence; she settled for a watered-down version of a portion of the truth. 'I think he was lonely and mixed up. A man who needed to feel important and in control of his life. It's about power, really – while he was making those calls, he could feel powerful and in control. And his wife has been sick,' she added.

Becca hadn't spoken for a long time; now she looked troubled. The euphoria that she'd felt earlier, the inexpressible relief at the end of a long ordeal, had been replaced by a more reflective mood. 'What will happen to him?' she asked in a low voice.

Misunderstanding the intent of the question, David was heartily reassuring. 'I'm sure he won't be bothering you again, Becca. They probably won't send him to prison, but they'll make sure that he gets treatment for his ... problem.'

'I feel sorry for Fred,' Becca said softly. 'He couldn't help it, I suppose. And I feel guilty as well. I knew his wife was sick, was in the hospice, but since I never met her I didn't ever go to see her. It's partly my own fault what happened. Maybe if I'd been more sensitive, had been a better Rector's wife ...' Her eyes filled with tears.

'Oh, Becca!' Stephen's voice was laden with emotion. 'How good you are! I wanted to kill him for what he'd done to you, and you've forgiven him already.' He went to her and embraced her. 'I love you so much,' he murmured. 'And I don't deserve you.'

'Come on, David darling,' Lucy said quickly, with admirable discretion. 'I think there's some washing-up waiting for us in the kitchen.'

'I stopped in South Ken on my way to the office,' David told Lucy as they tackled the washing-up. 'At home – at your house,' he amended conscientiously, 'I picked up your sketchbook and a few other bits and pieces of your artistic kit – I thought you might like to have it with you. And a few extra clothes.'

'Oh, darling, you read my mind!' Oblivious to the suds on her hands, she put her arms around him. 'How thoughtful of you.'

David savoured the moment, resting his cheek on the top of her head. 'That was before all this happened, of course,' he said. 'Now I suppose we really ought to go, and leave Stephen and Becca to get on with their lives.'

Lucy pulled away with a frown. 'But we still don't know who murdered Flora,' she reminded him.

Sighing, he drew Lucy back against his chest. 'It's not our business, love. And Stephen and Becca don't need us any longer. They need some time on their own.'

She still didn't know why she was so reluctant to return to London. 'One more day,' she insisted. 'Let's stay just one more day, and we can go home tomorrow night.' With sudden inspiration she added, 'I've got my sketchbook now, and I've been dying to make some sketches of those monuments in the church. I can do that tomorrow afternoon.'

'All right,' David agreed. 'One more day.' He kissed the top of her head.

'I've been thinking ...' said Lucy, still in his arms. 'If it wasn't Fred Purdy who killed Flora, it was probably someone else with a secret that she discovered. Maybe a woman. You know poison is a woman's weapon – maybe we've been looking at this all wrong, assuming that it was a man.'

David laughed fondly and hugged her. 'You're incorrigible, love.'

She detached herself from him with frosty dignity. 'You may laugh. But I'm serious, David. Maybe it was a woman.' She plunged her hands back into the hot soapy water. 'What about Marjorie Talbot-Shaw?'

'Marjorie Talbot-Shaw?' David frowned, trying to remember something. 'Oh! While I was home – at your house – I listened to the messages on your answerphone. Most of the messages didn't amount to anything, but there was one from Pat Willoughby. She said she had something she wanted to tell you about Marjorie Talbot-Shaw. She said to ring her back when you had a chance.'

'Why didn't you tell me sooner?' Lucy demanded, indignant.

'I didn't think it was that important.'

'Oh, honestly!' She shook the suds from her hands, dried them quickly on a tea towel, and went into the hall to the telephone. Too impatient to search out a copy of Crockford or a Church of England Yearbook, she rang Directory Enquiries and asked for the listing for the Bishop of Malbury; knowing George Willoughby, she was sure that it wouldn't be ex-directory.

David looked after her, shaking his head in bemusement.

The Honourable Patricia Willoughby, wife of the Bishop of Malbury, was well known for having her finger on the pulse of the diocese. One of her particular interests was the clergy wives of the diocese, whom she treated like the daughters she'd never had. Why, thought Lucy as she dialled Pat's number, hadn't she thought to ask Pat about Marjorie Talbot-Shaw?

It was Bishop George himself, long-time best friend of Canon John Kingsley, who answered. 'Lucy!' he boomed in his hearty voice. 'We haven't seen you in Malbury for months! Why don't you and David come down some weekend soon? You know there's always room for you – both of you – at the Bishop's House. Your father would love to see you, and of course Pat and I would as well.'

'Thanks,' Lucy replied, knowing that the offer was made sincerely, and appreciating its kind intent. 'We'll come soon, I promise. But could I speak to Pat, if it's convenient?'

'I should have known that you didn't want to talk to me,' he grumbled good-naturedly. 'No one ever does, unless they've got a problem. I'll get Pat.'

His wife came on the line a moment later. 'Lucy, my dear! You got my message, then.'

'You said to ring. About Marjorie Talbot-Shaw?'

'That's right.' Pat laughed. 'I saw your father yesterday, and he said that you'd mentioned her. There seemed to be some confusion and I thought I might be able to clear it up.'

'I should have known that you'd be the person to ask,' Lucy said. 'It doesn't make any sense. Daddy described her as small and blonde and rather silly. But the woman I've met who calls herself Marjorie Talbot-Shaw is nothing like that – she's dark-haired and tall and bossy. I know that Daddy can be a bit vague at times,' she added fondly, 'but he was quite definite about it.'

Pat laughed again. 'Your father is quite right,' she said in her customary brisk way. 'And so are you.'

'But how?'

'Quite simple, really. Godfrey Talbot-Shaw's wife Marjorie, the one that your father knew years ago, died some time ago, not long after your dear mother. That's probably why your father didn't know about it, or didn't remember it – he had so much on his own mind at the time.' Pat Willoughby remembered that time very well: she had been a tower of strength for the bewildered widower John Kingsley and his four children, one of them a newborn baby.

'And ...'

'And unlike your father, Godfrey Talbot-Shaw married again, after a suitable period of mourning. A woman as different as could be from his first wife. Except for one thing, my dear.'

'Her name,' Lucy said, deflated.

'Exactly,' Pat chuckled. 'I suppose he liked the name Marjorie. It's as simple as that.'

Chapter 24

How long will ye give wrong judgement: and accept the persons of the ungodly?
Psalm 82:2

The following morning, for the first time since her marriage, indeed almost the first time she could remember, Becca Thorncroft decided to stay at home from church. She couldn't face the curious stares, she declared, in the wake of the sensational events of the past few days. By now everyone would know that Fred Purdy had been arrested and charged with making obscene telephone calls to her, and they would all be looking at her to see how she was taking it. 'Just for today,' she said, looking to her husband for approval.

Stephen concurred with her decision. 'There's no need for you to put yourself through that,' he said. 'People's memories are short, and who knows what may happen by next Sunday to replace it in everyone's mind?' He smiled wryly. 'God knows, I wish *I* didn't have to go! And God only knows what I'm going to say to them in my sermon. I'll have to rely on Him for this one.'

David, too, declared himself unequal to the ordeal, and opted to stay with Becca; he would give her a hand with lunch, he offered.

But curiosity drew Lucy to the service. Someone might just say or do something that would betray a guilty secret, she reasoned. So she sat at the back of the chancel on her own, and observed. She saw no guilty secrets betrayed, but there were a number of other things for her to take in. It wasn't a pretty sight, she admitted later: the jockeying for position, subtle and not-so-subtle, as Ernest Wrightman nabbed the vacant churchwarden's seat and wand; the craning of necks looking for Becca, and the disappointment at her non-appearance; the wagging of tongues before, after and occasionally during the service. No one was really expecting Fred Purdy to show his face though he was known to be out on bail, and no one could claim to have seen him since his arrest. Gill and Lou weren't there either, but they were now old news. Diana Mansfield had come; she sat at her husband's side and didn't once turn her head to look towards the organ. And Stephen preached a sermon which caught them all by surprise.

'Today's theme on this last Sunday of Easter, the Sunday before the Feast of the Ascension, is "Going to the Father",' he began. 'I intended to preach on the

New Testament lesson, that famous and wonderful passage from St Paul's letter to the Romans which tells us that we are "more than conquerors through him who loved us". But I don't believe that we're ready for that message of hope. Instead I'd like to share with you a few words of Our Lord, from the Gospel according to St Matthew.' He opened his Bible and read, '"This people draw nigh to me with their mouth, and honoureth me with their lips; but their heart is far from me ... Not that which goeth into the mouth defileth a man; but that which cometh out of the mouth, this defileth a man ... Do ye not yet understand, that whatsoever entereth in at the mouth goeth into the belly, and is cast out into the draught? But those things which proceed out of the mouth come forth from the heart; and they defile the man. For out of the heart proceed evil thoughts, murders, adulteries, fornication, thefts, false witness, blasphemies." I see you all looking at one another, and thinking perhaps of one or two who are not with us today. But Our Lord also said, " ... why beholdest thou the mote that is in thy brother's eye, but considerest not the beam that is in thine own eye?", and " ... let him who is without sin cast the first stone". Think about what I have read to you, about these words of Our Lord, and search your own hearts before you too readily condemn others. That is all I have to say.' Stephen sat down, leaving a stunned congregation.

'It was brilliant,' Lucy congratulated him over lunch. 'Just the right thing to say.'

Stephen, modest, was unwilling to take the credit. 'They were Our Lord's words, not mine,' he asserted. 'And I don't suppose they were listening anyway. It didn't seem to prevent them carrying on as if nothing had happened, after the service. Enid was giving Ernest a hard time about being so eager to take over as churchwarden, and Doris was needling Enid about the Mothers' Union. And then, of course, there was the fascinating topic of Fred Purdy.'

'Natural enough, really,' said David. 'I don't suppose it's very often that a churchwarden is jailed for making nuisance calls to the Rector's wife.'

'That reminds me.' Stephen turned to Becca. 'Now that, in effect, I'm down two churchwardens instead of one, you'll never guess who came up to me after the service to offer to stand for the vacancy.'

'Not Quentin Mansfield?' Becca hazarded. 'Or Ernest?'

'Enid Bletsoe herself.'

'Seriously?'

'Do you see me smiling?' Stephen shook his head. 'Unfortunately, it's no joke. That's just what I need.'

Becca having been at home, it was an early lunch, and Lucy went off straightaway after the washing-up, armed with her sketchbook, to sketch the Lovelidge monuments in the Lady Chapel of the church. The church was empty, which suited her very well; the ubiquitous Harry Gaze must be home tucking into his lunch, she decided.

Before she began, she examined the monuments again, recalling the day when she and David had first arrived in Walston and Harry had given them his narrated tour. She started with the Sir John who had been Gentleman of the Bedchamber to Charles II, remembering Harry's comments about the three wives named Sarah. 'He must have been wholly fond of that name,' Harry had said. Just like Godfrey Talbot-Shaw and the name Marjorie, Lucy said to herself, smiling ruefully at her own foolishness. She'd been ashamed to tell David of the ridiculous fantasies that her imagination had concocted, all because of that one simple coincidence: sinister imaginings of assumed identities and suspicious deaths. Had the woman known in Walston as Marjorie Talbot-Shaw murdered the real one and taken her name for some fell purpose, or had she just borrowed the name from a tombstone or an obituary to build a new life for herself after some horrible crime? And had Flora Newall, also from Shropshire, discovered the deception and threatened to expose her? Those were the sorts of theories that Lucy had been toying with on the previous day, only to be told that the truth was no more sinister than two wives with the same name. Not even three, like Sir John Lovelidge. At least, she thought, she hadn't disgraced herself by telling David. He often said that she should have been a detective; such a fanciful house of cards scenario would have damaged her credibility for all time.

Lucy moved to the large marble Sir John, with his curly wig and his uncomfortable position, reclining on his side with his head propped on his hand. She read through the list of his virtues, stopping short at the name of his wife: Augusta, daughter of Lord Hollingsworth of the County of Shropshire. She remembered, suddenly, what Enid Bletsoe had said that day, about the monument and various other topics. For a long moment she stared at the inscription, her mind working furiously as various puzzle pieces were reassembled into something that made a terrible sort of sense, albeit with a few pieces missing. Am I being fanciful again? she asked herself severely, but the answer this time seemed quite different.

Back at the Rectory a few minutes later, she went straight to the phone and rang the Bishop's House in Malbury, crossing her fingers that Pat would be in, and that her prodigious network of contacts, if not her astonishing first-hand knowledge, would provide the information that Lucy needed.

She was in luck, at least on the first point; Pat answered straightaway.

'It's Lucy again,' she said. 'I hope it's not a bad time for you. I'm not interrupting your lunch, am I?'

'Just the washing-up,' Pat assured her with a smile that could be heard down the phone. 'And George can carry on doing that by himself, so talk as long as you like.'

Lucy conjured up the entertaining and all-too-believable picture of the Bishop of Malbury in Pat's homely kitchen, purple sleeves rolled up and elbow-deep in suds. 'I've got a little question for you, Pat.'

'Fire away,' said the Bishop's wife.

'I was wondering whether you know Lord Hollingsworth – you must do.'

Pat laughed. 'Lord Hollingsworth! I should say so! I don't think it would be possible to live in Shropshire and not know Lord Hollingsworth. The largest landowner in the county, as he never tires of telling people. And with clout, and an ego, to match. Head of the county set, and as such a force to be reckoned with in the cathedral.'

'And have you ever met his daughter? Charlotte, I believe she's called?' Lucy asked, holding her breath.

'Quite recently, as a matter of fact,' Pat confirmed. 'She's away at university, but was home at Hollingsworth Park during the Easter Vac. And she brought her fiancé to Malbury to meet George. They're being married in the cathedral, needless to say – special licence and the lot – and George is preparing them for marriage. It wouldn't do for the daughter of Lord Hollingsworth to be married by anyone but a bishop,' she added in an ironic tone. 'She would have preferred the Archbishop of Canterbury, but I believe his diary was full. Silly man.'

'What is she like, then?' Lucy queried.

Pat chuckled. 'If you want my honest opinion, which is all you're going to get, she's a spoiled brat as well as being a bit of a bluestocking – a rather unfortunate combination. She brought her fiancé to tea here at the Bishop's House, so I had ample opportunity to watch her in action. Rather a prim little miss, but one who is in no doubt that she'll always get her own way. Lord Hollingsworth's *only* daughter,' she amplified. 'Only child, in fact. The sun rises and sets, as you might imagine.'

'And the fiancé? What is he like?'

'Jamie, his name is. He seemed inoffensive enough,' Pat told her. 'Good-looking, which I suppose is an important consideration for Miss Charlotte, and easily led, which is possibly even more important. She keeps him on a pretty short chain,' she added bluntly. 'I could see that. He knows better than to step out of line.'

'He's not county, then?' Lucy asked, knowing the answer.

'Oh, no – not at all. Rather a nobody, according to Lord H., and an orphan to boot. She met him at Cambridge. I don't think Daddy is particularly enamoured of her choice, but Charlotte wants him and that's all that matters.' Pat paused for breath. 'I hope that's been of some help. I'm not even going to ask you why you wanted to know.'

'One day I'll tell you,' Lucy promised. 'Thanks a million, Pat. You've been a great help.' Thank goodness she'd thought to ask Pat instead of her father, Lucy reflected; John Kingsley could never bring himself to say a bad word about anyone, true or not.

With a sigh of satisfaction, she went searching for David. She found him in the sitting room surrounded by Sunday papers which he was digesting slowly and with indolent enjoyment. He looked up when she came in. 'I thought you were sketching, love. You haven't been gone long – did you get bored? Or couldn't you bear to be away from me any longer?'

184

Lucy didn't waste time replying. 'Where are Becca and Stephen?' she asked.

'Upstairs,' he winked, 'if you understand me. I wouldn't disturb them if I were you.'

'Good. It's you I want to talk to.'

'I'm all yours,' he grinned. 'Especially if you want to go upstairs and do likewise.'

'Listen to me, darling.' For emphasis she crossed the room and plucked the paper from his hands. 'It's about Flora's murder.'

David sighed. 'Still on about that, are you?'

'Yes, I am.' She ignored his put-upon tone. 'Listen. I've been thinking. Earlier, when we were thinking about who might have killed Flora, we talked about motive and we talked about opportunity.'

'Yes?'

'But the one thing we didn't really consider, darling, was the means.'

'Digoxin,' David supplied. 'There isn't much doubt about that.'

Lucy's voice was impatient. 'Yes, darling, but the question is: where did the murderer *get* the digoxin? It's not something you buy over the counter at Boots, you know.'

'That's true,' he acknowledged. 'So where does that lead us?'

'To look for someone with a medical connection, of course,' Lucy stated. 'Someone with knowledge about and access to drugs. And who fits that requirement?'

'Dr McNair?' David said facetiously.

Lucy glared at him. 'Get serious, David! I'm talking about Enid Bletsoe!'

'Enid?'

'She worked for Dr McNair for years,' she reminded him. 'She must have learned a great deal about medicine – and about medications – in that time. And I'm sure she would have run the dispensary as well. So getting the digoxin would have been no problem at all for her.'

'That actually makes sense,' David admitted with some reluctance, beginning to be interested in spite of himself. He sat up from his semireclining position and moved the papers off the sofa to make room for Lucy.

She ignored the sofa, pacing up and down behind it in excitement. 'And that isn't all, darling. Just think about it: who was it who suggested to Dr McNair that they should test for digitalis? Who mentioned digitalis in the first place?'

'Enid,' David said slowly. 'But if she'd done it, why draw attention to it? Why not just let Dr McNair go on thinking that it was a natural heart attack?'

'As a bluff, of course! No one would ever think she'd done it if she'd suggested it. And she thought that she was throwing suspicion on Gill, as well. She hates Gill – that was just plain spiteful, but it also meant that no one would ever suspect *her*.'

He nodded thoughtfully. 'You really might be on to something, love. But we've come back full circle to motive. Apart from the rather thin motive of getting Gill into deep trouble, why would Enid have wanted to kill Flora? I thought that the two of them were in cahoots – having Bryony taken into care and all that.'

'This is the part that doesn't quite hang together yet,' Lucy admitted, sitting down at last. 'But I'll tell you what I've worked out so far. I think that it has something to do with Lord Hollingsworth.'

'Lord Hollingsworth?' he echoed. 'You've lost me, Lucy love.'

'If we go back to the supposition that Flora found out something that the murderer didn't want her to know,' she explained patiently, 'then that would mean that Enid had a secret. And the person she would be most likely to want to keep a secret *from* is Lord Hollingsworth.'

David's brow wrinkled. 'It's coming back to me. Her son was marrying Lord Hollingsworth's daughter?'

'Almost. It's her grandson. Jamie.' Lucy took a deep breath. 'Don't you remember that day at the church? How she kept wittering on about her grandson, and how he'd had a summer job in Nether Walston – or maybe it was her sister who said that. Anyway, the big thing that she wanted to let everyone know was about Jamie marrying Charlotte Hollingsworth.'

'So what does that have to do with Flora?'

'I'm getting to that.' Lucy tried to explain her reasoning. 'It's the biggest thing that's ever happened to Enid, I have no doubt, and she wouldn't want anything to happen to prevent it. *Anything*,' she emphasised.

'And what might happen to prevent it?'

'Well,' she said, 'Lord Hollingsworth might find out something about her, or more likely about her grandson, that would mean he wasn't a suitable husband for his beloved daughter.' She realised that she was getting ahead of herself. 'I've just spoken to Pat about Lord Hollingsworth,' she explained. 'And about his daughter. And the scenario is pretty much as I'd imagined it. He's none too thrilled that his daughter is marrying beneath her, and would probably be delighted if Jamie had somehow blotted his copybook in a way that would dissuade the lovely Charlotte from marrying him. A bit of a bluestocking, Pat said,' Lucy mused thoughtfully. 'What if young Jamie had a misspent youth, or even some youthful indiscretion, and Flora had found out about it?'

David closed his eyes and pressed against them with his fingertips, remaining silent for a long moment. 'Ah,' he murmured. 'Nether Walston.'

'I know there's no proof …' Lucy said uncertainly. 'And no way to get any either, I suppose.' She sighed. 'You'll tell me that I've let my imagination run away with me. I suppose I have. Even if it were true …'

'Good Lord,' David said, almost to himself. His eyes flew open and his voice cut across hers, suddenly decisive. 'Leave it to me,' he stated, getting to his feet. 'Give me a couple of hours.'

David hadn't allowed her to go with him, so to pass the time until his return and to keep out of Becca and Stephen's way, Lucy went back to the church to pursue her aborted plan to sketch the monuments. There was still no sign of Harry, to her relief. She settled down on a chair in the chapel and quickly became engrossed in her labours, dashing off several quick charcoal sketches.

After a while Lucy became aware that she was not alone, sensing a quiet presence behind her. She turned to find Roger Staines looking over her shoulder.

'Please, don't let me disturb you,' he said. 'Carry on. I just couldn't resist looking.'

Embarrassed, Lucy shielded her sketch from view. 'It's not worth looking at,' she demurred. 'Charcoal isn't really my medium. It was just an experiment, really, because I found the monuments so fascinating.'

'But it's marvellous!' the former churchwarden enthused. 'Have you done any others?'

She reluctantly showed him her sketchbook. 'They're just impressionistic sketches, really,' she apologised. 'Nothing polished.'

'But that's what's so good about them,' Roger Staines stated. 'They capture the spirit perfectly without being overworked or twee.'

Lucy smiled. 'Well, I'm pleased that you like them.'

'Honestly, I think they're wonderful.' He paused, deep in thought for a moment, tapping his forehead with his finger. 'You know about my book, I expect,' he said at last. 'My history of the village and the church and the Lovelidge family. I think that a set of your sketches would be just the thing to illustrate the book.'

'Oh, I don't know.' Lucy shook her head modestly.

'Do you mind if I watch you for a bit?' he asked.

'If you like,' Lucy agreed, turning over a fresh page.

'Will it bother you if I talk to you, or would you prefer me to keep quiet?'

Lucy would have preferred him to go away and leave her in peace, but she couldn't very well say so; she decided to be polite rather than honest. 'I don't mind. Talk to me if you like.'

Roger was silent for a few minutes, fascinated by her skill, then he spoke in a reflective voice. 'Actually, I've been wanting to talk to you,' he admitted. 'You're an outsider in Walston, but you know the people involved. And you're intelligent. I wanted your opinion about this murder business.'

Startled, Lucy turned and stared at him. 'What do you mean?'

He gave an embarrassed laugh. 'I've been thinking about it a great deal, you know. But there's no one to talk to about it. I've tried talking to Fergus McNair, but he just tells me to mind my own business. So I thought of you – you must have an opinion, Miss Kingsley.'

Lucy tried to keep the eagerness out of her voice. 'Tell me your thoughts, then. And please do call me Lucy,' she added.

'Well, then. You may think this is a bit far-fetched,' Roger said, sounding apologetic, 'but I was wondering about Fred Purdy. Not because of the phone calls,' he added hastily. 'It has nothing to do with that.'

'Oh! Then why?'

'Because Flora was churchwarden,' he explained, with more confidence. 'And that's a position of considerable power. I don't know how much you've picked up about the politics at St Michael's, Miss … Lucy. But Fred has some very definite ideas about things. I wondered whether Flora might have crossed swords with him along the line during her brief time as warden.'

'For instance?' Lucy queried, keeping an open mind.

Roger rocked back on his heels and put his hands in his pockets. 'Well, for one thing, Fred has it in his mind that we shouldn't pay our Quota.'

'Yes, Stephen did tell us about that.'

'If Flora had opposed him, he might have been angry enough to … eliminate the opposition. I'm not saying that she *did* oppose him,' he added quickly. 'I don't know that for sure. But she was a sensible woman, and she'd spoken to me about it. I explained to her how important it is for us to pay our Quota, and she seemed to take it on board.'

It seemed to Lucy a rather feeble motive for murder, but she nodded for him to continue.

'And there's the business with Ingram's, of course.'

She frowned. 'I don't know anything about that.'

'Ingram's is an agricultural processing outfit on the edge of town. They're only small at the moment, but they've been bought by a multinational company and are looking to expand. It's a fairly complicated matter, involving the churchwardens as trustees of the almshouses. Ingram's need a right-of-way through the grounds of the almshouses or they can't expand. Fred is all in favour – it would be good for the shop, you see. I was dead set against it, of course, so we were at a bit of a stalemate.' He paused. 'You see, don't you? Again, Flora undoubtedly would have taken the same line that I did. She was vegetarian, you know. All other considerations aside, she wouldn't have liked the idea of thousands of poultry carcasses rolling through the gardens of the almshouses. Stephen would know,' he added. 'He's the third trustee.' Roger looked at her expectantly.

'It's possible, I suppose,' she said at last, hating to disappoint him.

'People thought that Flora was a bit of a pushover,' he said, almost as an aside. 'Perhaps because she was relatively new and didn't really know the ropes. And because of her jolly-hockey-sticks manner. But she was intelligent, and a strong-minded woman underneath all that dither.'

Lucy seized upon that assessment; it fitted in very well with her own theory.

But Roger wasn't finished. 'To tell you the truth,' he confided, 'I had another idea about it. You might have heard that Enid Bletsoe was spreading rumours that Gillian English had poisoned *me* with digitalis and caused my heart attack as well as Flora's.'

'I did hear that.'

'Blatant nonsense, of course,' he said robustly. 'Even if she *had* poisoned Flora, she couldn't possibly have poisoned *me*. Gillian English didn't move to Walston until the day of my heart attack! But if it were Fred ...' Again he paused. 'You see what I'm saying, don't you? All the possible reasons that Fred had to want to be rid of Flora – they all applied equally to me. I stood in the way of his plans until my heart attack put me out of action. Then Flora was in the same position.'

'So you're suggesting that Fred *might* have poisoned you as well,' Lucy stated.

Roger gave a cautious nod. 'It's possible.'

'Well.' Lucy looked up at him, weighing his theory. It wasn't just because it had nothing in common with her own carefully constructed scenario that she was doubtful about it; there did seem to be one thing that he hadn't taken into account. 'You've made some valid points,' she acknowledged. 'But Flora was poisoned with digoxin tablets. Where would Fred Purdy have got them? Or known how to use them? Quite frankly, Mr Staines, Fred Purdy has never impressed me as being very bright. Certainly not clever enough to work out a way to substitute digoxin for artificial sweeteners.'

Frowning, pulling on his lower lip, Roger pondered her words. 'Unless he just happened to come across the tablets somehow, and practised on me, then perfected it with Flora.' He shook his head ruefully. 'No, you're right of course. Fred would never have had the brains to carry it off.' He gave an embarrassed laugh. 'Forget everything I just said. I'm afraid that I let my imagination run away with me.'

'I've been guilty of that myself,' Lucy sympathised, with a wry smile.

'Then you *have* thought about it.'

'Quite a lot,' she admitted.

'And have you got any theories that are better than mine?' The irony in his tone was directed at himself rather than her.

Lucy thought briefly about the wisdom of spreading her ideas any further afield than David at this point, but decided that there was no harm in cautiously sounding out a man like Roger Staines. He wouldn't laugh at her, and if there were an obvious flaw in her reasoning he would point it out to her before she made a fool of herself. 'Well, actually,' she said, 'I think that the medical connection points to Enid Bletsoe. Since she worked for so many years at Dr McNair's surgery, she would have had access to digoxin.'

Rocking back and forth on his heels, Roger nodded thoughtfully. 'You have a good point. I hadn't really thought about Enid, but she's certainly spiteful enough. If she had a good motive, I wouldn't put it past her at all. Any thoughts about a motive, then?'

'Well, I never!'

Roger turned, startled, to see Doris Wrightman emerging from the chancel; she had come to the church looking for her husband, and the acoustics of the building meant that she had heard, perfectly, the last exchange.

'How dare you say such things about my sister!' She glared at them accusingly, her hands on her hips and her voice quivering with indignation. 'Calling my sister a murderer! Don't think I'm not going to go and tell Enid about this – right now!'

189

Chapter 25

Whoso privily slandereth his neighbour: him will I destroy.

Psalm 101:6

As David drove the roundabout roads to Nether Walston, his mind was not on his route; several times he took a wrong turning and had to retrace his way. Fragments of conversations, little things to which he'd paid scant attention at the time, floated around in his mind, their significance still tantalisingly out of reach. He wasn't even yet sure what questions he needed to ask, or of whom, but he was fairly certain that Cynth was his best bet as a starting point.

He had little hope of finding Cynth in the Crown and Mitre on a Sunday afternoon, and his pessimism was borne out. As licensing hours drew to a close, the lounge bar was inhabited only by a few elderly hard-bitten drinkers and two younger men who were clearly escaping from the domestic bliss of a long Sunday afternoon in the bosoms of their families. The publican behind the bar looked at David as though he'd never seen him before. 'Too late, mate,' he said in a lugubrious voice. 'I've already called for last orders.'

'That's all right,' said David. 'I wasn't wanting a drink – I was looking for someone. A girl called Cynth,' he amplified. 'I've met her in here before. Could you possibly tell me where she lives?'

The publican shook his head. 'Can't help you there, mate. You don't expect me to know where all my customers live, do you?'

That was patently ridiculous in a village the size of Nether Walston. David turned to appeal to the other inhabitants of the bar, but they all ignored his existence, gazing steadfastly into their pints or engaging in sudden animated conversation with their fellow drinkers: the village closing ranks to protect its own against outsiders, he realised, giving it up as a bad job and leaving the pub.

Out in the road again, David stood for a moment in indecision. Without Cynth, where could he turn? There was only one answer to that, he knew, and one he'd hoped to be able to avoid. He didn't really want to talk to Lisa; he wasn't even sure that he could find her house again, even in tiny Nether Walston. But he would have to try. He frowned to himself, attempting to reconstruct the route they'd taken that night when he'd walked her home. On the other side of the village, it was, and it looked quite different in daylight. He set off tentatively, but there really was only one main road in Nether Walston, and before long he stood in front of the row of terraced modern cottages. Lisa had gone in at the door of the middle one, he remembered – the one with the clean lace curtains at the tiny window.

He hesitated in front of the door, unsure whether he was doing the proper thing, or indeed whether he had any right to intrude in a young girl's life this way. What business was it of his, really? But the instincts that made David a good lawyer reasserted themselves even as he turned to go: the truth, he told himself, was more important than the niceties. He raised his hand and rapped on the flimsy wooden door.

After a moment it opened a crack and Lisa peered out. She was as ethereally lovely as he remembered, and even paler, David thought, in the daylight than she'd been in the fuggy darkness of the Crown and Mitre. He could hear baby noises in the background, and the complex scent that wafted out told of Sunday lunch, overdone beef and cabbage, mingled with the acrid ammonia smell of nappies.

There was a momentary flicker of fear in her grey-blue eyes, replaced almost immediately by recognition. 'The man from the pub,' she said. Her voice was not welcoming, but at least it wasn't hostile.

'David,' he supplied. 'David Middleton-Brown.' He smiled in what he hoped was a non-threatening way. 'Would it be convenient for me to have a word with you, Lisa?'

She looked back over her shoulder. 'Mum's not here,' she said uncertainly. 'She's popped out to see Gran. I don't think Mum would like it, me entertaining gentlemen while she was out. Not ones that I met at the pub, anyway. Mum doesn't like me going to the pub.'

For a moment he thought about giving her his business card, to put it more on the footing of an official visit than entertaining a 'man from the pub', but decided that might frighten her even more. He smiled at Lisa. 'It won't take a minute,' he said, adding, as inspiration struck, 'and I'd really like to see Janie. I've heard so much about her.'

It was the right thing to say; Lisa's face was transformed by a smile of maternal pride. 'Oh, well then.' She opened the door wide to let him in.

The smell was stronger inside, but the house itself was relatively tidy, though extremely small. After passing through a postage-stamp-sized entry hall inhabited by a pushchair, Lisa showed him into a minute living room which was dominated by a playpen. She navigated expertly round the obstructions, though David stubbed his toe on the playpen as he headed for the Dralon sofa. 'Can I get you some tea?' she offered. 'Or would you like to see Janie first?'

David had no feeling at all for babies, having had almost no exposure to them, and could think of few things less appealing than the thought of being presented with one, but he knew he'd let himself in for it and had better get it over with. 'Oh, I'd love to see Janie,' he enthused.

Lisa smiled again. 'I've put her down for a nap, but she's not asleep. I'll get her.'

In the moment while she was gone, he nursed his throbbing toe and assessed his surroundings. The furniture was old and well-worn, though in reasonably good condition for a house with a baby, the carpet a revolting print with garish flowers battling it out for dominance with swirls of violent colour. But the overall impression was of care rather than neglect; the ornaments on the shelf over the electric fire were free of dust, the net curtains, as he had already observed, were clean, and the nauseating carpet showed evidence of recent hoovering. It was, though, a strange setting for a girl with Lisa's delicate beauty, a girl with the face of a Gainsborough portrait.

'Here she is,' announced Lisa from the door, holding Janie in front of her like a treasured offering. She skirted the playpen and thrust the baby into his arms.

'Oh, what a pretty girl!' David exclaimed, hiding his dismay. At least, he thought, she wasn't sticky or smelly. She was, in fact, as those sorts of creatures went, not at all unattractive: she had fat rosy cheeks and curly fair hair and sturdy little legs.

Lisa beamed. 'Isn't she just!'

'How old is she, then?' David asked; he held her gingerly, perched on the edge of the sofa, not sure whether his hands and arms were in the right place to keep her from falling or flopping about.

'She's nearly a year now,' Lisa said. 'She's started walking already. That's why we've got the playpen in here – she's started getting into things. And she's so clever – she can say a few words already, can't you, darling?'

Janie wriggled in his arms; clearly she wanted down. Her mother scooped her up and put her into the playpen. 'Janie want to play, then?' she cooed, dangling a fat teddy in front of her.

'Play!' Janie echoed, seizing the teddy by the ears.

David breathed a quiet sigh of relief and settled back on the sofa. He gave Lisa a few minutes to sit down and grow comfortable with him, chatting about Janie in a way that was calculated to lower the young mother's defences. But though Lisa clearly enjoyed talking about her daughter, she never really relaxed; she seemed fidgety and ill at ease, her attention drawn away from him alternately by the baby in the playpen, the clock on the shelf, and the front door. Worried about her mother's imminent return, David guessed. Perhaps he had better move things along before Mum came back and interrupted.

He knew, instinctively, that he could afford to be circumspect only up to a point; she would not volunteer certain information unless he shocked it out of her. But he built up to it gradually. 'Janie's at such a cute age,' he remarked, watching the mother watching the baby as she systematically tried to destroy her teddy, manually and with her teeth.

'She's more like a real little person than a baby now,' Lisa agreed, smiling fondly at her daughter. 'Even if it does mean that the house is a bit crowded, with the playpen and all. Mum moans about it, but I know she loves Janie. And I tell her that it will get better, when Janie's a bit older.'

'There's no chance of your ... moving out?' David suggested; he watched her and added deliberately, 'For instance, being with Janie's father?'

Lisa's reaction was controlled; only the nervous gesture of tucking her hair behind her ear betrayed anything. 'No, that won't be happening,' she said softly.

David kept his voice soothing. 'Cynth said that Janie's father isn't around any longer,' he remarked.

'Cynth talks too much.' Lisa bit her lip and blinked her eyes rapidly, speaking more sharply than she intended.

He could delay no longer; now was the time to strike. 'Lisa,' he said gently, 'I need to know this – it's important. Believe me, I wouldn't ask you if it weren't. Your baby's father is Jamie Bletsoe, isn't he?'

She gasped as if she'd been struck, staring at David in horror. 'But no one knows!' she choked. 'How did you find out? Who told you? Do you know Jamie, then? Did he tell you?'

'I don't know Jamie,' he assured her. 'And no one told me. I just sort of ... guessed.'

Lisa gulped. 'You mustn't tell anyone – please, Mr ... David. Promise me you won't tell!'

'But why is it so important that no one should know?'

'It's Jamie's gran,' she whispered, as large fat tears ran down her cheeks. 'She mustn't find out. Jamie said that she'd kill him if she ever knew.' She rubbed at the tears with the back of her hand. 'And he said that she'd want to take Janie away from me and raise her herself. He said that she could do it, too – she could say that I was an unfit mother. But I'd *die* if someone took Janie away!' she added passionately. 'So she mustn't find out!'

David leaned forward, careful not to touch her but willing her to look at him. 'Lisa,' he said, 'I'm not the only one to guess about Janie's father, am I?'

Caught by the tone of his voice, she raised her wet eyes to meet his. 'No,' she whispered. 'It was that social worker – Miss Newall. She guessed as well. She'd been on at me to tell her who Janie's father was, so that agency, the CSA she called it, could get some money out of him for child support. I wouldn't tell her – that wouldn't be fair to Jamie. But she guessed.'

'How did she guess?'

Lisa twisted her hands together in her lap. 'It was the name, partly. I called my baby Janie, to remind me of Jamie. It was silly of me, but I thought that no one would figure it out. And she knew his gran too. She told me that his gran's house is full of pictures of Jamie when he was small – and Janie is the spitting image of her daddy.' Her hands fluttered helplessly, like wounded birds. 'I made her promise that she wouldn't tell, that she wouldn't tell Jamie's gran or anyone else.'

'And did she keep that promise?' David held his breath.

Her answer was so quiet that he had to strain to hear. 'I don't know.' The tears were coming faster now. 'I don't know,' she repeated wretchedly. 'She died, didn't she? Right after that, she died.'

Bryony English was bored. Her mother had sent her outside to play, telling her not to come back into the house under any circumstances; she would rather have been inside watching television or reading a book, but Mummy was horrid sometimes and said that she needed fresh air. She skipped desultorily, wishing there were another little girl across the road for her to play with instead of that Mrs Bletsoe. Mummy didn't like Mrs Bletsoe, though Bryony wasn't at all sure why; her own experiences with Mrs Bletsoe had been uniformly pleasant.

So when Mrs Bletsoe appeared outside her house, smiling, Bryony didn't run away. 'Hello, Bryony darling,' said Mrs Bletsoe with a flash of teeth. 'Wouldn't you like some nice choccie biscuits, darling?'

Bryony weighed up her options. She could go back inside, defying Mummy's wishes, or she could go across and eat Mrs Bletsoe's chocolate biscuits, defying Mummy's wishes. As she was going to lose either way, it didn't seem much of a contest. And there was always a chance that Mummy wouldn't find out if she chose the second option, whereas she would most certainly find out about the first. 'Yes, all right,' she said, dropping her skipping rope in the garden. She remembered to look both ways when she crossed the road; it was a pity she wouldn't be able to tell Mummy how good she'd been.

'I feel so sorry for that poor kid,' David told Lucy a bit later. 'She's really had a raw deal – stuck with Jamie Bletsoe's baby and too terrified to tell anyone.'

'While he's off wooing the lovely Charlotte Hollingsworth,' Lucy said bitterly. 'All right for some.'

They had slipped into the church after Evensong in search of a quiet place to talk; this time Lucy was careful to stay in the nave, where they would have ample warning if anyone else entered the church. 'It's pathetic, Lucy love,' David sighed. 'She really loved him, you know. Stars in her eyes, and all that. She was only sixteen when they met. Real Romeo and Juliet stuff.'

'They met when he had that summer job in Nether Walston,' Lucy guessed.

'That's right. At the agricultural processing plant, she told me. Their eyes met over a turkey carcass and it was love at first sight.'

Lucy wrinkled her nose. 'How romantic.'

'Well, it was for them.'

'Does she know about the lovely Charlotte?' Lucy asked.

David shook his head. 'She knows that it's over between them, but she doesn't know the reason why. Apparently he promised to marry her at first, but later on he broke it off.'

'Presumably when the lovely Charlotte came on the scene,' Lucy surmised. 'What an opportunistic little toerag he is! And she's stayed loyal to him all this time in spite of it, refusing to name him as the father of her child.'

'But in all fairness, love,' David pointed out, 'she had her own reasons for keeping quiet. He told her that cock-and-bull story about his grandmother being able to take the baby away from her, and she fell for it. And I think that he probably *did* love her, at one time.'

Lucy frowned. 'Are you defending him? He deserves to be boiled in oil, as far as I'm concerned.' She looked up at the Doom painting, at the everlasting torments visited upon the damned. 'In fact, boiling in oil is too good for him.'

'Oh, no, I wouldn't defend him.' David shook his head hastily, all too aware that it was more than his life was worth to do so. 'He behaved abominably towards her – I'd be the first one to say so.' Still, though, he mused, it wasn't all that surprising that things had happened as they had, given the circumstances. It was almost like a fairy tale, though one without a happy ending: a young man falls in love for the first time, with a stunningly beautiful but poor girl, and nature takes its course. A baby is on the way and he promises to marry her, meaning it, if he can manage to get around his wicked grandmother. But then fate intervenes, putting a spoiled rich girl in his way, and the temptation is too great for him. Exit poor girl and baby, enter – what? 'If there's any justice in the world, and if Charlotte Hollingsworth is as frightful as Pat says she is, then I suspect that Jamie Bletsoe will get his just deserts,' David commented, lifting his eyebrows ironically and following Lucy's gaze up at the Doom painting. 'A lifetime with Charlotte Hollingsworth – that will be worse than any punishment that even you might be able to devise for him.'

Lucy smiled in satisfaction. 'I hope so.'

He rubbed his palms together as though dusting them off. 'Well, that's that then, love.'

'What do you mean, that's that?' she demanded. 'We've now got a case built against Enid Bletsoe: means, opportunity – and motive. In a neat little package. What are we going to do about it?'

David regarded her for a moment with a half-smile. 'Put a bow on it and give it to John Spring. As a leaving gift.'

'But John Spring isn't leaving,' Lucy stated, baffled.

'No, but we are. Have you forgotten?' Moving towards the door, he added, 'Come on, love. It's time to pack. Remember your promise? Back to London tonight, and it's getting late.'

'Supper is ready, lovey.' Gill put her head around the door of the sitting room, where Lou was rereading the business section of one of the Sunday papers. 'Where is Bryony?'

Lou looked up. 'Isn't she with you?'

'No.' Gill frowned. 'I sent her outside to play in the garden, but that was quite a while ago. I just assumed she'd come back in here to watch television.'

'Maybe she's gone up to her room,' Lou suggested.

Gill went to the bottom of the stairs. 'Bryony!' she called. 'It's time for supper, darling!' There was no reply; after a moment Gill went up the stairs.

Lou was waiting at the bottom when she returned. 'Not there?'

Gill shook her head, the beginning of a worried frown between her brows.

'Perhaps she's still outside.' Lou tried to sound reassuring; she went to the door, opened it, and called. 'Bryony! Where are you hiding, you little horror?'

Still there was no reply.

'Where could she have got to?' Gill chewed on her lower lip, the frown deepening.

'You don't suppose …' Lou began. 'Oh, never mind.'

Gill turned to her, demanding, 'What?'

'I just wondered,' Lou said slowly, 'if she might have gone across the road. To see that old bag with the chocolate biscuits.'

'I told her never to speak to Enid Bletsoe,' Gill snapped. 'Bryony wouldn't disobey me by going over there when I'd expressly forbidden it.'

'But if she's not there, angelface, where is she?'

Gill took a deep breath. 'I don't know. Oh, lovey, I'm scared.'

Lou gave her a fierce, protective hug. 'Well, I'm going over there,' she declared. 'If Bryony is there, I'll give that cow a piece of cud to chew on!'

Wasting no time, she stormed across the road to The Pines. The door was ajar; she rapped on it sharply.

There was no reply. 'Hey!' she shouted, hands on her hips. 'Is anyone at home?'

The house was silent. After a moment, Lou pushed the door open and poked her head inside. 'Bryony?' she called. 'Are you here?' Then, as another thought occurred to her, she added in a loud voice, 'You don't have to be afraid to come home, Bryony darling. You won't be punished for disobeying your mother. Just come on home now, darling. We're worried about you.'

Lou could see that the door to the lounge was open. Her certainty that Bryony was hiding somewhere in the house emboldened her to step into the hall, and from there into the lounge. Bryony wasn't there; the only figure visible was that of Enid Bletsoe, lying on the sofa.

'What have you done with Bryony, you miserable old cow?' Lou demanded, not caring that she was waking Enid from her Sunday afternoon nap.

But there was no chance at all that Enid would wake, either then or ever again, and this was soon horribly evident to Lou.

Gill, waiting anxiously at the door of Foxglove Cottage, heard her screaming from across the road.

Chapter 26

For my soul is full of trouble: and my life draweth nigh unto hell.

Psalm 88:2

'Well, it's been very kind of you to put up with us for so long,' David said, stowing their cases in the boot of his car.

'Not at all.' Stephen stepped forward to shake David's hand. 'It's been marvellous of you to give up over a week of your time to help us through a difficult patch. Becca and I will always be enormously grateful to both of you.'

Becca bit her lip and blinked back tears. She had very mixed feelings about their going: she and Stephen had a lot of catching up to do, best done in private, but she would miss Lucy dreadfully. Over the past days she had come to rely on Lucy's strength and wisdom, and to value her friendship.

'We'll be back, Becca love,' Lucy whispered in her ear, embracing her warmly. 'And you'll come to London to see us, won't you?'

'Yes, all right.' Becca nodded. 'And you'll ring me sometime?'

'Of course. And you can ring me any time you want to chat.'

As if summoned by Becca's words, the phone rang in the hall; they could hear its insistent chirp through the open front door. 'I'll get it,' Stephen said. 'I'll just be a minute, I'm sure – don't go until I'm back.'

By the time he returned, David and Lucy were in the car. 'Thanks again for your hospitality,' David said, winding down the window for a final farewell and turning the key in the ignition. Then he saw the look on Stephen's face. 'What's the matter? Who was it on the phone?'

'It was Gill. Enid is dead,' Stephen blurted. 'Lou found her body. And Bryony is missing.'

David switched the ignition off. 'Good Lord,' he said.

It was quickly decided that Lucy should accompany Stephen and Becca to Foxglove Cottage while David went to the police station to see what he could discover about Enid.

They found the road between Foxglove Cottage and The Pines choked with police cars and a mortuary van. Not unexpectedly, they also found Lou in a flat

197

spin, on the edge of hysteria, fluctuating between the twin themes of Bryony's disappearance and the discovery of Enid's lifeless body. 'Where could she be?' she wailed one minute. 'I just don't understand how a little girl could vanish like that!' The next minute she shuddered, 'It was horrible. Her face was all contorted. She looked so awful.'

Gill had managed to maintain, so far, an appearance of tranquillity, if only to keep Lou from going completely out of control. 'Well, she was no oil painting when she was alive,' she said in an attempt at gallows humour.

Lou was horrified. 'That's not funny, angelface! You didn't see her – the way her eyes were staring, and her mouth …' She gulped. 'I mean, I loathed the old bag, but I wouldn't have wished that on her. Not on anybody.'

While Becca and Stephen tried to deal with Lou's incipient hysteria, Lucy made herself useful by brewing a pot of strong tea. She added sugar in liberal quantities to two of the cups, for Gill and Lou.

'Thanks,' said Gill. 'My mother always said that there was nothing like a cup of strong, sweet tea to help you deal with shock. The best medicine going, she always said. And I must confess that it hits the spot – though I've always found cowslip tea to be very efficacious as a tranquilliser.'

Lou gulped hers gratefully, unconcerned that she was burning her tongue. 'Don't you try to come near me with any of that cowslip muck,' she warned. 'I wouldn't drink it for a bet.' She began pacing. 'When are the bloody police going to get here, then?' she fretted. 'It's been ages since I rang them. I suppose they're all over across the road. You'd think that a missing little girl would be more urgent than a dead old lady, wouldn't you?' She grinned suddenly, more like herself for just a moment. 'Though I *did* tell them not to bother to send that dickhead Sergeant Spring. What a bloody waste of space – he's worse than useless.'

A short while later, WPC Karen Stimpson arrived; if she was surprised to find so many people there, she didn't betray it. Recognising Lucy, Becca and Stephen, she greeted them and eliminated them as candidates for mother of the missing girl, but that still left two possibilities. 'Mrs English?' she said, looking impartially between the two and trusting in them to sort it out.

'Yes,' Gill acknowledged. 'I'm Mrs English.'

With Karen Stimpson's arrival, the atmosphere underwent an immediate change; she managed, with her matter-of-fact air of efficiency, to exercise a calming influence. Lou took an instant liking to her, which was a great help. 'Thank God they've had sense enough to send a woman,' Lou declared. 'We've got at least a reasonable chance of success. I hate to think what would happen with some cack-handed man in charge.'

The WPC acknowledged the implied compliment with a smile. 'I'll try not to be too cack-handed.'

'What are you going to do to find Bryony, then?' asked Stephen, the only male present.

'You're sure she's not in the house,' Karen Stimpson addressed Gill.

Lou took it upon herself to answer. 'She's not in the house, and she's not in the garden. We thought she might have wandered off somewhere in the village, but I've done a quick recce and haven't found her. And Gill has rung round to a few of her school friends, but no one has seen her.'

'Well, then.' Karen Stimpson pushed her fingers through her mop of curls. 'If you've exhausted all the immediate possibilities, we'll have to start thinking in terms of – something else.'

'And what exactly does that mean?' Lou asked sharply.

The WPC tried to phrase it to cause as little alarm as possible. 'Well, if Bryony hasn't wandered off under her own steam, we'll have to assume that she's gone off with someone else.'

Lou's expressive hands flew up in the air. 'Kidnapped! Oh, God! You think she's been kidnapped!'

'I didn't say that.' Karen's tone was reassuringly matter-of-fact. 'She might have seen someone she knew and gone with them – a school friend, for instance, or someone else from the village.' She paused. 'But just in case, we'll be putting a tracer on the phone line straightaway.'

'Ransom demands,' Lou wailed. 'Oh, my God!'

'And of course we'll be instituting house-to-house enquiries in the village immediately. Someone in Walston is sure to know something. Don't worry, Mrs English,' she said in her most confident voice. 'We'll find your little girl for you.'

'Thank you,' Gill responded, still calm in spite of, or perhaps because of, Lou's histrionics; the only indication of her inner turmoil was the manner in which she clutched Bryony's discarded skipping rope, hanging on to it like a talisman.

WPC Stimpson found an opportunity to speak to Lucy alone in the kitchen, under the guise of helping to make more tea; in her previous experience with Lucy she had been impressed with the other woman's ability to stay cool under pressure, and decided to take advantage of that quality by enlisting her as an ally. 'I don't want to alarm Mrs English or her friend,' she confided quietly, 'but under the circumstances we have to be prepared for the worst scenario here. In nine cases out of ten these things sort themselves out quickly – the child turns out to have wandered off to see a friend or just loses track of the time. But I don't get the feeling that Bryony is that sort of child.' She paused. 'And as I'm sure you know, Mrs Bletsoe, across the road, has died in – suspicious circumstances. If she's been murdered – well, it occurs to me that it's possible that Bryony was playing outside and saw someone coming or going, and was kidnapped by the murderer to keep her from talking.' She made a rueful face, shaking her head. 'It's not a nice thought – I'd never say it to the little girl's mother. Because if that's what happened, our chances of finding her alive and well are … not so good. I'm sorry to burden you with this, but I wanted to tell you just in case, so that you'll be able to help them through it if need be. You're staying around, are you?'

'Oh, yes,' Lucy promised, alarmed. 'I won't be going anywhere as long as I can be of some use to Gill and Lou. But you don't really think …'

Karen gave her a little pat on the arm and a reassuring smile. 'It's just a possibility, and a remote one at that. But I'll feel better about everything if you're around.'

Not long after that, they all migrated to the kitchen to keep vigil around the silent telephone. Eventually the phone rang; Lou pounced upon it. It was David, wanting a word with Lucy, and she gave him short shrift. 'We can't have you tying up the line,' she said irritably. "Bryony's kidnapper might be trying to get through with a ransom demand.'

'Kidnapper?' he echoed, startled.

Karen Stimpson stepped in, catching Lucy's eye. 'Tell him to ring through on my mobile,' she instructed, supplying the number.

Lucy took the mobile phone through to the sitting room for privacy. 'Things here are dreadful,' she told David when he rang again. 'Lou is practically bouncing off the walls, she's so wound up.'

'How is Gill, then?'

'Calm. *Too* calm by half,' Lucy confided. 'I mean, it's her child who's missing and she's sitting around as though Bryony were in the other room watching television. It's worrying.'

'Stress affects people in different ways,' David reminded her. 'Anyway, love, I've got some news.' He paused for effect. 'It looks as though Enid Bletsoe killed herself.'

'Suicide!'

'Exactly. But guess how she did it?'

'Digoxin,' Lucy said slowly.

'You've got it in one, clever girl. Digoxin,' he amplified, 'dissolved in bitter lemon. Much the same idea as putting it in a gin and tonic, as suggested by my friend Chloe – the quinine in the bitter lemon would hasten the effects of the poison. Would potentiate it, in medical terms. A very efficient way to kill oneself, if not a very pleasant one.'

'Ah.' Lucy exhaled on a long breath, thinking through the implications. 'We were right, then?'

'Oh, yes.' David paused. 'But credit where credit is due, Lucy love. *You* were right. She's left a suicide note,' he added, 'admitting everything. She doesn't say why she did it, of course, but she admits poisoning Flora, and says that she's now ending it all because she's suffering remorse, and because people are beginning to talk about her and suspect her. It would be only a matter of time, she said, before she was caught, and she preferred to end it herself.'

Time ceased to have much meaning for those who waited at Foxglove Cottage, as the minutes stretched into hours and still there was no word of Bryony. WPC Stimpson left to supervise the house-to-house enquiries; her quiet strength was

200

missed. And David joined them, having learned as much as he could about Enid's death. He managed to distract the others, to a certain extent, by imparting what he had found out: that Enid had killed herself, and had also been responsible for Flora's death. But what would ordinarily have been a matter of great interest seemed secondary in the light of Bryony's continued absence. Through it all there was a great deal of tea-drinking, though at one point David said wistfully, 'I don't suppose there's a chance of a whisky, is there?'

Gill got up to go for the bottle, but Lou stopped her with a hand on her shoulder. 'Not now,' she said in a voice that would brook no argument. 'We all need our wits about us.'

It was nearly ten when Karen Stimpson returned, going through to the kitchen to find Gill. 'I have some news,' she said, smiling.

Gill's face lit up. 'You've found Bryony.'

'Well, not exactly. But we do have a lead.'

'Tell us!' Lou demanded, on her feet.

'I've spoken to a Mr Gaze, who lives near the church.'

Lou waved her hand in rapid circles to speed the narrative up. 'Yes, we know who he is. What did he say?'

'He saw a strange car in Walston this afternoon.' Karen watched Gill's face as she spoke. 'It was a red sports car, though he wasn't sure of the make. But he did give us a good description of the driver: a man in his thirties, well dressed in a light grey suit, with short fair hair and a moustache. He thought,' she added, 'that there was a little girl in the passenger seat, but he couldn't swear to it.'

'Adrian,' Gill said softly, moistening her lips with her tongue. 'My ex-husband. Bryony's father. It must be.'

'Adrian!' Lou exploded in a savage shout. 'I told the bastard I would break every bone in his body if he came near Bryony!'

Karen Stimpson smiled, ignoring Lou's outburst. 'We're almost there, then, Mrs English. If your ex-husband has got Bryony, we'll have her back in no time. If you can just give me his address ...'

'But what if he hasn't taken her there?' Lou interrupted. 'What if he's scarpered? Left the country or something?'

'We'll find him,' Karen said with reassuring certainty. 'If he's not at home, we'll circulate his description, and Bryony's, and the car's, to every port and airport in the country. Take my word for it, Mrs English. You'll have your little girl home with you by tomorrow morning.'

'Thank you,' Gill breathed, closing her eyes. It was only then that the effects of the shock caught up with her: she began trembling violently, wracked with gasping sobs. 'Oh, Bryony!' she wept. 'Oh, my little girl!'

And it was only later, when she'd calmed down sufficiently to talk, that she said to Lou, 'When did you speak to Adrian, then? To tell him that you'd break every bone in his body if he tried to see Bryony?'

Lou had the grace to look shamefaced. 'I didn't tell you,' she muttered defensively. 'But it was the day Flora died. Adrian had rung up to talk to you not long before that – remember? So I went to London to see him, to tell him to piss off and stay out of our lives. I didn't tell you because I knew you'd be upset. After all, we agreed never to mention the bastard's name in this house.'

'The day Flora died?' Gill looked at her in wonder. 'But oh – I wish you'd told me! You don't have any idea what terrible things I've imagined about where you were that day, and why you wouldn't tell me!'

Lou's hands fluttered and went to her face. 'I think it's time to get out the whisky,' she said in a very small voice.

Chapter 27

Out of the mouths of very babes and sucklings hast thou ordained strength,
because of thine enemies: that thou mightest still the enemy, and the avenger.
Psalm 8:2

Karen Stimpson was as good as her word: she delivered Bryony back to Foxglove Cottage the next morning. Bryony, though, was withdrawn and subdued, a far cry from her usual sunny self; she endured the tears and fussing, avoided the questions, and at the earliest opportunity slipped upstairs to her room.

Lou went off to her office to work while Gill saw Karen Stimpson to the door. 'I just don't know how to thank you,' Gill said quietly. 'You've been brilliant.'

'Just doing my job, Mrs English.'

'That may be, but you've done your job wonderfully well. And I'm so grateful.'

'You'll probably be seeing me again,' the WPC grinned. 'We'll have to take a statement from Bryony, I'm afraid. I couldn't get much out of her – all she would say was that she'd been playing in the garden and her daddy came along in his car so she went with him. She's probably afraid of being punished,' she analysed. 'We'll give her a bit of time to settle down, then I'll come back and have a word with her.'

Gill went upstairs to see to her daughter, finding Bryony in bed, still dressed, with the covers pulled up to her chin. All her efforts to coax her out of bed were in vain; the girl provided only monotone responses to Gill's questions and refused to leave her bed. 'Just leave me alone, Mummy,' she requested tearfully. 'I want to stay here.'

Reluctantly, Gill complied, going downstairs to make herself a cup of coffee. She sipped the coffee thoughtfully, then went to the phone and rang Fergus McNair. 'I hate to bother you,' she told the doctor, after explaining what had happened. 'But I'm a bit concerned about Bryony. She's been through an unpleasant ordeal, but this extreme reaction really isn't like her.'

'Bring her along, then,' Dr McNair instructed. 'I'll tell the receptionist to squeeze her in.'

'But that's just the problem, Doctor – she won't leave her bed.'

'I'll stop by after morning surgery, then,' he promised, and he, too, was as good as his word.

203

Fergus McNair had had a fair amount of experience in his years of family practice with children who were stroppy or difficult or frightened, not to mention those who were suffering or in pain; in addition he was blessed with a naturally effective bedside manner. But Bryony English failed to respond to any of his usual tricks. He pulled funny faces, he made the tongue depressor vanish up his sleeve, he put the stethoscope to his own chest and listened in mock horror. All of his efforts were met with a blank stare from the child in the bed. She responded obediently enough to his request for her to put her tongue out, and she held the thermometer in her mouth until he removed it, and she answered his questions politely, but she seemed incapable of laughing or even smiling.

Gill hovered around the edge of the room and followed him back downstairs. 'Well, Doctor?' she demanded anxiously.

His reply was succinct. 'There's nothing wrong with the child,' he stated, raising his grizzled eyebrows. 'Nothing that I can measure, at any rate. Temperature normal, heart normal, reflexes normal. Everything as it should be.' Dr McNair gave Gill an appraising look. 'But she's not right in herself, Mrs English. You can see that as well as I can. Something is eating away at that child on the inside.' He tapped his own chest. 'And I can't do anything about that.'

Gill chewed on her lip. 'Then what do you suggest?'

'Let's give her another day or so,' he suggested. 'Then if *you* can't reach her, and she doesn't seem any better, we'll have to give it some further thought. I know a good man in Norwich, and I'll expedite the referral if need be.'

'A psychiatrist?' she whispered, appalled.

He gave her a reassuring pat on the arm. 'Let's not worry about it, my dear. It's likely just the shock, and by tomorrow she'll be right as rain. Try to get her to eat something, and I'll be in touch tomorrow.'

'I'd like to have just one more look round the church before we go,' Lucy said to David in a last-ditch effort to put off for even a few minutes what now seemed inevitable. After all, as he'd told her, all the loose ends had now been tied up, and there was nothing to keep them in Walston any longer: Becca's phone caller had been caught, Flora's murderer had confessed and taken her own life, and Bryony was safely back at Foxglove Cottage.

'Yes, all right,' David agreed. 'I'll put the cases back in the car and we can have a little wander round the church before we say goodbye to Becca and Stephen. Again,' he added wryly.

'I haven't signed the visitors' book,' she realised as they went in through the west door. 'We really ought to leave a record of our visit.' She picked up the biro provided for that purpose and flipped through the last few pages of the visitors' book, reading the entries. 'People really do come here from all over,' she remarked. 'London, Scotland, Norwich, Cornwall. New Zealand, Florida USA, Germany.'

'Well, it *is* a very famous church,' David pointed out. 'And rightly so. The architecture is spectacular.'

'But look at the comments.' Lucy pointed to the right-hand column on the most recent page. 'No one says "spectacular architecture" or "Perpendicular at its best". Not even "love the angel roof". They all say "peaceful". Look, darling – seventy-five per cent of the people who visit this church can't think of anything more original to say about it than "peaceful". I mean, what do they expect? Loud rock music or a motorcycle rally?'

David grinned. 'It shows how little they know about Walston if they think it's peaceful. We could tell them a thing or two, couldn't we, Lucy love?'

'True.' Lucy bent over the book to inscribe their names, then moved slowly down the centre aisle of the nave, her eyes fixed on the chancel arch. Suddenly she stopped, covering her face with her hands.

'Love, what's the matter?' David, frowning in concern, came up behind her.

'Oh, David.' She sat down and raised her face to the Doom painting. 'I feel so awful – so guilty.'

'But whatever for?' David sat beside her and took her hand between both of his. 'You haven't done anything.'

'Enid,' she said in a low voice. 'I feel … responsible for her death.'

'Good Lord!' He stared at her. 'What on earth do you mean?'

Lucy told him then about her conversation in the chapel with Roger Staines, looking not at David, but keeping her eyes fixed on the Doom painting, on those unfortunate souls writhing in the relentless grip of red-eyed devils. She concluded with her imprudent remarks about Enid which Doris had so unfortunately overheard. 'I practically accused Enid of murder,' she said, on the brink of tears. 'And Doris rushed off to tell her. You said the suicide note mentioned that people were beginning to suspect. That was *me*, David! I drove her to suicide!'

'Oh, love!' He held her awkwardly as she wept on his shoulder. 'You couldn't have known,' he murmured. 'You couldn't have known that Doris would hear you, or that Enid would react so drastically. You can't blame yourself, love.'

'But I *do* blame myself! I shouldn't have said the things I did! It was wrong of me, and I can't forgive myself!'

David turned at the sound of the west door opening, fearing that it was Harry. The last thing he needed now, he said to himself, was Harry Gaze, licking his lips in feigned horror over the news about Enid, all the while eagerly anticipating the next funeral at St Michael's. But the figure who entered moved with much less proprietorial assurance than Harry. It was John Spring, looking utterly alien and ill at ease in this setting. 'There you are, Dave,' he said with relief, moving up the aisle towards them. 'The Rector's wife said that I might find you here.'

Lucy lifted a tear-streaked face from David's shoulder, startled at the intrusion, and groped in her skirt pocket for a tissue. David kept a protective arm round her, looking enquiringly at the sergeant. 'John, you're the last person I expected to see here.'

'Never been in here before, mate,' Spring admitted, gazing round the stone walls and up at the angel roof. 'Big, isn't it? And quiet.'

'Peaceful,' David agreed, squeezing Lucy's shoulder. She giggled into the tissue in spite of herself.

Spring gave her a curious look, then followed her eyes up to the Doom painting. 'What's that, then?'

'A medieval wall painting,' explained David. 'The Last Judgment. God the Father at the top, with the Son and the Spirit. The righteous souls going to heaven on the right, and the damned going the other way on the left.'

'But some of those people don't have any clothes on!' Spring realised with relish. 'I had no idea that those medieval people painted racy things like that, Dave! And in church, too!'

'You'd be surprised.' David raised his eyebrows. 'But I don't suppose you've come here for a lecture about medieval church art.'

John Spring grinned. 'Right you are, Dave. Like I said, the Rector's wife told me to look for you here. She's a lovely little thing, isn't she? Looks familiar to me, as well.'

David rolled his eyes, prompting Spring to continue. 'But I digress. I found out something this morning that I thought you'd be interested in, and as you've been so … cooperative with my investigations, I wanted to let you know right away.'

'You just caught us,' David said. 'We're on our way back home to London in a few minutes. What is it, then?'

Spring stroked his moustache uncomfortably. 'That Mrs Bletsoe. You know I told you last night that she topped herself?'

David nodded. 'And you told me what was in the suicide note.'

'I was wrong, mate.' Spring pulled a doleful face. 'I thought it was in the bag. All nice and tidy. Mark the Newall case closed, and maybe a promotion for me out of it. But I was wrong.'

'What!' David half rose from his chair, and even Lucy turned to stare at Spring.

'I was wrong,' he repeated, seeming to take some perverse comfort from the phrase. 'Enid Bletsoe didn't top herself – she was murdered, just like Flora Newall. And whoever did it went to a lot of trouble to make it look like suicide – faked the note and everything.'

'But how do you know it was faked?' David demanded. 'How do you know that it was murder?'

Spring crossed his arms across his chest. 'The murderer made one little mistake. He would have got away with it, mate, and us none the wiser, except for one little thing. He wiped the glass clean. Didn't want to leave his own prints, and can't blame him for that, but there were no prints at all. And Mrs Bletsoe wasn't wearing gloves. So that adds up to murder. She sure as hell didn't drink that poisoned bitter lemon through a straw!' he added with a glimmer of a smile.

'Good Lord.' David sat down again, his hand absent-mindedly stroking Lucy's hair. 'Well, I'll be blowed,' he said, almost to himself.

Lucy sighed, her mind a jumble of conflicting thoughts and emotions. The cause for her own feelings of guilt had been removed, but it opened up a whole new set of problems, or rather reopened old ones. For if Enid hadn't killed herself, it meant that the murderer was still on the loose in Walston. And he now had not one but two deaths to his credit.

When they got back to the Rectory, Becca met them at the door. 'Did that policeman find you?'

'Yes,' David nodded. 'Thanks.'

'And you've had a phone call, Lucy.' Becca frowned. 'From Gill. It sounded important – she asked if you could ring her back as soon as possible.'

Lucy complied, and a moment later joined David and Becca in the kitchen, looking troubled. 'Gill wondered if I might come over,' she told them. 'She's worried about Bryony – she won't eat anything and she doesn't want to get out of bed. She thought I might be able to do something with her since she's seemed to take to me. Gill said maybe if I were to read her a story, or bring her something tempting to eat ...'

'How about chocolate biscuits?' Becca suggested. 'She's got a weakness for chocolate biscuits, and Gill never keeps any in the house.' Glad that she could do something practical, Becca went to her pantry and came back with an unopened packet. 'Here. See if these will tempt her.'

Lucy wasted no time, going straight to Foxglove Cottage; Gill met her at the door and ushered her upstairs to Bryony's room, then crept away to leave them alone together.

'Hello, Bryony,' Lucy said softly. 'I'm so glad that you're home safe and sound, and I thought I'd like to read you a story.'

Bryony assented in a listless voice. 'All right.'

'One of your favourite fairy tales, then?' Lucy selected a book from the girl's well-stocked bookcase and settled down by the bed. 'You liked this one, I remember. It's the one about the beautiful miller's daughter and the wicked little man, Rumpelstiltskin.'

'No, not that one,' Bryony muttered, tears trickling out of the corners of her eyes. 'I don't want the one about the wicked man.'

'All right, then. How about *The Three Little Pigs*?'

Lucy read the story well, with appropriate voices and sound effects, but Bryony listened indifferently, her eyes closed. 'Do you want another story, then?' Lucy offered when she'd finished.

'It doesn't matter.'

Well, how about showing me your dolls, then? You promised you'd let me play with your Barbie,' Lucy tempted her.

'No.' Bryony's mouth was set in a stubborn line. 'I'm not getting up. Not now, and not ever.'

'But you're missing school,' Lucy pointed out. 'One day doesn't matter too much, but tomorrow …'

'No!' The little girl turned her face into her pillow. 'I'm not going outside! The horrible man will get me!'

Lucy wasn't surprised that she felt such strong negative feelings about her father, under the circumstances; she judged that it was time to distract her with chocolate biscuits. 'Look, Bryony,' she said sweetly, producing the packet of biscuits and putting them on the bed. 'Look what Becca sent to you. Some lovely chocolate biscuits – your favourite sort!'

'No!' Bryony shrieked, grabbed the biscuits and flung the packet across the room. 'Take them away! And leave me alone!'

'It didn't go very well,' Lucy admitted to Gill downstairs. 'She let me read her a story, but she got upset when I suggested that she might get up, and very agitated indeed when I offered her chocolate biscuits.' Ruefully she extended her hand with the smashed packet. 'I'm sorry, Gill. I don't seem to have helped much.'

'Do you have time for a cup of tea?' Gill looked at her beseechingly.

'Of course.'

They settled down in the kitchen with the pot of tea between them. 'What about Lou?' Lucy said in a way that was open to interpretation.

'She's working in her office.' Gill looked down into her tea. 'To tell you the truth, Lucy, Lou isn't being much help. She says that Bryony is just putting it all on, playing up to get attention. She says that if we ignore her she'll snap out of it. But I think that Lou can't cope – I think she's denying that there's a problem because she doesn't want to deal with it.'

'And what *is* the problem?' Lucy invited.

Gill shook her head. 'Where do I begin?'

'At the beginning?'

'You're sure you don't mind?' she said wistfully. 'Only I really don't know what to do.'

'If you can't talk to Lou,' Lucy pointed out, 'you've got to talk to someone. Tell me what's bothering you.'

Gill gave a weary sigh. 'It's a long story,' she warned.

'I'm not going anywhere.'

'Well.' She tore open the biscuit packet and tipped its contents onto a plate. 'Have a biscuit. Or the crumbs thereof.'

'Might as well,' Lucy agreed, taking half of a broken biscuit.

Gill sat still for a moment, as if gathering up her strength. 'All right,' she said at last, and launched into her story. 'Adrian and I were married for nearly five years. It wasn't so bad at first – I liked the idea of being married, and when we had Bryony I was over the moon. But Adrian was jealous of the attention I paid to Bryony, and he wanted her to be *his* little girl. That's when he started hitting me.' Her voice was matter-of-fact – horrifyingly so. 'Adrian was clever. He was always careful to stop just short of breaking anything, and he usually tended to hit me where it didn't show. So it went on for a few years like that.' Her eyes were turned in Lucy's direction, but they weren't focused, looking through her into a past of remembered pain. 'No one would have believed it, anyway – everyone thought that we were the perfect couple, with our lovely little girl. And people don't think that things like that happen in … good families. But one day I had had enough. He hit me once too often, and I got out. I was one of the lucky ones,' she added with a small smile. 'You'd never believe how many women put up with the most horrific abuse, just because they don't feel that they have any options – they're economically and emotionally tied to a man who, having already completely destroyed their self-esteem, tries his best to kill them at every opportunity. But I got out. I took Bryony and went to a shelter for battered women. That's where I met Lou,' she said, looking at Lucy rather than through her. 'She was a volunteer at the shelter. And she was splendid.'

Lucy nodded. 'She would be.'

'She helped me – us – to put our lives back together. She gave me myself back again,' she said simply. 'Then I divorced Adrian, and moved in with Lou.'

'There was no problem with the divorce?' Lucy asked.

'It was a stalemate situation. He threatened to tell the court about … well, about Lou. And I had a counterthreat, that I would tell about the abuse. So we both agreed to keep our mouths shut, and it went through.' She shook her head. 'But he wouldn't leave us alone. He kept coming round to Lou's house, supposedly to see Bryony – he had visitation rights, so he had every right to see her. But he would demand to see me as well, saying that I was his wife and he wanted me back. Lou hates his guts, of course, and most of the time she managed to keep him away from me.' Gill refilled Lucy's teacup, gathering her courage for the next part.

Lucy prompted her to continue. 'Most of the time?'

'Then there was the once – the awful time. Bryony was at school, thank God. And Lou was home sick from work – she had flu very badly. She was weak or she wouldn't have let it happen. Lou may be small, but she's very strong,' Gill added with a fond smile.

'What happened?'

Gill sighed and continued. 'Adrian came – he'd expected to find me alone. He said he wanted me and Bryony back, that I was still his wife, that we were a family. When I said no, he called me names. Dreadful names. He called Lou names. By then she'd dragged herself out of bed, but she was too weak …' Gill's voice trailed off, then she forced herself to go on, speaking with clinical calmness. 'He raped me. In front of Lou. He hit me, and then he raped me. It was horrible – more horrible than I can tell you.'

'Oh, Gill!' Instinctively Lucy put out a hand and touched her arm. Power, she said to herself. It was all about power.

Gill took a deep breath. 'After that, of course, we knew that we had to leave London,' she continued. 'To move away and not tell Adrian where we were going. Walston seemed the perfect place – out of the way so he'd never be able to find us. I could grow my herbs, and Lou could work from home, and we could bring up Bryony in peace. And then, then that interfering old woman across the road had to get in touch with Adrian and tell him where we were!' It was the most emotion that she'd displayed so far. 'After that, it was just a matter of time before he came. I should have expected it, I suppose.'

There were so many questions that Lucy wanted to ask. What about Bryony? What was his relationship with her? Did he ...?'

'He never hit Bryony,' Gill said quickly. 'Never touched her. He adored her, or adored the *idea* of her, liked seeing himself as the perfect father. He would have spoiled her rotten if he'd had the chance. And Bryony has always loved her father.'

Lucy was incredulous. 'Even with the way he treated you?'

'Oh, she didn't know about that.' Gill smiled bravely. 'That was between me and Adrian, and I didn't think it was fair to poison her mind against her father, just because of what he did to me. But after ... what happened that last time ... I just couldn't bear to see him again. And I didn't want Bryony to see him either. It might not have been right, and I couldn't help feeling guilty about it, but I just couldn't bear it.'

'No one would blame you,' Lucy declared. 'Any mother would have felt the same.'

Gill sighed and closed her eyes, suddenly weary. 'But now I just don't know what to think,' she said softly.

'What do you mean?'

'I'm just so terrified that he's ... done something to Bryony,' she confided, reaching the nub of the problem at last. 'The way she's acting – it's not normal. Something has traumatised her, and I'm so afraid that Adrian has ... hit her. Or ... something worse. God knows, he's capable of it. I didn't think he'd ever hurt her – but what if I was wrong? Don't you see?' She looked at Lucy imploringly. 'I don't know what to do. I can't talk to Lou – I can't tell her what I'm afraid of. If she even thought he'd done anything to harm Bryony, she wouldn't stop at breaking every bone in his body. She'd kill him, Lucy! She'd tear him limb from limb!'

There was no question, Lucy told David, of leaving Walston while Bryony was in such a state. And Gill, she added: for whatever reason, Gill had confided in her and no one else, and she must now remain available to help her see it through.

210

'But love,' David remonstrated later that afternoon. 'It's Monday already. We can't just stay indefinitely. And you don't know how long it will take for things to sort themselves out.'

'I'm not going,' Lucy stated. 'Not today. Gill needs me, and Bryony needs me.'

'And the office needs *me*! Love, I've got work to do!'

But in the end he gave in, as she knew he would. 'One more day, then,' David agreed, sighing.

Lucy was never quite sure, afterwards, at exactly which moment during the long night she realised that Bryony held the key to the Walston murders, or what it was that had triggered the realisation. But positive she was, and in the morning she managed to persuade David that she was right.

'But how will you get her to tell you?' he demanded. 'The poor kid is obviously terrified.'

Lucy smiled her closed, secret smile; not for nothing had she spent the early hours of the morning lying awake beside him, her brain in ferment. 'I've got a plan,' she assured him. 'Trust me.'

She waited until Tuesday afternoon before she went to see Bryony again. The girl was still refusing to get out of bed, though hunger had driven her to eat some ice cream and eventually a cheese sandwich. Fergus McNair had come and gone, shaking his head. 'She's not a happy lassie,' he told Gill. 'And it's not getting much better. I'll get on to the chappie in Norwich – perhaps he'll be able to see her tomorrow.'

For the success of Lucy's plan, it was essential that she should be alone with Bryony. 'Stay in the kitchen,' she directed Gill. 'I'm going to try to get her out of the house, and you mustn't be about.' She went up the stairs and approached Bryony's bed. 'I've brought you a present,' she said, holding out empty arms.

In spite of herself, Bryony was intrigued. 'What is it? I can't see anything?'

'That's because it's an invisible cloak,' Lucy explained, shaking it out and smoothing the folds in the air. 'And when you put it on, *you'll* be invisible, too!'

Bryony sat up in bed. 'Where did you get it?'

'Never you mind,' Lucy said mysteriously. 'But I want you to put it on, and then we'll go for a walk.'

'And no one will be able to see me?'

Lucy gave a solemn nod. 'No one. Not Mummy, or Lou, or Doctor McNair. Not even me.'

'Or the horrible man?' Bryony said in a small voice.

'Especially not the horrible man.'

Bryony got out of bed. 'Where are we going?'

'You'll see. We're going somewhere special, and when we get there I'll tell you a special story.' Lucy made swirling motions in the air around the little girl. 'There – how does that feel? It must be working – I can't see you!'

'It feels fine.' Bryony wrapped her arms around herself.

'Do you have your shoes on?'

Bryony giggled. 'No. But Mummy won't be able to see that I'm barefoot, so she can't tell me off.'

'You'd better put your shoes on,' Lucy urged. Bryony complied, then took Lucy's hand.

'I'd better hold on to your hand, so you know I'm still here,' the little girl suggested. 'Good idea.'

They went down the stairs and out of the house, hand in hand, through the village and towards the church. Lucy held her breath, hoping that they wouldn't encounter anyone who would speak to Bryony. But her luck held; they reached the church without seeing another soul, and slipped inside. Not leaving the emptiness of the church to chance, she locked the huge wooden door from the inside; David, primed to cooperate, had already decoyed Harry away by inviting himself to tea at Harry's cottage.

Bryony breathed in deeply, savouring the fragrance of the church. 'This *is* a special place,' she agreed. 'It even smells special. And I love the angels!' She pointed up to the angel roof, then giggled. 'I forgot. You can't see me!'

'You can take the cloak off now,' Lucy suggested. 'We're all alone, and no one will bother us in here.' She made a show of unwrapping the little girl and folding up the cloak. 'Let's put it right here, shall we, so you can wear it on the way home?' She led Bryony down the aisle of the nave, stopping halfway; she sat down and pulled the little girl onto her lap gently. 'Let's make ourselves comfortable, shall we?'

Bryony settled in Lucy's arms. 'You promised to tell me a story.'

Smiling, Lucy stroked her hair. 'You said that you loved the angels,' she began.

'They're wonderful,' Bryony agreed, looking roof-wards. 'All shiny, and singing invisible songs.'

'There are some angels up there, as well.' Lucy pointed over the chancel arch at the Doom painting. 'See there? On the right?'

Bryony nodded. 'I never noticed that before.'

'Well, I want to tell you the story of that picture, which some people painted way up there a long, long time ago. It shows God – can you see God?'

'In the middle?'

'That's right. Did your Mummy ever tell you that you must be good, because God knows if you're good or if you're bad?'

'Yes.' Bryony nodded solemnly. 'Sort of like Father Christmas, only God is real even though we can't see him.'

Lucy smiled. 'Well, Bryony darling, this picture shows what happens to the people who are good and the people who are bad. The good people are on the right, with the angels. The angels are taking them to heaven, where they'll live with God for ever and ever.'

'And what about the bad people?'

'They're on the other side.' Lucy pointed to the left. 'The devils are taking them away, and they'll be punished.'

Bryony turned to look at her. 'Is that what happens to bad people?'

'It's called the Last Judgment,' Lucy explained. 'It says in the Bible that it will happen one day, maybe a long time from now. And the bad people will be punished as surely as the good people will go to be with God.' She paused, choosing her words carefully. 'But until then, darling, God relies on us to help him, so that bad people can't go around being bad all their lives, and hurting other people. If we know that someone has hurt us, or hurt someone else, God wants us to make them stop.'

The little girl held her breath. 'How?' she whispered.

Lucy hugged her tightly. 'That's why there are policemen, and other strong people. To put the bad people in jail.'

'But I'm only little,' Bryony whimpered. 'I'm not strong.'

'Then you must tell me, darling. Tell me about the horrible man.'

'But he'll hurt me! He'll come and get me!' she wailed, terrified. 'I can't tell you!'

Lucy tightened her arms around the little girl. 'Don't forget the cloak,' she said softly. 'The horrible man won't be able to find you. And God will protect you,' she added.

Tears trickled down Bryony's cheeks. 'All right,' she whispered. 'I'll tell you. If you'll promise that he won't get me.'

'I promise,' Lucy breathed.

Chapter 28

The Lord careth for the strangers; he defendeth the fatherless and widow: as for the way of the ungodly, he turneth it upside down.

Psalm 146:9

Later that afternoon, after Bryony had been safely delivered home, David and Lucy had a long talk, sorting out all the anomalies that made sense at last. They walked along the footpath in the direction of Walston Hall, and were enchanted to find that the little wood was carpeted with bluebells.

'I should have paid more attention to Karen Stimpson,' Lucy admitted, stopping amidst the bluebells and sitting on a tree stump. 'She said the other night that Bryony might have seen something. But she linked it to the kidnapping, which was what threw me off: right after that we knew Bryony's father had taken her, so her warning seemed irrelevant.'

'And we thought that Enid's death was suicide at that point,' David added. He leaned against a tree and looked at Lucy.

'So it never crossed my mind that Bryony could have seen the murderer, and when she started talking about the "horrible man", I just assumed that she meant her father.' Lucy twisted a curl round her finger. 'And it turned out that she not only saw the murderer from across the road, she was actually in the house with him.'

'And she got a good look at him?'

'Oh, yes.' Lucy nodded. 'She didn't know his name,' she admitted, 'but her description was spot on.' She went on to repeat Bryony's story: how the girl had joined Enid Bletsoe for chocolate biscuits in spite of her mother's orders to the contrary. When the doorbell had rung, Lucy told him, the girl had been frightened that it was her mother or Lou, come looking for her, so at Enid's urging she'd run to the kitchen to hide under the table. The man had come into the kitchen: she'd seen him plainly, and had watched as he'd fixed Enid a drink, stirring the tablets into the bitter lemon. She'd waited until he'd gone before emerging from her hiding place, but when she'd returned to the lounge she'd found Enid writhing in the throes of her last agony. Bryony had fled from the house in terror, only to be snatched by her father before she could reach home. And of course there were so many reasons that she couldn't tell her mother – couldn't tell anyone – what had happened and what she'd seen.

David listened carefully, without interrupting. 'She actually witnessed the murder, then?' he said when she'd finished.

'Yes, the poor little thing. It's no wonder she was terrified, darling.' Lucy's voice was full of compassion.

'And the kidnap by her father was a fluke – a real red herring,' David stated, shaking his head. 'It's no wonder you didn't make the connection.' He chewed on his thumb nail pensively. 'So now we know who, and we know how. But what I still don't understand, Lucy love, is *why*. What on earth was his motive?'

'I've been thinking about it,' she said slowly. 'And I think that the answer is power.'

'Power?'

'I've been thinking about something Roger Staines said,' Lucy explained. 'That being a churchwarden is all about power. And I think that he was right about something else: Flora Newall died because she was churchwarden, and for no other reason. Not because she was a social worker, and not because she had access to people's secrets or had learned something that someone else wanted kept quiet. Because she was churchwarden.'

'It's an extremely powerful position,' David agreed. 'And one that people seem strangely reluctant to give up, in my experience.' He ran his fingers over the rough bark of the tree. 'But what about Enid? Why did she have to die?'

'To take the blame for Flora's murder, I suspect,' Lucy postulated. 'There might have been more to it than that, of course – perhaps she *did* find something out that would threaten him. Maybe she even knew that he'd killed Flora. And don't forget what Stephen said on Sunday: that Enid had volunteered to stand for churchwarden. Maybe he couldn't cope with that.' She stood up, brushing moss from her skirt. 'So what do we do now, darling?'

David grinned at her. 'Why do I have the feeling that going to John Spring with what you've learned isn't exactly what you have in mind?'

'You must be joking!' She rolled her eyes. 'Apart from anything else, I don't see how we could even consider putting Bryony through any more than she's already suffered. Even if she *can* identify him. There's got to be another way.'

'Actually,' David admitted, 'I don't believe that her identification, or even her witnessing the murder, would hold up in court. It certainly isn't enough evidence to convict him on. And as you say, it wouldn't be fair to put her through it. But apart from what Bryony has told you, there isn't a shred of evidence against him. Nothing concrete. Nothing but supposition and guesses on our part.'

Lucy looked down the footpath towards the church. 'We need to have a meeting.' she announced. 'Tonight. We need to talk to Gill and Lou about it, and see if they have any ideas.'

'Stephen and Becca as well.' David suggested.

215

Nodding in agreement, Lucy paused. 'And how about Roger Staines?' she added. 'After all, David, he was the one who came closest to the truth about the murders.'

They all gathered at Foxglove Cottage late that evening, after Bryony was in bed. Lou had already opened the wine, and David accepted a glass with gratitude.

David and Lucy hadn't warned the others of the purpose of the get-together, so there was a certain amount of curiosity as they all settled down with their wine. Deciding to get to the point quickly, David told them that they were there to talk about the murders in Walston. 'We know who the murderer is,' he said, 'but we need to decide what to do about it.' As they all stared at him, disbelieving, he named the man.

Lucy explained that Bryony had seen, and described, the murderer. 'So there's no doubt about it. But there isn't any other evidence against him.'

'No.' Gill's voice was quiet but unmistakably firm. 'My daughter isn't to be involved in this. She's been through enough already. I'm not having the police pestering her, and she's not going into court to identify him. I won't allow it.'

'Actually,' David confessed, 'as I told Lucy, I don't think her identification would be enough anyway. They would discredit it as evidence.'

'Then what can be done?' asked Stephen. 'Surely the police, if they know who it is, will be able to prove it?'

Lou leaned forward, looking fierce. 'The police? They won't be able to prove a bloody thing!'

David decided to play devil's advocate. 'They might,' he said. 'They've got surprise on their side, at any rate – he doesn't suspect that anyone knows. So if they got a search warrant they might be able to find digoxin in his possession.'

'But that doesn't actually prove anything,' Lucy pointed out. 'Plenty of people have digoxin quite legitimately.'

'True,' admitted David. 'And there really isn't any other way of connecting him to the murders.'

Stephen was frowning, baffled, as he tried to puzzle it out. 'But why?' he interjected. 'Why did he do it? I just can't think of a reason. Can you explain it?'

David looked at Roger Staines. 'You know, don't you?' he suggested shrewdly. 'So much of what you said to Lucy was true, or very near the mark.'

'I think I do.' Roger gave a slow nod. 'It's about power, isn't it? I should have guessed. He *has* to be important. That's the most crucial thing.'

'Flora opposed the expansion of Ingram's, didn't she?' postulated David. 'She voted against granting them a right-of-way through the grounds of the almshouses, I'm willing to wager.'

Stephen nodded, but still without understanding. 'Yes, she was strongly opposed to it. We had the meeting the night before she died, I think, a meeting of the almshouses trust. The churchwardens and I are the sole trustees.' He took his diary from his pocket and checked. 'That's right. It was that night. We had a long, acrimonious meeting. She was vegetarian, as you know, and said it was wicked even to consider such a thing. Fred tried his best to persuade her to change her mind – he really has a vested interest in the expansion of Ingram's, you know. And then … oh …' His brow cleared as comprehension dawned. 'Oh, I see!'

'And that must have been when the tablets were substituted,' David went on triumphantly. 'That night, sometime during the meeting.'

'Everyone knew that Flora kept artificial sweeteners in her handbag,' confirmed Stephen. 'And we had coffee that night at the meeting. She had the container out, sitting on the table.'

'And what about Enid?' Becca asked. 'Why … ?'

Lou got up suddenly and began pacing behind the sofa. 'All right, let's cut the crap,' she said in a decisive voice. 'None of this matters. You can work this all out later and pat yourselves on the backs for being so clever. What we're here to talk about now is what to bloody do about it.' She stopped pacing and put her hands on her hips, surveying them all. 'I don't give a shit about the old bag across the road. And I don't really care about Flora, to be perfectly honest – I hardly knew the woman. But I *do* care about Bryony, and I want to make sure that the bloody bastard who scared the shit out of her pays for it. I want to be damned sure that he's sorry he was born!'

David had thought about it and had an idea. 'A confession,' he said. 'There's no evidence, so we'll have to get him to confess.'

'But how?' Gill asked. 'Why would he confess?'

'Blackmail,' David said succinctly. He outlined his plan: he would ring the murderer and tell him that he had discovered his crimes, and the price of his silence would be a sum of money, to be handed over at a specified time and place. He would meet him, with a tape recorder in his pocket, and get him to talk. The police would be nearby, as a safeguard, and could arrest the man on the spot.

'But wouldn't that be awfully dangerous?' Lucy asked anxiously, concerned for David's safety. 'He's killed two people already, darling. I wouldn't want you to take any chances.'

'The police wouldn't let anything happen to me,' he assured her.

'Stuff the bloody police!' Lou snapped, pacing again. 'They're worse than useless. That dickhead Sergeant Spring, with his tight trousers – he's made a balls-up of everything so far. 'We're leaving him out of it!'

David turned to her. 'What do you suggest, then?'

'We'll do it ourselves – all of us. We'll deal with him, and hand him over to the police, signed, sealed and delivered.'

After that the plans came together rather quickly, with a free sharing of suggestions and ideas, although Lucy continued to have reservations, feeling that David was the one at risk. The amount of money demanded was to be modest, better to ensure compliance, and the meeting was to take place in the church on the following evening, thus allowing time for the money to be found. David would wait in the chancel, and the rest of them would be in the chapel, where, as Lucy could verify, they would be able to hear what was said, and thus be witnesses as well as being in a position to respond should there be any trouble, and prevent their quarry from escaping.

'But someone will have to stay here at home with Bryony' Gill pointed out. 'Perhaps it should be Lucy.'

'If David is in danger, I want to be there,' Lucy protested.

'I want to go as well.' They all turned to see Bryony standing in the doorway, perfectly self-possessed and speaking with assurance. She had evidently been there for some time. 'If you're going to catch the horrible man, I want to go.'

Gill's response was automatic and reflexive. 'No! You're not going anywhere near that church, young lady!'

Every trace of Bryony's former fragile state had vanished. 'But I must, Mummy,' she insisted stubbornly. 'I'm the one who saw him, and I should be there.'

Lou nodded. 'She's right, angelface. She ought to be there, to see it through. Don't worry about her,' she added, more gently. 'She'll be all right. He'll never even know she's there. And I'll be there to protect her, I swear it.'

'All right,' Gill gave in, trusting Lou's judgment as well as her ability to keep her promise.

So all that remained was for David to make the phone call. Having learned, as he remarked with an ironic smile, from Becca's experiences, he did it in a muffled voice, using a handkerchief over the receiver.

'I know what you did to Flora and Enid,' he said in a tone that was both confident and menacing, as much like an amateurish blackmailer as he could manage, going on to demand £500 for his silence, to be brought to the church at exactly seven p.m. on the following evening and left under King John's chair.

The next morning David was up early, leaving for London on a flying trip to his office. Ignoring his secretary's glares, he avoided all the work that had piled up on his desk and spent the day researching the laws on trusts, checking with the Charity Commissioners for the specific terms of the Walston Almshouses Trust. Everything that he learned reinforced the conclusions that he and Lucy had reached concerning the motivation behind Flora Newall's murder; he digested it all as he drove back to Walston to arrive in time for his appointment in the church.

They were all in place well before the appointed hour, crouching quietly among the twilit shadows of the Lovelidge tombs. David waited at the opening between the chancel and the chapel, vigilant; he looked at his watch as, at precisely seven o'clock, the west door opened a crack and a lone figure slipped in and moved up the aisle of the nave. Under the Doom painting he passed, in through the screen and towards King John's chair.

He was exactly as Bryony had described him, David observed: small and ginger-haired, with little black eyes, a mean-looking pinched mouth and a wispy moustache. Ernest Wrightman's movements were furtive as he slid a thick manila envelope under the chair and turned to go.

David stepped out of the shadows. 'Good evening, Mr Wrightman,' he said in a conversational tone.

The other man gasped in surprise, taking a step backwards, but he quickly recovered himself. 'Oh – hello. I wasn't expecting to see anyone here.' He darted an involuntary covert look over his shoulder towards the chair. 'I was just ... ah ... making sure that everything was all right. Sometimes the Rector forgets to lock up after Evensong – just as well that I checked.' He gave a high-pitched giggle and went on with more than a little of his customary pomposity. 'Sometimes I wonder what the Rector would do without me. He often tells me that he couldn't run the church without me, and you can see why.'

Behind him, David heard a faint muffled sound which he correctly interpreted as a protest from Stephen; he hoped that Ernest hadn't heard and that the young priest would be able to control his indignation until the proper moment. 'It looks as though you've dropped something, Mr Wrightman,' he said smoothly, moving into the chancel. Picking up the envelope, he turned it over and inspected it, then deliberately slipped it into his shirt pocket, smiling at Ernest all the while.

'Oh!' Ernest took another step backwards and stared at him as realisation struck. 'You! It was you!' He stood still for a moment, then gave an unpleasant laugh. 'Very high-principled, aren't you? Just like every other lawyer I've ever met. Most of them aren't this obvious about it, though.'

The barb hurt, in spite of the injustice of it, but David betrayed nothing. 'Every man has his price, they say,' he sneered, matching the other man's tone.

'And your price is surprisingly low. I suppose, though, that you intend to make this a habit – that this is only the first instalment.'

'No.' David's eyes didn't move from Ernest Wrightman's face. 'This will be it. On one condition, Mr Wrightman.'

'And that is?' Ernest's jaw went out pugnaciously.

'That you tell me why you did it. For my own information.'

Ernest folded his arms across his chest. 'You're so clever, Mr Lawyer-man. You tell *me*,' he challenged.

'All right, I will.' David spoke clearly, watching the other man's expression. 'You had it easy with Father Fuller, didn't you? He pretty much let you do as you pleased: choosing his churchwardens for him and running the trusts to suit yourself. As clerk of the trusts you had a great deal of clout. You didn't need to be churchwarden yourself – you had all the power without the title. Fred was no problem – you could handle him easily enough. And you thought Flora Newall would be a pushover. That's why you chose her: so that she would be your puppet, especially when it came to the trusts. It didn't matter that you weren't a voting member of the trustees, as long you could control the churchwardens. But Father Thorncroft wasn't going to roll over and play dead at your command like Father Fuller had done, so it was important that you found a churchwarden who would do your bidding.'

'Very clever.'

'But Flora wasn't a pushover,' David went on inexorably. 'She was a strong-minded woman with her own opinions. And when it came to Ingram's, you couldn't get her to see it your way.'

There was a sharp intake of breath. 'Stupid woman,' Ernest said. 'She didn't understand how important it was.' He continued, as if he needed to explain himself. 'I promised them, you see. I promised the owners of Ingram's that I'd fix it for them, that it was in the bag. They trust me – people do, you know. They know that if I promise something, I'll deliver. Ernest Wrightman is a man of his word – ask anyone. The people at Ingram's know that. They respect me. They took us for a cruise on the Broads, and they promised that in the summer we could have a holiday at their corporate villa in Spain. Doris was looking forward to that. And that woman, with her silly vegetarian scruples, tried to wreck it. Without even knowing what she was doing.'

'You couldn't stand to lose face, could you?' David probed.

'She was going to make a fool out of me with Ingram's, and nobody makes a fool out of Ernest Wrightman,' the little man said firmly.

'And Enid?' David went on. 'Was she going to make a fool out of you too?'

'She made fun of me on Sunday morning, saying that I just couldn't wait to carry the churchwarden's wand. And *she* was threatening to stand for churchwarden,' Ernest acknowledged. 'That would have been even worse than Flora Newall. But she asked for it, as well. She said she knew who had killed Flora, and I couldn't take the chance that she was just showing off, trying to wind Doris up.' He gave his curious high-pitched giggle. 'It was very neat, wasn't it? I found out from Doris that your nosy lady friend was beginning to suspect Enid, and that gave me the idea. If she committed suicide and took the blame for Flora's death, then no one would ask any more awkward questions. So I went round to see her and offered to fix her a drink.' He giggled again, pleased with himself. 'That was it for Enid. I never liked her, anyway.'

That was when Bryony appeared in the opening from the chapel, surprising both men. 'You put pills in Mrs Bletsoe's drink!' she shrieked. 'I saw you do it, you horrible man! And God saw you too, and he'll punish you!'

Ernest spun to face the girl; instinctively he lunged at her. David tried to intercept him but missed. At that moment Lou flew out of the chapel like an avenging angel and launched herself at Ernest Wrightman. 'You lay one finger on her and I'll kill you!' she bawled, placing a well-aimed kick at a particularly tender portion of his anatomy. He went down, groaning in agony, and looked up to see a curious vision as the forms of the others who'd been concealed in the chapel came into sight above the dado, like the dead at the Last Judgment rising from their tombs. Gill rushed forward to embrace her daughter in a protective hug, while Lou sat on Ernest. 'I've got him!' she announced triumphantly to David. '*Now* you can call the police!'

Epilogue

God is gone up with a merry noise: and the Lord with the sound of the trump.
Psalm 47:5

Thursday was the Feast of the Ascension, celebrated at St Michael's Church, Walston, in great style: at half past six in the morning the choir, under the direction of Cyprian Lawrence, sang Orlando Gibbons's setting of 'O clap your hands' from the top of the soaring Perpendicular tower, the bells rang out and everyone proceeded into the church for the First Mass of the Ascension.

As the early morning sun streamed in through the medieval glass of the east window, Father Stephen Thorncroft celebrated the Mass in the traditional words of the Book of Common Prayer, eschewing for once the more modern version of the liturgy. He observed another archaic practice as well, quite deliberately, knowing that he would probably be criticised for failing to live up to Father Fuller's standard of liturgical correctness: he extinguished the Paschal candle in the old Catholic way immediately after the reading of the Gospel in which Christ was taken up into heaven, rather than leaving it burning until the day of Pentecost as the current practice decreed. But it seemed to him fitting that the Paschal candle – the visible sign of Christ's presence on earth from His Resurrection to His Ascension – should now be put out. So much had happened since the candle had been lit at Easter; now it was time for a fresh start and a new period in the life of St Michael's. With a full heart he watched the grey smoke from the dead flame spiral upwards towards the angel roof; the gilded angels looked down and sang their silent song as they had done for over five hundred years.

After Mass, all those who had been involved in the events of the previous evening were invited back to the Rectory for breakfast. Becca was observably and unusually, even for her, pale and quiet, so others stepped into the breach to help her with breakfast. Lucy saw to the eggs while Gill cooked the bacon and sausages, David made toast and Roger Staines brewed pots of strong coffee. Stephen laid the table, with Bryony's assistance, leaving Lou to comment on the whole procedure.

She was, not unnaturally, still fixated on the previous night's events. 'Did anyone ever find out where Ernest Wrightman got the poison?' she queried.

'That's an easy one,' said David, cutting the toast into neat triangles. 'It was his own medication – he'd had a heart condition for years, and even had a heart attack several years back. That was why he'd had to stand down as churchwarden – just like Roger.'

Roger Staines turned at the sound of his name. 'And that reminds me,' he interjected. '*Did* Ernest poison me with digoxin? I'm a bit curious about that!'

David laughed. 'As a matter of fact, he admitted that he had done. It was on the spur of the moment, he said – he'd been helping you with some chore at church, and you'd been talking about the expansion of Ingram's.'

'I remember.' Roger nodded. 'That was when I told him that I'd never support it. We stopped for a cup of tea at his house afterwards – that must have been when he did it. Actually,' he recalled, pulling a face, 'I seem to remember thinking that Doris didn't make a very good cup of tea! It *was* rather bitter!'

'And because the digoxin was in the tea, which acted as an antidote,' David concluded, 'and because he wasn't very scientific about the dosage, it didn't actually kill you.'

'Though it came pretty close.'

'But the next time, with Flora, he was luckier,' put in Gill.

Lucy caught David's eye. 'It *was* luck, wasn't it?' she said. 'Luck that the herbal tea came along. Otherwise it wouldn't have killed her either. He wasn't as clever as he thought he was – or as *we* thought he was.'

'Ernest wasn't very clever at all.' David raised his eyebrows and his mouth twisted in a wry smile. 'He *thought* he was clever, all right. Just look at the situation with Ingram's: he was so thrilled that he was important to them, that they trusted him to deliver the goods. But at the end of the day he was their pawn. That expansion, if it had gone through, would have brought them an enormous amount of money. And what was it costing them to buy Ernest? A day on the Broads and a bit of ego-stroking. Pretty good value, I'd say.'

Stephen, who had been quite silent up to that point, put in the last, apposite, word. 'In other words, like Esau, our friend Ernest sold his birthright for a mess of pottage.'

'What's pottage?' Bryony asked.

'A sort of stew, I think,' Stephen explained. 'Like a thick soup.'

Bryony wrinkled her nose. 'I wouldn't eat any soup that was called pottage, especially "mess of pottage". It sounds horrible and messy. Yucky. Like worms, or guts, or something rotten.'

'That's enough, young lady,' her mother said in a firm voice. 'We're just about to eat breakfast.'

Becca left the room suddenly; Lucy saw her go out of the corner of her eye and followed her, concerned. She caught up with her in the corridor.

'Becca, love, are you all right?' Lucy asked anxiously as she got a look at the colour of the other woman's complexion. 'You look terrible!'

'Oh, Lucy.' Becca gulped and smiled, transforming her face from the inside to a vision of radiance in spite of her extraordinary pallor. 'Lucy, I'm pregnant!'

'Oh, Becca!' Lucy embraced her. 'How wonderful for you! You *are* happy about it, aren't you?'

Becca blinked her eyes rapidly as tears of joy clung to her lashes, and her voice was half laughing, half crying. 'Thrilled. Even though I feel like death at the moment. It was the pottage that finished me off.'

'When did you find out?'

'Just yesterday,' Becca said, admitting, 'I went to see Dr McNair yesterday afternoon without telling anyone.'

'Stephen knows?'

Becca smiled. 'I told him this morning before Mass. You wouldn't believe how ecstatic he was.'

'I thought he had a real glow about him during the service,' laughed Lucy, tongue in cheek, 'but I attributed it to holiness.'

'Oh, Lucy.' Becca squeezed her friend's hand. 'I just wish that you didn't have to go. I know I've said it before, but now it's different. Dr McNair says I won't feel this awful for very long, but at the moment I can't even face the thought of food. I need you here to help me, to make sure that poor Stephen doesn't starve to death.'

'Stephen is quite capable of looking after himself,' Lucy reminded her. 'After all, he was on his own for a long time before you came along.' But her voice didn't sound very convincing, and she had to avert her eyes from the disappointment on her friend's face.

Some time later, after breakfast, in the general hilarity of the washing-up, David realised that Lucy wasn't in the kitchen. Assuming that she'd probably gone upstairs to pack, he waited for a few minutes, then went up to the guest room to find her. She wasn't there. He returned to the kitchen and asked if anyone had seen her, but no one seemed to know where she was. On a hunch, David slipped out of the Rectory and went to the church.

The west door was open a crack; silently he pushed it open and stepped inside. It would have been difficult to miss seeing Lucy: she was standing by the rood screen looking at the Paschal candle, and the morning sun which streamed through the east window struck sparks from her hair, turning it into a gilded halo of red gold. David's heart constricted within him.

She turned, sensing rather than hearing his presence, and he moved quickly to her side.

'About ready to go, then?' David said in a hearty voice.

Lucy gave him a half-smile. 'I've been talking to Roger Staines at breakfast,' she replied obliquely. 'He wants me to do some charcoal sketches of the church to illustrate his book.'

'That's nice.'

She looked away, not meeting his eyes. 'I'm going to stay on here for a bit,' she said. 'To do the sketches.'

'But surely there's no hurry,' David pointed out. 'That book has been years in the writing, from all I've heard. Surely a few more weeks won't make a difference – and we can come for the weekend soon.'

'No.' Lucy moistened her lips with her tongue, still not looking at him. 'Becca is pregnant, darling. She's feeling awful, and she's begged me to stay for a while longer to help her get things sorted.'

'How nice for them,' he said, feeling inadequate – and beginning to panic. 'But surely they'd be better on their own.'

'Becca needs me,' Lucy stated.

David touched her hand; it was cold. 'So do I,' he reminded her gently. 'Remember me, Lucy? The man who loves you?'

She averted her face from him and spoke so softly that he could scarcely hear. 'I don't deserve you, David.'

'What are you saying, love?' He put a finger under her chin and turned her face towards him; her greeny-blue eyes were bright with unshed tears. 'What on earth is the matter?'

Taking a deep, shuddering breath, Lucy spoke in a low and passionate voice. 'I was responsible for a woman's death. I can't just walk away from that, David.'

'What are you talking about?'

'Enid,' she choked. 'You heard what that dreadful little man said last night – that I had given him the idea to kill Enid!'

Words were inadequate, and denial would be spurious; David put an arm round her shoulder. 'Oh, poor love,' he murmured.

Lucy laid a hand on the Paschal candle, feeling its smooth waxiness under her fingers. 'Can't you see, David? I've got to stay here, at least until Enid's funeral. I owe her that much.'

'All right,' he said, thinking quickly. 'I'll ring my secretary and tell her to jig things for a few more days. Or perhaps I could arrange to take a week of my annual leave.'

'No.' Her voice was firm. 'You've got to go back, David. Today, now. And I've got to stay.' She looked at the candle and went on softly. 'You know what this means – the Paschal candle. Now that it's been extinguished, it's the period of darkness before the Comforter comes. This is my period of darkness, darling. I've got to get through it before I can come out on the other side.'

'Let me stay with you,' he begged. 'Let me help you through this.'

She shook her head. 'It's my own purgatory. You can't go there with me – I've got to get through it alone. Please, darling,' she added. 'Go now.'

'You'll come back to me?' He took her icy hand from the candle and held it between his own. 'Soon?'

'As soon as I can.' She looked up at him, smiling in spite of herself at the stricken look on his face. 'Don't worry, darling.' A tiny laugh bubbled up from the back of her throat, transforming her face and lifting David's heart. 'I'm afraid you can't get rid of me that easily.'

Clerical Crime titles from Ostara Publishing

C A Allingham: *Archdeacons Aloat* ISBN 9781906288068

Victor Whitechurch: *The Crime at Diana's Pool* ISBN 9781906288051

D M Greenwood: *Clerical Errors* ISBN 9781906288099

D M Greenwood: Unholy Ghosts ISBN 9781906288105

D M Greenwood: *Idol Bones* ISBN 9781906288242

D M Greenwood: *Holy Terrors* ISBN 9781906288235

Veronica Heley: *Murder at the Altar* ISBN 9781906288136

Veronica Heley: *Murder By Suicide* ISBN 9781906288143

Lightning Source UK Ltd.
Milton Keynes UK
UKOW031859050912

198550UK00011B/79/P